Teaching the New English

Published in association with the English Subject Centre
Director: Ben Knights

Teaching the New English is an innovative series concerned with the teaching of the English degree in universities in the UK and elsewhere. The series addresses new and developing areas of the curriculum as well as more traditional areas that are reforming in new contexts. Although the series is grounded in intellectual and theoretical concepts of the curriculum, it is concerned with the practicalities of classroom teaching. The volumes will be invaluable for new and more experienced teachers alike.

Titles include:

Gail Ashton and Louise Sylvester (*editors*)
TEACHING CHAUCER

Richard Bradford (*editor*)
TEACHING THEORY

Charles Butler (*editor*)
TEACHING CHILDREN'S FICTION

Ailsa Cox (*editor*)
TEACHING THE SHORT STORY

Robert Eaglestone and Barry Langford (*editors*)
TEACHING HOLOCAUST LITERATURE AND FILM

Michael Hanrahan and Deborah L. Madsen (*editors*)
TEACHING, TECHNOLOGY, TEXTUALITY
Approaches to New Media and the New English

David Higgins and Sharon Ruston (*editors*)
TEACHING ROMANTICISM

Andrew Hiscock and Lisa Hopkins (*editors*)
TEACHING SHAKESPEARE AND EARLY MODERN DRAMATISTS

Andrew Maunder and Jennifer Phegley (*editors*)
TEACHING NINETEENTH-CENTURY FICTION

Peter Middleton and Nicky Marsh (*editors*)
TEACHING MODERNIST POETRY

Anna Powell and Andrew Smith (*editors*)
TEACHING THE GOTHIC

Andy Sawyer and Peter Wright (*editors*)
TEACHING SCIENCE FICTION

Gina Wisker (*editor*)
TEACHING AFRICAN AMERICAN WOMEN'S WRITING

Forthcoming titles:

Heather Beck (*editor*)
TEACHING CREATIVE WRITING

Lesley Jeffries and Dan McIntyre (*editors*)
TEACHING STYLISTICS

Fiona Tolan and Alice Ferrebe (*editors*)
TEACHING GENDER

Teaching the New English
Series Standing Order ISBN 978–1–4039–4441–2 Hardback
978–1–4039–4442–9 Paperback
(*outside North America only*)

You can receive future titles in this series as they are published by placing a standing order. Please contact your bookseller or, in case of difficulty, write to us at the address below with your name and address, the title of the series and the ISBN quoted above.

Customer Services Department, Macmillan Distribution Ltd, Houndmills, Basingstoke, Hampshire RG21 6XS, England

Teaching the Short Story

Edited by

Ailsa Cox
Reader in English and Writing, Edge Hill University, UK

palgrave
macmillan

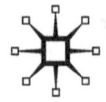

Introduction, selection and editorial matter © Ailsa Cox 2011
Individual chapters © contributors 2011

All rights reserved. No reproduction, copy or transmission of this publication may be made without written permission.

No portion of this publication may be reproduced, copied or transmitted save with written permission or in accordance with the provisions of the Copyright, Designs and Patents Act 1988, or under the terms of any licence permitting limited copying issued by the Copyright Licensing Agency, Saffron House, 6–10 Kirby Street, London EC1N 8TS.

Any person who does any unauthorized act in relation to this publication may be liable to criminal prosecution and civil claims for damages.

The authors have asserted their right to be identified as the authors of this work in accordance with the Copyright, Designs and Patents Act 1988.

First published 2011 by
PALGRAVE MACMILLAN

Palgrave Macmillan in the UK is an imprint of Macmillan Publishers Limited, registered in England, company number 785998, of Houndmills, Basingstoke, Hampshire RG21 6XS.

Palgrave Macmillan in the US is a division of St Martin's Press LLC, 175 Fifth Avenue, New York, NY 10010.

Palgrave Macmillan is the global academic imprint of the above companies and has companies and representatives throughout the world.

Palgrave® and Macmillan® are registered trademarks in the United States, the United Kingdom, Europe and other countries.

ISBN 978–0–230–57369–7   hardback
ISBN 978–0–230–57370–3   paperback

This book is printed on paper suitable for recycling and made from fully managed and sustained forest sources. Logging, pulping and manufacturing processes are expected to conform to the environmental regulations of the country of origin.

A catalogue record for this book is available from the British Library.

Library of Congress Cataloging-in-Publication Data

Teaching the short story / Ailsa Cox.
   p. cm. — (Teaching the new English)
  Includes index.
  ISBN 978–0–230–57370–3 (pbk.)
 1. Short story—Study and teaching. I. Cox, Ailsa. II. Title. III. Series.
PN3373.T428 2011
809.3'1071—dc22   2011003947

10 9 8 7 6 5 4 3 2 1
20 19 18 17 16 15 14 13 12 11

Contents

Series Preface vi

Notes on Contributors viii

Acknowledgements x

A Chronology of Significant Works xi

Introduction 1
Ailsa Cox

1 Short Shorts: Exploring Relevance and Filling in Narratives 13
　Paola Trimarco

2 Questioning Short Stories: Joyce, Barnes and Simpson 28
　Michael Greaney

3 Raymond Carver and the Power of Style 43
　Martin Scofield

4 Women Writers 60
　Linden Peach

5 The Postcolonial Experience: The South East Asian
　Short Story in English 76
　Dean Baldwin

6 The Science Fiction Short Story 96
　Andy Sawyer

7 Story and Film 117
　Peter Wright

8 Why Teaching the Short Story Today is a Thankless Task 147
　Charles E. May

9 Postgraduate Research 161
　Ailsa Cox

Appendix: Film Adaptations 174

Further Reading 185

Index 199

Series Preface

One of many exciting achievements of the early years of the English Subject Centre was the agreement with Palgrave Macmillan to initiate the series 'Teaching the New English'. The intention of the then Director, Professor Philip Martin, was to create a series of short and accessible books which would take widely taught curriculum fields (or, as in the case of learning technologies, approaches to the whole curriculum) and articulate the connections between scholarly knowledge and the demands of teaching.

Since its inception, 'English' has been committed to what we know by the portmanteau phrase 'learning and teaching'. Yet, by and large, university teachers of English – in Britain at all events – find it hard to make their tacit pedagogic knowledge conscious, or to raise it to a level where it might be critiqued, shared or developed. In the experience of the English Subject Centre, colleagues find it relatively easy to talk about curriculum and resources, but far harder to talk about the success or failure of seminars, how to vary forms of assessment, or to make imaginative use of virtual learning environments. Too often this reticence means falling back on received assumptions about student learning, about teaching or about forms of assessment. At the same time, colleagues are often suspicious of the insights and methods arising from generic educational research. The challenge for the English group of disciplines is therefore to articulate ways in which our own subject knowledge and ways of talking might themselves refresh debates about pedagogy. The implicit invitation of this series is to take fields of knowledge and survey them through a pedagogic lens. Research and scholarship, and teaching and learning are part of the same process, not two separate domains.

'Teachers', people used to say, 'are born not made'. There may, after all, be some tenuous truth in this: there may be generosities of spirit (or, alternatively, drives for didactic control) laid down in earliest childhood. But why should we assume that even 'born' teachers (or novelists, or nurses or veterinary surgeons) do not need to learn the skills of their trade? Amateurishness about teaching has far more to do with university claims to status, than with evidence about how people learn. There is a craft to shaping and promoting learning. This series of books is dedicated to the development of the craft of teaching within English studies.

Ben Knights
Teaching the New English Series Editor
Director, English Subject Centre
Higher Education Academy

The English Subject Centre

Founded in 2000, the English Subject Centre (which is based at Royal Holloway University of London) is part of the subject network of the Higher Education Academy. Its purpose is to develop learning and teaching across the English disciplines in UK Higher Education. To this end it engages in research and publication (web and print), hosts events and conferences, sponsors projects and engages in day-to-day dialogue with its subject communities.
http://www.english.heacademy.ac.uk

Notes on Contributors

Dean Baldwin is Professor of English at Penn State Erie, The Behrend College, Pennsylvania, US, where he teaches Shakespeare, British literature, postcolonial literature and the short story. He is the author of books on H. E. Bates, V. S. Pritchett and Virginia Woolf, and the editor of *The Riverside Anthology of Short Fiction* and co-editor of *An Anthology of Colonial and Postcolonial Short Fiction* (Houghton Mifflin).

Ailsa Cox is Reader in English and Writing at Edge Hill University, Lancashire, UK. She is the author of *Alice Munro* (Northcote House, 2004) and *Writing Short Stories* (Routledge, 2005). She is also the editor of *The Short Story* (Cambridge Scholars), and of the journal *Short Fiction in Theory and Practice* (Intellect Press). *The Real Louise and Other Stories* is published by Headland (2009).

Michael Greaney teaches at the University of Lancaster, UK. His interests lie in modern/contemporary fiction and theory. His first book, *Conrad, Language, and Narrative* (Cambridge University Press, 2002), received the Joseph Conrad Society of America's Adam Gillon Award for the most significant work in Conrad studies from 2001–2004. *Contemporary Fiction and the Uses of Theory* (Palgrave, 2006) is a study of the reception and representation of theoretical ideas in literary fiction since the 1960s. His current research is on narratives of insomnia in contemporary fiction and film.

Charles E. May is Professor Emeritus of Literature at California State University, Long Beach, US. He is the author of *The Short Story: The Reality of Artifice* and *Edgar Allan Poe: A Study of the Short Fiction,* and the editor of the pioneering study, *Short Story Theories*, and its revised version, *The New Short Story Theories*. He has published over 200 articles on the short story and short story writers in countless books and journals.

Linden Peach is the author of many books and essays on twentieth century and contemporary writing, including studies of Virginia Woolf, Angela Carter and Toni Morrison. *Contemporary Irish and Welsh Women's Fiction: Gender, Desire and Power* was published by the University of Wales Press in 2007. Professor Peach is Dean for the Faculty of Arts and Humanities, University of Wales, UK.

Andy Sawyer is the Librarian of the Science Fiction Foundation Collection at the University of Liverpool, UK, (the largest such collection in Europe). He teaches science fiction at both undergraduate and MA level. He co-edited the collection of essays, *Speaking Science Fiction* (Liverpool University Press, 2000) and is Associate Editor of the forthcoming *Encyclopedia of Themes in Science Fiction and Fantasy* (Greenwood Press). He has also served as a judge on the Arthur C. Clarke Award panel and the 2003 Clarke-Bradbury International Short Story Competition organized by the European Space Agency.

Martin Scofield is a Senior Lecturer at the University of Kent, UK. He is author of *The Cambridge Book of the American Short Story* (Cambridge University Press, 2006) and of articles on the short fiction of Henry James, Raymond Carver and Tobias Wolff. He has also edited *Ghost Stories of Henry James* (Wordsworth Classics, 2001).

Paola Trimarco is Lecturer in English at University Campus Suffolk, UK. She writes fiction and stage plays, and has also authored three books for Penguin EFL Readers.

Peter Wright is Reader in Speculative Fictions at Edge Hill University, UK, where he teaches courses in both Literature and Film Studies. He is the author of *Attending Daedalus: Gene Wolfe, Artifice and the Reader* (Liverpool University Press, 2003) and editor of *Shadows of the New Sun: Wolfe on Writing/Writers on Wolfe* (Liverpool University Press, 2007). He is also the co-editor of *British Television Science Fiction* (2005). He is currently editing *The Critical Companion to Science Fiction Film Adaptations*, with John Cook of Glasgow Caledonian University.

Acknowledgements

I should like to thank Professor Ben Knights and Jane Gawthrope at the English Subject Centre for their support for this project, which takes its place within the 'Teaching the New English' series of teaching guides developed by the English Subject Centre. I should also like to thank Paula Kennedy, Christabel Scaife and Steven Hall at Palgrave Macmillan and, most of all, the contributors to this volume. Special thanks go to Fred Leebron, Susan Lohafer, Clare Hanson, Laurent Lepaludier and all those short story writers and scholars who have participated in short story conferences hosted by the Society for the Study of the Short Story and the University of Angers and Edge Hill University. Finally, my thanks go to my husband, Tim Power, for his patience and support.

Extracts from 'The Revolutionist' reprinted with the permission of Scribner, a Division of Simon & Schuster, Inc., from *The Short Stories of Ernest Hemingway*. Copyright 1925 by Charles Scribner's Sons. Copyright renewed 1953 by Ernest Hemingway.

A Chronology of Significant Works

1839	William Fox Talbot reveals a system for making photographic prints
1839	Edgar Allan Poe, 'The Fall of the House of Usher'
1841	Edgar Allan Poe, 'The Murders in the Rue Morgue'
1842	Edgar Allan Poe's review of Hawthorne's *Twice Told Tales*; Ivan Turgenev, *The Sportsman's Sketches*
1850	Herman Melville, *The Piazza Tales*
1854	Elizabeth Gaskell, *Liza Leigh and Other Tales*
1857	*Atlantic Monthly* (periodical)
1850–1859	*Household Words* (periodical edited by Charles Dickens)
1861–1865	**American Civil War**
1865	Mark Twain, 'Jim Smiley and His Jumping Frog'
1868	Bret Harte, 'The Luck of Roaring Camp'
1871	Guy de Maupassant, 'The Necklace'
1886	Robert Louis Stevenson, 'The Strange Case of Dr Jekyll and Mr Hyde'
1886	*Scribner's Magazine* (periodical)
1888	Thomas Hardy, *Wessex Tales*; Rudyard Kipling, *Plain Tales from the Hills*; Arthur Conan Doyle, 'A Study in Scarlet'; Oscar Wilde, *The Happy Prince*
1890	Ambrose Bierce, 'An Occurrence at Owl Creek Bridge'
1891–1950	*The Strand Magazine* (periodical)
1892	Charlotte Perkins Gilman, 'The Yellow Wallpaper'
1892–1894	*The Yellow Book* (periodical)
1895	H. G. Wells, *The Stolen Bacillus*
1895	**Invention of moving film**
1898	Henry James, 'The Turn of the Screw'
1899	Joseph Conrad, 'Heart of Darkness'; Anton Chekhov, 'Lady with Lapdog'

xii A Chronology of Significant Works

1900	Jack London, *The Son of the Wolf: Tales of the Far North*
1901	**Death of Queen Victoria**
1901	Cornelia Sorabji, *Love and Life Behind the Purdah*
1904	M. R. James, *Ghost Stories of an Antiquary*
1905	Willa Cather, *The Troll Garden*
1906	O. Henry, 'The Gift of the Magi'
1908	Munshi Premchand, *Soz-e vatan* (Passion for the Fatherland)
1909	Gertrude Stein, *Three Stories*
1911–1913	*Rhythm* (periodical)
1912	Saki (H. H. Munro), *Chronicles of Clovis*; Stephen Leacock, *Sunshine Sketches of a Little Town*
1914–1918	**First World War**
1914	James Joyce, *Dubliners*; D. H. Lawrence, *The Prussian Officer*
1915	Franz Kafka, 'Metamorphosis'; *Best American Stories* founded (annual anthology)
1916	Rabindranath Tagore, *Hungry Stones*
1918	Katherine Mansfield, 'Prelude'
1919	Sherwood Anderson, *Winesburg Ohio*; Virginia Woolf, *Kew Gardens*; P. G. Wodehouse, *My Man Jeeves*
1920	F. Scott Fitzgerald, *Flappers and Philosophers*
1921	Somerset Maugham, 'Rain'
1922	**BBC begins radio broadcasts in the UK**
1923	Jean Toomer, *Cane*; *Weird Tales* (periodical)
1925	*The New Yorker* (periodical)
1925	Ernest Hemingway, *In Our Time*
1923–1955	*The Adelphi* (periodical)
1926	Zora Neale Hurston, 'Sweat'; H. P. Lovecraft, 'The Call of Cthulhu'; *Amazing Stories* (periodical)
1927	Jean Rhys, *The Left Bank*
1928	**British women gain the vote**
1930s	**Depression era**

A Chronology of Significant Works xiii

1931	William Faulkner, 'A Rose for Emily'; Frank O'Connor, 'Guests of the Nation'
1932	Seán Ó Faoláin, *Midsummer Madness*
1934	Samuel Beckett, *More Pricks Than Kicks*; Langston Hughes, *The Ways of White Folks*; Stanley Weinbaum, 'Martian Odyssey'
1935	Graham Greene, *The Basement Room*
1936	Frank Sargeson, *Conversations with My Uncle and Other Sketches*; University of Iowa Writer's Workshop founded
1937	Glyn Jones, *The Blue Bed*; Edith Wharton, *Ghosts*
1939–1945	**Second World War**
1939	Robert A. Heinlein, 'Life Line'; Katherine Anne Porter, *Pale Horse, Pale Rider*; A. E. Van Vogt 'Black Destroyer' (later incorporated into *The Voyage of the Space Beagle*, 1950)
1940	Dylan Thomas, *Portrait of the Artist as a Young Dog*
1941	Eudora Welty, *A Curtain of Green*
1943	Mary Lavin, *Tales from Bective Bridge*
1945	Elizabeth Bowen, *The Demon Lover*
1947	**Indian Independence**
1947	Raja Rao, *The Cow of the Barricades*
1950s	**Television becomes widely available**
1950	Isaac Asimov, *I Robot*
1951	Ray Bradbury, *The Illustrated Man*; Arthur C. Clarke, 'The Sentinel'; Doris Lessing, *This Was the Old Chief's Country*; Carson McCullers, *The Ballad of the Sad Café*. Muriel Spark wins the *Observer* short story competition with 'The Seraph and the Zambezi'.
1952	Daphne du Maurier, *The Apple Tree; The Paris Review* (periodical)
1953	John Cheever, *The Enormous Radio*
1954	Isaak Dinesen, *Seven Gothic Tales*; Tom Godwin, 'The Cold Equations'
1955	Flannery O'Connor, *A Good Man is Hard to Find*

1956	Mavis Gallant, *The Other Paris*
1957	Samuel Selvon, *Ways of Sunlight*
1958	Bernard Malamud, *The Magic Barrel*; Muriel Spark, *The Go-Away Bird*
1959	Mulk Raj Anand, *The Barber's Trade Union*; Walter M. Miller, *A Canticle for Leibowitz*; Grace Paley, *The Little Disturbances of Man*; Alan Sillitoe, *The Loneliness of the Long Distance Runner*
1960	J. G. Ballard, 'Chronopolis'
1962	Jorge Luis Borges, *Ficciones* and *Labyrinths* (first publication in English); John Updike, *Pigeon Feathers*; Paul Bowles, *A Hundred Camels in the Courtyard*
1963	Khwaja Ahmed Abbas, *The Black Sun*; Janet Frame, *The Reservoir* and *Snowman, Snowman*; Frank O'Connor, *The Lonely Voice* (criticism)
1964	Patrick White, *The Burnt Ones*; Michael Moorcock becomes editor of *New Worlds* (SF magazine, founded 1946)
1965–1973	**Vietnam War**
1965	James Baldwin, *Going to Meet the Man*
1966	Philip K. Dick, 'We Can Remember It for You Wholesale'; Joyce Carol Oates, 'Where Are You Going, Where Have You Been?'
1967	Harlan Ellison, 'I Have No Mouth and I Must Scream'; LeRoi Jones (Amiri Baraka), *Tales*
1969	Robert Coover, *Pricksongs and Descants*; Mary Morissey, *A Lazy Eye*. *The Saturday Evening Post* ceased publication (periodical, founded 1821)
1970	Wilson Harris, *The Sleepers of Roraima*; Margaret Laurence, *A Bird in the House*; John McGahern, *Nightlines*
1971	Alice Munro, *Lives of Girls and Women*; Cynthia Ozick, *The Pagan Rabbi*
1972	Chinua Achebe, *Girls At War*; Joanna Russ, 'When It Changed'
1973	Clark Blaise, *A North American Education*

A Chronology of Significant Works xv

1974	Edna O'Brien: *A Scandalous Woman*; V. S. Pritchett, *The Camberwell Beauty*
1975–1981	*Bananas* (periodical)
1975	Ruth Jhabvala, *How I Became a Holy Mother*; Arun Joshi, *The Survivor*; Ursula K. LeGuin, *The Wind's Twelve Quarters*; Ian McEwan, *First Love, Last Rites*; James Tiptree Jr, *The Women Men Don't See*; William Trevor, *Angels at the Ritz*
1976	Ann Beattie, *Distortions*; Elizabeth Jolley, *Five Acre Virgin*; Alistair Macleod, *The Lost Salt Gift of Blood*
1977	Alice Walker, *You Can't Keep a Good Woman Down*
1979	Angela Carter, *The Bloody Chamber*; Jayne Anne Phillips, *Black Tickets*
1980	Anita Desai, *Games at Twilight*; Nadine Gordimer, *A Soldier's Embrace*
1981	Adam Mars Jones, *Lantern Lecture*; Tobias Wolff, *In the Garden of the North American Martyrs*
1982	W. P. Kinsella, *Shoeless Joe Jackson Comes to Iowa*; Bernard MacLaverty, *A Time to Dance*; Bobbie Ann Mason, *Shiloh*; R. K. Naryan, *Malgudi Days*; Graham Swift, *Learning to Swim*
1983	Jane Gardam, *The Pangs of Love*; Alasdair Gray, *Unlikely Stories, Mostly*; James Kelman, *Not Not While the Giro*; Jamaica Kincaid, 'Girl'; Shena Mackay, *Babies in Rhinestones*
1984	Raymond Carver, *Cathedral*; Sandra Cisneros, *The House on Mango Street*; Ellen Gilchrist, *Victory Over Japan*; Rose Tremain, *The Colonel's Daughter*
1985	T. C. Boyle, *Greasy Lake*; Lorrie Moore, *Self Help*; Carol Shields, *Various Miracles*
1986	William Gibson, *Burning Chrome*; Olive Senior, *Summer Lightening*; Kim Stanley Robinson, *The Planet on the Table*; Shapard and Thomas (eds), *Sudden Fiction: American Short-Short Stories*; Cynthia Ozick wins the first Rea Award for the Short Story
1987	Martin Amis, *Einstein's Monsters*; A. S. Byatt, *Sugar*; Richard Ford, *Rock Springs*; Michael Joyce, *afternoon*

	(hypertext); Rohinton Mistry, *Tales from Firozha Baag*; Tim Winton, *Scission*
1988	Ruskin Bond, *The Night Train at Deoli*; Raymond Carver, *Where I'm Calling From* (posthumous); Mary Gaitskill, *Bad Behaviour*
1989	Julian Barnes, *A History of the World in 10½ Chapters*; Donald Barthelme, *40 Stories*; John Crowley, 'Great Work of Time'; David Foster Wallace, *Girl with Curious Hair*; Amy Tan, *The Joy Luck Club*
1990	Merle Collins, *Rain Darling*; Carol Emshwiller, *The Start of the End of It All*; A. L. Kennedy, *Night Geometry and the Garscadden Trains*; Pauline Melville, *Shape-Shifter*; Steven Millhauser, *The Barnum Museum*; Tim O'Brien, *The Things They Carried*; Helen Simpson, *Four Bare Legs in a Bed*
1991	Margaret Atwood, *Wilderness Tips*; Anne Enright, *The Portable Virgin*; Janice Galloway, *Blood*; A. M. Homes, *The Safety of Objects*; Will Self, *The Quantity Theory of Insanity*
1992	**Introduction of the World Wide Web**
1992	Robert Olen Butler, *A Good Scent From a Strange Mountain*; *The Stories of John Edgar Wideman* (republished 1993 as *All Stories Are True*)
1993	Leslie Marmon Silko, *Yellow Woman*
1994	Alice Munro, *Open Secrets*; Salman Rushdie, *East, West*
1995	Leonora Brito, *dat's love*; Chitra Banerjee Divakaruni, *Arranged Marriage*; Alan Spence, *Stone Garden*
1996	Andre Dubus, *Dancing After Hours*; Junot Diaz, *Drown*; Siân James, *Not Singing Exactly*; Geoff Ryman, *253* (hypertext version); Irvine Welsh, *The Acid House*
1997	Hanif Kureishi, *Love in a Blue Time*
1998	*McSweeney's* (periodical)
1999	Claire Keegan, *Antarctica*; Patrick McCabe, *Mondo Desperado*; David Mitchell, *Ghostwritten*
2000	Shashi Deshpande, *The Stone Women*; Jhumpa Lahiri, *Interpreter of Maladies*; Dan Rhodes, *Anthropology and a Hundred Other Stories*; David Sedaris, *Me Talk Pretty One Day*

A Chronology of Significant Works   xvii

2001	Destruction of Twin Towers. 'War on Terror'
2001	Talat Abbasi, *Bitter Gourd*; Rick Moody, *Demonology*
2002	Kate Atkinson, *Not the End of the World*; Ted Chiang, *Stories of Your Life and Others*; Kwame Dawes, *A Place to Hide*; Aamer Hussein, *Cactus Town*; Shelley Jackson, *The Melancholy of Anatomy*; Nancy Lee, *Dead Girls*; Toby Litt, *Exhibitionism*; 'Save Our Short Story' campaign founded in the UK
2003	Oscar Casares, *Brownsville*; Karen Joy Fowler, 'What I Didn't See'; Nell Freudenberger, *Lucky Girls*; ZZ Packer, *Drinking Coffee Elsewhere*; Ali Smith, *The Whole Story*
2004	Cyril Dabydeen, *Play a Song Somebody*; Edwidge Danticat, *The Dew Breaker*
2005	David Constantine, *Under the Dam*; Patrick McGrath, *Ghost Town: Tales of Manhattan Then and Now*; E. A. Markham, *Meet Me in Mozambique*. Yiyun Li wins the first Frank O'Connor International Short Story Prize for *A Thousand Years of Good Prayers*
2006	Dave Eggers, *How We Are Hungry*; Jackie Kay, *Wish I Was Here*; Nicholas Royle, *Mortality*; Karen Russell, *St Lucy's Home for Girls Raised by Wolves*; George Saunders, *In Persuasion Nation*; Charles Stross, *Accelerando*; Tamar Yellin, *Kafka in Bronteland*. James Lasdun wins the first National Short Story Prize for 'An Anxious Man'
2007	Tessa Hadley, *Sunstroke*; Miranda July, *No One Belongs Here More than You*; Clare Wigfall, *The Loudest Sound and Nothing*. Colm Tóibín wins first Edge Hill Prize for *Mothers and Sons*.

Introduction
Ailsa Cox

The short story is fiction at its most intensive and compact – in the words of the Scottish writer, A. L. Kennedy, 'small in a way that a bullet is small' (Kennedy, 2009). Or, to use another telling metaphor, from publisher Ra Page, it is 'a laboratory where just about all the structures, forms and tricks available to writers [...] can meet' (Page, 'A Publisher's View').

Short fiction was at the heart of the modernist experiment, through the work of Joyce, Mansfield, Faulkner and Woolf; and later canonical figures – Angela Carter, Margaret Atwood – have done some of their most innovative work in this field. Yet the short story has also been integral to the development of popular genres, including science fiction, tales of the supernatural, crime fiction and horror. Its roots lie as much in the oral tradition, in myth, fable and the tall tale, as with the literary avant-garde.

As a self-contained form, the short story lends itself particularly well to close reading and seminar discussion. Questions of style, imagery, structure and narrative strategy can be addressed through a single text. This is why short stories are often used in introductory modules, training students in the skills of textual analysis or to illustrate key themes and concepts. Later on, those same students may encounter short stories within more specialised options – on women's writing, for instance, or Irish literature.

Dedicated modules on the short story, especially the American short story, are delivered at a growing number of institutions in Britain and the US. But while individual short stories and their authors are studied across a great variety of courses, and at all levels, short story teaching has often been embedded within the general area of prose fiction. Academic criticism has tended to conflate short fiction with the dominant prose form, the novel, mirroring common misconceptions amongst publishers and readers. That situation is changing. The generic specificity of the short story – for a many years championed by an impassioned minority – is now being acknowledged by the literary and scholarly establishment.

In universities, a renewed interest in the short story has been largely triggered by the expansion of Creative Writing programmes. The 'laboratory' of the short story is where many new writers learn their craft, and many departments now publish the best undergraduate and postgraduate work in their own magazines. It has long been common practice in the US to associate Creative Writing programmes with prestigious literary journals such as *The Kenyon Review*. While this pattern is less widespread in the UK, *Stand* magazine is now based in the School of English at Leeds, while the University of Plymouth's *short FICTION* is, as the title suggests, devoted to the short story.

Since its early days as a maverick subject, regarded with suspicion by more conservative colleagues, Creative Writing has become an integral part of the English curriculum, experienced, in some form or another, by a significant proportion of undergraduates. Meanwhile, the teaching of Creative Writing has diversified to include an increasingly sophisticated interrogation of the relationship between reading and writing, and between creative and critical approaches. Nowadays modules on the theory and practice of the short story are routinely offered by writing staff in English departments, generating further possibilities for teaching and research across the creative/critical divide. Some literature teaching now includes transformative writing or 'textual intervention' (see Knights and Thurgar-Dawson, 2008; Pope, 1994), encouraging students to interpret texts by attempting to rewrite them. In an undergraduate literature module I have designed for Edge Hill University, literature students form editorial committees, researching and selecting four short stories for a mini-anthology on a theme agreed amongst themselves. They are then assessed on an Introduction which they write individually. While some students find the transition from standardised essay writing to a less formal type of discourse problematic, most enjoy the challenge of addressing a more personal response to a general readership.

Another reason behind the short story revival is its timeliness. The short story is the perfect form for a heterogeneous and fragmented culture, not – as sometimes is argued – because it is a quick fix for those with short attention spans, but for the more complex reasons outlined by William Boyd:

> The well-written short story is not suited to the soundbite culture: it's too dense, its effects are too complex for easy digestion. If the

zeitgeist is influencing this taste then it may be a sign that we are coming to prefer our art in highly concentrated form. Like a multi-vitamin pill, a good short story can provide a compressed blast of discerning, intellectual pleasure [...] – a sort of aesthetic daisycutter bomb of a reading experience that does its work with ruthless brevity and concentrated dispatch. (Boyd, 2004)

Boyd's 'daisycutter bomb' evokes Kennedy's 'bullet'. When trying to define the short story, writers frequently reach for their metaphors, an indication perhaps that while we all know a short story when we see one, naming its essential qualities is quite a different matter. As Joyce Carol Oates has said, 'Formal definitions of the short story are commonplace, yet there is none quite democratic enough to accommodate an art that so readily lends itself to experimentation and idiosyncratic voices' (Oates, 1998: 47). Oates's own guideline, concerning 'a concentration of imagination, and not an expansion' (ibid.), is one of the simplest and most pragmatic, distancing the short story from more discursive prose forms.

Line by line, the short story is not an 'easier' read than the novel. On the contrary – students looking for surface meaning may sometimes feel defeated by the ambiguities and ellipses of the literary short story. As Boyd suggests, this type of text calls for an especially active response from the reader. But if accessibility does not simply equate with the superficial and undemanding, then the short story can be made accessible. At an English Subject Centre symposium on Teaching Victorian Literature, attention was drawn to the benefits of using short stories, rather than simply sticking to weighty canonical novels (Maunder, 2005). What applies to Dickens, Hardy or Gaskell might also apply to their successors in the twentieth century and the contemporary canon. Taught widely both at A level and on undergraduate courses in the UK, Ian McEwan's *Atonement* embodies the discursive properties of the conventional novel, exploring the evolution of subjective identity through time and memory. Whatever its merits as a novel, it is far less accessible to students than McEwan's short story collections, not merely on account of word length, but also because intense, high-impact prose has greater immediacy than the discursive mode.

This accessibility is heightened even further by the new technology. Websites such as *East of the Web* (http://www.short-stories.co.uk) provide whole banks of both new and classic fiction, alongside discussion forums and questions for students. The English Department at Durham University backs up its second year survey module on the short story with its own hypertext resources; while in his essay 'Teaching Short Fiction with Computers' (May, 1998) Charles E. May describes his *Hyperstory* software which forces the reader to pause and consider at crucial points in the text – in other words encouraging students to read below the surface.

There are a number of British and North American universities offering short story options as part of their literature programme ('The American Short Story' at Stirling, 'The Early Twentieth Century Short Story' at Queen Mary, University of London). At the University of Hertfordshire, 'Reading the Short Story' is a compulsory first year module in the BA English Literature course. In the US, departments such as those at Iowa have long-standing reputations for short story scholarship and teaching, in association with Creative Writing programmes. At the University of Nebraska Kearney, students can take not only a genre study on the short story but a special topic on the short story sequence, while the course on literary adaptation looks at examples drawn entirely from short stories. At McGill in Canada, there are final year courses on the American short story, on nineteenth-century realist short fiction and Alice Munro, which may also be taken by graduate students. There is also a graduate course at Alberta on the novella.

The purpose of this volume is to explore the potential of the short story in the classroom, introducing some of the key issues which inform the teaching of this rich and diverse genre. The short story's antecedents go back at least as far as Boccaccio, Chaucer and the *One Thousand and One Nights*; since it would be impossible to cover every conceivable aspect, the focus is on twentieth century and contemporary authors; and (with some significant exceptions) on the short story in English. The book is also intended to stimulate further debate concerning the current status of the short story and, indeed, the whole purpose of teaching contemporary literature, and to suggest future directions for short story teaching and scholarship. Before introducing its contents, it will be useful to contextualise this volume with a brief survey of short story criticism.

Short story theory was pioneered by its practitioners and, perhaps uniquely in the field of literary studies, continues to be the product of close collaboration between the academy and creative writers. The concept of the short story as a distinctive genre, self-consciously differentiated from the novel, was, as is well-known, introduced by Edgar Allan Poe. In his 1842 review of Hawthorne's *Twice-Told Tales,* Poe claimed that because a short story can be read in one sitting it achieves a poetic intensity unattainable in a longer, discursive form. His prescription for a unique and aesthetically rigorous genre, based on 'unity of effect or impression' (Poe, 1994: 60) was formulated as part of a nationalistic project to initiate an elite modern culture in the US, founded on the magazine. Poe's aesthetic counterposed the vibrant new American short story against what he saw as the dead weight of the English novel, published throughout most of the nineteenth century in three hefty volumes. He is, as Levy expresses it, 'the patron saint and the neighbourhood bully of the American short story' (Levy, 1993: 10); and short story criticism has followed his agenda, which is to raise the status of the short story by defining its nature as an independent genre with unique characteristics. This desire was shared by practitioners in the twentieth century, as the market for short stories in large circulation magazines began its decline. In book publishing, the novel is the dominant mode, and short story writers from Katherine Mansfield to Alice Munro have felt a need to prove their credentials by attempting full length fiction. Their 'failures' have produced new and innovatory types of short fiction instead of the conventional novels their publishers might have preferred.

Short story theorists have responded to these pressures by going on the offensive, demonstrating the short story's difference to the novel, not only in quantity but in kind. Poe implied an affinity with painting, Elizabeth Bowen with film and many others, including Nadine Gordimer and Jackie Kay, with poetry. This desire to distance the short story from the novel, identifying a unique set of characteristics for the short story genre, became the ultimate goal of short story criticism – mostly found in essays, book introductions, articles, interviews and reviews written by practitioners including, notably, V. S. Pritchett, Seán Ó'Faoláin, Flannery O'Connor and Raymond Carver.

One of the most influential studies of the short story by a practitioner is the Irish writer Frank O'Connor's *The Lonely Voice* (1963). O'Connor argues that the short story belongs to outsiders, thriving amongst marginalised cultures, such as his own, lacking in a unified social consensus. As the title implies, he also suggested that the short story captures individual isolation, the existential loneliness of subjective experience. O'Connor's identification of formal fragmentation with a fractured interior consciousness may be related to the modernist sensibility which informed the development of the literary short story in the twentieth century. The epiphanic short story, turning on a moment's fleeting insight, became the template for the literary short story in the twentieth century. In her influential study *Short Stories and Short Fictions* (1985) Clare Hanson differentiates between the traditional plot-driven story and the image-based short fiction shaped by the modernist aesthetic.

The 1980s saw an awakening of interest in short story theory signalled by Hanson's work in the UK, and heralded in the US by Charles May's *Short Story Theories* (1977). Other landmarks include John Gerlach's *Toward the End: Closure and Structure in the American Short Story* (1985) and Susan Lohafer's *Coming to Terms with the Short Story* (1983). *The Journal of the Short Story in English*, a joint venture between the University of Angers, France and Belmont University, Nashville, US was founded in 1982; and the Society for the Study of the Short Story initiated regular international conferences during this period, publishing its papers in edited volumes (see Chapter 9).

The starting point for many of this new generation of scholars and practitioners was the ongoing quest for generic specificity. While an awareness of the short story's distinctive qualities continues to inform most criticism, it has become increasingly obvious that the search for a closed definition must be self-defeating. In one of several essays addressing this issue in an important volume, *Short Story Theory at a Crossroads*, Norman Friedman (1989) in 'Recent Short Story Theories: Problems in Definition', accuses theoreticians of setting up a priori distinctions, blithely excluding examples that do not conform to a preconceived system. He points out that some allegedly defining features of the short story might merely be aspects of periodicity – notably the affinity with the passing moment, which also applies to the modernist novel or poem. In their contributions, Mary Rohrberger and Douglas Hesse defend the usefulness of generic guidelines, while accepting that there will always be exceptions to the rule. Hesse's suggestion that we regard a genre as a cluster of characteristics, rather than a fixed taxonomy, provides a workable approach to generic identity. By the turn of the twenty-first century, short story scholarship had moved beyond its initial, defensive position. While some researchers are still concerned with formal characteristics, and are doing productive work in this field, we no longer need to preface every argument with a declaration of specificity.

The present volume brings together a range of writers with substantial expertise in teaching the short story within dedicated modules, in creative writing, in the wider study of prose fiction, and alongside other genres such as poetry and film. Several argue for the short story as a potential challenge to current orthodoxies in teaching. Charles May, Michael Greaney and Martin Scofield all claim that the short story resists conventional styles of literary analysis, encouraging teachers to liberate classroom discussion from instrumentalist attitudes towards literature. All the contributors explore the potential of the short story in the classroom, discussing some of the key issues, and the rewards, it may bring. The short story is treated not only as an object of study in its own right, but as a tool in the wider curriculum. This volume provides essential background knowledge and an introduction to the resources available for those relatively new to the short story, or who wish to put their current teaching within a broader context.

The first two chapters take formal and generic characteristics as their starting point. In 'Short Shorts: Exploring Relevance and Filling in Narratives', Paola Trimarco describes how tutors can use the very short story when teaching English Language, Literature and Creative Writing. Beginning with some definitions of a form also known as 'flash', 'sudden' and 'micro' fiction, she goes on to demonstrate how relevance theory enables students to treat literary works as acts of communication. Relevance theory works on the presumption that all communication has an underlying relevance; what, on a first reading, appears to be background information or added detail, in fact introduces additional meanings and inferences. Drawing on her experience of the Open University's 'The Art of English' course, Trimarco shows how these connections can be pursued through readings of examples by Kate Chopin, Ernest Hemingway and the contemporary American writer, Fred Leebron.

Chapter 2 considers the resistance of the short story sequence to the kind of interpretative questions that commonly direct classroom discussion and generate essay questions. The story sequence or cycle of interlinked stories has become especially popular amongst publishers, as a means of bridging the gap between short fiction and the novel. Its roots lie in Sherwood Anderson's *Winesburg, Ohio* (1919) and of course Joyce's *Dubliners* (1914). In 'Questioning Short Stories: Joyce, Barnes and Simpson', Michael Greaney reflects on the experience of teaching *Dubliners* and two contemporary short story sequences, Julian Barnes's *History of the World in 10½ Chapters* (1989), and Helen Simpson's *Hey Yeah Right Get a Life* (2000). If the short story is a definitively laconic genre, one whose habit of leaving its governing ideas unsaid seems to solicit the collaborative input of a self-conscious reader, then it would seem to be the ideal text for classroom discussion. On the other hand, it might be argued that the last thing that this evanescent, fragmentary and minimalist genre needs is to be smothered by discussion and analysis.

As Greaney shows, the stories of Joyce, Barnes and Simpson enact this paradox in different ways, each collection fostering a quizzically self-conscious attitude to the question of reading itself. The search for underlying themes is a comfortable and reassuring task for students, and for many teachers, and the short story sequence does invite thematic interpretations, for instance through recurring images of paralysis in *Dubliners*, the Biblical reworkings in Barnes, or Simpson's focus on the experience of motherhood. However the emphasis on unity risks reducing each of these books to another kind of novel, at the expense of generic specificity. Greaney suggests that we initiate classroom discussions by asking students to identify those 'common denominators' weaving the stories together, but then, through detailed textual analysis, discuss the resistance to narrative unity brought about by ellipses and silences.

Greaney's insistence on extensive close reading as the central activity in short story teaching is shared by all the contributors to this volume. The short story sequence, with its heightened ambiguities and resistance to closure, could even be said, in his words, to 'school' the student in more subtle ways of reading. Greaney's own textual analysis provides a model for reading the silences without imposing homogeneity. Applying the lessons of this chapter, instructors might consider how we formulate discussion questions and assessment titles which are not, ultimately, reductive or predetermined; and which in some cases may invite a more personal response than is usually sanctioned by the academy.

Martin Scofield also places active reading at the core of short story teaching, as demonstrated in his chapter 'Raymond Carver and the Power of Style'. Since his death in 1988, Raymond Carver has become a major canonical figure, and the greatest influence on the teaching of the American short story, both in theory and in practice, since Edgar Allan Poe. Scofield pays special attention to Carver's beginnings, to the rhythms of his prose, to irony, and to image and symbol. Advocating the primacy of those elements which are loosely called 'style', Scofield goes so far as to say that we do not need to 'teach' anything beyond the skills of careful reading.

In an increasingly visual culture, where information travels fast and snap judgements are quickly transmitted, students often need to be trained in the art of slow reading and the necessity of re-reading, skills which are demanded by the form itself. 'Reading' can be experienced in several ways, including listening to the spoken text. As I have already suggested, IT offers numerous benefits to short story teaching, including podcasts of authors reading their work and online chat rooms, encouraging student discussion of texts. May's *Hyperstory* software, navigating the online text, forcing the student to pause and re-read, is a sophisticated version of common practice; the instructor scrolls back and forth through the online text during seminars and lectures, extracting shorter passages for closer scrutiny.

Regardless of the pedagogical benefits of IT, and whatever the future may hold for the electronic book, most short stories are still written to be read as hard copy. The experience of reading online does not replicate the experience of reading continuous text on the printed page. This is a point that needs stressing in our pedagogical practice, since both students and educators are increasingly favouring the virtual learning environment. Nicholas Carr's book, *The Shallows* (2010) discusses the cognitive impact of the new technology, including the implications for reading habits and the processing of written texts. While Scofield does not address this debate explicitly, his defence of simplicity in the classroom prompts such considerations. Why not just read the story, or parts of it, out loud? Or even ask the students to prepare short readings? Reading aloud may seem old-fashioned, but it revives the short story's oral properties, the sounds and the rhythms of the spoken text. Even more importantly, it is a strategy for slow reading. Scofield leaves us to decide exactly how we facilitate close reading, but his approach to Carver maps points at which we encourage students to pause, consider, re-read and listen to the words.

The next two chapters focus on representation. Linden Peach's chapter on 'Women Writers' argues that the range and scope of women's writing provides an introduction to the diversity of female experience which will prove useful to students exploring the connections between gender and genre. Women's texts have given voice to experiences that were previously marginalised or not written about at all. As part of this process, writers as diverse as Elizabeth Bowen, Virginia Woolf, Grace Paley, Eudora Welty, Jean Rhys and Lorrie Moore have appropriated, and in many instances reinvented, the aesthetics of the short story. Through a reading of Katherine Mansfield's 'The Doll's House', Peach suggests introducing students to the political subtext in modernist short stories. Recent writing from a new generation of Welsh and Irish writers, including Siân James and Emma Donoghue, continues to push back the boundaries of short fiction. Peach shows how contemporary women's writing from the 'margin' can be used to generate wider discussion of the aesthetic challenges involved in exploring difference and taboo; and to question the possibility of representing 'real life'.

The short story has also played an important role in postcolonial studies, providing an outlet for suppressed or emergent voices in the Caribbean, Africa, Australasia and elsewhere. Like the previous chapter on gender, 'The Postcolonial Experience: The South East Asian Short Story in English' is a case study, focusing on specific trends and 'local' variants chosen from a wider field. The course on which Dean Baldwin has based his chapter is one of several offered by Penn State University, which now requires undergraduates to study some aspect of non-Western culture. Before discussing what can be learnt from the authors and their stories, Dean Baldwin considers the rewards, problems and strategies involved in teaching them to US students who have barely, if ever, encountered any culture but their own. After a brief outline of the origins of the short story in India and Pakistan, he surveys a range of writers and their work from the struggle for independence to the present. All the material he uses is available in the US and UK; authors include Anita Desai, Ruskin Bond, Mulk Raj Anand, Vikram Chandra, R. K. Narayan, Chitra Divakaruni, Raja Rao, Salman Rushdie and Kushwant Singh. This chapter will be especially useful to those who, like Baldwin, are teaching stories from India and Pakistan as an introduction to an unfamiliar literary and cultural tradition, perhaps within an interdisciplinary context.

'The Science Fiction Short Story' is another detailed case study, chosen this time to explore the short story as popular fiction. Drawing on his experience as a teacher and as Librarian of the extensive Science Fiction Foundation Collection at the University of Liverpool, Andy Sawyer charts the development of the science fiction short story, indicating key themes and useful texts for classroom discussion. He invites teachers and students to ask why science fiction writing is usually excluded by literary anthologies, and from the place that it deserves in the history of the genre. He also suggests approaches to reading and evaluating the varying strands within science fiction – the scientific romance in the Wellsian tradition; the 'hard' SF problem story (Godwin's 'The Cold Equations'); the new wave and alternative histories. Sawyer shows the importance of relating texts to their production and circulation, for instance the role of magazines and their editors in the shaping of content and narrative strategy. Instructors who are not science fiction specialists will find Sawyer's chapter a useful introduction to teaching this vitally important sub-genre either as a specialised module or as an element in the development of the genre as a whole.

The emphasis on sub-genre and on popular forms continues into the next chapter, in which Peter Wright looks at story and film. The short story often translates to the screen with relative ease. Examples range from Nicolas Roeg/Daphne du Maurier's *Don't Look Now* to Robert Altman/Raymond Carver's *Short Cuts* to Bernard Rose/Leo Tolstoy's *Ivansxtc*. But does film adaptation simply impersonate prose forms, or does it engage with our imagination in a different way? How can you pictorialise Borges? British director Alex Cox's *Death and the Compass* was

Introduction 11

originally commissioned by the BBC in 1992, as part of a planned series of Borges adaptations for TV. Later reworked for cinematic release, it is an ambitious attempt to replicate Borges's narrative strategies in visual terms. With close reference to Cox's adaptation, the chapter discusses how we can teach students to conceptualise the switch between what we read and what we see. The chapter also includes a comparative table which can be adapted as a template for analysing other story-to-film adaptations. (A list of short story film adaptations appears as an appendix to this volume.)

In 'Why Teaching the Short Story Today is a Thankless Task', Charles E. May argues that the short story is an inherently poetic artwork, eluding simple-minded sociological or political interpretations. Because its natural territory is the liminal and mysterious, it is marginalised by an increasingly utilitarian view of literature, which privileges the socially conscious novel. His provocative title is a rallying call for a passionate re-engagement with literature in the classroom.

The final chapter looks at new directions in short story research, pointing to growing areas of interest and suggesting starting points for postgraduate students. In such an extensive field of study, no survey could be exhaustive; despite the pessimism of some of the contributors, research into the short story is expanding and, just as importantly, becoming increasingly visible. This volume indicates just some of the possibilities for both teachers and researchers. Its intention is to stimulate ideas about short story teaching, its content, its methodology and its intentions, rather than determining a universal pedagogical approach. Above all, it aims to communicate the short story's potential to reinvigorate the teaching of English.

Works Cited

Boyd, William. 'Brief Encounters', *The Guardian*, review section, Saturday, 2 October, 2004.
Carr, Nicholas. *The Shallows: What the Internet is doing to our Brains*. New York: W. W. Norton and Co., 2010.
Friedman, Norman. 'Recent Short Story Theories: Problems in Definition', in *Short Story Theory at a Crossroads*, ed. Susan Lohafer and Jo Ellyn Clarey. Baton Rouge: Louisiana State University Press, 1989. 13–31.
Gerlach, John. *Toward the End: Closure and Structure in the American Short Story*. Tuscaloosa: University of Alabama Press, 1985.
Hanson, Clare. *Short Stories and Short Fictions, 1880–1980*. Basingstoke: Macmillan – now Palgrave Macmillan, 1985.
Kennedy, A. L. 'Small in a Way That a Bullet Is Small', in *The Short Story*, ed. Ailsa Cox. Newcastle: Cambridge Scholars, 2009. 1–9.

Knights, Ben and Chris Thurgar-Dawson. *Active Reading: Transformative Writing in Literary Studies*. London: Continuum, 2008.
Levy, Andrew. *The Culture and Commerce of the American Short Story*. Cambridge, MA: Cambridge University Press, 1993.
Lohafer, Susan. *Coming to Terms with the Short Story*. Baton Rouge: Louisiana State University Press, 1983.
May, Charles E. *Short Story Theories*. Athens, OH: Ohio University Press, 1977.
May, Charles E. 'Teaching Short Fiction with Computers', in *The Tales We Tell*, ed. Barbara Lounsberry, Susan Lohafer, Mary Rohrberger, Stephen Pett and R. C. Feddersen. Westport: Greenwood Press, 1998. 141–6.
Maunder, Andrew, 'Teaching Victorian Fiction', *English Subject Centre Newsletter*, Issue 8, June 2005.
Oates, Joyce Carol. 'The Origins and Art of the Short Story', in *The Tales We Tell*, ed. Barbara Lounsberry, Susan Lohafer, Mary Rohrberger, Stephen Pett and R. C. Feddersen. Westport: Greenwood Press, 1998. 47–52.
O'Connor, Frank. *The Lonely Voice: A Study of the Short Story*. New York: Melville House Publishing, [1963] 2011.
Page, Ra. 'A Publisher's View', http://www.theshortstory.org.uk/thinkpiece/index.php4?pieceid=6.
Poe, Edgar Allan. 'Poe on Short Fiction', in *The New Short Story Theories*, ed. Charles E. May. Athens, OH: Ohio University Press, 1994. 59–72.
Pope, Rob. *Textual Intervention*. London: Routledge, 1994.

1
Short Shorts: Exploring Relevance and Filling in Narratives

Paola Trimarco

Miniature fictions under the title of 'short shorts' began to be anthologised in English in the 1980s, growing in popularity and prominence over the past few decades. Very short short stories existed long before then, however, with noteworthy examples found in Ernest Hemingway's *In Our Time*, Jorge Luis Borges's *The Book of Imaginary Beings* and Franz Kafka's *Parables and Paradoxes*. A novelty in the repertoire of short stories, these briefer fictions were not studied as belonging to a genre in their own right, but rather they were studied as representations of the writing of a particular author, stories that could be linked thematically to other more prominent longer prose works, such as novels and autobiographical writings.

Short shorts go by many names, including: sudden fiction, flash fiction, instant fiction, prose poems, microfiction, postcard fiction and nanofiction. There is widespread disagreement over precisely what constitutes a short short and whether these different terms denote different categories. Bulman suggests that a short story is traditionally defined as a prose narrative of at least 2000 words, implying that anything less is some sort of short short (2007: 205). Thomas proposes that sudden fiction is around 1750 words, while flash fiction is approximately 750 words or less (1992: 12). Microfiction is described in one instance as 'a few hundred words' (Gessell, 2004) and in another as 500 words (by the literary magazine *Prairie Fire*). While length is the overriding criterion for labelling a story as a short short, this seems inadequate. As noted by Pratt (1994: 95) when writing about all short stories, 'The problem with shortness, of course, arises from a sense that literary genres ought to be characterised by aesthetic properties, and shortness seems altogether too quantitative, too material a feature to be given top billing.' In the case of short shorts, narratives and other stylistic features, such as intertextual referencing, emerge in ways somewhat distinctive to the form. Literary theorists noted this problem of definition before short shorts grew in popularity. One of the stories used in this chapter, Hemingway's 'The Revolutionist', has been referred to as a prose vignette or 'sketch' (Scholes, 1985: 41); yet Scholes also recognised 'a little narrative to be constructed from this text', suggesting that 'sketch' is an insufficient term.

With consideration to narrative structure and stylistic features suggesting one genre or another, these short fictions raise discussion points for classroom activities and essay assignments. For instance, 'Water' by Leebron, also in this chapter, has been taught as part of an exercise in questioning generic categories, debating whether the piece is prose, poetry or a prose poem.

What can be stated in broad terms about short shorts, however, is that at the surface level, the stories provided to readers are often incomplete or suggestive of a much larger, less anecdotal, story. To fully comprehend and appreciate these stories, readers often need to infer from social narratives, traditions of literary symbolism or other relevant background information, such as historical or political knowledge. Moreover, in the case of short shorts found in e-zines and other multimodal settings, readers might make inferences from the visual images accompanying the stories.

Given this general characteristic of short shorts, for university students of English language and literature, these stories aid in the development of reading strategies of texts where narratives require filling in, or in some way completing from what is in the texts and what is notably absent. From a theoretical standpoint, knowing what to fill in can be described at a cognitive level by relevance theory. In the classroom this use of relevance theory could be presented in its original context as developed by Sperber and Wilson (1995) from Grice's Co-operative Principle of Communication in the maxim of Relation; alternatively, it could be presented on its own so that any missing information or narrative is sought on the basis that 'language has an in-built guarantee that it is relevant' (O'Halloran, 2006: 365). Yet, this application of relevance alone could still leave open any number of interpretations of texts. Narrowing this down is often achieved through applying background knowledge of the historical or political settings of these stories, knowledge of the author or of social narratives (Hurley and Trimarco, 2008) as well as through intertextual references to common literary themes or symbols.

In this chapter I will show how the comprehension and appreciation of three short shorts are achieved for students using the approaches outlined above. Hemingway's 'The Revolutionist', Kate Chopin's 'Ripe Figs' and Fred Leebron's 'Water' are presented with a view to filling in missing narratives through relevance and background knowledge. Moreover, with students of English language in mind, I have included as part of the approach to 'The Revolutionist' a socio-semiotic approach based on Greimas (1983) and Halliday and Matthiessen (2004) which is used in a course at The Open University.

Although any one of these approaches has points which could also be employed by students of creative writing, with the focus more on the production of texts, these students benefit primarily from using short shorts as models for writing. Such stories prove useful for demonstrating the idea that a writer can leave gaps for readers to fill in for themselves. This addresses the impulse of many student writers to over-write and stifle their creative work through the provision of too much information. Short shorts, such as 'Water', illustrate the resonance that can be achieved through the judicious use of narrative silences.[1]

Ernest Hemingway's 'The Revolutionist'

Published in 1925 in Ernest Hemingway's collection of vignettes and stories, *In Our Time*, 'The Revolutionist' was a much-neglected Hemingway story. Like other miniature fictions of notable writers, it had been approached as part of a collection, in this case *In Our Time*, a collection exploiting the 'modernist aesthetic of fragmentation and juxtaposition' (Strychacz, 1996: 60). Other approaches have grouped this 371 word story with 'A Very Short Short Story' and 'Soldier's Home', under the uniting theme of the disorientation of the post-war world. (Strychacz, 1996; Smith, 1989).

'The Revolutionist' gives an account of an unnamed and seemingly rootless character wandering through Europe in the years following the First World War and the Soviet Revolution:

> In 1919 he was traveling on the railroads in Italy, carrying a square of oilcloth from the headquarters of the party written in indelible pencil and saying here was a comrade who had suffered very much under the Whites in Budapest and requesting comrades to aid him in any way. He used this instead of a ticket. He was very shy and quite young and the train men passed him on from one crew to another. He had no money, and they fed him behind the counter in railway eating houses. (Hemingway, 2003: 81)

The story goes on to record his love of Italy, especially its Renaissance paintings, and his enduring revolutionary optimism expressed in a brief conversation with the first person narrator. The story closes with that optimism undimmed by the encounter with the rather more taciturn and pessimistic narrator:

> […] his mind was already looking forward to walking over the pass while the weather held good. He loved the mountains in the autumn. The last I heard of him the Swiss had him in jail near Sion.
> (ibid: 82)

Before seeking relevance for interpreting this story, the reader needs to grasp at least the theme in order to have points to which things could relate. From the perspective of themes, 'The Revolutionist' could be explored in the light of Smith's comment on this story as being a 'narrative of disillusionment' (1989: 31), an approach used with students on an online course (www.bridgewater.edu). While this is true, it is a limited notion which could end in an analysis of the title alone in the context of intertextual knowledge, the idealistic revolutionary chasing an elusive goal.

More specifically, the reader is presented with a brief narrative, which superficially could be stated along the lines of Scholes' summation: 'the story of a young man who has been imprisoned for the political cause of revolution ... but who has come to Italy with his revolutionary faith and joy in life undiminished; this story ends with him in prison again, but in Switzerland where the conditions should be better' (Scholes, 1985: 41–2).

But this is a deceptively complete narrative, and Hemingway gives us more than that. He presents the reader with an ambiguous character who does not so readily fit the mould of the idealistic revolutionary. Montgomery (2006) sums up the ambiguity by noting that the idea of a revolutionist character 'conventionally includes traits such as "heroism", "energy", "ruthlessness" and "single-mindedness". And yet, if such traits are signalled by the title, they are scarcely supported by the text' (129).

Montgomery's analysis has been used on university courses within language and literature degrees, including the Open University's 'The Art of English' course. Montgomery analyses this character ambiguity employing two models from the field of literary stylistics: Greimas's actant scheme (1983) and a transitivity analysis using Halliday's functional grammar (Halliday and Matthiessen, 2004). With the Greimasian actant scheme it is easily revealed that as a SUBJECT, the revolutionist is not very active. After all, he is *sent* by the Party, carrying their message; he is *received* by the trainmen, who transport and feed him; he is *helped* by comrades, including the narrator; and he is *opposed* by Horthy's men and the Swiss police. The Greimasian scheme also highlights OBJECTS of desire for this unlikely revolutionist, these being world revolution and art. (Montgomery, 2006: 130)

Using a transitivity analysis from functional grammar, Montgomery categorises 32 clauses, nearly the whole of the story, in which the revolutionist is a participant. Halliday divides participant roles according to the types of processes they occur in – the four basic processes being material, verbal, mental and relational. To sum up Montgomery's findings: in material processes, the revolutionist is AGENT seven times and AFFECTED four times; in verbal processes, he is SAYER eight times and RECIPIENT twice; in mental processes, he is SENSER six times; and in relational processes, he is in the dominant role of CARRIER three times, once the POSSESSOR and once the POSSESSED. The important point to come from this is that 'the revolutionist is a SAYER, SENSER and AGENT in roughly equal proportions', and is not acting in the conventional revolutionist role, 'where we would expect many more AGENTS than SAYERS and SENSERS'. (Montgomery, 2006: 134–5).

Given this deeper understanding of how language functions here to articulate the revolutionist as a character driving the plot, we can return to the notion of relevance to help fill in the gaps in the narrative. As it is unlikely contemporary students will know the historical and political references made in the first and third paragraphs, such information needs to be conveyed about the Hungarian counter-revolution in 1919 and the 'White Terror' which was led by Admiral Horthy. This could be summarised on a whiteboard or given as a pre-reading research activity. Although it needs to be said that without full knowledge of these references, students might still grasp the basic plot line, I have nonetheless included these historical and political points as some students will be seeking relevance of the proper names and because such background knowledge does increase appreciation of the story.

The more notable points in this story, which at first appear irrelevant and cue the reader to seek relevance, are the references to painters from the Italian Renaissance: Giotto, Masaccio, Piero della Francesco and Mantegna. The revolutionist admires the first three, even buying reproductions, but is averse to Mantegna. All four worked mostly with religious themes, including the passion of Christ (Scholes, 1985: 45). But according to Scholes, 'Mantegna was more preoccupied with martyrdom and hence with torture than the others' (45). Knowledge of other Hemingway works, including *A Farewell to Arms* and *For Whom the Bell Tolls*, support the idea that for the author Mantegna represented 'bitterness' and the 'nailholes' of the martyr (Johnston, as cited in Scholes, 1985: 45–6). More striking still is the fact that the narrator tries to interest the revolutionist in Mantegna and mentions him twice in his account of the main character, emphasising the philosophical divide between the story's awkward hero and the narrator, a character himself identified halfway into the story.

With this understanding the revolutionist could be interpreted as a Christ figure. As noted above with help from a verbal transitivity model, the revolutionist might not fill all of the criteria of a hero, but he nonetheless does possess some agency and his tale is worth telling with the focalisation on him. He is also dominant in the participant role as SENSOR as he *believed*, he *liked*, he did *not like*, he was *looking forward* and he *loved*. This fits the Christ image as a being moved more by belief and sensitivity than by bloodthirsty action. Despite being tormented for his beliefs, he still held them and travelled like a wandering pilgrim by the support of others who held the faith.

Along these lines, for students seeking relevance for all of the pieces of this jigsaw to fit, they will notice the detail of the revolutionist's final destination in the story as Sion, Switzerland. This could possibly be a play on 'Zion' (Strychacz, 1996: 72). This interpretation would be in keeping with the religious meaning in the text, supporting the narrative of the revolutionist as a Christ figure, who eventually ends up being held in 'the city of God' (a summation of the various biblical interpretations of the meaning of Zion).

Students might also be seeking relevance in order to find the significance in the information given about the way the revolutionist travels with reproductions of these Renaissance paintings wrapped in a then-modern newspaper, called *Avanti* (Italian for *forward*). This could be interpreted symbolically as old world ideas about religion and martyrdom being wrapped, perhaps disguised, in present day politics.

To sum up, what is common to all of the interpretations offered in this reading of Hemingway's 'The Revolutionist' has been attention to elements that are not immediately relevant to the prominent story. This has been followed by suggestions of interpretations that would fill in the gaps in the narrative in ways that are most relevant to the storyline and characterisation, making it more accessible to readers.

Kate Chopin's 'Ripe Figs'

Like Hemingway's 'The Revolutionist', Kate Chopin's 'Ripe Figs' has 'received relatively little critical comment possibly because of its brevity' (Branscomb, 1994: 165). It first appeared in *Vogue* magazine in 1897 and was published again in the same year in the collection *A Night in Acadie*.

Ripe Figs

Maman-Nainaine said that when the figs were ripe Babette might go to visit her cousins down on Bayou-Boeuf,[2] where the sugar cane grows. Not that the ripening of figs had the least thing to do with it, but that is the way Maman-Nainaine was.

It seemed to Babette a very long time to wait; for the leaves upon the trees were tender yet, and the figs were like little hard, green marbles.

But warm rains came along and plenty of strong sunshine; and though Maman-Nainaine was as patient as the statue of la Madone, and Babette as restless as a humming-bird, the first thing they both knew it was hot summer-time. Every day Babette danced out to where the fig-trees were in a long line against the fence. She walked slowly beneath them, carefully peering between the gnarled, spreading branches. But each time she came disconsolate away again. What she saw there finally was something that made her sing and dance the whole day long.

When Maman-Nainaine sat down in her stately way to breakfast, the following morning, her muslin cap standing like an aureole about her white, placid face, Babette approached. She bore a dainty porcelain platter, which she set down before her godmother. It contained a dozen purple figs, fringed around with their rich, green leaves.

'Ah,' said Maman-Nainaine, arching her eyebrows, 'how early the figs have ripened this year!'

'Oh,' said Babette, 'I think they have ripened very late.'

'Babette,' continued Maman-Nainaine, as she peeled the very plumpest figs with her pointed silver fruit-knife, 'you will carry my love to them all down on Bayou-Boeuf. And tell your tante Frosine I shall look for her at Toussaint – when the chrysanthemums are in bloom.'

Common to the few treatments of this story are 'the importance of contrasts, natural imagery and cyclical patterns in the plot'. (Branscomb, 1994: 165) Any of these points could be topics for short essays by students.

At its most obvious level this is a coming of age tale where the child Babette learns about patience from her godmother, Maman-Nainaine.

The godmother is presented to the reader as 'stately', wearing a proper cap, owning silver and good china. It is suggested that she would want her goddaughter to appear as properly raised. By the end of the story, Babette has achieved this propriety when she makes a pretty and 'dainty' display of the figs on the good porcelain plate and carries it in without dancing about.

It is a gently humorous account of the way the concept of time seems different to the young than it does to the older generations. This theme could be developed in a classroom language-based activity whereby students identify words and phrases that highlight the contrasts between the girl and her godmother. Examples of this would include Babette being 'as restless as a humming-bird', whereas Maman-Nainaine was 'as patient as the statue of la Madone'. Similarly, Babette 'walked' and 'danced', whereas Maman-Nainaine 'sat'.

But for the reader seeking relevance in the use of natural images, what emerges is another level of interpretation about the child preparing for the sexual maturity of adulthood. This extension of what would appear to be anecdotal into something larger and more meaningful is not uncommon in literary practice. Pratt (1994: 99) sums up this characteristic of short stories, 'One of the most consistently found narrative structures in the short story is the one called the "moment-of-truth."' These are moments of crisis in the central character's life, the moments that turn events forever and lend new perspectives on life.

The reader is invited from the start to see the story from Babette's point of view, with the childish diminutive name for her godmother, literally *dwarfy-dwarfy Mummy*. With the focalisation coming from Babette's perspective, the first lines offer an idea that is presented as irrelevant because Babette herself does not see the connection between figs being ripe and being allowed to visit her cousins. But in such a brief story, the reader knows that there is some connection to be made, that is, the reader seeks relevance. Drawing from social narratives, assuming that Babette is young and needs to follow the orders of her elders, such as Maman-Nainaine, the reader can interpret that it is Babette who is not ready, or mature enough, to make the visit.

A sexual interpretation of this maturity process emerges from the presence of natural imagery in this seemingly irrelevant opening paragraph. The cousins are 'down on Bayou-Boeuf, where the sugar cane grows', suggesting phallic symbols, while the ripening of the figs, or any fruit, has a likely female sexual reference. In Romance culture, figs symbolise the female pudenda and fertility – a meaning Chopin's readership would have been well aware of. Arriving at such interpretations combines the need to find relevance in these details along with intertextual references drawn from Western literature and art over the centuries. With this, Babette's walking slowly beneath the fig trees, 'carefully peering between the gnarled, spreading branches' suggests the emergence of sexual awareness.

Supporting this sexual interpretation is knowledge about the author and the context in which the text was written. Chopin's other stories were often about sensual artistic women; her best known book being *The Awakening*. Moreover, the sociocultural context at the time this story was written reflected an era when sexual content, especially that related to women, was taboo. As one Chopin biographer puts it, by the time 'Ripe Figs' was written, Chopin had 'discovered that she could publish stories hinting at sexual matters ... but only if she placed her characters in quaint locales, and if she veiled through vague words what they actually did' (Troth, 1999: 142). In a similar vein, other biographical information sees this story as reflective of some aspect of Chopin's own life, given that her daughter was thirteen at the time of the story's first publication.

The extent to which such biographical support is needed to interpret the imagery and simple plotline as sexually metaphorical is arguable. Some lecturers using this story have not relied on such background information, but instead have allowed the story to be interpreted in such a way intertextually, with reference to literary tradition of texts mentioned above.

A related theme of entering adulthood is hinted at with the references to the passing of time in predictable stages, such as the seasons. In addition, the story has Babette presenting the ripened figs to her godmother in a ritualistic manner, akin to the coming of age ceremonies of many traditional societies: '... Babette approached. She bore a dainty porcelain platter, which she set down before her godmother.' In following a relevance approach, much of this detail could be regarded as not directly related to construction of the narrative.

In a similar vein, the reader is informed that the godmother 'peeled the very plumpest figs with her pointed silver fruit-knife'. This too could be part of the ritualistic tradition whereby it is the elder who is empowered with the sharp, potentially dangerous, object to prepare the child for the adult world, represented by the peeled fruit.

The story ends with the godmother giving Babette instructions for the younger woman's adventure to the Bayou. In the final sentence, like the opening ones, the reader is given another deceptively irrelevant remark, one which could be seen as not contributing to the narrative: 'And tell your tante Frosine I shall look for her at Toussaint – when the chrysanthemums are in bloom.' But if the reader seeks relevance, this comment becomes a reference to the final stage of adult life, which the older women, an aunt and a godmother, are likely to share. 'Toussaint' which appears here as if it were a place name, translates roughly into 'all saints', the holiday marking the eve of the day of the dead. Some background knowledge might be given to students to help them decode 'Toussaint', which is not an actual place in Louisiana (where all of the stories from *A Night in Acadia* are placed). There are certainly indications from the text that Maman-Nainaine is unwell or nearing death; she has a 'pale face' and a cap 'like an aureole' or halo.

The choice of chrysanthemums is also suggestive of death. In some European and East Asian countries, white chrysanthemums are a symbol of death and are only used at funerals and graves. In a similar vein, these flowers symbolise the month of November, the penultimate month in both the Roman and Gregorian calendars. These symbolic interpretations support the idea of the older women in the story coming to the ends of their lives. With this in mind, an alternative interpretation of Maman-Nainaine's act of peeling the figs is that the older woman is relinquishing the world as she nears death. Given that she is instructing Babette, with talk about chrysanthemums at the same time as peeling the figs, the connection between the ideas is plausible.

As with the interpretation of 'The Revolutionist', background information about the author and her time, as well as intertextual references to the commonly held symbolism of natural images, would need to be provided. Without such information a great deal could still be comprehended by inferring from social narratives about the passing of time and the coming of age.

While inferring from biographical information, knowledge of symbolism and social narratives could be said to fill in most of the gaps in this story, there remain other issues, cued by questionable relevance, that are more open to interpretation. Given the significance in the choices of place names and natural images, the reader might be left looking for relevance in Babette wanting to see her 'cousins' at the Bayou. There is no indication of the cousins being male, where such a visit could suggest, given the French-Louisianne culture of the time, that Babette would return married to a cousin. Equally puzzling is the premise of the girl being raised by her godmother. There seems to be a missing story taking place before the time of the main story in which Babette is orphaned or left to live with her godmother for some reason. Naturally, the reader wonders why this story is not about a mother and daughter as the themes and suggested symbolic meanings would be the same.

Such open-ended interpretations are often characteristic of short shorts, which in their deliberate brevity leave many strands of meaning to be explored.

Fred Leebron's 'Water'

This next story was taken from the anthology *Flash Fiction: 72 Very Short Stories* (1992).

Water

She touches his hair by the river.

I am in our apartment, working. Her hand moves down his back.

I empty the trash and unclog the kitchen sink. His former girlfriends have turned into lesbians.

I take the key to his apartment, which he gave me so I could water his plants during the summer. He bends his kissing face to hers.

I walk over to his apartment, just two blocks away. Their legs dangle in the river.

I unlock the door and bolt it behind me. The room smells of feet and stale ashtrays. In the kitchen is a gas stove. I turn it on without lighting it.

Down by the river is a flock of geese, which they admire while holding hands. Soon he will take her back to his apartment. Soon they will lie there, readying cigarettes.

I relock the apartment and slip into the street. The air smells of autumn, burnt. In the sky, birds are leading each other south.

I know there is nothing left between us, that she looks at me each morning as if I were interrupting her life.

This story presents two narratives, one involves the two lovers and takes place in the present by the river and in the future in an apartment, a scene conjectured by the narrator, and the other narrative involves the actions of the narrator as a character. This in itself raises interesting pedagogical issues in the teaching of focalisation and perspective along with the Bakhtinian notion of heteroglossia. It is possible that the narrator as 'I' is only telling their narrative, while the second narrative, the lovers' story set at the river, is being told by a second omnipotent narrator. In other words, from the perspective of 'I' the lovers are out of the apartment and nothing more is known, while knowledge of the lovers at the river is shared between the other narrator and the reader.

24 *Teaching the Short Story*

The reader infers that the 'I' narrator in the story has deliberately left the gas on in the man's apartment with the intention of blowing up the man and his lover when they light post-coital cigarettes. Largely this can be seen as an inference required for the comprehension of the text brought on by the reader needing to link the action of leaving the gas on to the couple's habit of smoking after sex. This could at first be misinterpreted as giving the reader irrelevant information, but in effect it causes the reader to seek relevance for these two propositions to be placed in the same story.

As with other examples discussed in this chapter, there are gaps in the story and points that cue the reader to seek relevance. In this case the reader has to infer from social narratives. Namely, who is this non-gendered 'I'? This could refer to an ex-girlfriend, perhaps one who has become a lesbian, as this reference to lesbians does not otherwise move the plot forward and therefore seeks relevance. Drawing from social narratives, the 'I' could be a former girlfriend of the man's current lover, a male friend whose girlfriend has been stolen by the man, or even the man's mother. All of these interpretations are plausible in the context of the story in which 'I' commits an act that would kill the lovers; and the likely motivation is jealousy. The only clues given to the reader are the statements about the narrator still having a key to the apartment and that the narrator senses animosity from the girlfriend. This does reduce the possibilities to someone the man knows and trusts with his apartment keys. The identity of the narrator enables the reader to complete the narrative by providing a motive for the planned killings.

Another point for which students might seek relevance is in the title. Why is it called 'Water'? Water is mentioned directly in the text only once and is referred to twice in reference to the river. Possible interpretations for this are wide ranging. For example, having to 'water' the plants being the man's undoing. This would be relevant in the context of the story, making the tale ironic and darkly anecdotal. Another interpretation would have this story being about the opposition between water, suggested by the lovers at the river, and the impending fire at the apartment, also alluded to in the phrase 'The air smells of autumn, burnt.' Such an interpretation would make this a larger, less anecdotal story, perhaps signifying a greater inner turmoil or perhaps the nature of love.

Similarly, the river also poses points seeking relevance: What do the river and the geese and the birds leading each other south have to do with this story? This could be suggesting the changes of the seasons, as autumn has already been referred to, and winter, the time when things die, that is around the corner. In these ways, the inferences could be seen as akin to those employed when reading poetry. Miniature fictions can be so weighted with symbolism that many are classified as prose poems.

This particular short short has been used at Salford University in the teaching of creative writing. 'Water' along with other examples from the *Flash Fiction* anthology has been employed to emphasise innovation within the short story form, from the perspective of questioning genre and encouraging students to test generic assumptions in their own practice.

Conclusion

In this chapter three short shorts have been examined in the context of relevance theory and the ways readers interpret gaps in narratives often left open in these miniature texts. It has been shown that such approaches could be used to facilitate critical reading strategies required for comprehending and appreciating these pieces of writing. So much is left up to inference that the reader is required to do much more than many longer fictions demand. With the more open-ended stories, such as 'Water', readers can be seen actively creating the text, using their autonomy, assuming power over what happens, what they interpret and what they want it to mean.

With all three stories, attention has been equally paid to linguistic points of interest to university students of English language. These stories lend themselves to analyses that reveal the way language functions in social and literary contexts. This has been demonstrated by borrowing from Montgomery (2006) in his approach to 'The Revolutionist', which itself extended on the works of Greimas (1983) and Halliday and Matthiessen (2004). Such approaches could also be applied to 'Ripe Figs' and 'Water'. Although here, in the interest of space, attention has been drawn to other linguistic points in 'Ripe Figs' and 'Water', such as words and phrases of lexical opposition.

It has also been shown that additional information might be required, giving students political, historical, biographical and intertextual literary background. Examples of how to disseminate this information have been given in this chapter to include in-class hand-outs and outside of class research activities. Other methods deserving mention include the use of pictures; for example, in teaching 'The Revolutionist' photos of paintings by the Renaissance painters mentioned in the story could be brought in for students to arrive at their own conclusions about their meaningful role in the story. Accompanying texts, such as other works by the same author could also be used to explore themes. With consideration to students who have a more auditory-prominent learning style, the brevity of these stories makes them suitable to be read aloud in class; on the Open University course 'The Art of English', an accompanying CD-ROM has the story 'The Revolutionist' read by an actor.

On creative writing courses, stories such as those presented here encourage student writers to avoid the trap and pitfalls of overwriting and to explore new forms of the short story genre. On this last point it is worth mentioning the importance of short shorts in this light given 'the relative unpopularity of the short story within the publishing industry' as noted by Hurley (2007), because of the 'slight cottage industry feel' and 'cookie-cutter mould' of the output of many novice writers. In response to this, teachers of creative writing face the challenge of how to teach forms that work and at the same time encourage innovation. Perhaps it is here that short shorts are at their most valuable in English pedagogy.

Works Cited

Bakhtin, M. M. *The Dialogic Imagination: Four Essays*, ed. Michael Holquist, trans. Caryl Emerson and Michael Holquist. Austin: University of Texas Press, 1981.

Branscomb, Jack. 'Chopin's "Ripe Figs"', in *Explicator*, Vol. 52, 1994. 165–77.

Bulman, Colin. *Creative Writing: A Guide and Glossary to Fiction Writing*. Cambridge: Polity, 2007.

Chopin, Kate. 'Ripe Figs', in *A Night in Acadie*, 1897. (Out of copyright, available at http://classiclit.about.com/library/bl-etexts/kchopin/bl-kchop-ripefigs.htm).

Gessell, Paul. Column in *Ottawa Standard* as cited in http://www.wordspy.com. 2004.

Greimas, A. J. *Structural Semantics: An Attempt at a Method*. Trans. D. McDowell, R. Schleifer and A. Velie. Lincoln: University of Nebraska, 1983.

Halliday, M. A. K. and Christian Matthiessen. *An Introduction to Functional Grammar*. London: Edward Arnold. 2004.

Hemingway, Ernest. *In Our Time*. New York: Scribner, 2003.

Hurley, Ursula. 'Teaching the Changing Story', *Writing in Education*, Issue 43, 2007. 57–61.

Hurley, Ursula and Paola Trimarco. 'Less is More: Completing Narratives in Miniature Fictions', *21: Journal of Contemporary and Innovative Fiction*, Issue 1, 2008. http://www.edgehill.ac.uk/english/21/index.htm.

Leebron, Fred. 'Water', in *Flash Fiction: 72 Very Short Stories*, eds James Thomas, Denise Thomas and Tom Hazuka. New York: W. W. Norton and Company, 1992. 157–8.

Montgomery, Martin. 'Understanding Actants on a Hemingway Short Story', in *The Art of English: Literary Creativity*, eds Sharon Goodman and Kieran O'Halloran. Basingstoke: Palgrave Macmillan and The Open University, 2006. 128–37.

O'Halloran, Kieran. 'The Literary Mind', in *The Art of English: Literary Creativity*, eds. Sharon Goodman and Kieran O'Halloran. Basingstoke: Palgrave Macmillan and The Open University, 2006. 364–89.

Prairie Fire. http://www.prairiefire.ca.

Pratt, Mary Louise. 'The Short Story: the Long and the Short of It', in *The New Short Story Theories*, ed. Charles E. May. Athens: Ohio University Press, 1994. 91–113.

Scholes, Robert. *Textual Power: Literary Theory and the Teaching of English.* New Haven and London: Yale University Press, 1985.

Smith, Paul. *A Reader's Guide to the Short Stories of Ernest Hemingway.* Boston: G. K. Hall, 1989.

Sperber, Dan and Deirdre Wilson. *Relevance: Communication and Cognition*, 2nd edn. Oxford: Blackwell, 1995.

Strychacz, Thomas. '*In Our Time*, out of season,' in *The Cambridge Companion to Ernest Hemingway*, ed. Scott Donaldson. Cambridge: Cambridge University Press, 1996. 55–86.

Thomas, James. 'Introduction', in *Flash Fiction: 72 Very Short Stories*, eds James Thomas, Denise Thomas and Tom Hazuka. New York: W. W. Norton and Company. 1992. 11–14.

Troth, Emily. *Unveiling Kate Chopin.* Jackson: University Press of Mississippi, 1999.

Notes

1. This point on using short shorts with creative writing students comes from Ursula Hurley at Salford University.
2. In later editions, this place name was replaced with 'Bayou LaFourche.'

2
Questioning Short Stories: Joyce, Barnes and Simpson

Michael Greaney

University instructors in English are continually vexed by the question of how much reading we can legitimately require students to undertake. Most courses involve a weekly trade-off between what we would like students to read and what would make for a successful seminar discussion. The student who would take a month to trek through *The Faerie Queene*, for example, might reasonably be expected to rattle through a manageable number of Spenser's sonnets in a week. Like the lyric poem, the short story is unintimidatingly approachable; its brevity compares encouragingly with the huge three-decker novels and epic poems that dominate the landscape of literary studies. What is more, short stories are quick to consume but slow to digest; they are pithy, succinct and readable, but tantalisingly resonant with unspoken emotion or delicately understated themes that a seminar discussion can unpack; it is therefore never too difficult to persuade ourselves that short stories are somehow commensurate with more inconveniently long-winded forms of literary expression. And given that university-level teaching of English literature is typically propelled by questions – What kind of text are we dealing with? What is it saying? What is it doing with language? Why is it doing these particular things in these particular ways? – then it is useful for our purposes that the short story is very often a question-provoking genre. The modern literary short story is often studiedly enigmatic: stories by writers such as James Joyce or Ernest Hemingway, for example, often revolve around puzzling non-events that invite a quizzical response about what did or did not happen. The questions provoked by this genre are intensified when the stories appear as part of an interrelated sequence, since the 'story sequence' is itself an imperfectly understood, notably under-theorised genre. Lying somewhere between a novel and an anthology, the story sequence confronts us with a problem of aesthetic categorisation that neatly illustrates Niall Lucy's contention that the literary text always exists *as a question*: the inspirationally enigmatic 'question of itself' (Lucy, 1997: 37–8). Taking some inspiration from Lucy, this chapter will consider three story sequences, James Joyce's *Dubliners*, Julian Barnes's *A History of the World in 10½ Chapters* and Helen Simpson's *Hey Yeah Right Get a Life*, as examples of texts that implicitly raise the 'question of themselves'. And rather than offering programmatic assertions about how these texts should be taught, I propose to explore the ways in which they school the reader in the art of negotiating the repetitions, variations and interconnections of the story sequence.

James Joyce, *Dubliners*

Published in 1915, *Dubliners* is one of the most celebrated story sequences in the language. Its strikingly unsentimental portrait of Joyce's home city is notable for deploying all the resources of the story sequence – the capacity for enriching repetition and satisfying interconnection – to create a portrait of Dublin as a place of sterile repetitiveness and alienated disconnection. Silence, paralysis, frustration, underachievement and failure are what tie the threadbare lives of Joyce's Dubliners together. Life, in this book, has none of the virtues or pleasures of art, and for this reason it is difficult not to sense a vein of magisterial cruelty in Joyce's artistry. The mood of the collection oscillates queasily between the airless claustrophobia of Dublin and the agoraphobic glimpses of the vast world that lies beyond its horizons. The predicament of the average Dubliner is to be unable to act on his or her longing to escape, and to be taunted by the sense that any ambition to 'see a little life' (Joyce, 1992: 36) can only ever be a tawdry small-town fantasy. For Joyce, Dublin is a small world that is afraid of its desire for bigness. The self-infantilising Maria in 'Clay' clings protectively to her self-image as a 'very, very small person indeed' (95), whilst Little Chandler in 'A Little Cloud' is convinced that he might cut a more impressive figure on a grander stage, but timidly submits to the innocuous anonymity of Dublin life. Dandling his bawling baby on his knee at the end of a typically frustrating day, Little Chandler's fate says something about the straitened littleness, the cruel minimalism of these stories; they are anti-epics, 'adventureless tales' (105) in which the wider horizons are ruthlessly closed down.

One of the chief sources of claustrophobia in *Dubliners* is Joyce's pared-down fictional style. The young narrator in 'The Sisters' is told by Father Flynn that the Church fathers have elucidated doctrinal mysteries in 'books as thick as the *Post Office Directory* and as closely printed as the law notices in the newspaper' (5). Here, Joyce's text is obviously casting an ironic sidelong glance at oppressive, encyclopaedic efforts to explain mystery; its own methods are, by comparison, calculatedly minimalist. Ezra Pound famously praised Joyce's stories because he 'carefully avoids telling you a lot that you don't want to know' (Pound, 1967: 28). It is true that these stories are not overburdened with superfluous detail, but no matter how grateful we are to be spared an encyclopaedic surfeit of non-essential information, few would deny that at the same time Joyce withholds a lot that we *would* like to know. The precise nature of Father Flynn's decline in 'The Sisters', for example, is never made clear, although the story strongly invites us to form our own conclusions on the basis of its numerous dark hints of impropriety or perversion. Silence in *Dubliners*, as Jean-Michel Rabaté has pointed out, is often designed to solicit the active imaginative involvement of the reader: the 'silences of the writing', he maintains, '[are] caught up by the silent reading-writing which transforms a collection of short stories into a text' (Rabaté 1982: 46).

Almost the first image we are confronted with in *Dubliners* is that of a paralysed priest, and it soon becomes clear that these stories are variations on the theme of paralysis: from 'Eveline', where the heroine freezes on the very cusp of escape from Dublin, to 'The Dead' with its emotionally frozen hero Gabriel Conroy. And it is in 'The Dead' that we get to hear a memorable anecdote about a horse that has spent so long tethered to a mill that it cannot help but walk round and round a statue of King Billy in central Dublin (208–9). This horse is, of course, a kind of equine counterpart to Joyce's Dubliners, trapped as they are in cycles of futile repetition. In 'Counterparts', for example, where a bullied underling goes home to play the role of abusive parent, it is significant that Farrington is a *copyist* – he makes a living from textual repetition even as he lives out a desperately repetitive life. And often Joyce's Dubliners are not just paralysed but paralytic; the book is full of enthusiastic drinkers, and its innumerable *rounds* of drinks provide us with yet another image of futile circularity. So relentlessly does Joyce circle around the theme of paralysis that we might begin to suspect that we are dealing with 15 versions of the same story. Could it be that *Dubliners* is paralysed by the idea of paralysis? In *Fiction and Repetition*, J. Hillis Miller adapts from Deleuze a distinction between 'Platonic' and 'Nietzschean' repetition; that is, between difference-within-sameness (multiple instantiations of some unified, archetypal truth) and sameness-within-difference (accidental resemblances between items with no genuine common denominator) (Hillis Miller 1982: 5–6). Sometimes repetition in *Dubliners* seems to effect a satisfying consolidation or amplification of meaning; the savvy reader, one who makes the effort to track the recurrence of key images or motifs, will be rewarded by an exponential increase in the text's repertoire of possible meanings in a text that might otherwise seem like an exercise in unprecedentedly stingy naturalism. Sometimes, however, repetition seems to obey a law of diminishing returns, whereby each new appearance of a given word, image, motif or event seems to drain away some of its meaning or impact; the desperately lacklustre imagery of Dublin life is steadily devalued by Joyce, like a currency in oversupply. When Farrington continually retells the same anecdote in 'Counterparts', for example, we can sense something of this lingering disintensification and attenuation of narrative significance.

The imagery of tears that occurs in many of the tales is a similar case in point. 'My eyes burned with anguish and anger' (28), says the narrator at the end of 'Araby'. 'A Little Cloud' ends with a child's sobbing and with Little Chandler's 'tears of remorse' (81), whilst Joe is blinded by tears of sympathy for Maria at the end of 'Clay' (102). In 'The Dead', Freddy Malins cries with laughter at one of his own anecdotes (186), Aunt Kate is moved to tears by Gabriel's speech (206), Gretta is similarly affected by a rendition of *The Lass of Aughrim* (219), and the story ends with Gabriel's 'generous tears' (224). This sequence of tales that literally end in tears is obviously designed to make a point about Dubliners' capacity for sentimentality and lachrymose self-pity. But there is also a key distinction being made here between the habitually blurred vision of Joyce's tearful characters and the hard, unsentimental clarity of perspective shared by the author and his readers. What seems to be the case in *Dubliners* is that Joyce is taking a world where the content is full of futile repetitiveness – a world of 'Night after night ... night after night' (1), 'time and again', 'over and over' (33), 'up and down ... up and down' (134) – but where the literary *form* uses repetition creatively to derive symbolic meaning from this sterile cityscape. Which is to say that *Dubliners* keeps an artful distance from its world of blank, futile 'Nietzschean' repetition by means of its recourse to a style of revelatory 'Platonic' repetition enjoyed by its active readers at the expense of its paralysed heroes.

Julian Barnes: *A History of the World in 10½ Chapters*

Any discussion of *A History of the World in 10½ Chapters* is bound to begin with the question of the book's provocatively quirky title. The idea of encompassing the entire history of the world in just ten-and-a-half chapters seems like a wildly eccentric and manifestly unfeasible project; it would take a miracle of historical condensation to get anywhere near to squeezing even a fraction of such an unthinkably vast topic into such a compact framework. And what exactly is that half-chapter doing there? Untidily, the book seems to be both hopelessly under-length and ever so slightly too long. But, then again, what scale of narrative or archive would be big enough to encompass the sum total of human history? Would ten volumes be enough, or ten libraries? If we accept that the history of the world is always going to be incalculably larger than even the most encyclopaedic historical account, then perhaps an arbitrary ten chapters is as good a size as any for Barnes's purposes. And of course because we have picked Barnes's book up from the fiction shelves then we will understand, even before we open it, that we are dealing not with an intellectual folly by a hugely overambitious historian but rather with a work of fiction that is masquerading as, and in all probability spoofing, traditional historical discourse. When we begin reading the book, however, we are confronted with a different problem of classification: *A History of the World in 10½ Chapters* takes the form of a set of stories that are dramatically self-contained but thematically interlinked. The stories take place at different moments in history, from Biblical times to the present day, and there is virtually no overlap between them in terms of specific characters or storylines (unless you count the moment at the end of 'Project Ararat' where the astronaut-turned-archaeologist Spike Tiggler discovers the skeletal remains of a character whose death, almost a century and a half earlier, concludes an earlier story, 'The Mountain'). There are also enormous stylistic and generic differences between Barnes's ten-and-a-half chapters, which include a mischievous reinvention of a Bible story ('The Stowaway'), a deadpan pastiche of fifteenth-century ecclesiastical court proceedings ('The Wars of Religion'), a one-sided epistolary narrative ('Upstream!'), an informative piece of art history ('Shipwreck'), a disarmingly personal meditation on love ('Parenthesis'), and an ironic afterlife fantasy ('The Dream'). Barnes's text even includes a fold-out reproduction of *The Raft of the Medusa* to illustrate the discussion of Géricault's painting in 'Shipwreck'. The image of the perilous sea voyage is the most conspicuous of the various motifs that tie together the disparate chapters of *A History of the World*. Wittily characterised as an 'ark-ological' text by Jackie Buxton, this book harbours a veritable flotilla of arks, ocean-going liners, cruise ships, ferries and life rafts, all of which function as metaphors for the fragile, vulnerable status of human life in face of the violently unpredictable tides of history (Buxton, 2000: 66).

History, for Barnes, is dominated by struggles for survival; but there is also an important sense in which history *is* survival, inasmuch as history represents the survival of the past into the present, whether in the form of personal memory, written record, or cultural artefact. History is the specialist academic discipline devoted to remembering, reconstructing and monumentalising the past; but in deciding what gets remembered the historian is also in the business of deciding what gets forgotten. All historians, however little they acknowledge the fact, are both archivists and amnesiacs. With this paradox in mind, it seems appropriate to think of Barnes as consciously playing the role of metahistorian or anti-historian; not because his take on history purports to 'fill the gaps' or 'set the record straight', but because it interrogates the conventions that produce those gaps and distortions in the first place. We can hardly read 'The Stowaway', for example, as representing the 'correct' version of happened on the ark, since only a strictly fundamentalist reader of the Bible would deny that the story of Noah is anything but fiction. What is more, it seems likely that more of Barnes's readers will have derived their knowledge of this fiction from illustrated children's books rather than directly from Genesis 8:4, which means that Barnes's story is not simply a fiction about another fiction, but a fiction about popular *versions* of another fiction. What is at stake here, then, is not what 'really happened' on the ark, but what symbolic significance we attach to this archetypal story of human survival; and what is crucial, for Barnes, is the startling truth that a story about the partial extermination of humankind has survived as an innocuously child-friendly story of divine providence. 'The Stowaway' is thus a startlingly effective act of literary defamiliarisation, designed to make us a little less willing to believe the stories we tell each other about the past.

A History of the World in 10½ Chapters is notable for its resistance to mythic, historical and fictional narratives that promote violently one-sided versions of the truth. In mounting this resistance, Barnes makes a virtue of two distinctive qualities of the story sequence: the 'smallness' of its constitutive elements, and its capacity for generic and stylistic heterogeneity. The virtues of smallness are obviously highlighted by the woodworm's-eye view of history in 'The Stowaway', and it soon becomes apparent that a positive infestation of termites, beetles and sundry creepy-crawlies are swarming their way through Barnes's text, from the woodworm that devour the bishop's chair in 'The Wars of Religion' to the '80000000000000 mosquitoes' (Barnes, 1989: 201) that feast on Charlie, the obnoxious letter writer of 'Upstream!'. Barnes clearly relishes the havoc and distress inflicted by undersized and microscopic vermin on authoritarian or self-important characters. The woodworm who are so fiercely abominated by the prosecuting counsel in 'The Wars of Religion' are probably as close as this text gets to a 'hero'; and as Alan Clinton points out, it seems as though, in Barnes's imagination, 'the woodworm forms a counterpart to the bookworm' (cited in Guignery, 2006: 69–70). The woodworm thus function as a kind of collective proxy for their bookish creator, and as a visual shorthand for his emphasis on the aesthetic and ethic of smallness that seems to characterise his text's relationship to oppressive grand narratives. Overblown myths and 'official' ideologies that pass themselves off as absolute truth are among the primary satirical targets of *A History of the World*; its miniature fictions gnaw their way through these grand narratives without setting themselves up as new, 'authoritative' truths.

Barnes's orchestration of his sequence of subversive micronarratives might therefore be said both to exemplify and to extend Mary Louise Pratt's definition of the short story as a 'countergenre' to the novel (Pratt, 1994: 99). It is virtually impossible to define the short story without measuring it against longer narrative forms, especially the novel; but if the short story inevitably seems to come off worse in any such bluntly quantitative comparison, there are also qualitative features – such as its suggestive 'incompleteness', its thematic concentration, its rich affinities with folk tale and oral tradition – in which the short story compares favourably with the novel. Novels and short stories thus seem to enjoy a 'countergeneric' relationship, whereby the latter are defined by their parasitic dependence on, and subversive tension with, the former. In the case of *A History of the World*, the range of 'countergeneric' qualities exhibited by Barnes's stories is particularly rich, because they exhibit a parasitic, woodworm-like relationship not just with the novel, but with the grand narratives of official history and Biblical tradition.

The other prominent subversive quality of Barnes's text is its stylistic heterogeneity. Crossing the boundaries between historical and novelistic discourse, verbal and visual narrative, realism and fantasy, *A History of the World* is an ostentatiously unclassifiable text – not because its methods are *sui generis*, but because it seems to belong to so many recognisable categories simultaneously. In a well-known essay, Roland Barthes makes a valuable distinction between the conventionally self-contained 'Work' and the radically open-ended 'Text', where the latter is constituted by 'its subversive force in respect of the old classifications' (Barthes, 1977: 157). Barnes's text certainly seems to provide us with an exemplary illustration of the Barthesian 'Text'. None of the labels that we might attach to it – novel, story collection, prose miscellany – are demonstrably 'wrong', but it seems as though the best way to classify *A History of the World* is in terms of its own resistance to classification. It is an unapologetically 'impure' text, a bastardised cross-breeding of myth, history, fantasy and autobiography. And this cross-generic experimentation is by no means an exercise in formal experimentation for its own sake. The impure 'unclassifiability' of *A History of the World* represents a flamboyant rejection of the ideologies of 'purity' in whose name appalling crimes have been perpetrated over the centuries. The demise of mythical cross-breeds – the basilisk, the griffon, the sphinx, the hippogriff – during the ark's voyage in 'The Stowaway' ominously foreshadows the violent intolerance of 'impurity' that will produce any number of pogroms and ethnic cleansings in human history. The Flood is itself a colossal act of cleansing, of purification-through-extermination; Barnes's version of the Flood story initiates a string of references to violent attempts to separate the 'clean' from the 'unclean' (pp. 10, 44, 121, 184) perpetrated by those in pursuit of sinister policies of racial purity or ontological hygiene. This fanatically intolerant mania for purity produced its most atrocious consequences in the Holocaust, an event that haunts Barnes's narrative, and is addressed and most directly discussed in the section of the chapter 'Three Simple Stories' dealing with the tragic voyage of the *St Louis*, the cruise ship that left Hamburg in May 1939 with 937 Jewish refugees on a desperate search for asylum. It is worth noting that in its treatment of this sobering material, Barnes's text forcefully belies postmodernism's reputation for moral and intellectual frivolousness, and powerfully illustrates Robert Eaglestone's contention that 'postmodern thought is shaped explicitly or implicitly by the Holocaust ... [and] engages with and shapes how we understand the Holocaust' (Eaglestone, 2004: 12).

It is clear that Barnes's text focuses sympathetically on the fate of those who have been written out of history on the grounds of their supposed ontological inferiority. But a final question that is worth raising about *A History of the World* relates to the position of *gender* in all of this. One of the major lessons of feminist thought is that traditional versions of human history have been lopsidedly patriarchal and male-dominated, consistently downplaying or ignoring women's experience. And it would certainly be possible to align Barnes with this feminist critique of patriarchal historiography, not least with reference to his satirical portrait of Franklin Hughes, the philandering media historian in 'The Visitors'. If Barnes's text spoofs the masculine discourse of history, however, it does not always find room for female alternatives. The epistolary narrative in 'Upstream!', for example, is an archive of Charlie's self-letters, which are going unanswered by his female addressee; and whilst this chapter is obviously designed as an exposé of Charlie's infantile self-indulgence, it does nevertheless seem to constitute female subjectivity as a gap or silence around which male discourse circulates. The same pattern seems to be evident in the most 'personal' chapter in this text, 'Parenthesis', in which the insomniac author fretfully ponders questions of love, survival and history while his female partner sleeps. Whether this recurring conjunction between male discourse and female silence means that *A History of the World in 10½ Chapters* is simply another product of what Jacques Derrida calls the 'patriarchive' (Derrida, 1996: 4 n.1) is one of the abiding questions raised by this endlessly quizzical text.

Helen Simpson: *Hey Yeah Right Get a Life*

Clare Hanson suggests that one reason the short story has been amenable to feminists is that it has appealed to those writers who 'wanted to open up new areas of experience without having any a priori commitment to a particular type of social analysis' (Hanson, 1985: 165). Helen Simpson's *Hey Yeah Right Get a Life*, a collection of interlinked short stories about the lives of thirty-something mothers in suburban London, is a notable example of this kind of undogmatic, 'experiential' feminist storytelling. Simpson seems to bring to this collection a partly ironic sense that the short story might be a peculiarly 'appropriate' genre for the maternal experience, in the sense that her self-effacing heroines are too overwhelmed by domestic responsibilities to claim anything but a small portion of narrative to themselves. Her collection might also be read as a literary response to the demand, made by Julia Kristeva in 'Stabat Mater', that 'one needs to listen, more carefully than ever, to what mothers are saying today, through their economic difficulties [...] through their discomforts, insomnias, joys, angers, desires, pains, and pleasures' (Kristeva, 1987: 256). It is clear that *Hey Yeah Right Get a Life*, with its vivid renditions of maternal discomforts, insomnias, joys, angers, desires, pains and pleasures, answers, very precisely, Kristeva's demand that we cease viewing female subjectivity as some mystifying terra incognita; and, crucially, the collection listens to what mothers are saying without filtering out the background noise that makes it so hard for those maternal voices to be heard. 'Get a life!', the sarcastic playground taunt of the title, seems to follow Simpson's permanently harassed mothers around as they negotiate conflicting professional and domestic responsibilities, minister to the relentless, unignorable demands of young children, and make the best of frayed relations with their husbands. 'Life', in this collection, seems to have become a desperately scarce commodity; the idea of enjoying time and space to oneself is, for Simpson's heroines, a half-forgotten luxury. The possibility that mothers have no life or no story – in the sense that marriage and childbirth might be seen to represent the end of the 'story' of a woman's life or the absorption of her life into that of her family – is one that provides significant motivation for her art.

The opening story in the collection, 'Lentils and Lilies', sees the world through the scornfully unforgiving eyes of an independent-minded teenager, Jade Beaumont, who is poised confidently on the cusp of a young adulthood during which she expects to soar free from the dismally uninspiring ordinariness of bourgeois suburbia. Jade seems to be a gifted reader: she is getting to grips with Wordsworth, Coleridge and Keats for her A Levels, and is acutely responsive to the visual cues offered by the world around her, coolly appraising everything from the glitter on a young woman's shoes ('au pair') to the pelmeted curtains hanging in suburban windows ('so bourgeois') to a mother's heels protruding from her sandals 'like hunks of Parmesan' (Simpson, 2000: 7). But Jade also misreads or under-reads her environment. After her firsthand involvement in one of the unglamorous emergencies of maternal life (she reluctantly helps out a slightly panicky woman whose young daughter has got a lentil stuck up her nose), Jade recoils fastidiously from this aesthetically displeasing business of tears, screaming and mucus. Sharpened by her enthusiastic contact with Romantic poetry, Jade's 'hyperaesthetic teenage eyes' (7) are too dazzled by visions of her own imagined future to see anything but lacklustre uniformity and mildly disgusting physicality in the lives of the women around her. Positioned at the opening of the collection, Jade is an exemplary bad reader who can perceive no story in the life of the unnamed mother whom she halfheartedly assists: *her* story is simply not happening, or is one that has come to a premature and undignified end. By highlighting the limits to Jade's vision in this way, Simpson's story solicits the sympathetic attention of an implied reader who is prepared to listen more patiently than its heroine to the humdrum stories of suburban domesticity. It is important also to note that the mother, who appears solely as an anonymous, flustered and overwhelmed foil to Jade in 'Lentils and Lilies', reappears in the very next story, 'Café Society', where she is named (Frances) and where we are granted access to her back-story, the names of her children, and the anxieties and responsibilities that prey on her mind.

Several of Simpson's characters appear in more than one story: Jade's mother, Nicola Beaumont, is a subject of gossip in 'Hey Yeah Right Get a Life', but appears as the central character in 'Burns and the Bankers', whilst Jade herself reappears for a walk-on part as the babysitter in 'Hey Yeah Right Get a Life'. Dorrie and Max have a fraught anniversary dinner in the title story, and an equally difficult family holiday in 'Hurrah for the Hols'. These overlaps and reappearances create an engaging sense of diegetic continuity between the various tales in Simpson's collection. Whereas a story collection like *Dubliners* seems to reproduce the fragmented state of the atomised modern city, *Hey Yeah Right Get a Life* conjures a pleasing illusion of an integrated, three-dimensional social world whose citizens we bump into with dependable regularity. Simpson uses the story sequence to develop an incremental and, as it were, 'random' model of characterisation in which we acquaint ourselves with her heroines through a series of chance encounters in the course of which they are gently but vividly de-anonymised. At the same time, she obviously takes some pleasure in banishing Jade to the margins of the collection, emphatically devoting her attention to the lives of the thirty-something women about whom the self-centred teenager of 'Lentils and Lilies' is so notably incurious.

When Jade fantasises about 'the long jewelled narrative which was her future', she can see no further than 'about thirty-three or thirty-four' because '[t]his was about as far as any of the novels and films took her' (4). Pointedly correcting our culture's habit of consigning married women to narrative invisibility, the stories of *Hey Yeah Right Get a Life* insert themselves, vividly, in the blind spot of the novels and films that Jade has been naively consuming. The theme of visibility is directly raised by the epigraph to *Hey Yeah Right Get a Life*, which is an excerpt from *War and Peace* that describes the changed appearance of Natasha after she has children: 'stouter and broader', Tolstoy's heroine has become an almost unrecognisably different version of the 'slim, mobile Natasha of old days' to the extent that often 'her face and body were all that was to be seen, and the soul was not visible at all' (xi). It is worth noting that there is something comically incongruous about Simpson's choice of epigraph: the contrast in scale between Tolstoy's gigantic historical novel and her decidedly slender collection of suburban *petits récits* could scarcely be greater, and it seems fair to read this epigraph as an ironic glance at the oppressive, lumbering bulk of the epic novel from the perspective of an altogether more 'weightless', economical literary genre. But the contrast between bigness and smallness also prepares us for the question of the maternal body as it is raised by many of Simpson's stories. Tolstoy represents Natasha as a kind of flesh-and-blood Russian doll, a mother whose ample proportions conceal younger, slimmer versions of an 'original' self that is now all but invisible. The epigraph from *War and Peace* is thus presented by Simpson as symptomatic of a sense of alienation from the maternal body that is all too prone to be shared by women themselves. If Tolstoy's Natasha becomes difficult to recognise as she grows older, Simpson's heroines have trouble recognising themselves: Lois in 'Cheers' steels herself against the moment 'when middle age came and sat down on you with its enormous bum' (125), whilst Dorrie, the mother of three in 'Hey Yeah Right Get a Life', feels as though she has become a 'big fat zero' (39). Both Lois and Dorrie seem to have internalised the gaze of patriarchal society and turned it, disapprovingly, on their own bodies; the upshot for both is an alienating tendency to think of the maternal body as pure biology, as surplus flesh – a 'big fat zero' with no sharply defined identity and, crucially, no voice.

Simpson's stories are full of images of reticent, tongue-tied and silent women: Sally and Frances exchange fewer than two hundred words during an hour of child-interrupted conversation in 'Café Society'; Janine bites her tongue while a fellow opera-goer whispers unfunny asides during a performance of *Orpheus and Eurydice* in 'Opera'; the lachrymose speechifying and aggressive, alcohol-fuelled banter of male professionals dominate proceedings in 'Burns and the Bankers', a tale that implicitly and mischievously includes Robbie Burns himself in its rogues' gallery of insufferably loquacious males. Powerful emotions in *Hey Yeah Right Get a Life* often remain unspoken and even unformulated, not because Simpson's heroines are lost for words but because any potential listeners are childishly uncomprehending, selfishly indifferent, or impossibly distracted. Simpson's stories are designed to amplify those female silences, to make them resonantly audible, and to relate them to the broader question of the literary and cultural silence about women above 'thirty-three or thirty-four'. Her writing thus offers itself as a form of compensation, albeit consciously belated and inadequate, for the linguistic freedoms that are withheld from her heroines; and the short story seems an appropriately unassuming, sotto voce mode in which to break that silence without presuming to erase it or pretend that it never existed.

In Simpson's hands, the short story also raises striking questions about the position of maternal subjectivity in geographical and cultural space. In 'Hurrah for the Hols', Dorrie's husband Max enjoys a solo expedition to a hermit's island that he 'conquer[s]' and 'pattern[s] with his footprints' (176). Max's afternoon of splendid isolation from care and responsibility sharply reminds us that there is no comparable opportunity for his wife to play Robinson Crusoe; indeed, Simpson's allusion to the expansive horizons of Defoe's adventure narrative can only emphasise the restricted ambit of her suburban miniatures. And *Robinson Crusoe* is by no means the only grand narrative by which *Hey Yeah Right Get a Life* finds itself briefly overshadowed. Tolstoy's *War and Peace*, as we have already seen, is positioned imposingly at the head of a collection that constantly samples or 'overhears' snatches of much grander, male-authored or male-dominated narratives, including Shakespeare, Romantic lyric poetry, opera and classical myth. Jade Beaumont's mind buzzes with lines from Wordsworth as she strolls to a job interview; fragments of the libretto of *Orpheus and Eurydice* strike poignantly home for Janine in 'Opera'; Dorrie's squabbling children in the title story live through 'as many variants of passion as occur in the average Shakespeare play' (25) before breakfast on a typically fractious morning. Though there is clearly some comic effect in these juxtapositions, Simpson's goal is not simply to create easy opportunities for high art to 'upstage' everyday life. Rather, her repertoire of high cultural allusions position her stories, and her heroines, at the interface between the sublime and the humdrum, from which vantage point it becomes possible to appreciate that suburbia has its own poetry. Simpson's writing shimmers with unexpected lyricism; its delight in the 'myopic blue dazzle of forget-me-nots' (10), the 'menthol coldness' of a spring morning (20), and a sun that 'glared with the blanched fluorescence of a shaving light' (174) continually reminds us that flashes of poetry are there for the taking amidst the colourless prose of everyday life. In this context it seems as though Simpson's feminism finds its most distinctive expression in the vein of surreptitious hedonism that runs through these stories. In 'Opera', Janine surmises that the role of music is to provide inner release: 'while on the outside you moderated and rationalised and subdued, in your secret self you were allowed to live with an intensity not otherwise sanctioned' (120). The stories are explorations of that interior, secretive pleasure, of the rare opportunities for hedonistic self-absorption enjoyed by those who are expected to minister ceaselessly, selflessly and wholeheartedly to the needs of others. Nowhere is this theme more excitedly explored than in 'Wurstikiget', which is the only first-person narrative in *Hey Yeah Right Get a Life*, and quite the most 'selfish', or unapologetically self-indulgent, story in the collection. 'Wurstikiget' – which loosely translates as 'sausageness', or 'not giving a sausage' – is the story of a lunch-time shopping spree at a hyper-exclusive London boutique accessible only by means of a secret password. This Aladdin's cave of flamboyantly unconventional 'apotheosis clothes' (157), where two female friends enjoy something like temporary freedom from their city jobs and relationships, provides what is Simpson's most memorable visual shorthand for those 'restricted spaces' where the 'secret self' is allowed pleasures not otherwise sanctioned. And her story collection might be thought of as performing a similar kind of function, providing a space for hedonistic pleasure for those who feel as though they are being squeezed into tiny corners of their own overcrowded lives.

Conclusion

I began this chapter by citing Niall Lucy's extremely suggestive comment that every work of literary art confronts the reader with the 'question of itself'. In the case of story sequences like *Dubliners*, *A History of the World in 10½ Chapters* and *Hey Yeah Right Get a Life*, the question of the text's fragmentary unity can never be far from the reader's mind. Whenever I teach these texts, I ask students if they can identify a 'common denominator' that binds together the various stories of a given collection. And whilst plausible answers to this question – 'paralysis', 'survival', 'maternity', for example – are not exactly hard to find, a supplementary question soon presents itself: in supplying a thematic common denominator for these texts, are we wrapping them up in precisely the kind of metanarratives that they aim to resist? It is by no means untrue to assert that Barnes's text is 'about survival', for example, or that Simpson's is 'about maternity'; but in boiling these texts down to a single master theme we are certainly losing something of their calculated heterogeneity. To use Jean-Michel Rabaté's terms once more, the process of 'reading-writing which transforms a collection of short stories into a text' may involve a deeply problematic assimilation of difference to sameness. The temptation that constantly presents itself to the scholarly reader, whether student or instructor, is to rewrite the story collection as a seamlessly integrated and monologic narrative. A focus on unacknowledged silences and unresolved contradictions is, as I have suggested in this chapter, one of the best ways of keeping these heterogeneous texts 'open' and avoiding the tendency to rewrite the story sequence as a novel manqué.

Works Cited

Barnes, Julian. *A History of the World in 10½ Chapters*. London: Cape, 1989.
Barthes, Roland. 'From Work to Text', in *Image, Music, Text*, trans. Stephen Heath London: Fontana, 1977. 155–64.
Buxton, Jackie, 'Julian Barnes's Theses on History (In 10½ Chapters)'. *Contemporary Literature* 41:1 (2000). 56–86.

Derrida, Jacques. *Archive Fever: A Freudian Impression*, trans. Eric Prenowitz. Chicago: The University of Chicago Press, 1996.
Eaglestone, Robert. *The Holocaust and the Postmodern*. Oxford: Oxford University Press, 2004.
Guignery, Vanessa. *The Fiction of Julian Barnes: A Reader's Guide to Essential Criticism*. Basingstoke: Palgrave Macmillan, 2006.
Hanson, Clare. *Short Stories and Short Fictions, 1880–1980*. London: Macmillan – now Palgrave Macmillan, 1985.
Hillis Miller, J. *Fiction and Repetition: Seven English Novels*. Oxford: Blackwell, 1982.
Joyce, James. *Dubliners*. Harmondsworth: Penguin, 1992.
Kristeva, Julia. 'Stabat Mater', in *Tales of Love*, trans. Leon S. Roudiez. New York: Columbia University Press, 1987. 234–63.
Lucy, Niall. *Postmodern Literary Theory: An Introduction*. Oxford: Blackwell, 1997.
Pound, Ezra. *Pound/Joyce: The Letters of Ezra Pound to James Joyce, with Pound's Essays on Joyce*, ed. Forrest Read. London: Faber, 1967.
Pratt, Mary Louise. 'The Short Story: the Long and the Short of It', in *The New Short Story Theories*, ed. Charles E. May. Athens: Ohio University Press, 1994. 91–113.
Rabaté, Jean-Michel. 'Silence in *Dubliners*', in *James Joyce: New Perspectives*, ed. Colin MacCabe. Sussex: The Harvester Press, 1982. 45–72.
Simpson, Helen. *Hey Yeah Right Get a Life*. London: Cape, 2000.

3
Raymond Carver and the Power of Style

Martin Scofield

The Question of Style

Apart from its discussion in a specialised field of linguistics, 'style' does not often these days get singled out for literary critical attention. Of course teachers and critics acknowledge in a general way the importance of 'form', and in short story theory there is still a marked concern with generic definitions. But 'style', that broad term that connotes various elements that distinguish an individual writer – 'manner', 'tone', 'voice' and so on – tends to get left out of the discussion.

This has something to do with an understandable desire to concentrate on 'substance', on what a writer has to say, his or her view of the world. (And yet how can that view be detached from its precise expression?) It may also have something to do with an awareness that has grown in the past 30 years or so that generic pressures on the one hand and the pressures of general linguistic context on the other may play as much a part in the particular formation of a writer's 'style' as distinctively individual features. The Comte de Buffon's now proverbial phrase 'Le style est l'homme même' – 'Style is the man himself' (Buffon 1954: 503b, quoted in Brown, 1997: 806) is still, I believe, suggestive; but criticism has more recently become especially aware how both style (and indeed 'the man himself') may be formed to a great extent by the surrounding forces in his society and culture.

There is also the sense that 'style', to the extent that it can be adopted and changed at will, can be something superficial and derivative. But nevertheless, we still, I think, need an idea of authentic style which will focus on that distinctive element in writing which signals the quality of an individual writer (however it comes about), that quality which, when we read a sentence, might make us say, 'that must be' such and such a writer. This stylistic 'signature' ought to be something we can communicate to students.

When 'teaching' Raymond Carver (whose work needs no teaching, only careful perusal, weighing and discussing) we need to be able to identify his recurring preoccupations (with the nature of love or the purpose of telling stories; with what gives value to life or what destroys it; with the dullness of mere everyday existence and the simple and surprising things that can lift that dullness) and organise our sense of his work around those identifications. But we also need to look closely at 'the words on the page', the way he puts down that word (and not another) after the one that went before, and the way he frequently revised his stories to achieve more precisely the effect he wanted.

Carver had a lot to say in essays and interviews about the question of style, though he questions the emphasis on the particular term:

> Some writers may have a bunch of talent; I don't know any writers who are without it. But a unique and exact way of looking at things, and finding the right context for expressing that way of looking, that's something else [...] Every great or even every very good writer makes the world over according to his own specifications.
>
> It's akin to style, what I'm talking about, but it isn't style alone. It's the writer's particular and unmistakable signature on everything he writes. It is his world and no other. This is one of the things that distinguishes one writer from another. Not talent. There's plenty of that around. But a writer who has some special way of looking at things and who gives artistic expression to that way of looking: that writer may be around for a time. (Carver, 1986: 22)

So in this chapter I shall demonstrate approaches to Carver's style as a unique 'way of looking at things', with particular attention to 'looking', the visual activity; but also with attention to hearing, and the sound of language: and beyond those elements again, with focusing on those details in everyday life that Carver gives attention to.

Beginnings

'Endings are elusive, middles are nowhere to be found, but worst of all is to begin, to begin, to begin': so says Edgar, the writing-student narrator, in Donald Barthelme's story 'The Dolt' (Barthelme, 1991: 91). Carver's beginnings are always distinctive and important, and he has often said in interviews that, however much he may revise a story, the first line usually stays (See for example Gentry and Stull, 1990: 127). He tells in *Fires* how the first line of 'Put Yourself in My Shoes' came to him before he had any story to go with it; 'He was running the vacuum cleaner when the telephone rang' (Carver, 1986: 26). (In the published version of the story the sentence is 'The telephone rang while he was running the vacuum cleaner.')

What could be more ordinary, more banal, as a way of starting a story? Why would any particular story grow out of that? But look what it actually contains: yes, banal activity, the humdrum of empty uneventful life (there may even, in retrospect, be something significant about the vacuum cleaner); and then the advent of something from outside: the telephone. Something has entered the vacuum, disturbed the solitary activity.

Telephone calls are often pivotal or in some way momentous in Carver, a kind of catalyst: the phone call from the unknown woman in 'Are You a Doctor?' (Carver, 1985); the call from the narrator to his girlfriend and the end of 'Where I'm Calling From' (Carver, 1995) (rounding off the story by giving one of its meanings to the title); the mysterious overheard phone call in 'Blackbird Pie' (Carver, 1995); the phone conversation between the narrator and her husband, Stuart, at the end of the later, longer version of 'So Much Water So Close to Home' (Carver, 1995), where she finally voices a reason for the deep aversion her husband's behaviour has caused her. A ringing telephone is a voice from the outside, a signal of change. The short story can focus especially well on these small details that signal or set in motion great events. Here the ringing telephone is simply a call from the narrator's wife inviting him to an office party, which leads to a drink in a bar, which leads to the visit to their old landlord and the encounter which is the subject of the story. At the beginning he was 'between stories' and felt despicable: at the end the vacuum is filled.

But let's look a little more closely at the rest of that first paragraph:

> He had worked his way through the apartment and was doing the living room, using the nozzle attachment to get at the cat hairs between the cushions. He stopped and listened and then switched off the vacuum. He went to answer the telephone. (Carver, 1995: 74)

There is a thoroughness, and methodicalness, about this character, even a touch of obsession. 'Using the nozzle attachment ...' (There's something very ordinary but oddly satisfying about that nozzle attachment – you feel he finds it satisfying. But it's also tedious, time-filling activity: Meyers is, after all, 'between stories'.) 'He stopped and listened ...' 'He went to answer ...' Paratactic sentences, taking one thing at a time, even the 'unimportant' things. (Although the cat comes back as one of the points of contention between the Myers and their old landlord: the details usually function in more than one way.)

A short story writer does not have much time or space to get things across, so the first few sentences must tell, must be charged with some distinctive feeling. Carver once pointed out that, among other considerations, editors get sent so many stories, they often make their decisions on the strength of the first paragraph or two. Take the opening of 'Fat' (Carver, 1995):

> I am sitting over coffee and cigarettes at my friend Rita's and I am telling her about it.
> Here is what I tell her.
> It is late of a slow Wednesday when Herb sees the fat man at my station. (Carver, 1995: 50)

What we get is the narrator's voice – intent, deliberate, telling us what she told Rita. It is important that the story is told in the first person: the narrator is talking to us now, and she is also presenting her story as happening now; so although the voice is quiet and unexcited – the opening is not 'dramatic' in any loose sense – the telling is still dramatic in the sense that we are listening to a story being told now, and we are there also in the present of that story. The paragraphing, too, increases the deliberateness and intentness: three separate paragraphs for each of those first three sentences. The story will go on to tell of an encounter which means more to Rita than she can quite articulate or understand, so that tone of deliberateness, that measured pace, is important. Even though we don't yet know why this means so much to Rita, we know from her tone that it does, and we want to find out why. So we (or that editor) read on:

> This fat man is the fattest person I have ever seen, though he is neat-appearing and well dressed enough. Everything about him is big. But it is the fingers I remember best. When I stop at the table near his to see the old couple, I first notice the fingers. They look three times the size of a normal person's fingers – long, thick, creamy fingers. (Carver, 1995: 50)

Much of the sense of the importance this has for Rita comes from the repetition. Not 'This man is the fattest ...' but 'This fat man is the fattest.' And the next sentence has 'big'. And then there are the 'fingers' – the word is uttered three times. And 'three times the size' is followed by three adjectives, at the end of the sentence for emphasis: 'long, thick, creamy fingers'. This focus on the fingers plays no small part in establishing what emerges as Rita's combination of admiration at the fat man's courtliness and a curious sexual attraction or sympathetic self-identification that will finally reveal itself at the end of the story. 'Long' suggests something of the courtliness; 'thick', the sensuality; and 'creamy' is perfectly judged to evoke the connection with food (soon the man will order sour cream with his baked potato and later will have an extra dish of ice cream with his dessert), and also a hint of voluptuous sexuality.

Endings

The short story has been called an 'end directed form' (see Gerlach, 1985). That is to say it 'starts near the end' as it were, or is focused from the first on the ending, which usually clinches or drives home the story in some way. Carver himself has said:

> Most of my stories start pretty near the end of the arc of the dramatic conflict. I don't give a lot of detail about what went on before; I just start it fairly near the end of the swing of the action. (Gentry and Stull, 1990: 229)

And the ending must connect – in some way – with the beginning. Robert Louis Stevenson, himself a master of the form, put it memorably when he compared a long story with the shorter form:

> The denouement of a long story is nothing; it is just a 'full close', which you may approach and accompany as you please – it is a coda, not an essential member in the rhythm; but the body and end of a short story is the bone of the bone and the blood of the blood of the beginning. (Stevenson, 1924, IV: 95, quoted in Shaw, 1983: 30)

So the ending of Carver's 'Fat' takes up, changes and confirms that beginning I have just analysed. Rita the waitress is back home with her husband:

> I get into bed and move clear over to the edge and lie there on my stomach. But right away, as soon as he turns off the light and gets

into bed, Rudy begins. I turn on my back and relax some, though it is against my will. But here is the thing. When he gets on me, I suddenly feel I am fat. I feel I am terrifically fat, so fat that Rudy is a tiny thing and hardly there at all.

That's a funny story, Rita says, but I can see she doesn't know what to make of it.

I feel depressed. But I won't go into it with her. I've already told her too much.

She sits there waiting, her dainty fingers poking her hair.

Waiting for what? I'd like to know.

It is August.

My life is going to change. I feel it. (Carver, 1995: 54)

'Rudy begins': the weary commonplaceness of that says everything about Rita's sexual feelings. 'But here is the thing' – that colloquial intentness tells us that the 'point' is coming, though it turns out to be a feeling rather than a 'meaning'. The fat man's fatness, combined with his courtliness – his combination of gross size and a kind of feminine delicacy – has had this strangely empowering effect on Rita, a shift of consciousness. Carver doesn't try to explain why this happens, just how it happens. He has said: 'People's actions seem to be of most [sic] interest, finally, than *why* they do things' (Gentry and Stull, 1990: 146). His style conveys the feeling that something is there underneath. Rita does not know what to make of it (and her 'That's a funny story' is itself funny) but the reader does, or at the least s/he knows that there is something there to ponder and work out. Rita waits 'her dainty fingers poking her hair' (the dainty fingers, fidgety, vague, contrast with the fat man's 'long, thick, creamy fingers' which handed her the menu or arranged his napkin with an aplomb we infer from the whole description of his actions). '*Waiting for what?*' is comic, too, in the way its exasperation is partly at odds with the fact that Rita has not, after all, tried to sum up the point; though not entirely at odds, because really she, and Carver, has told us enough. And she is also waiting for the change she knows is coming (whatever it's going to be – changing her job, having a child, leaving her husband?). It's that feeling of change that is the 'point' of the story, a feeling that is there in the very paragraphing of the ending, just as a presentiment of it was already there in the emphasis of the opening: 'Here's what I'm telling her.'

Much has been written about moments of 'epiphany' in the short story – those moments of revelation or realisation that come to the protagonist and the reader (sometimes just to the latter). Carver famously kept a three-by-five card on his desk with a quotation from Chekhov: '... and suddenly everything became clear to him' (Carver, 1986: 23). But often with Carver's endings there is a kind of 'anti-epiphany', where the revelation is felt to be implicit even though it never quite becomes realised, or the reader has to work at the meaning. In 'Why Don't You Dance?' (Carver, 1995), for example, the story of the young couple who buy furniture from a man having a sale in which he has put his whole bedroom suite out in his front yard, ends with the girl dancing with the man and saying 'You must be desperate or something' – which is a kind of realisation, but only an obvious or partial one, which does not get to what the incident means for the girl. But then there is a kind of coda:

> Weeks later, she said: 'The guy was about middle-aged. All his things right there in his yard. No lie. We got real pissed and danced. In the driveway. Oh, my God. Don't laugh. He played us these records. Look at this record-player. The old guy gave it to us. And all these crappy records. Will you look at this shit?'
> She kept talking. She told everyone. There was more to it, and she was trying to get it talked out. After a time, she quit trying. (Carver, 1995: 130)

Something about the experience – the strange encounter with despair made public, the inside becoming the outside – clearly haunts the girl. And what haunts her especially, we infer from the style of the coda, is the sense of her own involvement with the man, her being drawn to this despair and in some way implicated in the possibility of it. The short sentences, the sense of something ridiculous and perhaps humiliating ('Don't laugh') and the unexpected vehemence of 'crappy' and 'shit', suggest an emotional involvement and even a kind of implicit self-disgust at having got caught up in this, and a sense of something previously unknown in herself. Without the matter ever being explicitly clinched the reader gets the sense of the momentousness of the event for the girl, and the sense of the fascination of the man's despair as a possibility for any human life.

Again, in 'One More Thing' (Carver, 1995), L. D. is leaving his wife and daughter after a violent argument in which he has thrown a jar of pickles through the kitchen window. The story is a tragi-comedy of verbal abuse, and the desire on both sides to win the contest verbally. The comedy comes partly from verbal inadequacy, and from the attempt to say something final and devastating being undermined by illogic and mixed metaphor: 'You're nuts here, anyway. This is a nuthouse. There's another life out there. Believe me, this is no picnic, this nuthouse' (120). L. D.'s aim is for finality, closure, but even his smallest actions undermine him. Carver gives in detail his obsessive attempts to pack, and occasionally slips into free indirect discourse, which suggests both the writer's closeness to the protagonist and his detachment from him: 'He couldn't get the shaving bag closed, *but that was okay*' (121, my italics). And then at the end he squares up for a final confrontation:

> He put the suitcase down and his shaving bag on top of the suitcase. He drew himself up and faced them.
> They moved back.
> 'Watch it, Mom,' Rae said.
> 'I'm not afraid of him,' Maxine said.
> L. D. put the shaving bag under his arm and picked up the suitcase.
> He said, 'I just want to say one more thing.'
> But then he could not think what it could possibly be. (Carver, 1995: 122)

The vain attempt to assert authority is there in the bodily movements (that shaving bag persists to the end as a kind of fetish of control); and the final assertion and failure – the clinching non-revelation of awareness and authority which is the logical culmination of the movement of the story – is there in the anti-epiphany of the last line. Suddenly, one might say, nothing became clear to him.

Rhythm

Carver spoke often of the physical impact on him of Hemingway's prose: '[...] the prose hit me. I would read and reread those stories and feel a physical excitement. The way the words fell on the page, their sound, was exciting' (Gentry and Stull, 1990: 83). And one could sum up the quality of that sound, that falling on the page, in the term 'rhythm'. Rhythm in a story is a matter of single sentences, and also a matter of the curve of a whole story. It is usually established in the very first paragraph, is maintained throughout and then confirmed or sometimes modified or reversed at the end. Take the opening of 'Elephant' (Carver, 1995), a story about a well-meaning man hopelessly exploited by his relatives:

> I knew it was a mistake to let my brother have the money. I didn't need anybody else owing me. But when he called and said he

couldn't make a payment on his house, what could I do? I'd never been inside his house – he lived a thousand miles away, in California; I'd never even *seen* his house – but I didn't want him to lose it. He cried over the phone and said he was losing everything he'd worked for. He said he'd pay me back. February, he said. Maybe sooner. No later, anyway, than March. He said his income-tax refund was on the way. Plus, he said, he had a little investment that would mature in February. He acted secretive about the investment thing, so I didn't press for details.

'Trust me on this,' he said. 'I won't let you down.' (Carver, 1995: 386)

The rhythm helps establish the tone, and it is the tone which makes this story, which is one of Carver's funniest. The short sentences (Carver's sentences are characteristically short) and repeated syntactic and rhythmic patterns help build the tone of anxious explanation, which simultaneously asserts and undermines the speaker's claim that his actions were unavoidable ('I knew it was ...', 'I didn't need ...', 'But when he called ...', 'What could I do? I'd never been ...'). Those metrical opening phrases later break up into looser but still metrical patterns, as if the assertiveness of the opening rhythms is beginning to crack ('I'd never even seen ...', 'He cried over the phone ...', 'He said he'd pay me back'); and then looser still in the last three sentences of that first paragraph. And then there's the way the very short staccato phrases echo the brother's own phrases (which comically undermine themselves), shifting into free indirect discourse in the last two sentences here: 'He said he'd pay me back. February, he said. Maybe sooner. No later, anyway, than March.' And the way the last apologetic sentence of the first paragraph contrasts risibly with the earnest direct speech of the next line, the comic and rhythmic climax of the whole passage: '"Trust me on this," he said, "I won't let you down."'

This rhythmic pattern of firmness followed by break-up, followed in turn by renewed firmness, continues throughout the story, embodying the comic rhythm of the narrator's helpless, decent, weak, generous feelings towards his brother – comic in the sense both of risible and in some curious way heartening. The repeated-with-variations questions 'What could I do?', 'I was sore ... who wouldn't be?' 'Her kids had to eat, didn't they?' 'I had a job, didn't I?' 'What else could I do?' 'It's the stuff kids like to eat, right?' 'What could he do?' act as a kind of musical refrain of helpless appeal throughout the story. The rhythm and tone are crucial in establishing the essential comic, helpless good nature of the narrator. And then in the last part there is a kind of long closing movement of about two pages, a vigorous presto or allegro which affirms the nature of the protagonist's faith in life. The narrator goes for a walk, and the sentences swing into a confident stride which keeps up the momentum even when the sense or phrasing ('not to mention') adds a momentary comic deflation:

> I kept on walking. Then I began to whistle. I felt I had the right to whistle if I wanted to. I let my arms swing as I walked. But the lunch pail kept throwing me off balance. I had sandwiches, an apple, and some cookies in there, not to mention the thermos. (Carver, 1995: 400)

The basic anaphoric pattern ('I kept ...', 'I felt ...', 'I let ...', 'I had ...') keeps an underlying positive rhythm, broken only by the changed syntax of the deflating phrase ('But the lunch pail ...'). Even the 'redundant' phrases 'in there' and 'not to mention' add a sympathetically comic sense of over-assertion. The narrator stands outside a café, and a friend stops by to give him a lift and decides to show him what his car can do. In the last paragraph, the narrator seems to reveal a new confidence, a new sense of reckless enjoyment:

> 'Go,' I said. 'What are you waiting for, George?' And that's when we really flew. Wind howled outside the windows. He had it floored, and we were going flat out. We streaked down that road in his big unpaid-for car. (Carver, 1995: 401)

In addition to the narrator's jokey question (George is already giving it 'everything he could'), his renewed optimism is there in the rhythm as well as the sense, in those repeated metrical tetrads of stresses with a final extra beat in the last: ('He had it floored', 'going flat out', 'streaked down that road', 'big unpaid for car.')

A large part of a writer's rhythm depends on punctuation. And Carver has more than once quoted Isaac Babel's famous dictum (from Babel's story 'Guy de Maupassant'): 'No iron can pierce the heart with such force as a period put just at the right place' (Carver, 1995: xi and 1986: 24). One could illustrate this from innumerable places in Carver's stories, particularly the endings. Punctuation is crucial for the endings of 'Fat' and 'Why Don't You Dance?' as we have already seen; and one could add the endings of 'What We Talk About When We Talk About Love', or 'Errand' (Carver, 1995). Carver is fond (though not so much that it becomes a mannerism) of ending with short, staccato sentences punctuated with full-stops, when he wants a sense of closure. Conversely he can end with a longer sentence with lingering, parallel subordinate clauses when he wants a sense of things growing and opening up, as in the marvellous last sentence of 'The Calm' (Carver, 1995). But perhaps Carver's most striking use of 'the period [...] in just the right place' comes at the end of 'Nobody Said Anything' (Carver, 1995). This story of a boyhood exploit of coarse fishing, a fight to the death between two boys and a summer steelhead trout (with surely a humorous nod towards Hemingway's 'The Old Man and the Sea') might have ended simply on a note of black farce and bathos. After the young narrator has vainly tried to show his parents his mangled trophy of half a fish, the scene breaks down with the father's shouting, swearing and recrimination. But then the boy goes back outside; and the prose, the anaphora, those periods, that paragraphing, register what is surely a moment of paradoxical triumph:

> I went back outside. I looked into the creel. What was there looked silver under the porch light. What was there filled the creel.
> I lifted him out. I held him. I held that half of him. (Carver, 1995: 15)

Epiphany does seem the right word here: a revelation (for us and the boy) of strange beauty in the midst of ugliness and strange heroism in the midst of farce; a revelation pierced home by those periods.

Irony or Absence of Irony?

One of the most interesting questions about Carver's style in terms of its tone is its relation to irony. If irony means a tone in which the author's attitude to what is said is meant to be in some way superior to that of the narrator or speaker, or where the author implies a subtler meaning behind his words, aimed only at the initiated, then perhaps irony is not generally prevalent in Carver. At any rate he normally avoids an irony in which the position of the narrator (or, behind him or her, the author) is one of superiority. The classic exemplar of this kind of irony might be Henry James. Carver by contrast has said that he is uncomfortable with it:

> I see irony as a sort of pact or compact between the writer and the reader in that they know more than the characters do. The characters are set up and then they're set down again in some sort of subtle pratfall or awakening. I don't feel any such complicity with the reader. [...] I'm much more interested in my characters, in the people in my story, than I am in any potential reader. I'm uncomfortable

with irony if it's at the expense of someone else, if it hurts the characters. (Gentry and Stull, 1990: 185)

So Carver is generally on a level with his characters, feeling with them rather than against them. And yet this can hardly preclude a stance in which the writer, and through him the reader, sometimes knows more than the character, or has a different perspective on the characters than they do themselves. In the story I've already discussed, 'Elephant', the comedy of the haplessly generous narrator relies on us having a slightly different sense of him than he has of himself. We can smile, or indeed, like Carver's audience when he read the story in a small Seattle bookshop, laugh outright at the convolutions of his self-justification or his anxiously repeated refrain 'What could I do?' (Stull and Carroll, 1993: 107). But it is a sympathetic not a contemptuous laughter; our sense of his naivety is balanced against our sense of his generosity. We could all be in that position; and indeed it seems that Carver often was.[1] So Carver's irony here is as much a self-irony as anything else, or an irony which seems to rise above classifying one group of people above another, and to see the human condition as subject to a perpetual ironic discrepancy between self-awareness and reality.

One could take examples from innumerable places in Carver's stories, but the narrator of 'Cathedral' (Carver, 1995) will illustrate the point. He tells the story of the visit of his wife's blind friend in a tone of frank and baffled incomprehension, an inability to come to terms with his feelings of discomfort, his feeling that there is something uncanny about Robert. At one point he tells of Robert's marriage to Beulah, and of Beulah's death from cancer not long after:

> It was a little wedding – who'd want to go to such a wedding in the first place? – just the two of them, plus the minister and the minister's wife. But it was a church wedding just the same. It was what Beulah had wanted, he'd said. [...] She'd died in a Seattle hospital room, the blind man sitting beside her bed and holding on to her hand. They'd married, lived and worked together, slept together – had sex, sure – and then the blind man had to bury her. All this without his ever having seen what the goddamned woman looked like. It was beyond my understanding. Hearing this, I felt sorry for the blind man for a little bit. (Carver, 1995: 295)

Clearly there is irony here in that the author presumably does not share the narrator's naïve attitude. ('Who'd want to go to such a wedding ...?';

'the goddamned woman'; and the subtle registering of discomfort being shaken off: 'had sex, sure'). But we are so much taken inside the mind of the narrator that we can at least share his feelings even while we are demurring from them; and the last sentence gives the sense that he is already divided between discomfort and an awareness of some responsibility of compassion. The irony towards the narrator is gently comic rather than satirical: we are so taken inside his mind that we feel with and cannot entirely repudiate him.

In other places the 'irony' – if one should still call it that – is barely perceptible as a kind of deadpan humour, particularly in the rendering of banality. The opening of 'What's in Alaska?' (Carver, 1995) is typical:

> Jack got off work at three. He left the station and drove to a shoe store near his apartment. He put his foot up on the stool and let the clerk unlace his work boot.
> 'Something comfortable,' Jack said. 'For casual wear.'
> 'I have something', the clerk said.
> The clerk brought out three pairs of shoes and Jack said he would take the soft beige-coloured shoes that made his feet feel free and springy. He paid the clerk and put the box with his boots under his arm. He looked down at his new shoes as he walked. Driving home, he felt that his foot moved freely from pedal to pedal. (Carver, 1995: 55)

'Is this the beginning of a story?' a reader might ask incredulously. 'I mean, how dull does this guy sound? Beige-coloured shoes? [Later, his wife doesn't like the colour either.] And 'his foot moved freely from pedal to pedal'? Wow, some big deal!' And yet the reader might later reflect, this is the kind of thing he does. (Well, maybe not the beige shoes). After reading a certain amount of Carver we recognise this kind of thing as the comedy of everyday life. (There is also the very slight overstatement, the unnecessary flourish, or smugness, in the clerk's 'I have something'). The triviality of the actions in this opening is a common enough triviality. The emptiness that lies behind the story (and in Alaska) is the emptiness of a great deal of life.

'The Main of Life is, indeed,' said Samuel Johnson, 'composed of small Incidents, and petty Occurrences' (Johnson, 1963: 208). If Carver's sense of things here is ironic, one might call it the irony of petty occurrences.

Detail, Image, Symbol

> I never start with an idea. I always see something. I start with an image, a cigarette being put out in a jar of mustard, for instance, or the remains, the wreckage, of a dinner left on the table. Pop cans in the fireplace, that sort of thing. And a feeling goes with that. And that feeling seems to transport me back to that particular time and place, and the ambience of the time. But it is the image, and the emotion that goes with that image – that's what's important. (Gentry and Stull, 1990: 154)

Carver's statement aptly defines the way his creative imagination seizes on details. His style is full of material objects, usually of the most mundane sort. His method is based on plain and literal description. He rarely describes the appearance of his characters in detail, but what is important is the ambience that surrounds them. Nor is he given to metaphor and simile, figurative writing in the usual sense. Instead the physical details – or one particular physical detail – will take on a significance which come to sum up a whole story (and often gives the title of the story). And although Carver is not a symbolist writer, this detail often comes to have a symbolic charge. Carver was a great admirer of William Carlos Williams, and the principles of the earlier twentieth century poetic Imagists are – as they were with Hemingway – relevant to his work. Pound wrote: 'I believe that the proper and perfect symbol is the natural object', by which he meant the object that arises naturally in the course of literal description, so that its 'symbolic function does not obtrude' and that it still makes sense to someone who only sees the literal meaning – to whom, as Pound put it 'a hawk is a hawk' (Pound, 1960: 9).

So in Carver's story 'Vitamins' (Carver, 1995) the vitamins are the door-to-door sales goods of the narrator's wife, Patti; the material objects around which the story develops. Patti sells the vitamins and runs a group of saleswomen; the out-of-work husband nearly has an affair with one of the women, but it is nipped in the bud by an encounter in a bar with a disturbed Vietnam veteran; the vitamin business goes flat and Patti begins to get desperate. The vitamins provide a pretext and a structure, but with their suggestion of vitality and health they also suggest the vitality of the women, especially Patti, and the decline of sales is also a decline in Patti's well-being. At the end of the story the narrator comes in from his last meeting with Donna to encounter his wife having a nightmare about her job, screaming she is late for work ('But there was no sample case, no vitamins'). He is in the bathroom and starts looking for aspirin in the medicine chest; and the story ends:

> I knocked some stuff out of the medicine chest. Things rolled into the sink. 'Where's the aspirin?' I said. I knocked down some more things. I didn't care. Things kept falling. (Carver, 1995: 213–4)

The final detail is entirely natural and the story ends as if in mid-action: but the relation of the medicine to the vitamins, and the wider suggestiveness of 'Things kept falling', make the ending a rounding off of the whole theme. Similarly in 'The Bridle' (Carver, 1985), though more explicitly, the bridle that the narrator finds left behind in one of the rooms of the building where she and her husband are apartment-managers suggests – through her perception of it – the order and discipline with which, in her small way, she tries to live; and the end of the story is a kind of unforced summation: 'When you felt it pull, you'd know it was time. You'd know you were going somewhere' (433). Other contingent details of the story have similar effects: the way the narrator writes her name, Marge, on some fifty-dollar bills she's been given, and imagines people who own them later thinking 'Who's this Marge?' (421), suggesting her incipient puzzlement at her own identity; or her disapproval of the lottery game at the party of a drunken lawyer, where the prize is a free divorce-handling.

Many of Carver's stories are about his characters' distinct but very faint awareness of their predicaments – the chaos, or emptiness, or restrictedness of their lives – and his technique of metonymy, as it might be called, in which a particular object or a very small incident comes to stand for a larger whole, is especially fitted to that preoccupation. It is a technique that frequently allows some glimpse of hope, or at least possibility, in an otherwise gloomy world. The glimpse of possibility is rarely fulfilled, but it is there; and perhaps is all the more charged because it comes to nothing. In 'Feathers' (Carver, 1995) the narrator Jack and his wife Fran have dinner with Bud and Olla and their fat, 'ugly' baby. Bud and Olla keep a peacock, a bird the narrator and Fran have never seen, and the latter couple are deeply struck by its beauty and strangeness. After a richly satisfying meal in a room decorated by a cast of Olla's teeth on the TV, and an incident in which the peacock 'goes for' the baby (it turns out to be a harmless game), Jack finds himself closing his eyes and wishing 'that I'd never forget or otherwise let go of that evening' (290). And when they get home Jack and Fran, strangely stirred, make love. The story ends with Jack looking back on the event from the standpoint of some years later: the child conceived on that night has grown up with a 'conniving streak'; Jack and Fran scarcely talk any more. Jack remembers the evening with obvious nostalgia – the peacock, the friendliness and warmth, Olla giving Fran some peacock feathers – although Fran recalls it as the beginning of a change for the worse ('Goddamn those people and their ugly baby'). Peacock feathers: it's been said that they bring bad luck, which is clearly how Fran sees it. But the image from early in the story is not entirely negated:

> The bird moved forward a little. Then it turned its head to the side and braced itself. It kept its bright, wild eye right on us. Its tail was raised, and it was like a big fan folding in and out. There was every color in the rainbow shining from that tail.
>
> 'My god,' said Fran quietly. She moved her hand over to my knee.
>
> 'Goddamn,' I said. There was nothing else to say.
>
> The bird made this strange wailing sound once more. *'May-awe, may-awe!'* it went. If it'd been something I was hearing late at night and for the first time, I'd have thought it was somebody dying, or else something wild and dangerous. (Carver, 1995: 275–6)

The passage, sticking to the detail and movement of the event with only the most commonplace metaphors ('like a big fan', 'every color in the rainbow'), has undeniable poetic force. It epitomises the story's sense of the combined beauty and danger of life, of its equal possibility of fulfilment and failure, good and evil. It is not surprising that the short story as a form has so often been compared to the lyric poem: it needs a comparable precision of structure and language and a comparable intensity of feeling. And Raymond Carver's plain, colloquial, unromantic prose gives us these qualities more than that of any other short story writer of the last half-century. It is the rhythm and texture of his prose that constitute our experience as we read, and we need to be able to talk about that.

Works Cited

Barthelme, Donald. *Sixty Stories*. London: Minerva, 1991.
Brown, Marshall. '"Le style est l'homme meme": the Action of Literature', *College English*, 59, No. 7 (November 1997). 801–9.
Buffon, George-Louis Leclerc, Comte de. *'Discours sur le Style'*, (address given to the Académie Française, 1753), in *Œuvres Philosophiques*, ed. Jean Pivoteau. Paris: Presses Universitaires de France, 1954.
Carver, Raymond. *The Stories of Raymond Carver*. London: Picador, 1985.

Carver, Raymond. *Fires: Essays, Poems, Stories.* London: Picador, 1986.
Carver, Raymond. *Where I'm Calling From.* London: Harvill, 1995.
Gentry, Marshall Bruce and William L. Stull, eds. *Conversations with Raymond Carver.* Jackson: University Press of Mississippi, 1990.
Gerlach, John. *Toward the End: Closure and Structure in the American Short Story.* Tuscaloosa: University of Alabama Press, 1985.
Johnson, Samuel. *Prose and Poetry.* London: Rupert Hart-Davis, 1963.
Pound, Ezra. *Literary Essays of Ezra Pound*, ed. T. S. Eliot. London: Faber & Faber, 1960.
Shaw, Valerie. *The Short Story: A Critical Introduction.* London: Longman, 1983.
Stevenson, Robert Louis. *The Letters of Robert Louis Stevenson*, ed. Sidney Colvin (5 vols.). London: Heinemann, 1924.
Stull, William L. and Maureen P. Carroll. *Remembering Ray: A Composite Biography of Raymond Carver.* Santa Barbara: Cape Press, 1993.

Note

1. Asked about the 'downtrodden' characters in his stories he once said: 'I do feel more kinship, even today, with those people. They're my people. They're my relatives, they're the people I grew up with. Half my family is still living like this.' (Gentry and Stull, 1990: 137–8).

4
Women Writers
Linden Peach

Women in virtually every country in the world are writing short stories. But this is not necessarily reflected in the academy or even, fully, in publishing. In many North American degree programmes, there are survey courses on the short story, but there are relatively few university courses on the short story in the United Kingdom. Courses on the short story by women writers are even scarcer. Anthologies, some consisting only of women writers, and collections of short stories by specific women writers are included on modules that are thematic, period based or author based such as modern writing, women's writing, crime writing, African American literature, Irish literature, postcolonial writing, lesbian and gay literature and so forth. Most creative writing programmes provide students with the opportunity to explore the short story from the practitioner's point of view and many of these require students to study examples of the form. But outside of the limited critical, reflective practice which these courses provide, few degree programmes offer literature students the space to reflect upon the short story as a genre, let alone the way that the genre has been developed by women. The knowledge of the short story, and certainly of the short story by women writers, which most students will take from their literary studies will have been put together piecemeal from a range of modules where stories were included among the set texts.

Thus, short stories written by women are read as part of literature and writing courses but in the former they tend to be studied as specific texts within a themed or period context and in the latter examined primarily from a practice-based perspective. Whilst these courses provide students with insights into narrative, structure and aesthetic considerations of the short form, few students have an opportunity to reflect upon the short story in a more advanced, theoretically informed way or to fully explore current debates and issues. Course descriptions tend to suggest that where there are modules on the short story they tend to be structured around a practice-based rather than theoretical approach. One of the reasons for this, as Tony Brown has pointed out, is that 'there has been relatively little theoretical, or even critical work, done on the short story as a literary genre, certainly if you compare it to the amount of theorising which has been applied to the novel' (Brown, 2001: 25–6). The situation has not changed much since Ian Reid complained over 30 years ago that the short story 'seldom receives serious critical attention' (Reid, 1977: 1).

The comparative lack of attention that the literary short story receives on degree courses in the UK reflects its low status in the larger publishing world and this was an issue that worried the majority of participants at the 2007 Edge Hill University Conference on the short story. Most would-be, and even experienced, authors recognise the difficulty of placing a short fiction collection with an agent or publisher. Many authors who have published important contributions to the development of the short story, such as Virginia Woolf and Angela Carter, are still better known for their novels, while many writers who start out publishing short stories aspire to writing a novel or only publish collections of short stories when they have earned a reputation with longer fiction. The reasons for this are that the novel is more highly valued as a literary achievement than the short story; that most writers relish the opportunities and challenges provided by the novel; and that few writers can earn a living from writing short stories.

Given the fact that few degree courses offer opportunities for students to study the short story as a genre, one might ask why single out short stories written by women? Certainly it would be impossible not to recognise the influence of male short story writers, Maupassant and Chekhov for example, on women writers such as Virginia Woolf, Katherine Mansfield and Katherine Anne Porter. Virginia Woolf, as Valerie Shaw has argued, 'aimed at the same effects of inconsequentiality and inconclusiveness that she admired in Chekhov' (Shaw, 1983: 231) and Katherine Mansfield studied Chekhov in German translation. But at the beginning of the twenty-first century there are good reasons for studying and researching the short story by women writers. First, the publishing of writing by women in the second half of the twentieth century has been a cultural phenomenon and the short story has featured in this renaissance, albeit not as strongly as in the case of the novel and poetry. This resurgence in women's writing has occurred for a variety of reasons: the world-wide feminist movement; creative classes at pre-degree, degree and post-degree level; publishing houses such as Honno in Wales and Arlen House and, subsequently, Attic in Ireland dedicated to women's writing; the increased presence of women in higher education, publishing and the arts.

The latter begs a question about the fact that the majority of women short story writers who are published in anthologies or have their own collections have had a university education. Second, as I have argued elsewhere, the history from which women's writing has emerged is not simply 'about women', or even 'about feminism'; it is about the way in which women and feminism are implicated in social structures (Peach, 2007: 7). Thus, such writing is about power, politics, nation, history, culture and community. It also shares with that of other marginalised groups a profound concern to create art that interrogates the different socio-cultural contexts in which we all live.

Despite the relative neglect of the short story in literary studies and the reluctance of publishers to accept collections of stories, the genre has proved an important form in women's literature in the twentieth century. One would hope that literature graduates had had opportunities to study at least some of the key writers such as Virginia Woolf, Katherine Mansfield, Doris Lessing, Katherine Anne Porter, Willa Cather, Jean Rhys, Elizabeth Bowen, Kate Chopin, Kate Roberts, Joyce Carol Oates, Bobbie Ann Mason, Nadime Gordimer, Alice Munro, Margaret Atwood, Jamaica Kincaid, Zora Neale Hurston, Toni Cade Bambara, Jackie Kay, Siân James, Catherine Merriman, Leonora Brito, and short story cycles by women, such as Louise Erdrich's *Love Medicine*.

This select list is far from inclusive but nevertheless demonstrates the range of women short story writers. Some of these names may be better known than others, others may be better known in specific countries such as Wales and Ireland, and others have stood the test of time as short story writers. This raises the interesting question, 'How will women short story writers be remembered?' Virginia Woolf made an important contribution to the development of the women's short story, but few critical accounts of her short stories do them justice, as opposed to her novels. Whereas this reintroduces the relative unimportance granted the short story compared with the novel, it hardly needs stressing that the 'test of time' is not innocent of gender, racial and class politics or of geocultural bias.

Anthologies provide useful insights into the influence of gender, ethnic and geocultural prejudices on the critical reputation and status of women writers. The extent to which women writers have been represented or underrepresented in anthologies of short stories has particularly vexed a number of women writers and academics. In her foreword to the anthology of women's writing from a Welsh feminist publishing house, the Welsh academic Jane Aaron has pointed out:

> So far, at least nine anthologies purporting to represent the best of twentieth-century Welsh short stories have been published. On average, about 17 per cent, or one in six, of the writers included in these collections have been women, a fraction which compares favourably enough with the usual allocation of space to women writers in literary anthologies, which is generally closer to the one in twelve mark.
> (Aaron, 1994: xi)

Ann Charters has suggested that it is possible to trace the development of particular types of short fiction, such as modernist experimental work from Chekhov and a more materialist type of writing from Maupassant (Charters, 1987: 358). However, the danger in this type of narrowing, particularly in looking at women's writing from different parts of the globe and from the various countries constituting the United Kingdom, is of eschewing particular historical, cultural and literary aesthetic contexts. Moreover, in much women's short fiction, the 'types' of story which Charters identifies are not always so readily separated.

It is difficult to ignore the influence of women modernists, especially Virginia Woolf and Katherine Mansfield, on the development of women's short fiction. However, they are more generally acknowledged in literary criticism for their contribution to modernist fiction than the women's short story as such. Reid attributes to them at least one 'essential' generic quality of the short form, 'that we are left uncertain about the nature and extent of the revelation, peak of awareness, that a character has apparently experienced' (Reid, 1977: 58). Valerie Shaw finds in Woolf the same interest as in Mansfield in 'the random qualities of life' and 'the unsatisfactory nature of human attempts to communicate inner experience' (Shaw, 1983: 231). Woolf's story 'Kew Gardens', succinctly described by Shaw as 'a narrative of sensation and sense-impressions' (ibid.), is one of the most written about of Woolf's stories, principally because it exemplifies some of the key objectives of modernism (Woolf, 1993). However, the links between the early- and the late-twentieth-century short stories by women, between what has come to be known, not uncontentiously, as 'first' and 'third' wave feminism to which I shall return shortly, are quite profound.

The critical approach that seems to have inspired the majority of collections and anthologies of women's short fiction in the late twentieth and early twenty-first centuries is one that focuses upon the exploration of women's lives in and through their particular socio-cultural and socio-economic contexts, a dimension that literary historical surveys tend to eschew or minimise. In an interview with Ann Charters, Grace Paley said that she turned from writing poetry to short stories when she 'began to think of certain subject matter, women's lives specifically' (Charters, 1987: 1314). She goes on to say that her story 'Goodbye and Good Luck' 'was about a lot of older women I knew who didn't get married, and I was thinking about them' (1315). On a cursory glance this emphasis upon 'context' and the material 'reality' of women's lives would appear to be at odds with the modernist interest in the sensitivity, perception and cadence of women's voices. However, there has been a tendency in criticism to overlook the 'political' in Woolf's and Mansfield's fiction in favour of the 'private' and to pay insufficient attention to the extent to which the 'private' in modernist writing is 'political'.

Mansfield's 'The Doll's House' (Mansfield, 2002) is a subtle and disturbing exploration of many of the themes that are painted in somewhat broader brushstrokes in the work of the later writers to whom I shall turn shortly: exclusion, intolerance and prejudice. For all its subtlety, it candidly examines the link between attitudes and behaviours among women and particular socio-economic 'realities'. The social perspectives of the well-heeled Burnell children, who live in a symbolic doll's house themselves, are determined by the home from which they come which is never described but is clear from their strong attachment to aspects of the actual doll's house. Their attitude and behaviour towards the children of the poor washerwoman are legitimised by the way in which the latter are seen within the school and the wider community as a whole. It explores the material and economic origins of exclusion and inclusion, including the socio-politics of 'refinement', by focusing upon a single and, in the wider scheme of things, trivial event – middle-class sisters acquiring a magnificent doll's house. Yet, as a new centre of community interest and gossip, the doll's house confirms, and possibly even redraws, social and economic boundaries for the school pupils which not only further excludes the poor Kelvey girls but permits them to be cruelly taunted and insulted. The Burnells, with the exception of Keiza, see as through the slit of a narrow door; but the reader sees the community and the Burnell household opened to a full gaze like the doll's house when the front is opened. It also exposes the way in which seemingly ordinary everyday details, upon which both Woolf and Mansfield construct their stories, like the way the Kelveys eat jam sandwiches out of newspaper, are in fact highly political. Mansfield's emphasis, which we can also see in Woolf's work, on the narratives of the everyday and upon movements of the mind could not be more relevant to women – especially those who experience not only gender but class, ethnic and sexual prejudice – who have to renew the struggle between empowerment and disempowerment upon a daily basis. At one level, it would be possible to see Keiza's rebelliousness as a reaction against her family but in fact she speaks from, and behaves according to, her own narrative. It is her idea, originating from nowhere else in the story, to invite the Kelveys to see the doll's house.

Editors of many of the late-twentieth-century ground-breaking anthologies of women's writing have sought deliberately to include not only a variety of different types of writing but the diversity of women's lives within different socio-economic contexts even within a particular, small(ish) country such as Ireland. The editors of the first American anthology of Irish women's writing, *Territories of the Voice* (1990), point out:

> We tried to ensure that the stories we selected provided portraits of, for example, urban women and rural women, women from the Republic of Ireland and women from the North, Catholic women and Protestant women, portraits of women who loved men and women who loved women, visions of elder women thinking back through their lives and portraits of young girls, adolescent women, mothers, widows, and women living alone. (DeSalvo et al., 1990: xii)

The anthology includes stories that explore the life experiences of Irish women caught up in situations that also break various taboos: a young Catholic mother in Northern Ireland; an IRA woman whose grandfather was an Ulster volunteer; a woman pregnant with her married lover's child who is forced to seek an abortion in England and a young woman in love with the nun who teaches her. The latter, Edna O'Brien's 'Sister Imelda', combines confession, a naïve narrative voice and unsettling female imagery in an exploration of a subject that has been previously marginalised:

> I had met Sister Imelda outside of class a few times and I felt that there was an attachment between us. Once it was in the grounds, when she did a reckless thing. She broke off a chrysanthemum and offered it to me to smell. It had no smell, or at least only something faint that suggested autumn, and feeling this to be the case herself, she said it was not a gardenia, was it? (DeSalvo et al., 1990: 142)

The publisher's blurb for a relatively recent collection of stories by the Welsh writer Siân James, *Outside Paradise* (2001), argues for her work in terms similar to those of the editors of *Territories of the Voice* that stress its 'relevance' and 'meaningfulness' to women especially. Thus, James's stories are 'a testament to women of all ages', and concern 'real women dealing with whatever life throws at them, whether stranded on a mountaintop or caught shoplifting'. In this respect, James's stories would seem to represent what has been identified as 'new' or 'third' wave feminism although James herself might not know the terms. For the 'third' wave links feminism to recognition of a new-found diversity, racial and sexual, as much as it is associated with an interest in 'popular' culture.

I teach James's short stories because students in one part of the United Kingdom are often ignorant of women's fiction being published and acclaimed in other parts. Her stories raise pertinent issues about national, social and community difference. Their view of Wales is aligned with Homi Bhabha's view of a nation: 'The nation reveals, in its ambivalent and vacillating representation, the ethnography of its own historicity and opens up the possibility of other narratives of the people and their difference' (Bhabha, 1990: 300). But James's work encourages students to think about the issues that actually lie behind the book's marketing – issues I have referred to above. What, one may ask, are 'real' (as opposed to 'unreal'?) women? Talk in these terms, and the emphasis upon the fact that the stories deal with 'women of all ages', inevitably raises issues around such topics as 'essentialism', 'diversity', 'woman' as opposed to 'Woman', and women's language. They open the floodgates to contemporary critical concerns and can become fault lines along which can be plotted the debates around 'post-Feminism', post-Gender, post-History, and even post-Self. I say 'debates around' because not only is the term 'post' contentious – does it mean a split from the term to which it is attached or imply some kind of linear development from it? – but the concepts to which it is invariably connected are themselves ambivalent, complex and often diffuse.

Students who want to write as well as study the short story might balk at the introduction of 'post' anything in a discussion of a writer's work, and be driven back to writing unreflectively about 'real' women without any wider sense of what this means. As David Dabydeen has said: 'The problem with postmodernist theories is that they tend to dismiss "presence" as a kind of metaphysical conceit and valorise "absence", "aporia" and "kenosis"' (Dabydeen, 1997: 135–51). The last thing James could be accused of is valorising presence. But given their scope and the diversity in the women's lives with which they deal, it is inevitable that the stories in *Outside Paradise* should challenge any singular conceptualisation of 'woman', gender, history, self and feminism. Indeed, even if the stories themselves are not especially postmodern in terms of narrative technique and structure (compare, for instance, Angela Carter), they have their origins in a socio-cultural context that is in many respects 'post' – postmodern, post-industrial and post-feminist – and this becomes particularly obvious when individual stories are read in relation to each other.

At the core of James's collection of stories are estrangement and the different ways in which this has been and can be defined for women and, as in *Territories of the Voice*, subjects that have been traditionally taboo. Many of the female protagonists in *Outside Paradise* are alone: the narrator of 'Not Singing Exactly' through circumstances brought about by an abusive parent and later by the imprisonment of her husband; the narrator of 'A House of One's Own' by family circumstance and inheriting a house in a village which is new to her; Hetty in 'Billy Mason from Gloucester' because of the amount of time she has given to being a carer; the teenager in 'Hester and Louise' because she has been sent away from her home in London to her grandmother in Wales by her busy parents; and the narrator of 'Strawberry Cream' because she is an only child in a small Welsh community. However, in a number of the stories in this book women are empowered by different female relationships, even if only temporarily: the narrators in 'Not Singing Exactly' and 'A House of One's Own' by their relationships with their mothers; Hetty in 'Billy Mason from Gloucester' by her friendship with the farmer's wife, Mrs Evans; the teenager in 'Hester and Louise' by the Arwel sisters; and the narrator when she was a pre-pubescent girl in 'Strawberry Cream' by the presence of an older, exotic girl who becomes her summer friend.

Thus, at one level, a postmodern, ahistorical approach to James's work is useful because it deconstructs many of the grand narratives – such as History, Nation, Woman, Family – but at another level it seems inappropriate because it would deny the 'materiality' at the heart of her stories. Poststructuralist deconstruction, which questions the taken-for-granted connections between 'language' and 'material world' appears much more relevant, if we are cautious about dispensing entirely with 'referentiality'. For the emphasis upon 'separateness' in James's stories allows her to reposition the gendered, female body in culture, language and society and to explore in her writing not so much 'language' and 'difference' as a 'language of difference'. For James, this language of difference is anchored in material, socio-economic contexts, which no doubt led her publisher to speak of 'real' women. This is evident in the ways in which two women, one working class and the other middle class, talk about their experiences of sex; in the ways in which a young woman of Welsh descent from Liverpool new to a Welsh village confronts the vicar, whose candidness she comes to respect, and her neighbour; and the assertiveness and disarming outspokenness of a young woman brought up in a tough part of South Wales:

> It's a brilliant dress too, gooseberry green crushed velvet and so tight you can see her belly button as well as her nipples and the cleft in her bum. (James 2001: 111)

> And I suppose he has got something too, because I starts thinking about sex, how I'm always turned on by words like fuck and shag. (112)

The short story seems to have enabled James to 'experiment' with different voices and to write a 'language of difference' which might not have been possible if she were writing a novel.

The voices which James explores in her short fiction are 'different' because they reveal what is involved in speaking the unspeakable and in the struggle towards self-assertiveness and self-definition in an oppressive domestic and/or community context. The narrator of 'A House of One's Own' tells the village clergyman:

> Why shouldn't I tell the Reverend the truth? Let him know something about the real world out there? Yes, I was sexually abused Reverend, from the age of – what? Three or four? [...] Oh, I remember the way he'd kneel over me, pushing his fingers into me front and back, pretending it was fun [...]. And then he'd get his big prick out and hurt me real bad. (78)

James's 'realism' is typical of much short fiction by contemporary Welsh, Irish and Northern Irish and Scottish women writers that seeks to push back the boundaries around gender, sexual identity, family and community. But the contemporary black Welsh writer Leonora Brito's first collection of stories, *dat's love* (1995), has more in common with the Nobel Prize-winning African-American novelist Toni Morrison than many Welsh short story writers, sharing her concern with how ethnic minority communities and mixed-race peoples can reclaim themselves as the subjects of their own histories and biographies rather than being the objects in other people's narratives. Writing from the perspective of a member of the Cardiff Bay community, Brito sees it, as Morrison sees Harlem in *Jazz* (1992), as a place where it is possible to be more than oneself, and, as Morrison says of Harlem, people can embrace their 'riskier' selves. The Bay, like Morrison's Harlem, is a place of violence, highly charged sexual relationships, and internecine conflict. However, it is also a place where spontaneity, improvisation and sexuality take their cue from the music that fills the bars. In 'Stripe by Stripe', one of the Bay's inhabitants remembers it as 'the New Orleans of a great coaling Metropolis' (Brito 1995: 117–18) where 'people have fought hard and played hard' (118). The Bay's spirit is epitomised in the 'good time girl' (115), Madame Patti, who is seen as 'rowing and drinking and causing trouble, painting her front door bright yellow while everyone else's was council house blue' (115).

Reading James's and Brito's stories together, and in context with the work of the Irish writer Emma Donoghue to whom I shall turn in a moment, gives the reader a true sense of what 'third' wave feminism, alluded to earlier, involves. Sometimes accused of reinventing the wheel, the kind of feminism we find in writers such as these is exciting because of the way in which the post-1990s women's short story brings together women of different countries, classes, backgrounds, cultures and ethnicities as well as women who are straight, gay, bi and transgender. 'Second' wave feminism, associated with the 1960s, 1970s and 1980s was by comparison hardly ever global and remained a largely middle-class affair. However, 'third' wave feminism is sometimes mistakenly disassociated from what had gone before and from a range of different contemporary contexts. Thus, Brito's work cannot be seen as separate from race-based movements of the mid and late twentieth century and also with the community and oral history projects of the 1980s and 1990s.

The number of neglected stories by women seems in Jane Aaron's eyes to parallel the wasted lives of women generally over the centuries; what she calls in her foreword to *Luminous and Forlorn* the 'convincing exposure of disappointment and the wastage of female potential on a massive scale' (Aaron, 1994: xiv). This sense of the way in which women have been written out of history by 'History' has inspired the Irish writer Emma Donoghue's first collection of short stories. *The Woman Who Gave Birth to Rabbits* (2002) is a watershed in Irish women's short fiction for the way in which it develops the possibilities arising from the diversity of women's experiences across different communities and different generations. It combines, as Donoghue says in the Foreword, historical research and imagination. Thus, in her words, it is 'a book of fictions, but they are also true'. It uncovers the lives of women, some with famous names and others that have been 'written off as cripples, children, half-breeds, freaks and nobodies'. In some respects, the project has grown out of her novel *Slammerkin* (2000) which was inspired by the few surviving facts about a young woman, Mary Saunders, who was executed for the murder of her employer Mrs Jones in Monmouth in 1764. But the short forms allow her to do something comparable to what Siân James has achieved in *Outside Paradise* because of the way in which a collection of short stories, as opposed to a novel, lends itself to multiplicity and polyphony. Donoghue's concern, like James's, is not with 'History', which is always written from particular preconceptions and vested interests, but with histories. Their stories ask, and encourage readers to ask, questions about the writing of history itself. In whose interests and from what standpoint is it conceived? Who is excluded and who is privileged as a result of the particular narrative perspective? How incomplete are particular histories and who is it that benefits and who is it that is disadvantaged by this incompleteness?

A further strength of the collections that we have been discussing is that not only do they highlight the polyphony of Western culture but the fact that culture itself is not fixed and static. Whereas women, and other previously marginalised groups, have been able to find hope and inspiration in this, at another level James, Brito and Donoghue demonstrate how different cultures at different times have had different ways of imposing conformity upon women.

Rosalind Miles says of the woman's novel:

> There is also much work for women writers still to do in continuing to explore the intimate aspects of their lives as women; as daughters, as mothers, in sexual relations with men, and with each other, or as women alone; besides the ongoing challenge of mapping those areas of experience still under patriarchal taboos. (Miles, 1990: ix–x)

The crucial concern in James's, Donoghue's and Brito's work is to free women from male referents in order for them to discover a 'truer' material identity. Angela Carter in the introduction to *Wayward Girls and Wicked Women* (Carter, 1986, 1997) argues:

> Most of the variously characterized girls and women who inhabit these stories, however, would seem much, much worse if men had invented them. They would be predatory, drunken hags; confidence

tricksters; monstrously precocious children; liars and cheats; promiscuous heartbreakers. As it is they are all presented as if they were perfectly normal. (Carter, 1986: ix)

She goes on to point out that 'wayward' and 'wicked' when applied to women in men's writing usually 'has nothing to do with ethics; it means sexual morality and nothing but sexual morality' (x). Thus, the stories Carter has selected from different parts of the world, including, Bessie Head's 'Life', Katherine Mansfield's 'The Young Girl', Ama Ata Aidoo's 'Plums' and Jamaica Kincaid's 'Girl', avoid what Carter calls 'sexual profligates' and women as victims. In her emphasis upon women of different nationalities, races and sexualities achieving control of their identities and bodies, their 'material' reality, through acquiring control over language and discourse, Carter bridges 'second' wave feminism, with its emphasis upon language and political action, with 'third' wave refocusing upon cultural discourse and diversity.

The way in which cultural discourse functions in specific social and material contexts is one of Donoghue's principal themes. For Donoghue one of the most important of these contexts is that created by medical-scientific discourse. Her short story 'Cured' is an imaginative reconstruction of a case of a young woman admitted to the 'care' of a famous Victorian surgeon Baker Brown (1812–1873), a pioneer of clitoridectomy who performed operations on not only young women but also children as young as ten. He conducts them, the story suggests, on women who come with ailments in other part of their bodies which he attributes to the clitoris. The young woman in this story is suffering from a back injury. The textbook upon which he relies is not neutral. It underlines a limited and condescending understanding of women's role in society: 'the patient becomes restless and excited, or melancholy and retiring; listless and indifferent to the social influences of domestic life' (Donoghue, 2002: 113). At the heart of the story is Donoghue's concern with power and meaning as constituted in language. The metaphor which most opens up this aspect of the story is the one that Donoghue uses to describe Baker Brown's internal examination of his patient: 'His hands moved like a pickpocket's, gliding, seeking' (112). He is as linguistically artful as the pickpocket is physically dexterous. The authority which he has over the woman's body is manifest in the control that he has over language. All his questions to her are leading questions, simultaneously distracting and manipulative:

'Are you ever sleepless,' he broke in, 'or do you wake in the middle of the night?'

'Only if my back is bad,' she said, aware that she was repeating herself.
'Unaccountable fits of depression?'
'Well. Not really.' She tried to think. 'Only a sort of lost feeling, once in a while, when I consider my future.'
'Attacks of melancholy without any tangible reason?' he said encouragingly.
After a moment, she shook her head. 'If I'm ever low in spirits, sir, it's for a reason.' (113)

By contrast, her language is naïve and deferential. He tries to draw her in a specific direction which she resists because she does not understand either the language or the situation that she is in: 'She thought perhaps if she could tell this doctor all her reasons, all the real and unreal worries that ever lowered her spirits, she would then be able to shake them off' (113). The pickpocket metaphor is particularly appropriate because the doctor steals a part of her body and of her very being.

Thus, short stories written by women bring to the fore women's struggles to free themselves from a range of distorting, restricting and marginalising discourses including those around sexuality, science and medicine, class, race, region and nation.

Drawing on the work of Clare Hanson, Tony Brown maintains that there are qualities in the short story that lend themselves to some of the 'most profound intuitions of marginalization, of loneliness and detachment, or at best an ambiguous relation to the culture and society that surrounds them' (Brown, 2001: 27). As Hanson argues:

> The formal properties of the short story – disjunction, inconclusiveness and obliquity – connect with its ideological marginality and with the fact that the form may be used to express something suppressed/repressed in mainstream literature. (Hanson, 1989: 2)

But we can go further than this and ask questions about what happens when a marginalised subject is brought from or emerges from the margins, whether it be a taboo subject like child abuse or a fetish; a body of writing that has been marginalised, as has been the case with women's writing from Wales and Ireland in the last century; or the experiences of women from particular faith or ethnic communities. What kind of space is entered and created by the movement itself? What are the dialectics and tensions within that space?

These are pertinent questions to ask of Angela Carter's short fiction. It is now a commonplace argument that Carter did not rewrite the fairy tale in *The Bloody Chamber and Other Stories* (1979, and republished in *Burning your Boats: Collected Short Stories*, 1995), but borrowed ideas around which to write new tales, on subjects that had been previously marginalised, which had a more actively sexual female subject and emphasised the violence and abuse of women. The stories address taboo subjects but do so in a way that challenges the conventional view, resisted even by 'first' wave feminists such as Woolf and Mansfield, that the dangers facing women are imposed purely from outside. Female sexuality in Carter's stories is active, chaotic and often savage whereas the learned femininity and sexual being in patriarchal narratives is, usually, submissive and masochistic. Thus, the space in which Carter is writing is one that is complex and ambiguous, resisting conventional notions of female sexuality, gender, desire, domination, submission, sadism and masochism.

The interest throughout the stories in *The Bloody Chamber* lies, as in Woolf and Mansfield's stories, in moments of rupture and/or awakening. Smith points out that Mansfield's stories are in fact written around and through various kinds of disruption although they are not as obvious formally as in Woolf's work (Smith, 2002: xxiv). Often Mansfield begins in the middle of something: 'Suddenly – dreadfully – she wakes up' ('The Wind Blows'); 'Oh dear, how she wished that it wasn't night time' ('The Little Governess'). However, Carter's approach is more at the level of myth and discourse which she delights in puncturing. The werewolf in Carter's story of that name is by definition an interruption of the human, or the human may be seen as an interruption of the monstrous.

'Werewolf' is not a rewrite of 'Little Red Riding Hood' as such; it is a tale written from an altogether different point of origin. It is written around the 'Other' to the mythicisation of femininity and female sexuality in Western discourse which serves to critique them. The child who journeys from her home to her sick grandmother is a daughter who resists the 'daughtering' of her mother who dutifully prepares a basket of oatcakes and butter. 'Dutifully' because her mother has successfully trained her to behave as a dutiful daughter, as she wishes to teach her own daughter. By 'daughtering', I mean the way in which a daughter is conditioned in subservient, passive acceptance and obedience. In an act suggestive of female castration of the male, the daughter cuts off the attacking werewolf's paw and immediately emasculates and infantilises him as he runs off sobbing. The paw which she cuts off is the hand of her grandmother that significantly wears the wedding ring. In effect what she does is to use her father's knife, which her mother has given her, to sever her mother's conforming influence upon her in order to free herself from being a child-object in her mother/grandmother's narrative so that she can be the subject in her own story. The grandmother has to die at the end not simply because she is suspected of being a witch but because she is a more controlling and influential presence in the 'socialisation' of her granddaughter than even the girl's own mother. The grandmother has succeeded in 'daughtering' one generation and that project is put at risk by the presence of fresh family blood. Thus, the grandmother can be seen as being in cahoots with the father figure who wants a subservient maternal line to better serve his own interests.

Thus, from Woolf and Mansfield through Angela Carter to late twentieth and twenty-first century women writers, the short story has allowed authors to pursue subjects that would not be sustainable in a longer form, or acceptable to a commercial publisher, and to explore and represent the diversity of women's experiences, backgrounds and voices. Whilst acknowledging that short fiction lends itself to marginalised subjects, it is important to ask questions about the nature of the space which what has been previously marginalised or silenced creates. The short story has proved an appropriate canvas for women writers to explore the complexity and anxiety within this space. When applied to the short form, Miles's contention that women writers have more 'to do in continuing to explore the intimate aspects of their lives as women' brings together modernist feminism, sometimes and not uncontentiously regarded as 'first' wave feminism, and the interest of third wave feminism in diversity and the material reality of women's lives. Woolf's interest in 'the narrative forms of everyday life', shared by Mansfield in 'The Doll's House', has a particular relevance even for twenty-first century women writers for whom the struggle between 'empowerment' and 'disempowerment' is enacted in different cultures and socio-economic 'realities' on a daily basis in every detail of life.

Works Cited

Aaron, Jane. 'Foreword'. In *Luminous and Forlorn: Contemporary Short Stories by Women from Wales,* ed. Elin ap Hwyl. Dinas Powys, Wales: Honno, 1994. ix–xv.

Bhabha, Homi. 'Dissemination: time, narrative, and the margins of the modern nation'. In *Nation and Narration,* ed. Homi Bhabha. London: Routledge, 1990. 291–322.

Brito, Leonora. *dat's love*. Bridgend: Seren, 1995.
Brown, Tony. 'The Ex-centric Voice: The English-Language Short Story in Wales'. *North American Journal of Welsh Studies*, Vol. 1, no.1, 2001. 25–41.
Carter, Angela. 'The Bloody Chamber and Other Stories'. In *Burning Your Boats: Collected Short Stories*. London: Chatto & Windus, 1995. 111–28.
Carter, Angela. *Wayward Girls and Wicked Women*. London: Virago, 1986.
Charters, Ann, *The Story and Its Writer: An Introduction to Short Fiction*. New York: St. Martin's Press, 1987.
Dabydeen, David. 'Teaching West Indian literature in Britain', in *Studying British Cultures: An Introduction*, ed. Susan Bassett. London: Routledge, 1997. 135–51.
DeSalvo, Louise, Kathleen Walsh D'Arcy and Katherine Hogan, eds. *Territories of the Voice: Contemporary Stories By Irish Women Writers*. London: Virago Press, 1990. (First published Boston, MA: Beacon Press, 1989).
Donoghue, Emma. *Slammerkin*. London: Virago, 2000.
Donoghue, Emma. *The Woman Who Gave Birth to Rabbits*. London: Virago, 2002.
Hanson, Clare, ed. *Re-Reading the Short Story*. London: Macmillan – now Palgrave Macmillan, 1989.
James, Siân, *Outside Paradise*. Cardiff: Parthian Books, 2001.
Mansfield, Katherine. 'The Dolls' House', in *Selected Short Stories*. Oxford: Oxford University Press, 2002. 350–6.
Miles, Rosalind. *The Female Form: Women Writers and the Conquest of the Novel*. London: Routledge, 1990.
Morrison, Toni. *Jazz*. New York: Alfred A. Knopf, 1992.
Peach, Linden. *Contemporary Irish and Welsh Women's Fiction: Gender, Desire and Power*. Cardiff: University of Wales Press, 2007.
Reid, Ian. *The Short Story*. London: Routledge (Critical Idiom Series), 1977.
Shaw, Valerie. *The Short Story: A Critical Introduction*. London: Longman, 1983.
Smith, Angela. 'Introduction', in Katherine Mansfield, *Selected Short Stories*. Oxford: Oxford University Press, 2002. ix–xxxii.
Woolf, Virginia. 'Kew Gardens', in *Selected Short Stories*. London: Penguin, 1993. 46–52.

5
The Postcolonial Experience: The South East Asian Short Story in English

Dean Baldwin

Historically speaking, the South East Asian short story in English has progressed from its tentative beginnings in the late nineteenth century to a more assertive present-day position, documenting along the way the political, social and personal struggles of the people of the subcontinent. Concerns about writing in English have largely given way to full confidence in the language's ability to convey the Indian and Pakistani experience, both at home and abroad. The brief survey below will hint at many of the rewards of teaching the Indian and Pakistani short story in English. The list of authors worthy of students' attention grows almost daily, as more and more collections of stories become readily available in the West. The success of the US-based Jumpha Lahiri, whose *Interpreter of Maladies* won a Pulitzer Prize, may even have widened the readership for such material.

Nevertheless, the very accessibility of the Indian short story in English masks some of its difficulties for Western readers, chief of which is ignorance of the Hindu sacred texts that lie behind many of stories. Direct references to gods and goddesses can, of course, be looked up; and often glossaries or notes provide at least rudimentary explanations of these. But what cannot be easily looked up are the mythic bases of many stories, the echoes of the *Mahabharata* or the *Ramayana* that would be obvious to any Hindu but are lost on Western readers. The ending of Arun Joshi's 'The Boy with the Flute', for example, may seem ludicrous to a Western reader who does not realise that the title refers to the god Krishna, who is literally the *deus ex machina* who answers Mr Sethi's prayer. Three central stories in Shashi Deshpande's *The Stone Women* refer directly to myths from the *Mahabharata* and are discussed as such by her in an Afterword.

Of more immediate import is students' ignorance of Indian history and geography, both before and after colonialism. None of the students

I teach in Pennsylvania are at all familiar with South Eastern culture. Over the years a few of them have seen a Bollywood film, and more recently there has been the Oscar-winning *Slumdog Millionaire*. Some are vaguely aware that India is the home of many call centres and computer programmers working for American businesses. But it is safe to assume that none of them has ever read anything by an Indian author or knows anything about South East Asian history, religion, art, music, food and so on. British students may be somewhat more knowledgeable than Americans about the general history of the Raj and of the pre-1947 independence movements, but most instructors will need to assign outside readings or give informative lectures to provide students with the essential historical context for reading the stories. Knowledge of India's caste system, its spiritual traditions, geography and social customs (especially arranged marriage and the taboos surrounding widows) are also essential. Many of these will emerge from the stories themselves, but many will not, again necessitating the instructor's guiding hand. Of course, in many classrooms there will be students of South Asian origin who can add their own knowledge and point of view – and sometimes their corrections – to the lecturer's material. Handling their contributions and questions requires considerable skill, above all to correct any impression that an individual student's view somehow represents *the* view of a particular religious, ethnic or racial group.

I take as a given that anyone teaching the Indian short story will be conversant with postcolonial theory and its relevance to the literature. But assuming familiarity with the theory does not solve the problem of confronting the stories as literature – that is, as objects of aesthetic as well as political interest. Each instructor will handle this tension individually, of course, but in my view at least it would be a mistake to focus so completely on issues of identity, mediation, language, politics, economics and feminism (to name just a few) that aesthetic issues are bypassed or ignored. The history of the Indian/Pakistani short story, as I understand it at least, shows an early preoccupation with social and political issues, but then a break in the 1950s and 1960s from these to 'existential' problems of identity, self-fulfilment and psychological complexity, although social issues never disappear and those associated with the diaspora emerge. Generally speaking, the South Asian short story focuses more on long-standing social problems within the subcontinent than it does on issues relating to colonialism. The relative absence of stylistic experiment among South Asian writers in English and the predominance of 'realistic' conventions may obscure the vitality of the language found in many of the writers, from the early struggles to find an indigenous idiom through English to the stylistic inventions of contemporary writers who have energised the language with brilliant originality. Instructors may find a parallel in Indian film, where movies such as *Once Upon a Time in India* (also known as *Lagaan*), *Born into Brothels*, *Water* and *The Namesake* can help students grasp not only the issues raised by the stories but also some of the colour, heat and tempo of Indian life that only film can capture.

Another profitable way for instructors to approach this material is by pairing stories by British writers with those of Indian origin. This is particularly effective with the late nineteenth and early twentieth-century material, where sharp and informative contrasts between British writers such as Kipling, Flora Annie Steel, Leonard Woolf and Alice Perrin can illustrate varying degrees of support for the Raj. A convenient source for stories of this kind is provided by *The Oxford Anthology of Raj Stories*, edited by Saros Cowasjee (1998), although I would supplement this with Kipling's 'The Man Who Would Be King'. Stories by Anand, Rao and Narayan can be especially effective with pre-independence comparisons.

The pleasures of teaching the Indian/Pakistani short story lie not only in its potential to help students see the world from a new and revealing perspective, but also to see in these stories the potency of the short story as a form. As has often been pointed out, the short story can be held in the mind as a whole, like a poem. As such, it requires a poetic sensibility in the reading – an acute awareness of language, nuance, form, subtlety and suggestion. This chapter introduces the reader through some examples of stories which will yield insights through this kind of close reading and analysis, placing them in their historical context. In the reading process, students can come to appreciate not only the politics and sociology of these stories, not only the cultural assumptions and practices imbedded in and expressed by them, but also the inner workings of literature as a form of art and communication.

The Beginnings of the Short Story in India

The origins of any literary genre are clouded in obscurity, but this clichéd observation is especially true of the South Asian short story, for not only are many of the essential materials lost or very difficult to obtain, but also the problem is complicated by the multitude of languages and dialects in the subcontinent. Moreover, many authors are bilingual or even multilingual in their reading and writing, so even dealing with the influences on a single author may be more than demanding.

The difficulties of tracing the origins and development of the Indian/ Pakistani short story are, however, no excuse for ignoring or slighting it. It is a complex and multilingual phenomenon to be sure, but for those reasons all the more rewarding to research and the more challenging and interesting to teach. The broad outlines are known; the major authors are widely agreed upon and accessible for study; but there are many details to be filled in, unknown authors to be discovered, and above all there are rich and rewarding opportunities for students to explore, enjoy and learn from Indian writers. In these stories are the many layers of an ancient and rich culture that for the past three centuries has been intimately entwined with the West. Exploring this culture, coming to terms with its problematic relations to the West, and discovering the richness and beauty of this body of literature offer teachers of the new English and their students a wealth of rewarding experiences.

Having noted the difficulties and rewards of the subject, I will add a tentative declaration; namely, that the Indian short story in whatever language is not simply a derivative of the European/American tradition. (I am going to speak in this section exclusively of the Indian short story, since the Pakistani story in English did not develop until after 1947 – when there was a Pakistan.) The available evidence suggests a complex and problematic relationship between the Western and Indian story. Like the European/American short story, the Indian variety was preceded by several forms that resemble the short story: folk tales, short narrative poems, self-contained episodes within epics and other long works. There are also brief character sketches and satirical pieces similar to classical and neoclassical satires in English (Suhrawardy, 1945: 206; Singh, 1934: 58). It is possible to argue, therefore, that the Indian short story evolved from much the same materials and perhaps even in a parallel way to the European story, but no one actually makes this claim. The question, therefore, is the nature and extent of European/American influence.

Literary historians commonly describe indigenous Indian literature as highly romantic – full of supernatural intervention, superhuman achievements, lofty and idealised sentiments, and fanciful style (Rubin, 2001: 6). Simplistically, the new realistic strain in late nineteenth-century Indian literature, of which the short story is an integral part, can be attributed to European influence, although Amit Chaudhuri points out that Indian literature has its own realistic traditions (2004: xxvi). Both realistic and romantic conventions can be found in Indian writers Premchand and Rabindranath Tagore, and we know that Tagore's older brother Jyotirindranath translated some of Maupassant's stories into Bengali (Dutta and Robinson, 1995: 39). Nevertheless, the only scholar to study the relationship between Tagore and Maupassant concedes that while there are similarities between the two, 'Tagore [...] was the initiator of the short story in Bengali. He had no model to imitate in his own literary tradition and had to open a new field' (Bhattacharya, 1989: 104-5). Whatever the case regarding Tagore, many Indian historians stress the effects of Continental literature as decisive in shaping the development of the Indian story. Among the European writers mentioned are Hugo, Dumas, Flaubert, Maupassant, Turgenev and Chekhov (Vatsyayan, 1957: 75; Ramakrishnan, 2000: xiv), while at least one critic favours the British and American connections through Kipling, Wells, Bennett, H. E. Bates, Saki, Poe and O. Henry (Viswanathan, 2000: 149). Thus, it would be wrong to discount the European or British influence entirely, for the evidence suggests a penchant for the mundane and realistic in early collections listed in Dorothy Spencer's *Indian Fiction in English: An Annotated Bibliography* (1960):

Sarala and Hingana (Tales Descriptive of Indian Life), 1895
Love and Life Behind the Purdah, 1901
Sun-Babies, Studies in the Child Life of India, 1904.

Whatever the influence from Europe or America, it is essential to consider the importance of Bengal. The most famous Bengali writer, and the first writer of short stories in Bengali, is Rabindranath Tagore (1861-1941). Among his prodigious output are over 200 short stories, with collections in Bengali published in 1894, 1895, 1912, 1915 and later (Trosky, 1987: 355-6). Four of these were translated into English between 1913 and 1925 (Trosky, 1987: 366). *Hungry Stones* (translated 1916) illustrates the difficulties of describing Tagore's stories and tracing the influences upon them. 'The Kingdom of Cards', for example, is a contrived allegory on the absurdity of the caste system; 'The Babus of Nayanjore' a combined fairy tale or fable and confessional story with elements of social satire and moralising. To a Western reader, Tagore's stories often seem diffuse and overly moralistic, but some, like 'The Cabuliwallah' are tight, objective and economical.

Tagore's fellow Bengali, Cornelia Sorabji (1866-1954), is indisputably among the earliest Indian writers of short stories in English. Like Tagore, she attended university in England, but unlike him completed her law studies and became the first Indian woman called to the bar. Her only work of short fiction, *Love and Life Behind the Purdah* (1901), has recently been reprinted (2003) and is hence widely available for the first time. The ten stories in the collection vary widely, from brief sketches to a substantial analysis of an Indian village during plague ('Pestilence at Noonday').

As the title indicates, however, all are focused on the lives of married women, whose plight the author deplores from a Westernised point of view. Sorabji attacks the denial of education to women, the practice of suti or suttee (a wife's ritual immolation with her husband's corpse), the self-sacrifice required of barren women, and the virtual imprisonment of a Rajah's wives. The women in these stories are constantly required to sacrifice their minds, bodies, personalities and even their lives to the dictates of a severe patriarchy reinforced by religion and tradition. Her method is essentially realistic, although her heroines are sometimes infused with romantic renunciation and heroic sacrifice.

Sorabji is an accomplished writer. Her characters are sharply rendered, her situations drawn from direct experience, and her sense of structure solid. To further her political ends, Sorabji often presents her characters as representatives of a class – the barren wife; the educated but frustrated Indian wife; the brisk and efficient memsahib; the traditional Indian woman and so forth – but these are used to good effect in stories that work effectively at both the personal and political levels. Postcolonial critics might fault her for advocating views that coincided with those of the Raj, but the abuses she exposes and the customs she criticises are those that progressive Indians have espoused for the past century or more. Sorabji's influence on subsequent writers has not to my knowledge been assessed, but in their methods and sensibilities her stories foretell the direction of Indian short fiction, the great majority of which will use realistic techniques to question and criticise Indian social mores and customs.

Sorabji's style is fluent but at times a little stiff and formal, as might be expected from one whose native language is other than English. It has, to my ears anyway, a Victorian flavour, a bit of women's magazine primness. Occasionally she slips into archaic formalisms such as 'She was up betimes', (61) and 'A *kunkun* party is a good old custom, and picturesque withal' (64). The dialogue she puts in the mouths of her uneducated Indian characters seems artificially formal and correct, though at times she ascribes to her speakers a kind of King James English that may attempt to convey an aspect of Bengali that cannot be otherwise represented in contemporary English:

> 'Of delicate sensibility art thou, oh pundit-je,' said I, somewhat sulkily, 'and yet carest nothing that that tree doth offend against my carriage, and my head, and my health!' (Sorabji, 2003: 106–7)

Stylistic issues such as these need to be addressed by a native speaker who can perhaps explain them and the effects they are intended to convey.

Another early writer is Premchand (Dhanpat Rai Srivastava), whose earliest collection, *Soz-e vatan (Passion for the Fatherland)*, appeared in Urdu. David Rubin describes it as follows:

> Patriotism and romantic love dominate Premchand's first short story collection, published in 1908. Britain is not specifically mentioned in the patriotic tales because of the increasingly strict government censorship. Instead, Premchand chose subjects from medieval times or foreign history [...] in which his opposition to British rule could be disguised by attacking past oppressors or glorifying other independence movements. This strategy did not forestall the banning of his collection in 1909 and the burning of all unsold copies. (Rubin, 2001: 168–9)

'Resignation' from that first collection illustrates Premchand's development up to that point, and also why the British burned the book. The story's protagonist, an overworked clerk named Feteh Chand, is 'a dumb animal', beaten by poverty, bad luck and British bullying. One night, summoned after working hours by his drunken boss, he endures physical abuse and humiliation, but later returns and replies in kind, exacting a promise from his boss that he will refrain from mistreating subordinates. The story is marred by obvious propaganda and what can only be called an unmotivated change of character in Feteh Chand, but it is briskly paced and vividly rendered.

Shortly after this, Premchand began writing in Hindi, presumably to gain a wider audience ('Dhanpat Rai Srivastava', 2002). He continued to use short fiction as a way of exploring and commenting on social issues and on India's struggle for independence. An early story, 'The Power of a Curse' (1911), is marked by sharp observations of village life and psychological insight, even as it is marred by a tendency to overt moralising. Still later, he examined Indian village life, 'not simply as a social problem but particularly as a stage for complex psychological drama of universal significance' (Rubin, 2001: 169).

Tagore and Premchand were separated by a generation in time, by language and by geography. Whether it is correct to argue, as some have done, that Tagore was the fountainhead of the Indian short story (for example Iyengar, 1962: 89–90) is a matter that requires further investigation, but it does seem fair to say that following Tagore, Sorabji and Premchand, the Indian short story, particularly in English, follows their combined example. This can be illustrated by examining the stories of Mulk Raj Anand (1905–2004), R. K. Narayan (1906–2001) and Raja Rao

(1909–2006), often referred to as the 'big three' of pre-independence fiction in English.

Anand, Narayan and Rao

Mulk Raj Anand claims that his interest in short stories began as a child with his reading of *Kathasaritsagar* (*The Ocean of Stories*) (Sethi, 1990: 42), but the years he spent in England studying philosophy and meeting many of England's leading literary figures must also have contributed to his development. Indeed, most of the stories collected in his short fiction debut in 1934, *The Lost Child and Other Stories*, were previously published in British periodicals. The following year saw the publication of his novel *Untouchable*, perhaps still his best-known work. Of that work, Anand reminisces that it was influenced by his reading of European and Russian writers: 'I am not sure whether the *Confessions* of Rousseau, which I had just read then, or some of the books of Russian writers, like Gogol, Tolstoy and Gorky, which I had pursued in India before going to London, were not then forcing me to acknowledge, what most Indian writers of the modern period, like Bankimchander Chatterji, Ratannath Sarshar and Rabindranath Tagore, had not accepted in their novels, that even the so-called lowest dregs of humanity, living in utmost poverty, squalor and degradation, could become heroes of fiction' (Anand, 1977: 6). He goes on to say that he had not yet read Premchand. Anand's early stories can be represented by 'The Cobbler and the Machine', a cautionary tale that nevertheless avoids the overt didacticism of Tagore. Its first-person narrator looks back on his boyhood enthusiasm for Western machinery – the railroad, the phonograph and even the sewing machine. As a boy, he pesters the cobbler, Saudagar, to abandon his traditional tools and obtain a sewing machine. Eventually he does, but to repay the loan by which he purchased the machine, Saudagar must work harder than ever, eventually becoming a slave to the very device that the boy thought would lighten his labour and enable the cobbler to make him a pair of English style boots:

> But to-morrow and to-morrow and to-morrow came and went, and as my old Indian shoes were completely worn out and discarded, I trudged barefoot to and from school, and cursed both my parents for not buying me a new pair of Angrezi [English] shoes and Saudagar for not completing the pair he had promised me.
> I couldn't realize that my parents were poor and could not afford to buy me a pair of English boots, and I was too obstinate to accept

a cheap pair of Indian shoes. But Saudagar's work was pledged to Lalla Sain Das for the money the cobbler had borrowed to buy the machine, and I was disgusted. (Anand, 1959: 78–9)

The cobbler eventually dies at his mortgaged machine.

In summary the story may sound too much like a thinly disguised parable, but the boy's naive voice, the economy of the narrative, and its complex linking of several themes raise this story above the level of political parable and make it also a personal tragedy and coming of age story.

Anand's fiction, like that mentioned above, continues in this engaged, socially conscious, Marxist-influenced but ultimately humanistic vein. He perpetually champions the underdog – victims of sexism, caste prejudice, economic exploitation, imperialism and corruption. Though a staunch Indian nationalist, he has few illusions about Indian politicians either before or after independence. Broadly, his theme is human suffering. He is most effective in conveying his themes when writing from the inside of his characters or narrators. A detached, omniscient point of view often produces a story that seems more contrived than organic. 'Mahadev and Parvati', (from *The Barber's Trade Union*), a tale about a married couple on a pilgrimage to resuscitate their failing marriage, is a case in point. It has drama and tension but lacks the immediacy of a story like 'Duty' (also from *The Barber's Trade Union*) in which a policeman's day in the blazing sun is realised through brilliant detail and a psychologically convincing act of random violence. Anand is capable of humour, too, as in the tragicomic 'A Pair of Mustachios'.

Anand, like Sorabji, faced the difficult problem of translating Indian experiences, culture and language into an English that could both be understood by non-Indians and recognised as 'Indian' by native readers. Vijay Mohan Sethi analysed Anand's stylistic tactics and concluded that he creates a kind of '"Pigeon-Indian" which conveys the Indian sensibility through the English language' (1990: 63). Among Anand's devices are using Hindustani words in contexts where they can easily be understood by English readers, direct translations of common phrases that result in unidiomatic English, hybrid formations that combine English and Hindi, and deliberate misspellings of English words to convey their Indian pronunciation. These and other devices that Sethi analyses (62–9) account for some of the strangeness English-speaking readers might feel as they read Anand's fiction, but they also represent an important aspect of Indian fiction in English – one acknowledged by other writers and commented on extensively by postcolonial critics.

R. K. Narayan (1906–2001) enjoyed a long and productive career as a novelist, travel writer, essayist and short story writer. Most of his fiction is set in a South Indian city he calls Malgudi that, for all its remoteness, represents the world at large. Like Anand, Narayan examines a wide range of characters, from high government (and usually corrupt) officials to lowly snake charmers and knife sharpeners. He has said of his own writing, 'I discover a story when a personality passes through a crisis of spirit or circumstances' (Narayan, 1982: 8). Unlike Anand, he makes little attempt to render Indian languages into English. Apart from the occasional untranslated word in Tamil, he writes standard English in a clear, brisk, largely unadorned manner that is at its best in probing the thoughts and feelings of his quirky characters. Early stories from *An Astrologer's Day* (1947) bear signs of Maupassant's gritty realism and O. Henry's penchant for surprise endings. Later stories largely avoid these influences but retain his early emphasis on character. Among the best of these is 'Naga', told through the eyes of a boy whose father is a snake charmer but also a rogue who frequently drinks and eventually abandons the boy, leaving him with only the ageing cobra Naga. Unable to coax the snake into ferocity, the boy tries to free it, only to rescue it again after seeing that it cannot survive in the wild. The parallel but contrasting plots involving abandonment make a powerful point while illuminating the boy's character and predicament.

Perhaps Narayan's most effective story is 'A Horse and Two Goats' (1970), which features an impoverished peasant, Muni, who daily tends his two surviving goats near the base of the village's abandoned statue of a mounted warrior. On this day, he encounters a lost American tourist who tries to communicate with Muni and of course fails, and during this hilarious 'conversation' bargains with Muni for the sale of the statue. Muni thinks the proffered money is for his two goats. In the end, Muni cannot explain to his exasperated and domineering wife how he came to possess one hundred rupees and still have his goats. The story illustrates both tragically and humorously the divide separating Western and Eastern cultures, as well as depicting the poverty and privation that continue to dominate rural India. Narayan's handling of his materials is faultless, from his depiction of the hapless Muni, to the dramatic encounter between Muni and the arrogant storekeeper to whom he owes money, to the story's bittersweet conclusion. Narayan's singular accomplishment is to create an entire community through his fiction, a community that, like Faulkner's Yoknapatawpha County, has a mythical reality and vibrant life, at once local and transcendent.

Raja Rao (1909–2006) was a relative latecomer to short fiction. Some of his early stories, like 'The Cow of the Barricades' (1947), deftly combine mythical elements and social realism. Briefly summarised, the story relates that the cow Gauri mysteriously appears in the village every Tuesday and allows herself to be fed only by 'the Master'. Her apparently supernatural comings and goings evoke veneration in the villagers and bring peace and compassion. But this is a time of political strife over independence. When the government's threats to the village provoke a violent response, the Master's Gandhian pacifism fails and a battle ensues. Inexplicably, Gauri appears and climbs to the top of the barricade, inspiring the villagers to lay down their arms. The government's troops, however, shoot her dead. With the end of hostilities, Gauri becomes a local icon, the subject of a venerated statue and children's pull-toys. As for Gauri herself, the Master says 'She will be reborn when India sorrows again before she is free' (41). One is tempted to describe this story as an early instance of magical realism.

Rao's later stories, however, move increasingly towards philosophical and religious exploration. 'The Policeman and the Rose' (1978) has only a faint storyline, a vague narrator/character who appears to be in search of truth, and little in the way of narrative development. It reads more like a speculative essay or obscure allegory, in which the policeman is perhaps a symbol for the body or the conscience and the rose a symbol of transitory life. One critic calls it 'a fantastic elaboration of the Advaitic idea of *Jiva* and the soul – one bound and the other liberated form of a single reality of the life-principle' (Chakoo, 2000: 135).

These five writers – Premchand, Tagore, Anand, Narayan and Rao – collectively span the period during which the Indian short story was born, grew and matured. Together, they mark the development of the genre from its beginnings to its flowering before and shortly after independence. After independence, the *Nayi Kahani* or 'New Story' movement reacted against the residual romanticism of earlier writers and became more pessimistic in tone and individualistic in outlook (Alter, 1995: 26). They were not, of course, the only writers of note or of influence, but they do illustrate some of the main influences and trends that led ultimately to the explosion of short fiction by talented Indian writers in the 1960s and after.

After Independence

The tumultuous events following independence and partition in 1947 spawned a great number of short stories and novels in English and other languages. Some of these, in both English and other languages, have been collected by Saros Cowasjee and K. S. Duggal in *When the British Left* (1987). Anand and Kushwant Singh are among the authors anthologised here, but one of the most effective is 'Exchange of Lunatics' by Saadat Hasan Munto. The story takes place two years after partition and the bloodshed it caused and focuses on the insane Bishen Singh, who, like the other inmates of the asylum, does not understand partition and does not want to move. Refusing to be part of either country, he plants one foot in India, the other in Pakistan. The next day he is found dead. The irony may be a bit heavy-handed, but the story, like others in the collection, effectively conveys the insanity of artificially dividing people by religion. The theme of sectarian violence is also treated in a recent collection, *Bruised Memories: Communal Violence and the Writer* (2002), edited by Tarun K. Saint. Among its most interesting inclusions is an experimental story by the editor, entitled 'Broken Mirror' in which shards of a broken mirror reflect incidents of Hindu–Muslim violence.

Anand, Narayan and Rao continued to write long after independence was achieved in 1947, and to consider them as purely pre-independence either in technique or content would be to do them a serious injustice. Indeed, all three remained potent forces in Indian literature – novels, stories, criticism, travel writing and journalism – until the very end of the twentieth century. But of course there were younger writers for whom the struggles for independence were of less immediate importance. Indeed, according to some observers, 'The Indian short story turned inward and introspective in the fifties and sixties' (Ramakrishnan, 2000: 212), traits that can be seen in a number of the writers who came to the fore during these decades.

Khwaja Ahmed Abbas (1914–1987) caught the optimism and hopefulness of the immediate post-independence period in a series of 12 novels and eight collections of stories, plus plays and films that made him an extremely popular voice among ordinary readers and a mere 'populariser' among many critics. *The Black Sun and Other Stories* (1963) illustrates his strengths and weaknesses. 'The Sword of Shiva' is narrated in the first person by an old woman, Chanda, an outcast in her village for having borne a son out of wedlock. One day, many years ago, she and her young son were caught in a lightning storm and hoped to find refuge beneath a neem tree, but they were prevented from doing so by four of the village's most prominent and respectable men, all of whom rejected her as despised by Allah for her sin. As the moneylender says, 'it is written in the holy books that lightning strikes people like you' (76).

Predictably, lightning instead strikes the neem tree, killing all four of the 'righteous citizens' beneath it. The story effectively captures the rambling of an old woman's recollections and the tragedy of her life, as well as the smug self-righteousness of the men who scorn her; but the ending is too pat and the story's moral too obvious.

Similarly, 'The Dumb Cow' focuses on the unfortunate youngest daughter of a middle-class family who is afflicted by stuttering and a disfiguring pox that leaves her unmarriageable. At school, however, a sympathetic teacher encourages her to develop her mind and her confidence so that she can speak without stuttering. When the family tries to palm her off on a rich old man, he, seeing her for the first time, rejects her unless the family provides a huge dowry. Sulekha, however, rejects him, speaking her mind eloquently without stuttering and announcing that as a qualified teacher she has no need for a husband. Again, the sentiment is laudable but the method is sentimental and clumsy. However, for many of Abbas's readers, these and similar stories would have caught the progressive mood of Gandhi's politics and the aspirations unleashed by self-government.

Exactly contemporary with Abbas is Khushwant Singh (b.1915), a Sikh writer in many genres with an outlook as coolly analytical, even satirical – as Abbas's is romantic and optimistic. There is a no-nonsense frankness about his style and subject matter, a directness that matches his almost proscriptive view of the short story, which to his mind must be short (3500 words is a good length) and tightly unified; have a distinctive beginning, middle and end; a message; and a 'scorpion's sting' at the end (Singh, 1989: xii). 'The Mark of Vishnu' meets all these criteria and delivers an emotional punch that many of his stories lack. It is narrated through the eyes of science-smitten schoolboys, who scoff at superstitious Gunga Ram and his love for the cobra Kala Nag, which he daily feeds a bowl of milk. When Kala Nag is driven from his hole by a violent rain, they beat it to a pulp, put it in a tin, and take it to their science teacher at school. When the teacher opens the tin, Kala Nag escapes. From nowhere, Gunga Ram appears with his daily bowl of milk, only to be bitten and killed by the angry snake. The story supports neither the religious scepticism of the boys nor the devotion of the pious Gunga Ram; the cobra remains a mystery, beyond both types of dogma.

Few of Singh's other stories reach this emotional pitch. Some satirise politics ('The Voice of God', 'Man, How the Government of India Run'); others focus on characters ('The Insurance Agent', 'Black Jasmine'); and still others on social problems or situations ('India is a Strange Country',

'Mr Singh and the Colour Bar'). All are lively, and some carry a genuinely satirical punch, but most remain on the surface, written in a style many have called journalistic. There is always a point, but the sting the author insists upon is too often less potent than Kala Nag's deadly bite. At his best, Singh can peel layers of hypocrisy from individuals and institutions, and he can be amusing, but often his stories lack emotional depth or intellectual punch.

Among the second generation was Anglo-Indian Ruskin Bond (b.1934), who is more in Narayan's humanistic vein than Anand's political tradition. His subjects are almost exclusively Indian, but his style is pure English, as he has no Indian language to flavour his native tongue. Two of his more popular stories will serve to illustrate.

'The Night Train at Deoli' (1988) is brief and lyrical, narrated through the eyes of a man looking back on a singular experience during his college days when he travelled from Delhi to Dehra for his summer vacation. His train always stopped at the hamlet of Deoli, and there he twice encountered a girl selling baskets. Her simple dignity and eloquent eyes make a deep impression, but after the second meeting he never sees her again, nor does he act on his impulse to interrupt his journey to look for her. She remains a memory, a loss, a wistful possibility, a mystery.

'Dust on the Mountain' is set in Bond's home district of Mussoorie and chronicles the efforts of young Bisnu to save his family from ruin by leaving his drought-stricken farmland to seek employment in the city of Mussoorie, where he first works as a tea boy in a movie theatre, then as a cleaner for a truck driver who hauls limestone. When the driver's truck is destroyed in an accident, Bisnu returns home to rejoin his family. The point of the story is less the struggles of Bisnu to provide for his family than the destruction of the environment he witnesses in his travels. Deforestation and the mining of pristine mountains where villagers once picked strawberries are Bond's perhaps too obvious targets.

The 1970s and 1980s

Ruth Jhabvala (b.1927) presents the historian with especially difficult problems of nationality, as she is most frequently regarded as an Indian writer, though born in Germany, educated in England, and Indian only in having married Cyrus Jhabvala and moving to India with him in 1951. Her early fiction focuses on Europeans in India with a Jane Austen-like satirical eye towards them, Indians and Indian society. Gradually, her initial love of India gives way to scepticism, a movement reflected in *How I Became a Holy Mother and Other Stories* (1976).

Among the best known writers of her generation is Anita Desai (b.1937). Although she began publishing successfully in the 1960s, her best-known novels and stories date from the 1980s: *Games at Twilight and Other Stories* (1980), *Baumgartner's Bombay* (1989), *Fasting, Feasting* (2000), *Diamond Dust* (2000). Like writers of the previous generation, she is typically more interested in a character's internal development or self-realisation than in politics, although 'Studies in the Park' from her first collection can be read on several levels. Suno is pressured by his family to study hard for his school exams so that he can enter university and eventually land a good job. Unable to study in his noisy home, he retreats to a nearby park and there, in a moment of epiphany, sees an old man tenderly ministering to a dying young woman. They communicate to him what it means to be alive, and from that moment he refuses to worry about or even to take school exams. At the personal level, it is a story of self-actualisation and knowledge, but from a political perspective it can be read as a revolt against the remnants of Britain's colonial system of educating docile civil servants.

The stories in *Diamond Dust* reflect Desai's move to America in 1987, for they are variously set in India, England, Mexico and America. Although some have social or political undertones, they mainly focus on individual crises; 'Winterscape' and 'The Rooftop Dwellers' having feminist implications. Moyna of 'The Rooftop Dwellers' is trying to carve out an independent life in New Delhi, working for a literary magazine. Ejected from the women's hostel for having a pet cat, she is forced to rent an overpriced *barsati* (rooftop apartment). Her movements are severely restricted by her gender, which dictates nearly everything about her life. As she struggles to navigate her circumscribed world and to help rescue the failing literary journal from collapse, we learn a great deal about life in New Delhi as well as what it means to be a woman in contemporary India. Desai leaves little doubt about her own preferences. At the end of the story, Moyna receives a letter from her mother, transparently inviting her to meet a potential suitor. Moyna dissolves in derisive laughter; she will remain a free agent.

Contemporary Writers and Trends

To cite any one author or work as initiating the explosion of Indian literature on Western consciousness would be dangerous and misleading, but Salman Rushdie's (b.1947) *Midnight's Children* (1981) is sometimes cited as performing this seminal task. His one collection of stories, *East, West* (1994) is in many ways typical of fiction by authors of the Indian diaspora. 'The Courter' is humorous, nostalgic and realistic all at once. Focusing on the unlikely characters of Certainly Mary (the narrator's grandmother) and her Eastern European friend Mixed-up, the story reveals the difficulties of language, culture and racism faced by early Indian immigrants to Great Britain. Like Rushdie and Ruth Jhabvala, many of the writers who form part of this movement are multinational, making it difficult to classify them by the traditional means of nationality or ethnicity.

Chitra Banerjee Divakaruni (b.1956) moved to America aged 20 but still locates her fiction among Indians and sometimes in India itself. In her collection *Arranged Marriage* (1995) she examines various aspects of this locus of cultural tension. 'Clothes' is a beautifully written study of a successful arranged marriage using clothing as a central metaphor of a young woman's development through marriage and moving to America. When her husband is murdered in a robbery, she boldly decides to remain in California, in her mind's eye discarding her white widow's sari for an almond-coloured skirt and blouse. *The Unknown Errors of Our Lives* (2001) is more diverse in its themes but like its predecessor focuses on Indians of the diaspora. 'Mrs Dutta Writes a Letter' shows the difficulties faced by an elderly mother trying to cope with her Americanised son and his family and with a culture that often baffles and confuses her. Finally admitting failure, she will return to India. The title story of the collection is a richly complex psychological study of Richira, a young Indian-American woman struggling not with America and its culture but with her own mysterious ambitions, needs and fears. Her quest for self-knowledge, first through a teenage diary aimed at self-improvement, then through paintings of Hindu deities, and finally and dramatically in an encounter with her fiancé's former and now pregnant lover, leads her to conclude that marriage 'is a long, hobbled race, learning the other's gait as you go' (Divakaruni, 2001: 234). Divakaruni has complete control of the short story form, with a rich, supple style and a tender-tough understanding of the human heart.

Similar to Divakaruni in many respects is Talat Abbasi, a Pakistani woman writer of great variety and power. *Bitter Gourd and Other Stories* (2001) contains stories set in Karachi and New York. 'Simple Questions' is an almost stream-of-consciousness narrative by a mother of five girls and two stillborn sons beside herself with worry over dowries for her daughters and her inability to bear a living son. Her simple question to the headmistress of her daughter's school is: What use is reading and writing to a girl whose primary need is for a dowry and a husband? The narrator's tumbling style and associative organisation underscore her frantic yearnings for these traditional signs of a woman's value. Those interested in pursuing other stories by Pakistani women writers in English may consult the collection edited by Muneeza Shamsie (2005).

We are probably too close to the contemporary scene to do more than guess at trends, but in the third collection of stories by Pakistani writer Aamer Hussein, *Cactus Town and Other Stories* (2002) there may be significant indications of present directions. Hussein writes about characters who move across borders, some of them apparently easily, without the angst of exile or crises of displacement that mark much fiction about the Indian/Pakistani diaspora. Stylistically, he makes few concessions to monolingual readers, including not just occasional words of Indian languages but frequently whole sentences, untranslated. In 'The Colour of a Loved Person's Eyes', a couplet from an Urdu poem is not translated, even though it is central to the narrator's understanding of his mysterious mother. The title story, 'Cactus Town', is a series of 17 fragments, loosely connected by recurring characters and the narrator's point of view. The 1971 civil war resulting in the partition of Pakistan and Bangladesh occurs in the background of some incidents. There is an uncompromising character to this and others of his stories, suggesting that even though English is the medium, the intended audience is multilingual Pakistanis or Indians for whom movement between languages is as natural as the characters' adaptations to various countries and cultures. One might almost call them post-postcolonial stories. Multicultural London is home to several of these stories; alienation and loss are frequent themes, but they seem to be treated more as a normal part of life than wrenching problems.

No survey, even one as incomplete as this, could close without acknowledging the explosion of short fiction (and novels) by women writers, some of whom have already been mentioned above. Fortunately, many of these have been conveniently collected; unfortunately, it is possible to do little more than suggest the dominant themes and to mention a few prominent collections. Thematically, the stories return us to the very beginnings of the story in India – to the restrictions and oppressions faced by women for hundreds of years. Jehanara Wasi's (2001) *A Storehouse of Tales: Contemporary Indian Women Writers*; Monica Das's (2003) *Her Story So Far: Tales of the Girl Child in India*; and *Daughters of Kerala* (Chandersekaran, 2004) represent just a few of the many collections available. Widowhood, child prostitution, arranged marriages and the problems of vocation and identity faced by contemporary women are among the issues treated. Any of these or similar collections could form the basis for profitable explorations into the legacy of East–West values conflicts that lie at the heart of so much postcolonial Indian fiction.

Works Cited

Abbas, Khwaja Ahmed. *The Black Sun and Other Stories.* Bombay: Jaico, 1963.
Abbasi, Talat. *Bitter Gourd and Other Stories.* Karachi: Oxford University Press. 2001.
Alter, Stephen. 'The Short Story in India', *Wasafiri* 21 (Spring 1995), 26–8.
Anand, Mulk Raj. *The Barber's Trade Union and Other Stories.* Bombay: Bhatkal, 1959.
Anand, Mulk Raj. 'The Story of My Experiment With a White Lie', in *Critical Essays on Indian Writing in English* (Silver Jubilee Students Edition) ed. M. K. Naik, S. K. Desai and G. S. Amur. Madras: Macmillan Company of India, 1977. 4–18.
Bhattacharya, France. 'Tagore and Maupassant: Two Worlds, One Medium: The Short Story', in *Rabindranath Tagore in Perspective: A Bunch of Essays.* Calcutta: Visva-Bharati, 1989. 104–17.
Bond, Ruskin. *The Night Train at Deoli, and Other Stories.* New Delhi: Penguin India, 1988.
Chakoo, B. L. *Social Play and Metaphysical Symbolism in Raja Rao's Stories.* Amritsar: Guru Nanak De University, 2000.
Chandersekaran, Achamma C. (ed.) *Daughters of Kerala: Twenty-Five Short Stories by Award-Winning Authors,* trans. Achamma C. Chandersekaran. Tucson, Arizona: Hats Off Books, 2004.
Chaudhuri, Amit (ed.) *The Vintage Book of Modern Indian Literature.* New York: Random House, 2004.
Cowasjee, Saros (ed.) *The Oxford Anthology of Raj Stories.* Delhi: Oxford University Press, 1998.
Cowasjee, Saros and Kartar Singh Duggal (eds) *When the British Left: Stories on the Partitioning of India.* New Delhi: Arnold-Heinemann, 1987.
Das, Monica (ed.) *Her Story So Far: Tales of the Girl Child in India.* Delhi: Penguin India, 2003.
Desai, Anita. *Games at Twilight and Other Stories.* London: Heinemann, 1978; New York: Harper, 1980.
Desai, Anita. *Baumgartner's Bombay.* London: Heinemann, 1988; New York: A. A. Knopf, 1989.
Desai, Anita. *Fasting, Feasting.* London: Chatto & Windus, 1999; Boston: Houghton Mifflin, 2000.
Desai, Anita. *Diamond Dust.* New York: Houghton Mifflin, 2000. London: Chatto & Windus, 2000.
Deshpande, Shashi. *The Stone Women.* Calcutta: Writers Workshop, 2000.
'Dhanpat Rai Srivastava'. *Contemporary Authors Online.* May 14, 2002. <http://www.galenet.com/servlet/GLD/hits?c=...Type&n=d&locID=psucic&NA=Premchand>.
Divakaruni, Chitra Banerjee. *Arranged Marriage: Stories.* New York: Anchor Books, 1995.

Divakaruni, Chitra Banerjee. *The Unknown Errors of Our Lives*. New York: Doubleday, 2001.
Dutta, Krishna and Andrew Robinson. *Rabindranath Tagore: The Myriad-Minded Man*. New York: St. Martin's, 1995.
Hussein, Aamer. *Cactus Town and Other Stories*. Oxford: Oxford University Press, 2002.
Iyengar, K. R. Srinivasa. *Indian Writing in English*. Bombay: Asia Publishing House, 1962.
Jhabvala, Ruth Prawer. *How I Became a Holy Mother and Other Stories*. London: John Murray, 1976.
Joshi, Arun. *The Survivor: A Selection of Stories*. New Delhi: Sterling, 1975.
Lahiri, Jumpha. *Interpreter of Maladies*. London: Flamingo, 2000.
Narayan, R. K. *An Astrologer's Day and Other Stories*. London: Eyre & Spottiswoode, 1947.
Narayan, R. K. *A Horse and Two Goats and Other Stories*. New York: Viking, 1970.
Narayan, R. K. *Malgudi Days*. London: Penguin, 1982.
Radice, William. 'The Poems and Stories of Rabindranath Tagore', in *Masterworks of Asian Literature in Comparative Perspective: A Guide for Teaching*, ed. Barbara Stoler Miller. Armonk, NY: M. E. Sharpe, 1994. 109–22.
Ramakrishnan, E. V. (ed.) *Indian Short Stories, 1900–2000*. New Delhi: Sahitya Akademi, 2000.
Rao, Raja. *The Cow of the Barricades and Other Stories*. Oxford: Oxford University Press, 1947.
Rao, Raja. *The Policeman and the Rose: Stories*. Oxford: Oxford University Press, 1978.
Rubin, David. 'The Short Stories of Premchand', in *Masterworks of Asian Literature in Comparative Perspective: A Guide for Teaching*, ed. Barbara Stoler Miller. Armonk, NY: M. E. Sharpe, 1994. 167–78.
Rubin, David. 'Introduction'. *The World of Premchand: Selected Short Stories*, trans. David Rubin. New Delhi: Oxford University Press, 2001.
Rushdie, Salman. *Midnight's Children*. London: Jonathan Cape, 1981.
Rushdie, Salman. *East, West: Stories*. London: Jonathan Cape, 1994.
Saint, Tarun K. (ed.) *Bruised Memories: Communal Violence and the Writer*. Calcutta: Seagull Books, 2002.
Sethi, Vijay Mohan. *Mulk Raj Anand: Short Story Writer*. New Delhi: Ashish Publishing House, 1990.
Shamsie, Muneeza (ed.) *And the World Changed: Contemporary Stories by Pakistani Women*. Delhi: Women United, 2005.
Singh, Bhupal. *A Survey of Anglo-Indian Fiction*. London: Oxford University Press, 1934.
Singh, Khushwant. *The Collected Stories of Khushwant Singh*. Delhi: Ravi Dayal, 1989.
Sorabji, Cornelia. *Love and Life Behind the Purdah*, ed. Chandani Lokugé. 1901. New Delhi: Oxford University Press, 2003.
Spencer, Dorothy M. *Indian Fiction in English: An Annotated Bibliography*. Philadelphia: University of Pennsylvania Press, 1960.
Suhrawardy, Saista Akhtar Banu. *A Critical Survey of the Development of the Urdu Novel and Short Story*. London: Longman's Green, 1945.

Trosky, Susan M. (ed.). 'Tagore Rabindranath', in *Contemporary Authors*. Vol. 120. Detroit: Gale Research, 1987.
Vatsyayan, S. H. 'Hindi Literature', in *Contemporary Indian Literature: A Symposium*. New Delhi: Shaitya Akademi, 1957. 70–90.
Viswanathan, S. 'The Indian Short Story: Towards a Location Chart', in *English and the Indian Short Story: Essays in Criticism*, ed. Mohan Ramanan and P. Sailaja. Himayatnagar, Hyderabad: Orient Longman, 2000. 146–51.
Wasi, Jehanara (ed.) *A Storehouse of Tales: Contemporary Indian Women Writers*. New Delhi: Srishti, 2001.

6
The Science Fiction Short Story

Andy Sawyer

Edgar Allan Poe wrote that at the heart of the short story was 'a certain unique or single *effect*' (Poe, 1950: 450). He himself can be seen as one of the originators of the science fiction (SF) short story (as well as the detective and horror stories), but while studies of the short story naturally include Poe, science fiction and its relatives seem to have got short shrift. Charles May's *The Short Story: the Reality of Artifice* (2002) mentions Poe, but no other SF writer – if we exclude Kipling and a tangential comment on Wells – other than Ray Bradbury. Yet few genres have helped to keep the short story alive as much as science fiction which is par excellence an example of 'effect'.

May's introductory 'chronology' gives a clue, perhaps, to this oversight. The single reference to Bradbury is to his 1980 *Collected Stories*, which is unhelpful in placing Bradbury in the tradition of the short story: the 1950 date of his *Martian Chronicles* might have been more informative. For a form which relied on magazines for its dissemination, little is said about the role of markets and audiences. What some histories of the short story might have regarded as significant dates – say, the founding of *The Strand* in 1891 – are passed over, despite the fact that a number of the authors discussed first saw publication in periodicals.

This is not a criticism of a useful handbook. Science fiction is but one stream in the history of the short story; and describing the role of the popular magazines in the late nineteenth and early twentieth centuries is not at all the same thing as a discussion of how specific writers achieved their effects. Nevertheless, there is an odd relationship between science fiction, a mode of writing that does the most extraordinary things with ideas of genre, reader expectation, metaphor and other 'literary' responses to fiction, and contemporary canonical literary studies. This chapter intends to redress the balance, providing an introduction to those teaching the short story who are not experts in science fiction; addressing key issues they should be aware of; and suggesting just some of the material at their disposal. SF is the subject of sustained and thorough critical attention, thanks in part (in the UK at least) to the various incarnations of the Science Fiction Foundation, whose journal *Foundation* has recently published its hundredth issue and whose library, internationally one of the most important collections of SF texts and critical materials, is now administered by the University of Liverpool where it supports a thriving MA in Science Fiction Studies. Other specialist journals include *Science Fiction Studies*, *Extrapolation* (from 1959 the longest-running critical journal devoted to science fiction), the *Journal of the Fantastic in the Arts* and the *New York Review of Science Fiction*; as well as the critical and review journals issued by the British Science Fiction Association and individual fans such as the British Peter Weston and the Australian Bruce Gillespie (see http://www.efanzines.com). All of these have established an informed and committed critical discourse among academics and general readers which most other literary fields would envy – a discourse cemented by the publication of the second edition of the *Encyclopedia of Science Fiction*, edited by John Clute and Peter Nicholls, in 1993. Conferences sponsored by the Science Fiction Research Association and the International Association for the Fantastic in the Arts, as well as a less regular series under the auspices of the Eaton Collection at the University of California, Riverside and the Science Fiction Foundation, have broadened and deepened these discussions. There is also a tradition of serious discussion of the field within the science fiction fan community's own numerous conventions (most notably the 'Academic Stream' at recent World SF Conventions, the 'Wiscon' feminist-SF convention, and the annual 'Readercons', but including many others). Yet despite this success, SF is frequently seen as something specialist, a branch of 'popular literature' rather than a mode which infuses literary responses to the century or more of change we have been living through.

While some areas of literary studies – particularly those concerned with postmodernism – have taken on board the fictions of writers like Philip K. Dick and William Gibson,[1] and one or two individual writers, such as Ursula K. Le Guin, are the subject of fairly intense critical attention, most students are unlikely to encounter science fiction stories in classroom anthologies. The author and teacher John Kessel wrote in 1989 that 'no matter how well an SF writer writes today, if he publishes in an SF magazine he can't get into this book [the 1988 *Best American Short Stories*]' (Kessel, August 1989).[2] In his introduction to the anthology *The Science Fiction Century*, the editor David G. Hartwell calls SF the 'characteristic literary genre of the [twentieth] century [...] the genre that stands in opposition to literary modernism' (Hartwell, 1997: 17). Kessel's explanation for the suspicion about SF seemingly held by many literary editors (see 'The Place of the SF Short Story', below) sheds further light on this issue.

Anyone teaching the history and development of the short story genre needs to include at least some consideration of the important contribution of science fiction writers. Later in this chapter, I will introduce some of the diversity of themes and techniques used by its practitioners. But first, to understand science fiction, it is necessary to know where it came from, how it works, and why it stands in such an uneasy relationship to the 'academy'.

Where SF Came From

On 10 March 1926 the first issue of *Amazing Stories* appeared on American newsstands and the world changed.

Or rather, it didn't. The kind of fiction *Amazing's* publisher Hugo Gernsback called 'scientifiction' was already published in popular magazines on both sides of the Atlantic. As Mike Ashley points out in the first chapters of *The Time Machines*,[3] the history of the SF short story is part of the wider history of wonder tales and fantasies in magazine format. By 1926, the story of 'pseudo-science' or technological marvel had mingled with utopian/dystopian satires and Jules Verne's imaginary voyages. What some British reviewers called 'scientific romances' had been identified in the 1890s and the term applied to the early works of H. G. Wells, such as *The War of the Worlds* (1898), itself the culmination of a fashion for 'future-war' fantasies since George Chesney's 'Battle of Dorking' ([1871] 2004).

Gernsback, an immigrant from Luxembourg engaged in exploiting new technologies like radio, had already issued a 'scientific fiction number' of his magazine *Science and Invention* in 1923. Stories of 'scientific fiction' were mainstays of American 'pulp' magazines such as *Argosy*, *All-Story*, or *Weird Tales* as well as earlier 'dime novels' like Edward S. Ellis's *The Steam Man of the Prairies* ([1868] 2004) and Luis Senares's lengthy 'Frank Reade Jr.' series, full of wondrous inventions powered by steam and electricity. These, (and their British equivalent, 'penny dreadfuls') were read by boys and young working-class men, but many of the American magazines of the 1880s and 1890s were aimed at a more sophisticated audience. It was the search for greater specialisation among the readership – what we would now call 'niche marketing' – that resulted in the fragmentation of the general-story periodical into genre-based magazines aiming at specific sub-audiences. While American pulps such as *Cavalier* and *All-Story* published writers like Garret P. Serviss, and Edgar Rice Burroughs, British magazines such as *Pearson's* or *The Pall Mall Magazine* published short stories and serials by H. G. Wells and George Griffiths, whose apocalyptic fantasies of air warfare preceded Wells's *The War in the Air* (1908). Although *The Strand* itself, the 'new kind of magazine [which] may be termed the Standard Illustrated Popular Magazine' (Ashley, 2006: 197) published less protoscience fiction than some of its rivals, its readers nevertheless were the first to experience Wells's 'The Country of the Blind' ([1904] 1998) and Conan Doyle's 'The Lost World' ([1912] 1995). Writers of speculative/ imaginative fictions of all sorts therefore had a ready market.

Thus a magazine dedicated to what we would call SF was something of a latecomer. By the time *Amazing* appeared there were already magazines dedicated to the detective story, the Western and the supernatural. What Hugo Gernsback did was to define a genre: 'the ordinary pleasure reading of the new technological world' (Hartwell, 1997: 18). 'Extravagant Fiction today ... Cold Fact Tomorrow' was the masthead of the editorial promising a 'new sort of magazine' – one that would entertain, instruct and introduce his audience of young would-be technicians to what he called 'scientifiction'; a mode identified by Gernsback's selection of examples and the *raison d'être* laid out in his editorial.

Amazing reprinted Verne's 'Off on a Comet, or Hector Servadac'; Wells's 'The Facts in the Case of M. Valdemar'; Wells's 'The New Accelerator'; and two stories that had appeared in Gernsback's own *Science and Invention*, plus a third from *All-Story*. Pointing to writers like Verne, Poe and Wells, Gernsback claimed that they were the masters of what he argued was a new form of literature for the age of inventions and the twentieth century. He defined this new form as 'a charming romance intermingled with scientific fact and prophetic vision' (Gernsback, [1926] 2006: 3). Gernsback promoted 'scientifiction' as not only an entertaining form but a didactic and prophetic one: one that would inspire its readers to *create* the future they could glimpse through these stories.

The SF Effect: the 'Sense of Wonder'

Much of this was sheer marketing hype: nevertheless Gernsback and his successors devoted their critical energies to encouraging what has become known as the 'sense of wonder' – the science-fiction version of

Poe's 'unique or single effect'. It is partly a sense of newness, of being opened up to new information about the world. It is partly a conceptual breakthrough: the world is *different*: the narrator of Arthur C. Clarke's 'The Sentinel' ([1951] 2001) has made a discovery that changes forever his, and humanity's, view of the universe. It is partly that moment of heightened consciousness or perception on realising that the world we are imaginatively involved in while reading a fiction differs not only considerably but *fundamentally* from our own: Farah Mendlesohn, in *The Cambridge Companion to Science Fiction*, when discussing a novel by Greg Egan, reminds us that at the same time as we are noticing the very human-like behaviour in his characters we have to keep in mind that 'these people are not us' (James and Mendlesohn, 2003: 7). It is partly the passion for the big, the new, the shiny. There is an entry in the Clute/Nicholls *Encyclopedia of Science Fiction* for 'Big Dumb Objects' and few SF readers beyond their early teens are really going to be excited in any meaningful way by the simple presence in a fiction of spaceships, robots, aliens or any other of the 'icons' of science fiction. But it has also been persuasively argued that the 'sense of wonder' is associated with the Romantic sense of 'pleasurable terror' on encountering ideas of the infinite or the sublime: the sudden realization that the universe is bigger, more awesome than we can possibly imagine. It is also the realisation that in this process of escape and exploration we are 'reading back' upon our world. The strange has become familiar and the familiar, strange.

Other kinds of writing may have similar effects, but with science fiction this is predominant; a good science fiction story, whatever its other faults, will instil this sense of wonder. More traditional 'literary' effects, such as the exploration of character, can be subordinate to this. For example, to cite two stories I will return to later, the effect of Tom Godwin's 'The Cold Equations' ([1954] 2003) would remain the same no matter what the characters were called. The story is designed specifically to prove the point that human personality and agency is as nothing against the universe: while the characters are written in a certain way to engage the reader in identifying with their dilemma, their individual psychologies are irrelevant and whether they are 'Barton' or 'Marilyn' or entirely different people does not matter. (It is relevant that despite having taught this story at least once a year for at least ten years I have had to return to it to look up the names.) On the other hand, an equally important story, James Tiptree Jr's 'The Women Men Don't See' ([1973] 1975) derives much of its effect from the nature of its protagonists. While the story is equally 'about' universals, it could not be told in this particular way were Don Fenton and Ruth Parsons not who they were. Each story has its appropriate technique: each, for a number of reasons, is particularly suitable for classroom and seminar, and I have used them – and other stories discussed below – in teaching SF and speculative fiction at undergraduate and MA level.

The 'sense of wonder' is, while a necessary requisite, thus not necessarily a sufficient factor for a good SF story. Brian Aldiss, in *Trillion Year Spree* calls Gernsback's own writing 'tawdry and illiterate' and says that 'the worst Gernsbackian SF neither thinks nor dreams' (Aldiss, 1986: 203–4). Algis Budrys ascribes to Gernsback the problem which underlines the reaction of so-called 'high culture' to SF: the confusion between *technology* and *science* (Budrys, 1996: 297). On the other hand, Gary Westfahl in *The Mechanics of Wonder* (1998) argues convincingly that Gernsback identified and promoted (and did much to form) 'the *idea* of science fiction' (my emphasis) as a more-or-less agreed upon kind of writing which could be relied upon by its readers to do certain things. True, what Gernsback wrote in his editorials about the educational value and social inspiration of the science in 'scientifiction' was undermined by the inability of many of his writers to isolate 'sense of wonder' from melodrama, and the insistence of his readers upon stories of fantastic adventure that lumpenly marvelled instead of questioned. Still, at its best, Gernsback's legacy is the ingenious explorations of science as an adventure playground to be found in the imaginative longings of modern space opera, and the romantic visions of technological utopias. At its worst, though, it is the reign of the stereotype, failure to explore moral and ethical dimensions, the popular misconception that science fiction is about 'predicting the future' and the refusal to consider whether romantic visions of technological utopias lead to *dys*topia.

The Wells Continuum: Science and the Future

One of Gernsback's positive achievements was to place Wells firmly at the genre's heart. In his short stories and novellas, Wells set the template for subsequent SF. While Wells is one of several putative 'fathers of science fiction' his utopianism was in many ways opposed to the inventor-worship of the Gernsback tradition. He denied Vernian 'forecasting' and saw the fantastic elements in his stories as being secondary to ideas; they 'aim indeed only at the same amount of conviction as one gets in a good gripping dream' (Wells, 1933: vii). Nevertheless, his scientific training enabled him to draw upon a vocabulary and a way of thought based upon the scientific method and the 'thought experiment'. Neither the crystal that turns out to be a Martian viewing device in 'The Crystal Egg' ([1897] 1998): nor the planet from outer space that narrowly misses the earth in 'The Star' ([1897] 1998) are serious speculations. But their symbolic relationship to Wells's Darwinian view of human evolution and the swipe at Victorian complacency is vividly implied. If it is not the threat of Martian invasion, or a new and dangerous star, it may well be some other catastrophe: the human race is no more privileged than any other species.

The two great science fiction authors of mid-twentieth century America, Robert A. Heinlein and Isaac Asimov, were men in whom Wellsian futures can be seen through different lenses. Heinlein's early flirtation with socialism ended in right-wing libertarianism but in many of his short stories those Wellsian futures can be seen adapted to the politics of post-Depression USA. 'The Roads Must Roll' (1973) gives us both Wellsian moving walkways and an examination of the question of labour: who should control the literal and metaphorical levers of power? Asimov, an altogether more liberal thinker than Heinlein, used Wells-like 'thought experiments' in his well-known 'robot' stories, but his 'Foundation' sequence, collected in three novels but originally published under the aegis of John W. Campbell as short stories in *Astounding*, is perhaps his greater indebtedness to the Wells continuum.

The expansion of the number of magazines dedicated to something called (after 1929) 'science fiction' did a great deal to establish the mode as a literature of ideas. From 1933 onwards, F. Orlon Tremaine's *Astounding* published what he called 'thought variants'. John W. Campbell, *Astounding* editor from 1937–1971, encouraged, developed and occasionally bullied a stable of writers – including the early Arthur C. Clarke – who were expanding SF's range. Campbell's habit of throwing out an idea to a number of writers to see how different the results were, or pushing a writer to realise the implications of an idea, enriched the field greatly. Yet the restriction of these kinds of stories not only to magazines but a particular *kind* of magazine resulted in a ghettoisation from which it was difficult to escape. Only a few writers, such as Ray Bradbury or Heinlein, managed to sell to the more upmarket (and higher-paying) 'slicks' such as the *Saturday Evening Post* or *Colliers*. And while the magazines in the USA waxed and waned, there was no dedicated science fiction magazine at all for the adult market in Britain until the short-lived *Tales of Wonder* in 1937. Only after the war, when *New Worlds* began in 1946 and, under John Carnell and (later) Michael Moorcock became the iconic British SF magazine, and *Authentic* and *Nebula* appeared in the early 1950s, was there established a solid British market.

A Short Story Medium

For most of its history from the 1920s, SF has therefore been predominantly a short story medium, with novels serialised or 'fixed up' out of stories, as in the case of Walter M. Miller's *A Canticle for Leibowitz* (1993), A. E. van Vogt's, *The Voyage of the Space Beagle* (1973), or Isaac Asimov's *I, Robot* ([1950] 2004). Charles Stross's *Accelerando* (2006) is a more recent example. Some authors, such as the prolific Harlan Ellison or, more recently, Ted Chiang, either do not write in longer form or are known specifically for their short stories. Several authors are known for a handful of short stories; even a single one. Godwin's 'The Cold Equations' is but one example: even well-read SF fans would be hard-pressed to name other stories by him. Economic as well as artistic motives made it a habit to expand or add to short stories, as Daniel Keyes did with 'Flowers for Algernon' ([1959, expanded 1966] 2006), later filmed as *Charley* in 1968.

The term 'fix-up', used in the *Encyclopedia of Science Fiction* for novels created out of linked short stories, has no pejorative implication; but in the foreword to *The Birthday of the World* Ursula K. Le Guin has pointed out that this ignores the *deliberate* intention to create 'a book of stories linked by place, characters, theme, and movement, so as to form, not a novel, but a whole' (Le Guin, 2002: xi). Perhaps more science fiction 'novels' are closer to this mosaic form than are usually thought, for until the post-war rise of the paperback, the default route into book publication (at least in American SF) was serialisation in the magazines. This reliance on a specialist readership hungry for both novelty and familiarity shaped the way SF became a literature of effect and allusion; how it developed a megatext (a shared world of concepts serving as conceptual shorthand for reader and writer alike), so that long pseudo-textbook descriptions of future technology could be replaced by words like 'warp drive', 'terraform', 'cyberspace' or 'ansible'.[4] A number of these words have entered the common vocabulary, as words that are in some way *needed*. It took 'robot' a matter of months after the first English language performance of Karel Capek's play *Rossum's Universal Robots* (1920: trans. 1923) to be used to illustrate ideas of alienation under industrialisation or bureaucracy; and 'cyberspace' leaked out of the works of William Gibson ('Burning Chrome', 1982) to become a cliché of everyday computerspeak.

Through interplay and competition between magazines and authors the SF story developed greater subtlety. The eclipse of magazine by paperback allowed the publication of single author collections or anthologies. From the 1970s onward the 'theme' anthology became a particularly strong segment of the market. The late 1960s 'new wave', associated in Britain with *New Worlds* magazine under the editorship of Michael Moorcock, and in America by younger writers like Harlan Ellison, who edited the influential anthology *Dangerous Visions*, allowed greater space for literary experimentation.[5] The limitations of 'science fiction' were (or so it was claimed) overcome by referring to *'speculative* fiction'. Meanwhile Judith Merril was deliberately looking beyond the confines of the magazines for her 'Year's Best SF' anthologies, published between 1956 and 1968. J. G. Ballard argued that spaceships and aliens were outmoded and that (psychological/symbolic) 'inner' rather than 'outer' space was the true domain of the science fiction writer. Michael Moorcock called for 'A New Literature for the Space Age' in his first editorial for *New Worlds* in 1964, arguing for greater openness in subject matter and style.

The difficulties in the attempts to 'mature' SF were sometimes due to the difficulty in defining the mode. The 'idea of science fiction' infusing the post-Gernsback magazines in the USA was very different from the British 'scientific romance'. Nonetheless, ambiguity added to the field's potential richness. So did division into identifiable sub-genres. The scientific romance, for example, has been identified as dealing with longer evolutionary scales, pessimistic or less hopeful endings, with a lesser dependence upon heroics. 'Hard' science fiction, relying on established or carefully extrapolated science for both plot and effect, linked Wells as a writer who *knew* science with Gernsback's fiction for technicians. It became identified as a shared 'game' between writers and readers where scientific thinking must be as scientifically accurate (or plausible) as possible. (Westfahl, 1996: 113). Such a story is Godwin's 'The Cold Equations': SF author and teacher James Gunn calls 'The Cold Equations' 'a touchstone story because if readers don't understand it they don't understand science fiction' (Gunn, 1986: 72).

The 'cold equations' are the objective laws of science that tell us that reality cannot be twisted to meet human desires. The universe is not *in itself* sympathetic to human concerns, and a stowaway on a spaceship carrying emergency medical supplies to a disease-stricken planet (a young girl who only wants to see her brother) *has* to be jettisoned. The story is milked for the utmost poignancy and sentimentality, but it can only have one ending: *we* may care for her, but the universe doesn't. Critical examination of the story reveals more than this simple dilemma. John Huntington (Huntington, 1989: 79–85) interrogates the story on the question of 'fairness', and Gary Westfahl in Chapter 6 of

Cosmic Engineers notes that Godwin wanted the girl to survive; it was the editor Campbell who insisted on revisions to create the 'logical' ending. From the viewpoint of popular literature, even of the 'hard SF' tale, the 'true' reading of the story is as a 'problem' like the traditional detective story. Somewhere in the text is the clue to an eventual solution. Just as the detective braves the labyrinth of clues and red herrings to identify the murderer, so the hard-SF hero (in cooperation or competition with the reader) uses his (it is usually 'his') scientific knowledge to solve a dilemma.

Campbell's own interpretation of 'The Cold Equations' is illuminating:

Science fiction begins when you take a divergent viewpoint, and make the reader gradually understand that that cockeyed viewpoint – that he strongly rejected at first – is a sound, wise, and rational way of life under the circumstance of the situation at hand.

'The Cold Equations' was a test of that idea. ('Letter to Philip Jose Farmer' in Chapdelaine 1985: 293)

So is the focus here on the 'cold equations' at all, or is it on 'cold ethics' – the 'culturally abhorrent' proposition that the sacrifice of an innocent may be the *right* cause of action in some circumstances? Would our reaction to the story have been any different if the stowaway had been a social undesirable instead of an 'innocent' girl? The novelty is that we are 'conditioned' to expect that a 'problem' story will result in the solution to that problem. 'The Cold Equations' is still a classic 'problem' story – but are we being misled as to the actual nature of the problem?

The tension between different interpretations of what the genre *means* makes up much (perhaps too much) of the critical response to science fiction, but it can be found in comparing the 'implied future' of the early SF magazines with later reaction to it. William Gibson's short story 'The Gernsback Continuum' ([1981] 1993) describes how the narrator, researching the 'futuristic' 1930s and 1940s architecture of American cities, discerns the 'semiotic ghosts' of the Gernsback magazines, leaking from the 'future that never was': the collective consciousness of the public who bought into the world of art-deco skyscrapers and airships and the assumption that technology per se would bring about utopia. The gadgets and cityscapes of the narrator's hallucinations are straight from covers of *Amazing* and *Wonder*. The 'smug, happy and utterly content' people who live in this dream show 'all the sinister fruitiness of Hitler Youth propaganda' (1993: 466). Gernsbackian imagery is embedded deep in our culture. The irony such a comparison shows, of course, is that Gibson's once cutting-edge genre of cyberpunk is equally embedded. Is, we may ask, the postmodern imagery of cyberpunk now equally a slightly creepy fashion item?

What does a Science Fiction Short Story Do?

Paul Kincaid in 'What is it we do when we read science fiction' discusses various aspects of what happens when we read science fiction by focusing on SF's neologisms. One of his examples is a phrase in which someone is described as having 'genemod perfect skin'. We can construct a meaning out of 'genemod' (which we can construe as a variant of 'genetically modified') even though the word – unlike 'cyberspace' or 'robot' – is meaningless in everyday discourse. Kincaid also discusses the way language is put together in new ways. He cites, for instance, Harlan Ellison's reaction to the phrase 'The door dilated' from a Robert A. Heinlein novel: 'Dear God, now I knew I was in a future world' (Kincaid, 2000: 72–82). Drawing on critics like Samuel R. Delany and Damien Broderick, Kincaid says that 'what we are doing when we read science fiction is allowing ourselves to be mystified'. We can model a new, invented reality out of the sometimes alienating language in which the story is built.

SF's ability to ask the simple question, 'What if?' leads to what has become perhaps the most influential way of considering how a science fiction story works. In her introduction to the *Norton Book of Science Fiction*, Ursula K. Le Guin cites Bob Shaw's 'Light of Other Days' as a classic example of the way a science fiction writer invents a technology and then extrapolates its effects. In Shaw's case, this is 'slow glass': through it, light may take days, months or years to pass. The result is a technology which, in its capacity to provide a literal 'window on the past' transforms the lives of the characters in the story (and provides a mechanism in which Shaw can examine other ways in which new technologies affect the world).

This is what Darko Suvin, in his definition of science fiction as 'the literature of cognitive estrangement'[6] calls the 'novum'. A 'new thing' has been introduced into this (fictional) world and changed the rules. In a science fiction story, we cannot assume that the fictional world is our world. (A useful rule of thumb for distinguishing SF from fantasy is that any change arises from the same laws of science as understood in our world. It is not 'magic'.) By experiencing these differences, and the 'estrangement' caused by their existence and extrapolation, we are invited to bring something unfamiliar into our realistic imaginative world, making us see it differently (and by implication, criticise it).

Le Guin herself, in many of her short stories, applies this process not to technology but society itself. (Anthropology is also a science.) In many of the stories collected in *The Birthday of the World*, for instance, Le Guin shows worlds that explore and extend our notions of gender. In 'Mountain Ways,' the world of O has a complex system of marriage:

> Marriage on O is a foursome, the sedoretu – a man and a woman from the Morning moiety and a man and a woman from the Evening moiety. You're expected to have sex with both your spouses of the other moiety, and not to have sex with your spouse of your own moiety. So each sedoretu has two expected heterosexual relationships, two expected homosexual relationships, and two forbidden heterosexual relationships. (Le Guin, 2002: 91)

This situation produces what Le Guin calls 'comedies of manners' which perhaps stand in the same relationship to traditional comedies of 'relationships' as Godwin's 'The Cold Equations' does to the traditional hard SF 'problem story'.

At the heart of the science fiction story, then, is speculation and extrapolation – the often playful examination of the implications of ideas. This can be found in the fascination for 'time paradox' stories (such as Bradbury's 'A Sound of Thunder' (2005), Heinlein's 'By His Bootstraps' (1973), or John Crowley's 'Great Work of Time' (2004)) in which the histories of individuals or societies are changed, and its close relation, the 'alternate history'.

As a mode apparently engaged with the future, science fiction's fascination with history nevertheless caused it to explore the past and the notion of historical change, whether by the interference of time travellers or by the postulation of a parallel world's influence. Popular divergence points ('jonbar points' from an early series by Jack Williamson) are, naturally enough, history's 'great moments' such as the result of the American Civil War or World War II, but there are other divergences. Kim Stanley Robinson's 'The Lucky Strike' ([1984] 2002) is about a refusal to go through with the Hiroshima bombing. Moments of 'historical change', moreover, do not have to be set in the past; Joanna Russ's 'When it Changed' (1972) considers the reaction of a future/alternative feminist-separatist world to the coming of men.

Such explorations of possibility are immanent in other significant themes of science fiction, such as the 'first contact' story – the perennial tale of conceptual breakthrough in which humanity's place in the universe is irretrievably altered. While 'aliens' frequently stand in for whatever threat readers prefer not to admit to fearing (racial and gender anxieties) they may also allow readers to confront and explore those ideas of Otherness. Stanley Weinbaum's 'A Martian Odyssey' ([1934] 1977) is sometimes described as the first story where the 'alien' is presented as interesting *because of* its alienness. Lost on Mars, an Earthman saves the life of a birdlike Martian. Having already set us up with repartee among the expedition (two Americans, a Frenchman and a German, allowing for verbal confusions), Weinbaum extends the problem. If three human cultures can have difficulty in understanding each other, how can a human understand an alien? But he concludes that communication between Jarvis and 'Tweel' is possible because each is a rational being who *wants* to communicate. 'Alien' may equal 'different', but 'different' does not necessarily equal 'hostile'.

Frederik Pohl's 'The Day After the Day the Martians Came', published in the 'taboo-busting' anthology *Dangerous Visions* (Ellison, [1967] 1987), offers a use for the encounter with the alien that oscillates between realism and metaphor. Pohl allows an African-American bellhop in a motel where reporters are watching the Martians on TV to make a wry comment about racism as jokes and bigotry are turned against a new target. Other SF writers see the 'holy grail' of the mode as what Gregory Benford describes as 'effing the ineffable' (Benford, 1986/7). SF's attraction to Otherness is a creative problem unavailable to writers in a natural mode. How can you fully describe what it might be like to live on a high-gravity world with methane seas? What emotions might sweep a species with three or more genders? The ability of science fiction to literalise the metaphor or to make what only *might* be real the subject of a fiction in the realist mode (in the words of Samuel R. Delany ([1977] 1999) to present 'subjunctive reality') allows vast potential.

'The Women Men Don't See' by James Tiptree Jr (the pen name of Alice Bradley Sheldon) is an example that, even more than Godwin's 'The Cold Equations', cannot be told except as a science fiction story. The narrator, Don Fenton, is on an aircraft which crashes in the Central American jungle. With him are two women, mother and daughter, who have earlier registered with him only as 'a double female blur' (Tiptree, 1975: 131). His attempts to play conventional 'hero' roles are inept. Following the crash, the women are distant – self-reliant, friendly but cool. For his part, Fenton is not attracted to them. Or so he says; but when he and Ruth Parsons (the mother) need to share sleeping arrangements he is smugly proud of himself for not acting on his sexual response. He and Ruth go to fetch water; he is injured. While she nurses him, Ruth and Fenton discuss the state of women in a patriarchal world. For Ruth, even 'women's lib' is a temporary alleviation which can be withdrawn at the next crisis: all women can do is survive 'in the chinks of your world-machine' (154). Her separatism repels him. 'Mrs Ruth Parsons isn't even living in the same world with me', he reflects (154). During the night he is awakened by light, strange voices. Later on, these 'voices' turn out to be aliens. The women leave with them.

In considering the idea of the alien, 'Women' is in some ways an *easy* story – it is very clearly about how (middle-class American) women feel alien. The word 'alien' in these last two sentences means slightly different things: the first use includes an all-encompassing meaning of the word: stranger, being from another world. The second is more of a metaphor. Put together, we have something like what Gary Wolfe calls one of the 'icons' of science fiction: the common stock of frequently used 'novums' whose very frequency allows writers to use them in numerous ways. The Martian alien can be, for instance, Wells's invaders which signify, among other things, the emotionless, evolved 'man of the year million' or the threat to Victorian complacency in the shape of other nations, races or classes; or it can, in 'A Martian Odyssey', suggest how alien life might exist in its own ecology which we have to learn to understand.

The Place of the SF Short Story

John Kessel, as a teacher of creative writing and a science fiction writer, is one of the few experts on both the short story itself and the SF short story. In 'Why SF is Not Welcome in the Parlor', he claims that 'SF has become, without knowing it, one of the last outposts of the traditional short story' (Kessel, August, 1989). While magazine sales are pitiful compared to 50 years ago, the marketplace nevertheless manages to support a number of 'dedicated' SF magazines; in Britain, *Interzone* is the longest-lived SF magazine the country has ever had. Even in its relatively shrunken form, science fiction remains a 'popular' art form. This, Kessel argues, is the answer to the question he poses about why 'mainstream' short story anthologies rarely if ever accept science fiction. With its origin among the short stories of H. G. Wells, we must remember that Wells took the opposing side to the 'modernist' camp, quarrelling with Henry James and Joseph Conrad. In his (1993) article 'The Brother from Another Planet', Kessel builds upon his argument by contrasting 'science fiction' and the 'mainstream' short story.

In comparing 'best of' anthologies of science fiction and 'literary' short stories, Kessel suggests that the SF story *is* different from the 'mainstream' story published in 'literary' magazines and studied in most academic courses on short fiction. Forgetting subject matter (one might *expect* SF to be about 'difficult' subjects like science and technology), a greater predominance of SF stories appear to be in the third person rather than the more immediate first person. Similarly, the combination of first person, present tense, increasingly found in literary fiction after 1960, is rarely present in SF. SF stories are also longer, more plotted, more concerned with the 'storytelling' virtues of beginning, middle, end; more dominated with 'big' ideas rather than the local, domestic or personal. 'SF stories direct attention away from the small to the large, from the plight of the individual to the underlying idea (feminist, economic, evolutionary, technological, political, social, etc.)' (Kessel, 1993: 8).

Yet SF manages to do some remarkably flexible and subtle things. Its 'double voicing' means that the SF writer is capable of a remarkable degree of complexity. Students are often confused by the intrusion of the 'real' aliens into 'The Women Men Don't See'; or wonder why Karen Joy Fowler's (2005) 'What I Didn't See' is included in a speculative fictions course when there are no apparent 'fantastic' elements in it.

The first point is to do with SF's literalising metaphor. It brings home the point that Parsons *really would* leave with aliens given the chance. Her 'alienation' is not an easy pun; it is real. The intrusion of the alien beings changes Fenton's paradigm in a way an encounter with a separatist-feminist would not. She really does live in a different world from him; he really is not the centre of the universe. And so as well as being an *obvious* story it is also a *difficult* story. Why do we *need* the actual arrival of the aliens? Surely it's only a metaphor – we women, the story says, *feel* like aliens; this surely isn't *our* world we are living in? – compounded by the viewpoint of the narrator, who really *does* see them as alien, or at least Other. Isn't the SF element one step too far into the fantastic?

The answer to this might go as follows: a version of this story – the *bad science fiction* version – would have it revealed that men and women *really are different species* so that we could marvel at a novel idea and remain with our prejudices unchanged. Don actually brings up this notion, to deny it. Students might compare this story to Ursula K. Le Guin's well-known novel, *The Left Hand of Darkness* (1969), in which individuals can be 'male' or 'female' at different times and so in whom gender as we know it does not exist. In reading 'The Women Men Don't

See' we are constantly oscillating between viewpoints. The story is narrated by a male who seems to be presenting a radical feminist stance. The author is male. Except that 'really' the author is female. (And Sheldon's sexual orientation, according to a recent biography may not have been entirely heterosexual.) *How does awareness of Tiptree's 'true' identity affect our reading of the story?*

The second point, regarding 'What I Didn't See', is that the story – by one of the founders of the James Tiptree award for 'SF that explores and extends the notion of gender', is redolent with Tiptree associations, from the echo in its title, to the jungle setting (it partly reflects an actual expedition which Tiptree's mother, the explorer and writer Mary Bradley took part in) as well as a whole range of fictions which involve women kidnapped by, or running away with, gorillas, from Tarzan to films like *King Kong* (1933) or Ed Wood's *Bride of the Monster* (1955). Like the Tiptree story, it features a woman apparently 'escaping' into another world. Unlike the previous story, this one has a female narrator whose viewpoint guides the reader. It is also supremely – consider again the title – about misdirection. We do not have to be told the subtext. This is a story that speaks SF even as it does not apparently utter a single science fictional syllable. If 'The Women Men Don't See' can only be told *as* science fiction, 'What I Didn't See' *needs* science fiction for its richness to fully blossom.

True, this estrangement can be overstressed. Metatextual effects can be embedded in traditional clichés and bad writing. Interesting, important ideas are no guarantee of original literary style. Reader expectation works both ways. A reader used to the generic tropes of the modern 'literary' short story may find Weinbaum's 'A Martian Odyssey' crudely cartoon-like, particularly in the repartee of the human characters, constantly interrupting the flow of the narrative with uneasy wisecracks. To some extent, this is justified. 'A Martian Odyssey' was Weinbaum's first science fiction publication, and the style and subject matter of what John W. Campbell was to try to turn into a probing, subversive literature was still being formed. On one level, the story *is* a traditional pulp product. For example, the default assumptions of this future – particularly the 'natural' assumption that of course this expedition would be made up of white males – are unquestioned. Yet if we look at the story closely, we may find that it is precisely this sort of pulpish masculinity that seems to be deconstructed in the relationship between Jarvis and Tweel, and the story becomes a fascinating study of unease.

This is, as I've suggested, a story about friendship, about how difference can be overcome. Jarvis knows that he and Tweel, though they do not *understand* each other, *like* each other. Like many examples of science fiction – then and since – all the characters are men, but is all this wisecracking a skirting around emotion? Is there a gender missing in the story? 'Fancy Long' the entertainer plucked from Jarvis's mind by the predatory dream-beast is the only female – that we can recognise as female – in the story. Jarvis's *denial* ('I know her pretty well – just friends, get me?') of a sexual connection is one thing, but the language he used to explain what has happened is quite another: 'The Dreambeast uses its victim's *longing* and *desires* to trap its prey' (Weinbaum, 1977: 29–30, my emphasis).

We might even consider the 'default' pronoun given to Tweel and the one Martian organism we see reproducing, the 'silicon beast', which seems to be asexual:

'They're his spores, or eggs, or seeds' (27). Why '*he*'? But Jarvis is clear on the use of the default pronoun: 'Thanks, Tweel. You're a *man*!'

Do gender roles slip into the narrative, even in the absence of characters from that gender? Brian Attebery, in *Decoding Gender in Science Fiction* (2002) discusses Weinbaum's novel of a mutant superman, *The New Adami*, as a novel of sexual anxiety. Is 'A Martian Odyssey' in this light also a story 'about' sex and gender? On one level (or more), no; it's clearly centred upon communication and is an essentially *humorous* revamping of the stereotype of the Martian. But it's also about the lack of, or partial lack of, communication. Anything female is fragmented. All Fancy Long does is smile and wave. Tweel is a male 'buddy' rather than a female, or even asexual, companion. The 'estrangement' in this story lies not so much in the fact that we are on Mars, nor even that there is an alien in it, but in the way that it asks new questions: Does the alien *have* to be a threat? Can we *embrace* Otherness rather than fear it? And do we in the twenty-first century *discover* new ways of reading stories like this or do we *impose* our current ideologies upon them just as the ideologies of the 1920s and 1930s were imposed upon them in the act of writing?

The place of the science fiction short story, though comparatively healthy, remains in limbo. On the one hand, American magazines such as *Analog*, *The Magazine of Fantasy and Science Fiction* and *Asimov's*, as well as the British *Interzone*, provide a solid market for writers, and on both sides of the Atlantic there is a thriving if unstable 'small press' market through which aspiring writers can make their routes and established writers can keep in touch with their audiences. 'Best-of-year' anthologies are still published, and occasional one-offs like the all-fiction hundredth issue of the critical journal *Foundation* provide variety. But on the other hand, circulations are down since their heyday, it is virtually impossible to find these magazines outside specialist shops, and the days are gone when a writer could make a living out of supplying the magazines with stories. The internet has, of course, taken up some of the space. In recent years, 'Hugo' nominations for best short story of the year have come from webzines as well as traditional print media, although webzines are by no means an economic concern, and it is unclear what the final shape of the field will be. Self-publishing is an option – probably too easy a one. Perhaps the best fiction webzine, the 'Sci.Fiction' department of the webzine Sci.Com was recently dropped, although the long-standing *Infinity Plus* (http://www.infinityplus.co.uk/) still remains, and still publishes important names, as does *Helix* (http://www.helixsf.com/). Other webzines, including *Strange Horizons* (http://www.strangehorizons.com/index.shtml) (which published one of the 2007 Hugo nominations), and *Fantastic Metropolis* (http://www.fantasticmetropolis.com/) publish fiction. Much short fiction is now found on authors' and publishers' websites.

The web remains tangled. Some authors go as far as encouraging the dissemination of their fiction through 'Creative Commons' licensing; others oppose strongly the unauthorised publication of their fiction on 'pirate' sites. The science fiction short story will certainly survive, but its journey to long-term survival will be choppy.

Works Cited

Aldiss, Brian W. *Trillion Year Spree*. London: Gollancz, 1986.
Ashley, Mike. *The Time Machines: the Story of the Science Fiction Magazines from the Beginning to 1950*. Liverpool: Liverpool University Press, 2000.
Ashley, Mike. *Transformations: the Story of the Science Fiction Magazines from 1950 to 1950*. Liverpool: Liverpool University Press, 2005.
Ashley, Mike. *The Age of the Storytellers: British Popular Fiction Magazines 1880–1950*. London: British Library, 2006.
Ashley, Mike. *Gateways to Forever: the Story of the Science Fiction Magazines from 1970 to 1980*. Liverpool: Liverpool University Press, 2007.
Asimov, Isaac. *The Complete Robot*. London: HarperCollins, 1983.
Asimov, Isaac. *Foundation*. London: HarperCollins, 1994.
Asimov, Isaac. *I, Robot*. New York: Bantam, 2004.
Attebery, Brian. *Decoding Gender in Science Fiction*. New York: Routledge, 2002.
Benford, Gregory. 'Effing the ineffable'. *Foundation* 38 (winter 1986/87): 49–57.
Bradbury, Ray. *A Sound of Thunder and Other Stories*. New York: HarperCollins, 2005.
Budrys, Algis. 'Paradise Charted'. *Visions of Wonder: the Science Fiction Research Association Anthology* edited by David G. Hartwell and Milton T. Wolf. New York: Tor, 1996: 292–338.

Chapdelaine, Perry A., Tony Chapdelaine and George Hay (eds). *The John W. Campbell Letters*, vol. 1. Franklin, TN: AC Projects, 1985.
Chesney, George. *The Battle of Dorking*. Whitefish, MT: Kessinger Publishing, 2004.
Clarke, Arthur C. *The Collected Stories*. New York: Tor, 2001.
Clute, John and Peter Nicholls. *The Encyclopaedia of Science Fiction*. London: Orbit, 1993.
Conan Doyle, Arthur. *The Lost World & Other Stories*. Herts: Wordsworth, 1995.
Crowley, John. 'Great Work of Time' in John Crowley (ed.) *Novelties and Souvenirs: Collected Short Fiction*. HarperCollins: New York, 2004.
Delany, Samuel R. *The Jewel-Hinged Jaw*. Elizabethtown, NY: Dragon Press, 1977. London: Gollancz, 1999.
eFanzines.com. http://www.efanzines.com.
Ellis, Edward S. *The Huge Hunter or The Steam Man of the Prairies*. Whitefish, MT: Kessinger Publishing, 2004.
Ellison, Harlan, (ed.) *Dangerous Visions* [1967]. London: Gollancz, 1987.
Fowler, Karen Joy. 'What I Didn't See' in *The James Tiptree Award Anthology 1*, ed. Karen Joy Fowler, Pat Murphy, Debbie Notkin and Jeffrey D. Smith. San Francisco: Tachyon Publications, 2005: 191–210.
Gernsback, Hugo. 'A New Sort of Magazine'. *Amazing Stories*, 1 (April, 1926): 3.
Gibson, William. 'The Gernsback Continuum'. *The Norton Book of Science Fiction*, ed. Ursula K. Le Guin and Brian Attebery. New York: Norton, 1993: 457–66
Gibson, William. *Burning Chrome*. London: HarperCollins, 1995.
Godwin, Tom. *The Cold Equations and Other Stories*. New York: Baen, 2003.
Gunn, James. 'The Readers of Hard Science Fiction', in *Hard Science Fiction*, ed. George Slusser and Eric S. Rabkin. Carbondale: Southern Illinois University Press, 1986: 70–81.
Hartwell, David G. *The Science Fiction Century*. New York: Tor, 1997.
Heinlein, Robert A. *The Best of Robert Heinlein*. London: Sigwick & Jackson, 1973.
Heinlein, Robert A. 'By His Bootstraps' in Robert A. Heinlein, *The Menace From Earth*. London: Corgi, 1973. 40–87.
Huntington, John. *Rationalising Genius: Ideological Strategies in the Classic American Science Fiction Short Story*. New Brunswick: Rutgers University Press, 1989.
James, Edward and Mendlesohn, Farah. *The Cambridge Companion to Science Fiction*. Cambridge: Cambridge University Press, 2003.
Kessel, John. 'Why SF is not Welcome in the Parlor' http://www4.ncsu.edu/~tenshi/Parlor.html. (Originally published in *Short Form*, vol. 2, no. 2, August 1989).
Kessel, John. 'The Brother from Another Planet'. *New York Review of Science Fiction* 55 (March 1993) 1: 8–11.
Keyes, Daniel. *Flowers for Algernon*. London: Orion, 2006.
Kincaid, Paul. 'What is it we do when we read science fiction?' *Foundation* 78 (spring 2000): 72–82.
Le Corbusier. *The City of Tomorrow and its Planning*. London: Architectural Press, 1987.
Le Guin, Ursula K. *The Left Hand of Darkness*. London: MacDonald, 1969.
Le Guin, Ursula K. *The Birthday of the World*. New York: HarperCollins, 2002.
May, Charles E. (ed.) *The New Short Story Theories*. Athens: Ohio University Press, 1994.
May, Charles E. *The Short Story: the Reality of Artifice*. London: Routledge, 2002.
Miller, Walter M. *A Canticle for Leibowitz*. London: Orbit 1993.

Moorcock, Michael. 'The March of the Whiteshirts'. *Interzone* 211 (July/August): 5–6.
Poe, Edgar Allan. 'Review of Nathaniel Hawthorne's *Twice-Told Tales*'. *Selected Prose, Poetry and Eureka*. New York: Holt, Rinehart and Winston, 1950: 447–55.
Robinson, Kim Stanley. 'The Lucky Strike' in *Vinland the Dream and Other Stories*. New York: HarperCollins, 2002.
Russ, Joanna. 'When It Changed'. http://www.scifi.com/scifiction/classics/classics_archive/russ/russ1.html. First published 1972 in Harlan Ellison's *Again, Dangerous Visions*.
Stross, Charles. *Accelerando*. London: Orbit, 2006.
Suvin, Darko. *Metamorphoses of Science Fiction*. New Haven: Yale University Press, 1979.
Tiptree Jr, James. 'The Women Men Don't See'. *Warm Worlds and Otherwise*. New York: Ballantine, 1975. 131–64.
van Vogt, A. E. *The Voyage of the Space Beagle*. London: HarperCollins, 1973.
Weinbaum, Stanley. *A Martian Odyssey and Other Stories*. London: Sphere, 1977.
Wells, H. G. 'Introduction'. *The Scientific Romances of H. G. Wells*. London: Gollancz, 1933.
Wells, H. G. *The Complete Short Stories*. London: Phoenix Press, 1998.
Wells, H. G. *The War of the Worlds*. Harmondsworth: Penguin, 2005.
Westfahl, Gary. *Cosmic Engineers*. Westport: Greenwood Press, 1996.
Westfahl, Gary. *The Mechanics of Wonder: the Creation of the Idea of Science Fiction*. Liverpool: Liverpool University Press, 1998.

Notes

1. See, for example, Fredric Jameson *Postmodernism, or, The Cultural Logic of Late Capitalism* (London: Verso, 1992) and *Archaeologies of the Future* (London: Verso, 2005).
2. The 2007 edition of this anthology series, edited by Stephen King, reprints 'The Boy in Zaquitos' by Bruce McAllister, from the January 2006 *Magazine of Fantasy and Science Fiction*. (Information from Gordon van Gelder *F&SF* editor, 19/07/2007).
3. The first part of a definitive four-volume history of science fiction of which three, *The Time Machines, Transformations* and *Gateways to Forever* are currently in print from Liverpool University Press. The forthcoming fourth volume will bring the story from 1980 to the present day. This account gratefully acknowledges and is indebted to the work of Mike Ashley, David Pringle and the members of the 'Fictionmags' e-list.
4. 'Warp drive' as a convenient shorthand for getting over the limitations of the speed of light and thus enable a (relatively) plausible explanation for faster-than-light travel dates back to the 1930s. 'Terraform', as transforming a world to make it earthlike and habitable, was coined by Jack Williamson in the 1940s. An 'ansible' is a faster-than-light communications device in the fiction of Ursula K. Le Guin and, subsequently, several others. It is also the regular newsletter of the science fiction community, edited by David Langford (http://news.ansible.co.uk/).

5. There were significant differences between British and American 'new waves', which like all 'movements' were made up of individuals with their own agendas rather than groups toeing a party line, but the term has survived to haunt the writers concerned.
6. '[A] literary genre whose necessary and sufficient conditions are the presence and interaction of estrangement and cognition, and whose main formal device is an imaginative framework alternative to the author's empirical environment.' *Metamorphoses of Science Fiction*, (Suvin, 1979: 7–8).

7
Story and Film
Peter Wright

For anyone interested in introducing students to the phenomenon of film adaptation, the short story provides an ideal form for the theoretical discussion of how prose fiction is translated to the screen. Unlike the novel, which frequently requires the excision of elements deemed extraneous to its adaptation, a short story may demand the insertion of additional material. Since the content of most short stories is insufficient to sustain a feature film, development is required not only to transform the story's verbal sign system into a visual sign system but possibly to expand or complicate its narrative events, characterisation, dialogue, narrative time or spatial distribution. The consequent differences between a story and its filmic version provide fertile ground for analysis and debate.

A significant proportion of screenplays are based on short stories, including Ford's *The Quiet Man* (1952) (from Walsh's 'Green Rushes' (1935)), and Hitchcock's *Rear Window* (1954) (from Woolrich's 'It Had to Be Murder' (1942)). Indeed, the tight dramatic structure of the well-plotted story may lend itself to adaptation because it can be mapped onto the three-act structure traditionally used by mainstream scriptwriters. Additionally, there has been an aesthetic comparability between film narrative and the short story prevalent since modernism. Both engage with the ongoing moment. Film narrative unfolds before our eyes; the short story reader encounters time as flux, rather than the sequenced evolution of the conventional novel.

Narrative, in film and the modern short story, is structured through the juxtaposition of images. Both are highly elliptical forms, able to move seamlessly back and forth between past and present – between impressions, memories, dreams and delusions. This capacity can be illustrated through a number of short story adaptations which display a high degree of spatio-temporal fluidity, often using shifting time frames to construct conflicting realities. Nicolas Roeg's *Don't Look Now* (1973) (based on the 1966 story by Daphne du Maurier), Kurosawa's *Rashomon* (1950) (a version of Ryunosuke Akutagawa's 'Yabu no Naka'/'In a Grove' (1922)) and, more recently, Sarah Polley's *Away from Her* (2006) (adapted from Alice Munro's 'The Bear Came Over the Mountain' (1999)) are all relevant examples.

Theoretical approaches to film adaptation have long since transcended value judgements based upon fidelity. Little can be gained from privileging the literary text over its adaptation. Indeed, generally speaking, prose fiction and film are in dialogue, each informing the other both in generic terms and in the interpretation of individual texts. According to Robert Stam, each text is an 'open structure', constantly re-read in a changing context: 'The text feeds on and is fed into an infinitely permutating intertext, which is seen through ever-shifting grids of interpretation' (Stam and Raengo, 2005: 15). These 'grids of interpretation' have given rise to textual adaptations that reach beyond the cinema into the realms of sequential art (both the comic and the graphic novel) and the roleplaying game.

Why Teach Short Story and Film?

Short stories and films are being studied alongside each other in various undergraduate and postgraduate courses, and not always in the context of literary adaptation. The short story's contribution to the development of popular genres ensures it a place on the interdisciplinary curriculum – for instance, the MLitt in The Gothic Imagination offered by the English Department at Stirling University. But there are other reasons for teaching these two forms in tandem.

First of all, Western culture is a screen-based culture. Film, television and other forms of digital technology are now the dominant media. Students are frequently familiar with the narrative devices used by film, and are often – consciously or unconsciously – sophisticated readers of visual texts. Hence, film can provide a useful means of helping students to analyse comparable strategies on the page, or to identify the specific properties of prose fiction by distinguishing them from those available in another medium.

Secondly, whether the practice is academically acceptable or not, many students will read literary texts through the prism of a film or TV version. Teaching has to acknowledge and engage with that process; it cannot be ignored. Any consideration of the publishing history of the short story, which has shaped the form, needs to consider the relationship it shares with other media, including radio, whose history is intertwined with that of film in the first half of the twentieth century.

Lastly, the postmodern dissolution of generic boundaries has to be considered. For the reasons outlined in the Introduction, short story criticism has tended to founder in generic specificity. But by erecting such limits it is possible academics, critics and commentators are constructing prisons for themselves. Narratives find their own forms, and sometimes these transcend, dissolve or complicate preconceived borders. Readers and viewers are seduced primarily by sheer narrative impetus, regardless of the fine lines between one generic form and another.

In the context of these considerations, it is often valuable to teach short stories that do not, apparently, lend themselves easily or readily to adaptation. By introducing the story as a source text prior to screening, teachers require students to pictorialise how the story may have been translated. If they experience difficulties in achieving this, it enables them to distinguish between the narrative strategies that are cinematic and those that appear non-cinematic. What is *translatable* and what requires *adaptation* becomes more apparent. In a larger context, such an exercise may explain to students why certain writers or works feature more prominently in any adaptation-based filmography. Of equal importance is the requirement to select stories that reject, challenge or subvert the generic conventions students recognise – and often accept uncritically – from their experiences of consuming Western film and television.

Of the many writers one might employ for this purpose, Jorge Luis Borges is perhaps the most challenging. Borges's arcane mental puzzles may not seem obvious cinematic material, but Borges's relationship with the cinema is extensive and well documented. Like Graham Greene, he was a film reviewer in the 1930s, at a time when the talking picture was evolving as an art form. More significantly, Borges's stories have been filmed consistently – and creatively – from the 1950s. With director Leopoldo Torre Nilsson, Borges adapted 'Emma Zunz' (1949) as *Días de Odio* (1954); René Múgica's *El Hombre de la esquina rosada* (1962) was based on 'Man on Pink Corner' (1933); and in 1971 Bertolucci filmed the most prestigious Borges adaptation to date, *Strategia del ragno* (*The Spider's Stratagem*), a version of 'The Theme of the Traitor and Hero' (1944). Borges himself returned to screenwriting in 1969 when he co-wrote, with Adolfo Bioy Casares, the screenplay for Hugo Santiago's

Invasión (1969), an Argentinean drama following a secret struggle against a totalitarian invader.[1]

Borges's most important influence on the cinema is more indirect. His preoccupations find their expression in what can be termed 'Borgesian' films. *Performance* (1970), Donald Cammell's unsettling essay on the mutability of identity, is situated in a suitably Borgesian realm: a labyrinthine abode seemingly vast yet claustrophobically infolded. Cammell's cinematic debt to Borges is signposted through a narrative punctuated with quotations and explicit tributes to the Argentinean writer. While Nicolas Roeg's *Don't Look Now* displays a similar thematic preoccupation with Borgesian notions of doubling and synchronicity, it eschews overt references in favour of a cinematic style that communicates Borges's characteristic concerns. The film's cinematography and editing transform a wintry Venice into a maze of shadowed alleys and chill, empty plazas where identity, time and reality become increasingly uncertain. Its narrative development and denouement, although faithful to du Maurier's eponymous short story, recall, perhaps coincidentally, Borges's detective story, 'Death and the Compass' (1942).

Unfortunately, the availability of Borges adaptations is limited. Most are either unavailable or inaccessible in translation. The exception is British writer-director Alex Cox's version of 'Death and the Compass', perhaps the most vibrant translation of Borges yet adapted for the screen.

Superfluous Symmetries and Maniacal Repetitions: Borges, Cox and Cinema's *Trompe l'Oeil*

'Death and the Compass' is, at one level, Borges's parody of the detective genre, as practised by Conan Doyle and in Poe's tales of Auguste Dupin. Cox's adaptation was originally intended to be one of a short series for BBC2's *Tales from Borges* (tx 17–21 October, 1993), a season commemorating the centenary of Borges's birth. However, Cox's film, shot in Mexico in 1992 as a 50-minute adaptation, was broadcast on 5 August 1992 as a *Screenplay* presentation on BBC2. Following this, as Cox explains, the producer Karl Braun asked him to shoot additional scenes. Consequently, a further 40 minutes of material was filmed in Mexico in 1993 to bring the film up to feature length for release in 1996.[2] To students and scholars of film adaptation, the consequences of this double shoot for the film's narrative structure are particularly interesting. Where Borges's story and Cox's original version are largely linear narratives, the finished film is temporally complex. It features considerable use of analepsis, three interrelated narrative time frames, and a consequent ambiguity in character motivation.

It is no surprise that Cox was drawn to Borges's fiction. As Stam points out, even though Borges's works are 'less obviously carnivalesque' than those of other South American writers, he 'carnivalises European literary classics, by turning Dante's *Divine Comedy*, for example, into a "trivial" love story in *El Aleph* (1949), or by having his Pierre Menard rewrite *Don Quixote* (but without changing a word)' (Stam and Raengo, 2005: 318), or by parodying the detective genre in 'Death and the Compass'. Like Borges, Cox has often 'carnivalised' extant forms, particularly the conventions of Hollywood film-making. As Maximilian Le Cain observes, Cox is a 'true maverick whose political passion and passion for the cinema unite in an often anarchistic rejection of Hollywood norms – the "corporatisation of storytelling" – and Hollywood itself' (http://www.sensesofcinema.com/contents/03/24/cox_davies.html). In short, Cox is a carnivalesque director, writing back against the 'official power and ideology' of Hollywood. His *Death and the Compass* is rendered carnivalesque through its adaptation of a carnivalesque source, its 'use of humor to anarchize institutional hierarchies' and, to a lesser extent, its 'carnivalizing [of] film on a purely formal level' (Stam, 1989: 110), that is, in deliberately departing from Hollywood conventions.

Given the narrative complexity of Cox's adaptation, an understanding of the structural differences between the source text and its adaptation is essential. Indeed, the most productive starting point for any informed discussion of a particular adaptation is a straightforward comparative segmentation. Such segmentations assist in moving students away from 'faithfulness' as a measure of an adaptation's validity, relevance or aesthetic success towards other, more productive approaches. It achieves this by identifying the similarities and the disparities between a story and its visual correspondent without privileging either one.

There are varied methods for segmenting a film and, by extension, its source text. However, since the close reading of any adaptation requires a detailed analysis of narrative structure, it is often beneficial to segment the narratives by scene rather than by sequence. In the following table, the narrative events of the final cut of Cox's film are compared with those of Borges's story. The scenes filmed during the second Mexican shoot are italicised.

This segmentation allows for a discussion of the structural differences between the story and its adaptation and why such differences might exist.

	Death and the Compass (Cox, 1996)	'Death and the Compass' (Borges, 1942)
O	**Commissioner Treviranus's opening monologue** introduces Lönnrot and refers to 'the series of bizarre events that culminated at the villa Triste-le-Roy'.	Borges' extradiegetic narrator introduces Lönnrot and 'the bloody acts that culminated at the villa of Triste-le-Roy'.
C	**Credit Title**	
1	**Treviranus's apartment:**	
a	An aged, unstable Treviranus describes Lönnrot's character and reminisces on Red Scharlach's raid on the Used Money Repository.	
b	**Monochrome analepsis narrated by Treviranus:** *Scharlach robs the UMR.*	
c	A yellow-washed establishing shot of heavy industry highlights the nature of the South Side.	
d	A colour television shows Lönnrot vowing, 'No criminal is safe tonight.'	
e	A spiralling newspaper reports Lönnrot's vow in monochrome.	
f	In his apartment, Treviranus continues his dubious reflections on Lönnrot. He drinks heavily as he introduces a crime committed on Monday 3rd December.	
		Hôtel du Nord
		Doctor Marcel Yarmolinsky checks into the Hôtel Du Nord.

2 **Hôtel du Nord: 4th December**
a Lönnrot's car travels to and arrives at the Hôtel du Nord.
b **Yarmolinsky's room:**
   Lönnrot meets Zunz, editor of the 'Yiddish Zeitung'. Treviranus expounds his explanation for the murder. The first 'clue' is found in Yarmolinsky's typewriter: 'The first letter of the Name has been spoken'.

c **Lönnrot's car**
   Lönnrot studies Yarmolinsky's books as he returns to the police station.

3 ***Treviranus's apartment***
   Treviranus tries to exonerate himself from any accusation that he was complicit in Lönnrot's fate.

4 **Police station**
   Zunz is brought in for questioning.

5 **Lönnrot's office**
   Disengaged from the investigation, Lönnrot questions Zunz regarding rabbinical theosophy.

6 **Cutaway**
   Three men hang from a bridge in a blue-washed, night-lit city street.

7 **Triste-le-Roy**
   Scharlach watches Lönnrot receiving an award on television. In the same report, Zunz explains Lönnrot's lines of enquiry through the 'nomenclature of the Pentateuch'.

Hôtel du Nord
Yarmolinksy's body is discovered. Treviranus and Lönnrot discuss the case. Where Treviranus reads the murder as a bungled robbery, Lönnrot seeks 'a purely Rabbinical explanation' (118). The editor of the 'Yiddish Zeitung' is present. One of the police officers discovers the 'clue'.

Lönnrot's office
Lönnrot, 'indifferent' to the police investigation, studies Yarmolinsky's books. When, the editor of the 'Yiddish Zeitung' meets him to discuss the murder; Lönnrot prefers to 'speak of the diverse names of God'. (119)

(continued)

123

Continued

Death and the Compass (Cox, 1996)	'Death and the Compass' (Borges, 1942)
8 **Treviranus's apartment** Treviranus criticises Lönnrot's tendency to link events that had no connection. He introduces Azevedo, an aspiring politician and gangster, asserting that 'there was nothing to connect him to the Yarmolinsky murder'.	
9 **Railway tracks – 3rd January (night)** a Scharlach shoots Azevedo and paints the second 'clue' on a wall in his blood: 'The second letter of the Name has been spoken'.	**Deserted western suburb – 3rd January (night)** A gendarme discovers a second body lying outside 'an ancient paint shop'. Written on the wall 'upon the yellow and red rhombs' (p. 120) is the second 'clue'.
b **4th January (day):** Lönnrot and Treviranus visit the crime scene. As they leave, Treviranus refers to Lönnrot's 'thing' with Scharlach's brother.	**4th January (day):** Treviranus and Lönnrot attend the scene. The dead man is Azevedo.
c **Monochrome analepsis:** a montage of a card game, a beating and wanted posters for Scharlach. In voice-over Lönnrot and Treviranus debate the likelihood of Scharlach's involvement in the murders. Lönnrot considers the explanation 'too obvious'.	
d Lönnrot returns to his car, which has broken down.	
10 **Treviranus's apartment** Treviranus suggests that Lönnrot's affection for his car, 'a symbol of his pride ... his ultimate, tragic, self-destructive vice' led to his disappearance.	
11 **Railway tracks** Lönnrot saves two street thugs a life of crime.	

12 **Lönnrot's apartment**
   Lönnrot meditates. When he calls Zunz, he questions him regarding 'the ninth attribute of God'. Zunz informs Lönnrot that it is God's capacity to perceive infinity. Lönnrot asks him to uncover how many letters are in the name of God.

13 **Treviranus's apartment**
   Treviranus appears to be bribing someone over the telephone.

14 **Lönnrot's office – 3rd February (night)**
   Treviranus receives a call from a man calling himself Ginsberg.

15 **Liverpool House**
   Ginsberg claims he has information about the 'sacrifices' of Yarmolinsky and Azevedo.

16 **Lönnrot's office**
   Ginsberg is cut off. Treviranus has the call traced to the Liverpool House tavern. Together with Lönnrot and his men, they leave for Liverpool House.

17 **Establishing shot: city streets**
   Treviranus sends his men into the fray as political rivals supporting either the 'new king' or the 'old king' clash violently.

18 **Treviranus's apartment**
   Treviranus reads the memo that declared the neutrality of the police force and preserved it during the coup.

19 **Outside Liverpool House**
   The police storm the bar.

Treviranus's office – 3rd February (night)
The Commissioner takes a call from 'Ginzberg (or Ginsberg)' who claims to have evidence pertinent to the two 'sacrifices'. Treviranus traces the call to Liverpool House and contacts the owner, Black Finnegan, who explains that the last person to use the public telephone was his lodger, Gryphius.

(continued)

Continued

Death and the Compass (Cox, 1996)	'Death and the Compass' (Borges, 1942)
20 Liverpool House interior	**Liverpool House interior**
a Lönnrot and Treviranus interview the bar owner.	Treviranus interviews Finnegan and ascertains that Gryphius rented the room eight days earlier. Finnegan cannot describe Gryphius. Nevertheless, he explains how harlequins, whose costumes were composed of 'yellow, red, and green rhombs' (122) took his guest away in a coupé.
b **Monochrome prolepsis within the analepsis** The bar owner, now in prison clothing, confesses that he used the room he rented to Gryphius for prostitution.	
c **Monochrome analepsis** The bar owner rents the room to Gryphius ten days before the police raid.	
d During the interview, the bar owner cannot provide a description of Gryphius.	
21 Liverpool House exterior	**Liverpool House exterior**
One of Lönnrot's men interviews a prostitute.	Treviranus discovers the third 'clue': 'The last of the letters of the Name has been spoken' (122).
22 Liverpool House interior	**Liverpool House interior**
a **Monochrome analepsis** The bar owner collects money from the prostitute who rented the room before Gryphius. He shares his limited knowledge of Gryphius in voice-over.	Treviranus discovers the '*Philologus Hebraeo-Graecus* (1739)' in Gryphius-Ginsberg's room. Lönnrot is summoned and, while other patrons are questioned, he studies the book. He realises that the murders have been committed on the fourth day of each month because the Jewish day begins and ends at sunset.
b **Monochrome analepsis** The bar owner delivers Gryphius's food.	
c Lönnrot interrogates the bar owner.	
d **Monochrome analepsis** The bar owner recalls how two female harlequins arrived and took Gryphius away with them.	
e Lönnrot, Treviranus and their officers search Gryphius's room. They find the third clue on the wall.	

23 **Liverpool House exterior**
   Lönnrot and Treviranus leave the bar and Lönnrot explains that Gryphius, like the previous victims, has been sacrificed, by a Hasidic sub-sect. He also understands that the murders were committed on the fourth day of the month.

24 **Treviranus's apartment**
   Treviranus rambles about how he attempted to have Lönnrot placed on 'permanent medical discharge' so that 'whatever fate befell him might have been avoided'.

25 **Lönnrot's apartment**
   Lönnrot plays chess with his lover as he watches Scharlach pontificate about Treviranus and his 'criminal negligence'. Distracted, he loses the game.

26 **Establishing shot: police station exterior**

27 **Lönnrot's office**
   Miss Spinoza suggests that the murders are at an end since the three locations form an equilateral triangle. Lönnrot is unimpressed by Treviranus's sarcastic association of Spinoza's conjectures with his rabbinical research.

28 **Treviranus's apartment**
   Treviranus repudiates claims in newspapers championing Lönnrot.

29 **Police car (night)**
   Lönnrot's two closest colleagues leave the city at Treviranus's command.

30 **Treviranus's apartment**
   Treviranus criticises Lönnrot's complication of the case.

Media response
Several newspapers comment on the case; Scharlach accuses Treviranus of 'criminal negligence' (123).

Treviranus's office – 1st March
Treviranus receives a parcel from Baruj Spinoza containing a map marked with an 'equilateral and mystic triangle' uniting the murder scenes. He sends it to Lönnrot, who realises that the crimes were equidistant in time as well as space. Lönnrot solves the puzzle, realising a fourth crime is planned. He communicates this to Treviranus.

(continued)

Continued

	Death and the Compass (Cox, 1996)	'Death and the Compass' (Borges, 1942)
31	**Establishing shot: Lönnrot's apartment building**	
32	**Lönnrot's apartment** Lönnrot learns from Zunz that there are four letters in the name of God.	
33	**Cutaway: Aerial shot of the city**	
34	**Treviranus's office** Lönnrot explains his anticipation of a fourth murder. He believes the murderer is mapping landscape points describing a rhomboid. The final murder will occur at Triste-le-Roy. Treviranus conceals his decision to send Lönnrot's trusted colleagues away, depriving him of back-up.	
35	**Monochrome cutaway** A spiralling newspaper declares Treviranus's indictment.	
36	**Courtroom (monochrome)** Treviranus is questioned about his involvement in Lönnrot's disappearance. He denies all involvement.	
37	**Police station** As Zunz arrives, Lönnrot leaves the building.	
38	**Police station car pool** Lönnrot discovers that his car engine has been dismantled.	
39	**City streets** Zunz asks Lönnrot for an interview. Lönnrot rejects the opportunity, until he learns that it is for 'Madame Britannica'. Although he declares such publicity unimportant, he bundles Zunz into a taxi bound for the station.	

40 **Treviranus's apartment**
    Treviranus comments on how Lönnrot was 'content to be thought of as humble as long as he was also thought of as brilliant ... Whatever happened to him was entirely his own fault.'
41 **Train**
    Lönnrot and Zunz travel south.
42 **Station and open country**
    Lönnrot and Zunz walk to Triste-le-Roy.
43 **Triste-le-Roy exterior**
    Lönnrot gives Zunz a police radio. He leaves Zunz outside as he enters the empty building. Moments later, Lönnrot's colleagues try to warn him that 'there is a plot' and that he is in 'great danger'. Zunz tunes them out.
44 **Triste-le-Roy interior**
    Zunz enters the building.
45 **Treviranus's apartment**
    Treviranus admits that, following Lönnrot's disappearance, he and his colleagues concluded Lönnrot was on the take.
46 **Triste-le-Roy interior**
    Zunz explores the villa.
47 **Treviranus's apartment**
    Treviranus insists Lönnrot was crooked.
48 **Triste-le-Roy interior**
    Zunz and Lönnrot investigate the building. Lönnrot ascends a spiral stair to the top floor.
49 **Treviranus's apartment**
    Treviranus explains that his statement was given after he was accused of joining 'with forces that wanted to destroy Lönnrot' despite being Lönnrot's 'closest friend'.

─────────

Train
Lönnrot travels south.
Loading platform and open country
Lönnrot walks to Triste-le-Roy.
Triste-Le-Roy exterior
Lönnrot walks through the abandoned villa's grounds.

Triste-le-Roy interior
Lönnrot wanders the building. Climbing a spiral staircase, Lönnrot reaches the observatory. The windows are 'rhomboid diamonds' of red, yellow and green (p. 125).

(continued)

Continued

	Death and the Compass (Cox, 1996)	'Death and the Compass' (Borges, 1942)
50	**Triste-Le-Roy top floor**	**Triste-le-Roy observatory**
a	Zunz shoots Lönnrot.	
b	**Treviranus's apartment**	
	Treviranus's eye widens.	
c	**Triste-le-Roy top floor**	
	Scharlach and his two female accomplices, dressed as harlequins in red and yellow, shoot Lönnrot repeatedly.	
d	**Treviranus's apartment**	
	Treviranus is shot.	
e	**Triste-le-Roy top floor**	Lönnrot is captured and brought before Scharlach, who explains how he manipulated Lönnrot into coming to the villa by implying that the murders and a faked disappearance (Gryphius was Scharlach in disguise) were mystically connected in a rhomboid geometrically and temporally precise.
	Zunz reveals himself to be Scharlach. He informs the dying Lönnrot of his plot to lure the detective to his death.	
f	**Monochrome analepsis: card game**	
	Lönnrot interrupts a card game. His men shoot the players as Scharlach's voice-over explains how his brother, an innocent man, was injured in the raid and died later.	
g	**Triste-le-Roy top floor**	
	Lönnrot claims that no one is innocent.	
h	**Monochrome analepsis: card game**	
	Lönnrot watches the bodies passively.	
i	**Triste-le-Roy upper floor**	
	Scharlach admits that he was also shot during the raid.	

j **Monochrome analepsis: Triste-le-Roy** Scharlach recovers at Triste-le-Roy. He explains how his Catholic companion inspired an idea for revenge by continually repeating, 'All roads lead to Rome'.

Scharlach admits that his actions are revenge for the incarceration of his brother and his own injury at Lönnrot's hands. He was nursed back to health by an Irish Catholic, whose repetition of the 'axiom of the *goyim*: All roads lead to Rome' (p. 126) suggested how he might murder Lönnrot.

k **Triste-le-Roy top floor** Scharlach describes how he formulated a plot to murder Lönnrot 'personally and very well'. Conceiving of himself at an aleph point, he associated the cell where his brother died with where Lönnrot now lies dying.

In his delirium, Scharlach perceived the world as a labyrinth where all paths led to Rome, which was equivalent to the cell where his 'brother was dying and the villa of Triste-le-Roy' (p. 127).

l **Monochrome analepsis: gaol cell** Scharlach's brother is kicked to death as Lönnrot watches.

m **Triste-le-Roy top floor** Scharlach tells Lönnrot how he conspired with Azevedo to steal the Tetrarch of Galilee's sapphires.

Scharlach informs Lönnrot that Azevedo's bungled theft and Yarmolinsky's death inspired him to construct the trail of 'clues' that brought Lönnrot to Triste-le-Roy.

n **Monochrome analepsis: the Hôtel du Nord** Scharlach narrates as Azevedo blunders into the wrong room and kills Yarmolinksy.

o **Triste-le-Roy upper floor** Scharlach and his harlequins intone: 'The first letter of the Name has been spoken.'

p **Monochrome analepsis: the Hôtel du Nord – Yarmolinsky's room** Yarmolinsky types the fatal line.

q **Triste-le-Roy upper floor** Lönnrot realises that the sentence was merely an opportunity seized by Scharlach to manipulate him.

(continued)

Continued

Death and the Compass (Cox, 1996)	'Death and the Compass' (Borges, 1942)
r **Monochrome analepsis: the Hôtel du Nord – Yarmolinsky's room** Scharlach explains how he went to the Hôtel disguised as Zunz to discover what had gone wrong with the theft. There he found Lönnrot, who was taking the typed line seriously.	
s **Monochrome analepsis: print room** In voice-over, Scharlach spells out how he researched the Hasidim and published articles on the subject, articles he knew Lönnrot would read.	
t **Triste-le-Roy upper floor** Lönnrot realises Scharlach had Azevedo killed. Scharlach tells Lönnrot how he used his revenge on the bungling Azevedo to draw Lönnrot into his plot.	
u **Monochrome analepsis: railway tracks** Scharlach murders Azevedo and paints the message in blood.	
v *Treviranus's apartment* *An unseen assailant measures the dead Treviranus while another figure stands in the background.*	
w **Triste-le-Roy upper floor** Scharlach reveals that he was Gryphius and that one of his harlequins was Miss Spinoza. To complete his revenge, he only had to wait for Lönnrot at the villa. Lönnrot remembers the existence of an aleph in a mosque in Cairo, a place 'at which all things are visible ... where all times merge' and asks, should they meet in another life, that he be killed at that point. Scharlach agrees and fires.	Lönnrot sees 'the sky divided into rhombs of turbid yellow, green, and red' (p. 128). He suggests that when Scharlach hunts him in a later incarnation he uses a 'Greek labyrinth of a single straight line', an allusion to Zeno of Elea's 'race course' paradox of motion. Scharlach agrees and shoots Lönnrot.
E **End Credits**	

Borges's 'Death and the Compass' is essentially linear in structure. It is recounted by an omniscient, extradiegetic narrator whose ironic tone underpins the story's parodic intent. This changes only when Lönnrot visits Triste-le-Roy and Scharlach assumes the role of narrator. His homodiegetic metanarrative serves as an expository analepsis that explains the plot and reveals the overall story. Scharlach's account also functions metafictively, reminding the reader that the plot is an artifice of both author and villain. In turn, this draws attention to the nature of narrative itself. Scharlach (and Borges) create a series of key incidents (the 'clues') which Lönnrot follows to his death. Chatman terms such incidents 'kernels' since they 'cannot be deleted without destroying the narrative logic'; they are 'narrative moments which give rise to cruxes in the direction taken by events' (Chatman, 1978: 53). Cox's retention of these kernels preserves the tension – albeit parodic – existing between epistemological enquiry and ontological certainty found in Borges's story.

Importantly, aside from the commercial considerations of bringing the film up to feature length, Cox's second Mexican shoot allowed him to comment on these themes and to complicate the source text's linear structure. In contrast to Borges's measured, perhaps ironically methodical narrative, Cox employs 'a unique, truly anarchic narrative strategy' (Le Cain, http://www.sensesofcinema.com/2003/24/alex-cox/cox_davies/)). Analepses (and even a prolepsis within an analepsis) occur throughout, displacing the story's linearity and rejecting Hollywood narrative conventions.

The scenes in Treviranus's (Miguel Sandoval) apartment suggest a conspiracy (already implied by the departure of Lönnrot's (Peter Boyle) colleagues (Scene 29) and by the exchange in Treviranus's office (Scene 34)) beyond Scharlach's (Christopher Eccleston) more obvious plot. It becomes apparent, if elliptically, that Treviranus is involved in Lönnrot's disappearance. This is confirmed in Scene 50d when Treviranus is murdered (whether by Lönnrot's subordinates or by Scharlach's operatives remains obscure). As these scenes last less than a second, they are easily overlooked and the viewer may not apprehend Treviranus's complicity in Lönnrot's demise. Nevertheless, there is a further suggestion of Treviranus's guilt in the film's narrative structure.

An audience familiar with the techniques of cross-cutting or intercutting may view the scenes showing Lönnrot's investigation as accurate representations of Treviranus's memories. This interpretation suggests that Treviranus knows what happened to Lönnrot. However, his erratic behaviour and assertions of innocence undermine that reading. Accordingly, the film situates the audience paradoxically; the viewers perceive Treviranus as both reliable (through the narrative structuring) and unreliable (through Sandoval's performance). This situating extends the story's concerns with misinterpretation and the ambiguity of evidence into the viewing experience.

Ironically, the audience, like Lönnrot, has a wealth of evidence available from which to construct an interpretation. The narrative's extensive analepses, its varied character perspectives, and the confessional tone it adopts at various kernels, provide a seemingly omniscient position for the viewer. This is a false impression, however. Unlike Lönnrot, who finds the solution of the mystery is personal annihilation, the viewer is unable to formulate an unequivocal resolution. The reality that exists behind appearances, which is found in both the story and the genre it parodies, is absent from Cox's adaptation.

The impossibility of obtaining a solution emphasises the subjectivity of any interpretation and aligns the film with Barthes's notion of the death of the author. Barthes's concept is given a playful rendering in Scharlach's raid on the UMR (Scene 1b). As Scharlach escapes, Commandante Borges, 'the only blind detective on the city force', confronts him and is killed despite his absurd assurance that he is 'an expert sharpshooter'. With this Borgesian surrogate dead any attribution of authorial intent would normally pass to the director. However, Cox himself plays Borges. In engineering the on-screen 'deaths' of both author and screenwriter-director, Cox seemingly transfers responsibility for interpretation onto the audience, suggesting the independence of the filmic text. In this way, the film is liberated from restrictive readings based on concepts of fidelity to authorial vision or intended meaning. Nevertheless, there is sufficient evidence of Cox's preoccupations as a director to indicate that a poststructuralist approach would be of limited benefit in understanding the adaptation. The aforementioned 'deaths' of the authorial figures, for example, can also be read as a metaphor for Cox's anarchistic rejection of authority (see Le Cain).

Any structural examination of a text and its adaptation emphasises *conservation* (what is preserved from the source text) and *transformation* (how the source text is altered structurally). Clearly, notions of conservation and transformation transcend narrative events and serve as appropriate terms for considering the entire process of adaptation. In *The Novel and the Cinema* Wagner attempts to quantify similarity and difference by proposing 'three modes of adaptation': *transposition*, 'in which a novel is directly given on the screen, with the minimum of apparent interference' (Wagner, 1975: 222); *commentary*, 'where an original is taken and purposely altered in some respect. It could also be called a re-emphasis or re-structure' (223); and *analogy*, where a film uses analogous techniques, moves 'a fiction forward into the present, and makes a duplicate story' (226).

Although Wagner's application of this taxonomy results in dubious categorisations, it is possible to group adaptations under these headings. Nevertheless, his schema overlooks the crucial observation made in Bluestone's seminal *Novels into Film*: 'Between the percept of the visual image and the concept of the mental image lies the root difference between the two media [the novel and the film]' (Bluestone, 1957: 1). Here, Bluestone emphasises how there can never be a 'minimum of apparent interference' in any adaptation because the translation is from a linguistic to a visual sign system. Accordingly, to retain any value, Wagner's taxonomy requires qualification. *Transposition* maintains its relevance when it is applied *only* to those elements of a written narrative that require no translation into a visual language or which can be spoken by characters within a given film. Character names and functions, place names, narrative events, and direct speech or exposition taken and used as dialogue are all elements transposable from a source text. Accordingly, 'Lönnrot', 'Treviranus', and 'Red Scharlach' are all transposed pronouns. In terms of basic character functions, Scharlach is the antagonist; Lönnrot the protagonist, here treated ironically; and Treviranus the sceptic who favours prosaic explanations over arcane mysteries. The principal narrative kernels, including the murders and the faked abduction, Ginsberg's telephone call and the dénouement at Triste-le-Roy, are all preserved and sequenced according to Borges's story. Less apparent are those occasions where direct speech or exposition is employed as dialogue. Unfortunately, as a source of critical comment and as a means of understanding the process of adaptation, the notion of *transposition* is rarely productive; assessing *conservation* is less informative than examining *transformation*.

Bluestone's emphasis on the pictorialisation of prose during adaptation also has consequences for *commentary*. Conceiving commentary as a re-emphasis or re-structure of narrative material, Wagner overlooks the fact that all fiction requires alteration for the screen. This means that, proportionally, less material can be conserved in an adaptation than must be transformed. In *Novel to Film* McFarlane terms conservation *transfer* and transformation *adaptation proper*. He notes that where prose narratives are *narrated*, cinematic narratives are *enunciated*. Cinematic enunciation, he argues, 'is a matter of adaptation proper, not of transfer' (McFarlane, 1996: 23). In effect, 'enunciation' describes the translation of elements from the source text 'which involve intricate processes of adaptation because their effects are closely tied to the semiotic system in which they are manifested' (20).

The distinction between *transfer* and *adaptation* proper is implied in Barthes's 'Introduction to the Structural Analysis of Narrative'. Here, Barthes distinguishes between two forms of narrative function: *distributional* and *integrational*. He divides distributional functions further into *functions proper* and *indices*. *Functions proper* define actions and events linked linearly through a text; *indices* imply a 'more or less diffuse concept which is nevertheless necessary to the meaning of the story' (Barthes, 1977: 92) McFarlane explains that the 'concept [of indices] embraces ... psychological information relating to characters, data regarding their identity, notations of atmosphere and representations of place ... [they influence] our reading of narrative in a pervasive rather than a linear way' (McFarlane, 1996: 13). Where *functions proper* can be transferred, *indices* must be enunciated. Enunciation is required to transform a narrative using a linguistic sign system into a narrative communicated visually. As such, it is the cinematic means of narration.

In *Coming to Terms* (1990) Seymour Chatman provides a diagrammatic representation of the cinematic narrator. In so doing, he summarises the 'expressive apparatus' of enunciation as two channels, the auditory and the visual:

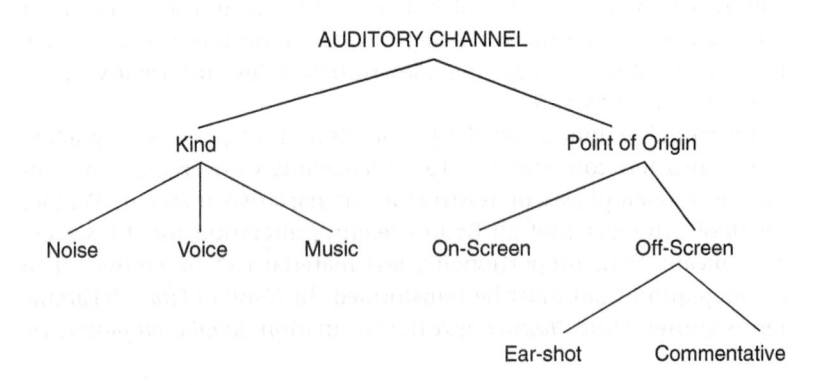

```
                    AUDITORY CHANNEL
                   /                \
                Kind              Point of Origin
              / |  \               /         \
           Noise Voice Music   On-Screen   Off-Screen
                                           /        \
                                       Ear-shot   Commentative
```

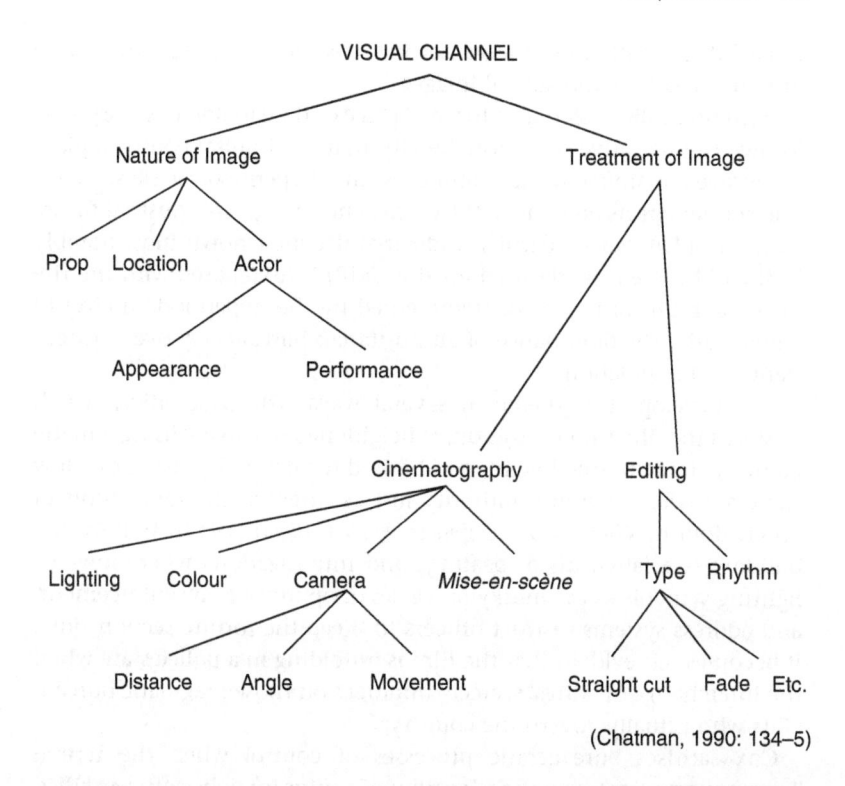

```
                        VISUAL CHANNEL
                       /              \
            Nature of Image          Treatment of Image
           /     |      \             /              \
       Prop  Location  Actor         /                \
             /          \           /                  \
      Appearance    Performance    /                    \
                              Cinematography          Editing
                           /    |      |      \        /    \
                      Lighting Colour Camera Mise-en-scène  Type  Rhythm
                                    / | \                   /  |   \
                              Distance Angle Movement  Straight cut Fade Etc.
```
(Chatman, 1990: 134–5)

In Cox's film, the auditory and visual channels dramatise and extend Borges's ironic and parodic treatment of detective fiction into a carnivalesque, often frenzied narrative that reminds the viewer of the film's status as artefact. Equally, the film's enunciation politicises Borges's story to foreground a parodic critique of the police state.

In his foreword to *Artifices*, later collected in *Ficciones*, Borges says that 'Death and the Compass' is set in 'a Buenos Aires of dreams' (95). The description of setting in the story is, nevertheless, minimal, due partly to the constraints of form but mostly to Borges's intention to privilege events over imagery. Only at Triste-le-Roy is the reader treated to Borges's spare yet evocative scene setting. The cinema is not so constrained. Richly detailed images, symbolically or thematically resonant, can be communicated directly through the visual channel. In film, less precise descriptions require visualisation and permit the film-maker considerable freedom in translating prose to image. For his adaptation, Cox employs a striking, often comic-bookish visual style that makes remarkable use of *mise-en-scène* (setting, costume, lighting, positioning of figures), colour and surreal imagery.

With no explicit references to a real place or time in Borges's story, Cox locates the narrative in a pastiche city that is, simultaneously, a place of decayed manufacturing complexes and hypermodern skyscrapers. The special effects emphasise the coexistence of a post-industrial future with a resplendent modernity. Industrial decline (shown most notably in the old cement works used for the UMR) is juxtaposed with the rise of the administrative sector (represented by the hypermodern city) to emblematise the dominance of authoritarian bureaucracy over a disenfranchised population.

Cox develops this theme in several ways. The post office, which serves as the film's police station, is heightened massively using a matte painting. Its imposing height, emphasised further with the use of a low camera angle, represents authority just as surely as the high stools of officialdom in Wiene's *Das Cabinet des Dr Caligari* (1919). Within, the building is a labyrinth of beatings and interrogations where low-key lighting symbolises the murky processes of oppressive law enforcement, and address systems instruct officers to 'Keep the torture section tidy'. It becomes self-evident that the film is unfolding in a police state when the interchange of 'kings' scarcely impinges on those pragmatic bureaucrats who actually govern the country.

Cox satirises bureaucratic processes of control when the retired Treviranus ruminates on the allocation of coffins for police officers killed on duty and on the impact of blunt pencils on administrative efficiency. Here, Cox extends Borges's parodic intentions to critique despotism, bureaucracy and the police state. The fact that Lönnrot represents this state indicates early in the film that he may not be the unsullied crusader presented by the media. Such political criticism is not uncommon in Cox's work. *Walker* (1987) is a direct attack on American imperialism and *Highway Patrolman* (1991) charts the corruption of an idealistic young police officer by the system. Cox himself is an outspoken critic of American foreign policy, capitalism and the war in Iraq.

If the addition of this political critique is evidence of Cox's adaptation as a commentary on Borges's story, his treatment of Triste-le-Roy shows how a film-maker may employ cinematic techniques analogous to literary description. Borges describes the villa as abounding 'in superfluous symmetries and maniacal repetitions' (125). Later, Lönnrot realises that the house is not as large as he assumed: 'It is only made larger by the penumbra, the symmetry, the mirrors, the years, my ignorance, the solitude' (125). Although Lönnrot voices this realisation in the film, the sense the audience has of the villa's symmetry and repetition is achieved entirely through location and cinematography. The derelict convent doubling for Triste-le-Roy is symmetrical; its halls and galleries, like Borges's Library of Babel, are periodic, repetitive. At various points, the camera positions, often situated at the junction of corridors, transform the geometry of the convent into a mirror-hall of converging lines. Blue light and deep shadows achieve Borges's 'penumbra'. The villa is a nightscape of uncertain angles, a labyrinth composed equally of architecture and light. Fluid cameras chart the journey through its shadowy expanse; static takes permit moments of reflection where the chill, otherworldly imagery is distinctly unsettling.

This echoing, melancholy space functions as a metaphor for Lönnrot's state of mind when he realises his hubris has proved fatal. In the loft, hand-held camera work visualises Lönnrot's mental disorder and Scharlach's anarchic posturing. The detective's mind reels not simply because he is fatally wounded but because his unshakable faith in his ability to apprehend the true nature of things has been shattered. Where he once considered the world an ordered place subject to investigation and quantification, he now recognises it as a chaotic realm where logic can be used against itself to dissolve authority and control.

Just as the minimalist *mise-en-scène* of Triste-le-Roy and the camera work therein externalise Lönnrot's mood, so the cinematography and set decoration of Treviranus's apartment convey the retired commissioner's mental condition. Each scene in his apartment is filmed using a hand-held camera. This hesitant, mobile framing communicates his confusion and reluctance to be 'on the level'. Jump cuts punctuate these scenes, suggesting Treviranus's fractured, disjointed memories, or else his editing of the truth. Equally, they imply his mental fracturing and feverish attempts at exoneration.

A framed portrait of Treviranus dominates his baroque apartment, which is a disorder of documents, books and statuettes. The portrait and Treviranus's preoccupation with historical figures connote his desire to be immortalised like Lönnrot. However, the muted apartment lighting parallels the yellow tones of old skin or parchment, indicating that Treviranus is merely a relic as aged and immobile as the artefacts surrounding him.

His apartment's opulence is reflected in his cavernous police office (Scene 34), which is adorned with photographs of himself. Again, Cox employs a hand-held camera to suggest Treviranus's unreliability but on this occasion he shoots through a wide-angle lens. The resulting distortion implies a corresponding distortion of truth. Accordingly, when

Treviranus tells Lönnrot that his subordinates are unavailable, the audience may question the commissioner's candour.

Situated within these resonant locations, Cox's principal characters are attired in primary colours. Treviranus is clothed in yellow except in the scenes in his office (Scene 34) and when he is in court (Scene 36) where he is in uniform; Lönnrot wears a pale blue suit; and Scharlach is a dandy in a red frock coat and ruffled shirt. Although it is tempting to read these colours symbolically, colour symbolism is ambiguous and culturally specific. Simple interpretations are inappropriate: Treviranus's suit does not simply imply cowardice nor does Scharlach's costume suggest only anger or passion. Rather, the ambiguity of colour connotes the ambiguity of the characters. Treviranus is a police commissioner, yet he is corrupt; Lönnrot is a crusading officer, yet he watches Scharlach's brother being beaten to death in custody; Scharlach is a killer, yet his revenge on Lönnrot is the only righteous act in the film.

In addition to emblematising ambiguity and complexity, such costuming establishes an intertextual link with Beatty's *Dick Tracy* (1990), a film Cox admires. By mirroring Beatty's comic-book style, Cox extends Borges's detective parody to a major character in American popular culture. The corrupt Treviranus's suit mirrors the incorruptible Tracy's trademark yellow trench coat. By implication, Cox is satirising the faith fostered in the police by Hollywood cinema. Reflecting on the American film industry, he observes, 'Hollywood exists to make the American public hate foreigners, prepare for war, love the police, and to encourage Yuppies to have babies, which were also the goals of the film industry of the Third Reich' (Cox cited in Broderick). It is not surprising to find a comparable critique in *Death and the Compass*.

The repeated use of yellow, blue and red functions as a motif throughout, reappearing on the harlequin costumes, on posters and on the masked windows of the loft at Triste-le-Roy. It substitutes for the yellow, red and green rhombs that reappear throughout Borges's story and which subliminally guide Lönnrot to the scene of the fourth, geometrically positioned murder. In Lönnrot's office, a city map is divided into three coloured sectors: yellow to the west, blue to the east and red to the south. Although this symbolises Scharlach's hideout to the south, such divisions are more important for emphasising not only the separateness of the characters (each has a personal agenda) but also their interconnectedness. In this way, Treviranus's connection with Scharlach is suggested elliptically, providing a visual clue to the less obvious association between the characters implied by the plot.

Cox's characterisation, and the actors' performance of their literary counterparts, is more significant than the characters' appearance however. Where Cox's Lönnrot mirrors Borges's detective, Treviranus and Scharlach are more developed. In the story, Treviranus appears to play Lestrade to Lönnrot's Holmes, although this paralleling becomes ironic when the reader recognises Treviranus's insights are often more perspicacious than Lönnrot's deluded investigations. Cox maintains this relationship yet invests his Treviranus with an egocentric, avaricious and cowardly nature. Treviranus's dreams of offices in the penthouse suite in the new 'civiscraper' identify him as a materialist ripe with corruption, a fact confirmed by his almost immediate indictment in the film. Sandoval's younger Treviranus is arrogant, fastidious and oily, a man whose self-absorption reaches its zenith in old age. Here Sandoval's performance, a combination of bitterness, hysteria, anger and melancholy, is poignant. His fall from grace, impelled by his jealousy of Lönnrot, makes him a tragic figure. Treviranus's decline into mania is symmetrical with Lönnrot's passage from respected cop to murder victim. Where Lönnrot's intellectual hubris is responsible for his demise, it is Treviranus's jealousy and greed that proves his undoing. Arrogance unites both characters and Scharlach exploits it mercilessly.

Eccleston's performance as Scharlach is a marked contrast to his portrayal of the bespectacled, mousy Zunz. His synthesised, distorted voice provides an otherworldliness that, together with his flamboyant posturing, marks him as a comic-book villain. However, the film's portrayal of Scharlach is far from one-dimensional. There is genuine pathos in Ecclestone's depiction of a vengeful anarchist seeking justice. At the conclusion of the film, the viewer understands his attack on the UMR is part of a larger anarchist plot to topple the existing system by exploiting its means (wealth) and its methods (rationalism and greed) against itself.

Caught between Treviranus and Scharlach, Boyle's Lönnrot is modelled closely on Borges's character. His dialogue is often extracted from the short story or else the story's prose is adapted as dialogue. Nevertheless, Cox and Boyle ensure that Lönnrot is read as a duplicitous, pretentious egotist. When Zunz is brought to the police station (Scene 4) in handcuffs, Boyle remarks, 'Those restraints are for your own good. There are many areas in this building which are off limits to civilians. Were you to wander into the wrong room, you might find yourself in serious trouble.' Boyle's toneless delivery indicates that he is playing the role of a concerned public servant, hypocritically excusing the draconian practices of the police state for the benefit of Zunz the reporter. It is only when the audience sees that Lönnrot is as capable of condoning brutality as Treviranus that the purpose of Boyle's lack of intonation becomes clear. His characteristic pretentiousness is shown in his apartment (Scene 12) when he tells his lover Natasha (Arianne Pellicer): 'It doesn't do to get attached to things. It doesn't do to grasp at things. If one gets attached to one's existence, it's just as stupid as being attached to non-existence. And just as impossible.' She counters his posturing prosaically, remarking, 'I'm not going to stop smoking. Don't care what you say.' In his commentary, Cox explains that Boyle wanted to play Lönnrot as Marlon Brando's Kurtz in *Apocalypse Now* from this point forward (Cox, [1996] 2002, DVD commentary, 28: 15–28: 22; Cox and Wool, 2002). However, Boyle's intonation actually recalls Dennis Hopper's mode of speech as the photojournalist in the same film. In short, Boyle mimics a character parroting second-hand philosophy from a madman. This intertextuality implies that Lönnrot, too, is aping poorly understood philosophy, something his vacuous observation to Natasha suggests. His inane meditations belie his reputation as a master detective and telegraph the possibility that he is self-deluded and egocentric enough to be duped.

The potentially disorientating effect of Cox's metaphorically and literally colourful characters, the visually discordant, often anarchic action, jump cuts and cross-cutting across various narrative times is mitigated by the fluidity of stylistically sophisticated long takes. Although the technique is common to many of Cox's films the long takes serve two particular functions. Firstly, during the raid on the UMR, they operate in conjunction with fluid camerawork to convey the pace and precision of Scharlach's operation. Secondly, they connote the inexorability of Lönnrot's destruction. Long takes and mobile cameras draw the viewer through the narrative labyrinth as Scharlach's plot drives towards its climax. Indeed, the appearance of the long take may indicate that Scharlach's intellect is shaping the events just as the jump cuts disrupting the scenes in Treviranus's apartment suggest his mental disintegration.

At the conclusion of the film, the takes are significantly shorter as the pace accelerates. Time and space seem to collapse as Scharlach's motive, the plot, and its consequences for Lönnrot and Treviranus, are revealed. For the audience at least, Scene 50 is an aleph, 'a point' as Lönnrot explains, 'at which all things are visible; a point where all times merge'. Lönnrot asks Scharlach if he will kill his reincarnated self at such a point in Cairo. Scharlach agrees. The camera pulls back, gaining height, as the circular loft of Triste-le-Roy is revealed to be the elevated centre of a shadowed labyrinth. The film's final irony is that Lönnrot fails to recognise that he has already been murdered in such a place. This closing image, another matte painting by Rocco Gioffre, ensures the audience recognise film as an artifice usually designed to give the impression of a reality viewed omnisciently 'from above'. Although there are a number of occasions on which such artifice is foregrounded (the use of jump cuts, analepses and so forth), the film's score is fundamental to the audience's recognition of the film as construct. Cox's use of the soundscape, including the score, diegetic and non-diegetic noises, and voice emphasises the artificiality of the film world.

Where the student recognises film dialogue as being the primary means of narrative communication, it is not uncommon for that student to overlook the role played by cinema's auditory channel in establishing mood and tone. Cox avoids this oversight by deploying a synthesised score by Dan Wool (credited by the band name 'Pray for Rain') that is, by turns, intrusive, emblematic and strident whilst often working in ironic counterpoint to the cinematic image.

The heavily layered Opening Titles score, played over images of a thematically and intertextually resonant maze, is composed predominantly of an off-key piano accompanied by metallic screams, whistles, a stuttering engine noise suggestive of electric trains, and a regular basso tone like the echoing of a muffled drum. The overall effect is of a sinister carnival riding a faltering train attended by a demented calliope-player. This unsettling discordance plays in counterpoint to the ordered regularity of the maze. The score and the image work to imply the existence of an anarchic composer beyond or above the labyrinth who maps its contours with manic precision. Consequently, the plot of the film is communicated suggestively: Scharlach is the anarchistic originator of the labyrinthine stratagem that eventually traps Lönnrot.

The soundscape is at its densest during Zunz's first visit to the police station. Screams echo, telephones ring, typewriters rattle and cattle prods crackle. Acoustic strumming and a regular synthesised rhythm suggest the implacable operations of the state and the machinery of oppression, yet its comparatively high key and upbeat tempo act in counterpoint to the events on screen. In this way, Cox refuses to provide the viewer with a consistent emotional perspective. On one hand, the visuals suggest a brutal and oppressive police state; on the other, the score's lighter tone invites an ironic perception of events. This hesitation is compounded further by an echo added in post-production (Cox and Wool, 2002 DVD commentary, 18:35–18:55) that conveys the empty, inhuman atmosphere of the building. By refusing to complement sinister events with appropriately ominous music, Cox estranges his viewers, indicating the film's existence as artefact while reminding them, metatextually, of the more usual practices of mainstream cinema scoring. The score also evokes the intertextuality of Borges's story. Where Borges references Holmes and Dupin through Lönnrot, the synthesised score alludes to police teleseries from the 1970s and 1980s, including *The Streets of San Francisco*, *Starsky and Hutch*, *Miami Vice*, and even *The Sweeney*, without sampling them directly. The soundtrack for *To Live and Die in L.A.* (Friedkin, 1985) is also a key source (Cox and Wool, DVD commentary, 2002, 27:40–27:50). Synthesisers imitate police sirens and this displacement of diegetic sound onto a non-diegetic source provides a sense of the unreal, reinforcing the comic-book visual style.

Death and the Compass is a useful text for introducing students to the concept of intertextuality. Where Borges's story derives its intertextuality from its ironic inversion of the Holmesian detective and the clue-puzzle mystery, Cox's adaptation celebrates its existence as cinema with a dense visual allusiveness. His primary sources are films noirs, spaghetti Westerns, *Dick Tracy* and dystopian SF films.

Clearly, adaptation results in a direct intertextual relationship between the source text and its new form. Once students understand what an intertext actually is, it is valuable to make a distinction between *source intertextuality* and *context intertextuality*. Source intertextuality defines those connections any adaptation shares with its source – character names, narrative events, direct speech and passages quoted as dialogue. Context intertextuality, on the other hand, is less specific, describing intertextual connections existing between the adaptation and other identifiable material, which may be textual, historic, cultural, autobiographical and so forth. Context intertextuality does not extend, however, to include broader artistic conventions or forms. Knowing that *Death and the Compass* shares an intertextual connection with narrative cinema tells the spectator very little about the adaptation itself.

Restricting interpretation to specific intertextual material, it is apparent that *Death and the Compass* shares a number of source intertexts with Borges's story whilst displaying a range of 'intertextual signposts' (Riffaterre, 1990: 56–8) to context intertexts ranging from the cinema, to The Sex Pistols (Lönnrot's observation that 'No one is innocent' is taken from the Pistols' song), to other Borges stories, including 'The Aleph' (1949), 'Emma Zunz' and 'The Rose of Paracelsus' (1986), to comic books and Cox's own films. Indeed, serendipity links Liverpool House, which features in Borges's story, to Cox's Liverpool background. More generally, however, both the story and its adaptation reveal a genuine affection for popular genres. Cox's fondness for crime films in particular can be observed in the costume, action and dialogue, which plays with the hyper-masculine conventions common to pulp detective writing. Although such intertextuality opposes a unitary interpretation, reminding the audience that meaning is a negotiated, contended phenomenon, Cox's self-consciously intertextual, anarchic and aestheticised adaptation reminds us that cinema, like Borges's story, is both artifice and artefact. It is, as Lönnrot says of Triste-le-Roy, a *trompe l'oeil*, a two-dimensional image contrived to appear three-dimensional. In this way, Cox's adaptation draws attention to its own enunciation. Moreover, the notion of film as a *trompe l'oeil* can be read as a metaphor for the process of adaptation itself, in which the 'two dimensional' page is rendered seemingly 'three dimensional' on screen through cinema's technical sleight of hand. Such metacinematic self-reflexiveness makes Borges's *Death and the Compass* one of the most productive texts for students of film adaptation.

Works Cited

Barthes, Roland. *Image–Music–Text*. Trans. Stephen Heath. Glasgow: Fontana, 1977. 79–124.

Bluestone, George. *Novels into Film*. London: The Johns Hopkins University Press, 1957.

Borges, Jorge Luis. *Ficciones*. Trans. Anthony Kerrigan. London: John Calder, 1985.

Broderick, Peter. 'The Comeback of Alex Cox or, How I Stopped Worrying and Learned to Love the Long Take.' http://www.filmmakermagazine.com/winter1993/comeback_alex.php

Chatman, Seymour. *Story and Discourse: Narrative Structure in Fiction and Film*. London: Cornell University Press, 1978.

Chatman, Seymour. *Coming to Terms: The Rhetoric of Narrative in Fiction and Film*. London: Cornell University Press, 1990.

Cox, Alex. [1996] *Death and the Compass* (DVD). London: 4Digitial Media, 2002.

Cox, Alex and Dan Wool. 'Audio Commentary' on *Death and the Compass* (DVD). London: 4Digitial Media, 2002.

Cozarinsky, Edgardo. *Borges in/and/on Film*. Trans. Gloria Waldman. Santa Fe: Lumen Books, 1988.

Le Cain, Maximilian. 'Interview with Alex Cox and Tod Davies' http://www.sensesofcinema.com/2003/24/alex-cox/cox_davies/

McFarlane, Brian. *Novel to Film: An Introduction to the Theory of Adaptation*, Oxford: Clarendon Press, 1996.

Riffaterre, Michael. 'Compulsory Reader Response: The Intertextual Drive'. In *Intertextuality: Theories and Practices*, (eds) Michael Worton and Judith Still. Manchester: Manchester University Press, 1990. 56–78.

Stam, Robert. *Subversive Pleasures: Bakhtin, Cultural Criticism and Film*, London: The Johns Hopkins University Press, 1989.

Stam, Robert and Alessandra Raengo, (eds) *Literature and Film: A Guide to the Theory and Practice of Film Adaptation*. Oxford: Blackwell, 2005.
Wagner, Geoffrey. *The Novel and the Cinema*. London: The Tantivy Press, 1975.
http://www.alexcox.com.

Notes

1. For a detailed discussion of Borges's relationship to the cinema, see Edgardo Cozarinsky, *Borges in/and/on Film*, trans. by Waldman, G., Lumen Books, 1988.
2. See http://www.alexcox.com/dir_deathandcompass.htm.

8
Why Teaching the Short Story Today is a Thankless Task

Charles E. May

Denis Donoghue has recently lamented that his students do not want to talk about literature, but rather large-scale public themes independent of the work:

> They are happy to denounce imperialism and colonialism rather than read 'Heart of Darkness', *Kim* and *Passage to India* in which imperialism and colonialism are held up to complex judgment. They are voluble in giving you their opinions on race and its injustices, but nearly tongue-tied when it is a question of submitting themselves to the languages of *The Sound and the Fury, Things Fall Apart,* and *A Bend in the River*. They find it arduous to engage with the styles of *Hard Times* and *The Wings of a Dove*, but easy to say what they think about industrialism, adultery, and greed. (Donoghue, 2006: 15)

I sympathise with Professor Donoghue. In my last semester before retirement a few years ago, I taught a postgraduate course on the twentieth-century short story in Canada, Australia, New Zealand and India, as well as several African and Caribbean countries. I told my students at the beginning that we were going to engage in close readings of the stories, analysing and evaluating them on the basis of their human complexity and aesthetic excellence. When my students ignored the texts and insisted on talking about general political issues of race and postcolonialism, I realised that 'close reading', 'human complexity', and 'aesthetic excellence' were strange and unfamiliar concepts to them.

Francine Prose's book *Reading Like a Writer* (2006) argues that to be a good reader and a good writer one must be knowledgeable about, and sensitive to, the craft of fiction – words, sentences, character, dialogue and details. However, paying close attention to language is not a politically correct definition of reading nowadays for many academics, who have in fact argued that once you give priority to close reading, you engage in the following socially irresponsible acts:

- You favour indirect expression over direction expression.
- You favour deep meaning over surface meaning.
- You favour form over content.
- And most unforgivably – you favour the elite over the popular.

However, over and over, Prose goes against the current academic trend and urges the reader to focus on words, rhythm and pattern – not subject matter. By relentlessly insisting on the importance of language and form, Prose reinforces what William H. Gass has argued: that the artist's fundamental loyalty must be to form. 'Every other diddly desire', insists Gass, 'can find expression; every crackpot idea or local obsession, every bias and graciousness and mark of malice, may have an hour; but it must never be allowed to carry the day' (Gass, 1996: 35).

Because of its formal characteristics and its generic history, studying the short story may be more apt to place one in such a politically incorrect position than studying the more socially responsible novel. It is unfortunate for the short story that an understanding of its form has been inextricably linked to that old interpretative manoeuvre called the New Criticism, also known as close reading, which has come under fire for being at best naive and non-theoretical and at worst, downright fascist. The problem I have faced is: how to rescue a highly formal genre from critics who find the very notion of form a dehumanised, tight-fisted, politically incorrect brand of right wing fundamentalism. It is no accident that many of the contemporary writers that Prose cites for the excellence of their fiction – Raymond Carver, Stuart Dybek, Deborah Eisenberg, Mavis Gallant, Alice Munro, Flannery O'Connor, William Trevor and Joy Williams – have specialised in the short story.

I agree with the old-fashioned convictions of José Ortega, who once said, 'The material never saves a work of art, the gold it is made of does not hallow a statue. A work of art lives on its form, not on its material; the essential grace it emanates springs from its structure [which] forms the properly artistic part of the work' (Ortega, 1956: 23). This seems so obvious it is difficult to see how anyone could deny it. But of course the idea that the excellence of the short story depends not on its content but its form is denied in classrooms around the world every day. In fact, the very idea of artistic form and excellence is often challenged in those classrooms.

In the early twenty-first century, as multicultural studies and postcolonial theories privilege the socially conscious novel, teaching the short story – a poetic form that has never been amenable to sociological or political criticism – becomes a difficult and thankless task. After briefly surveying the history of the short story as an asocial artwork, I will outline some of the generic characteristics that account for its current secondary status.

In what is perhaps the earliest published theoretical statement about the generic characteristics of short fiction, Friedrich Schlegel characterised Boccaccio's revolutionary short tale form in *The Decameron* – arguably the first example of short prose narratives that departed from popular oral folk tales and qualified as individual art – as 'a story which must be capable of arousing interest in and of itself alone, without regard to any connection with the nations, the times, the progress of humanity, or even the relation to culture itself' (Schlegel, 1965: 7). This notion of the story being detached from any cultural background, drawing its interest from the striking nature of the event itself rather than its context has, much to the chagrin of social and cultural critics, always been a perceived characteristic of short fiction. Schlegel notes that the modern retelling of already known traditional stories necessarily focuses the attention away from mythic authority and towards the authority of a point of view – the subjective point of view of the teller as he remodels the tale (7). An inevitable result of this shift in authority is a gradual displacement away from strictly formulaic structures towards techniques of verisimilitude that encourage credibility. However, because short fiction focuses attention on 'an experience', rather than on 'experience' more abstractly considered, the displacement from mythic authority is not towards man identified within a society, but rather towards the authority of a single point of view. Schlegel argues that short fiction is 'particularly suited to present a subjective mood and point of view, indeed the profoundest and most peculiar, indirectly and as it were symbolically and especially adapted to this indirect and hidden subjectivity because it tends greatly to the objective' (8). For these reasons the Boccaccio novella, noted for its 'news' of the real world, that is, real events detached from the former mythical world of the romance, retains some of its former romance magic – both by the subjectivity of the teller and by the formal symbolic pattern of the events.

The highly formal nature of the short story has always been criticised by those critics and novelists who have argued that literature has a responsibility to be socially aware and involved. The short story was attacked by American realistic writers in the nineteenth century, such as William Dean Howells, for being false to reality. James T. Farrell criticised the form in the 1930s for its failure to be a vehicle for revolutionary ideology. Maxwell Geismar lashed out against short story writers such as Salinger, Roth, Malamud and Powers in 1964 for the narrow range of their vision and their stress on the intricate craftsmanship of the well-made story. And in 1992, John Aldridge scolded short story writers for focusing too much on technique and too little on significance. All these complaints boil down to the same thing – that the short story is too much a matter of form and too little a matter of what social critics define as 'real life'. It is clear that such critics prefer the more socially conscious novel. However, the short story, both because of its folk tale ancestry and its shortness (which necessitates a tight structural patterning), is a form with generic characteristics precisely in a way that the novel is not.

Frederic Jameson has noted that because the novel is a way of dealing with temporal experience that cannot be defined in advance or dealt with any other way, no pre-existing laws govern its elaboration. Short stories, myths and tales, on the other hand, are characterised by a specific and determinate type of content; consequently, their laws can be the objects of investigation. Jameson reminds us that short stories or folk tales have a kind of object-like unity in the way they convert existence into a sudden coincidence between two systems: a resolution of multiplicity into unity, or a fulfilment of a single wish. Jameson says the short story is a way of 'surmounting time, of translating a formless temporal succession into a simultaneity which we can grasp and possess' (Jameson, 1972: 74).

Such a highly formal genre, of course, seems most amenable to a critical approach that values form over content. Such an approach, summarised at its most extreme by Victor Shklovsky in 1917 – 'Art is a way of experiencing the artfulness of an object; the object is not important' – is now scorned by contemporary cultural critics as narrow and even inhuman (Shklovsky, [1917] 1963: 6). However, formalism, broadly considered as an interest in literary form, rather than narrowly considered as the aestheticism of the Russian formalists or the conservatism of the New Critics, is not a fad, but rather – it seems superfluous to say – an essential requirement for studying literature. Moreover, it is absurd to argue that just because one is interested in the form of a work, one is not interested in its human meaning. The problem, of course, arises when statements like those of Shklovsky and other formalists lead the critic to ignore the human content of the work. The related problem is how to attend to the human content of the work without lapsing into the gratuitous oversimplification that the artwork is merely an information medium for the replication of everyday life or the rhetoric of ideology.

Umberto Eco says he looks to cultural history to explain why a particular literary work operates in a cultural context in such a way that routine notions and attitudes are broken down, and a new direction of consciousness emerges:

> In this way I hold that the formal analysis of a work's structural mechanics [...] does not lead one to treat the work as *an end in itself* [...] but serves to provide the instruments by which to understand the relations between work, cultural context and the personality of the writer [...] I don't believe that 'formal' consideration of a work means accepting any kind of aesthetic 'formalism' but rather the opposite: the formal approach is the sole way of correctly clarifying relationships between the work and the world of other values. (Eco, 1963: 142)

Georg Lukács has said that form is the really living content of a critic's writing and that his moment of destiny is that point at which things become forms – 'the moment when all feelings and experiences on the near or the far side of form receive form, are melted down and condensed into form. It is the mystical moment of union between the outer and the inner, between soul and form' (Lukács, 1970: 8). And Terry Eagleton has more recently noted that whereas realism, the most common modal perspective of the novel, is primarily a 'cognitive form concerned to map the causal processes underlying events and resolve them into some intelligible pattern, the short story, by contrast, can yield us some single bizarre occurrence of epiphany of terror whose impact would merely be blunted by lengthy realist elaboration.' As Eagleton notes, 'since realism is a chronically naturalizing mode, it is hard for it to cope with the ineffable or unfathomable, given those built-in mechanisms which offer to transmute all of this into the assuringly familiar' (Eagleton, 1995: 150).

Short prose narrative since Boccaccio has always been more structure than stuff, more form than content, more artifice than nature – which is simply to say, more art than reality. This fact of the form has always been a thorn in the critical side of readers who believe that the purpose of fiction is to provide as faithful a mirror to external reality as it is possible for language to do. Ever since Boccaccio's ten young storytellers fled plague-ridden reality for the language-bound world of story, short narrative has been characterised by its self-conscious creation of an alternate world of artifice. This focus on form, on the art of the short narrative rather than on its content, makes many critics distrust short fiction as too formal and thus too distant from the flesh and blood of ordinary reality. It has also made them distrust any approach to short fiction that emphasises form. However, the short story's traditional focus on experiences that are counter to the realm of everyday reality is one reason that the short story has had to be a tightly organised form. Edith Wharton expresses it this way: 'The greater the improbability, the more studied must be the approach, the more perfectly maintained the air of naturalness, the easy assumption that things are always likely to happen that way [...] the least touch of irrelevance, the least chill of inattention, will instantly undo the spell' (Wharton, 1925: 51).

No one knew this better than Edgar Allan Poe, the American writer often credited with being the first to acknowledge the short story's unique characteristics. Poe's theory of short fiction is based on the concept of unity as the fundamental principle of existence. As a result, for Poe, the purpose of literature is not to mirror the external world but to create a self-contained realm of reality that corresponds to the basic human desire for total unity. For Poe, 'plot' is not merely a series of sequential events to arouse suspense, but rather overall pattern, design, or harmony. Only pattern, not realistic cause-and-effect, can make the separate elements of the work meaningful. Moreover, Poe insists that only when the reader has an awareness of the 'end' of the work – that is, the overall pattern – will seemingly trivial elements become relevant and therefore meaningful. There is little doubt that Poe was always more interested in the work's pattern, structure, conventions and techniques than its reference to the external world or its social or psychological theme. His argument in the famous 1842 Hawthorne review is that the effect of the tale is synonymous with its overall pattern or design, which is also synonymous with its theme or idea. Form and meaning emerge from the unity of the themes of the story. Poe carries his concern with unity of effect even further in 'The Philosophy of Composition', asserting the importance of beginning with the end of the work, the possibility of which transforms reality into narrative discourse. The only narrative the reader gets is that which is already discourse, already ended as an event, so that there is nothing left for it but to move towards its end in an aesthetic, eventless way, by means of tone, metaphor and all the other artificial conventions of narrative.

One of the most significant of Poe's contributions to the development of the tight aesthetic unity of the short story form derives from one of his most typical themes: the theme of psychological obsession embodied in a first-person narrator. Poe transforms the ironically distanced and discursive first-person narrator familiar to readers of *Spectator* essays and the stories of Washington Irving into the voice of a narrator so obsessed with the subject of his narration that the obsession becomes the thematic centre of the story and thus creates the story's tight aesthetic unity. When one is obsessed, by definition, the obsession is the centre of the person's experience and perception. As a result, everything the person experiences or perceives is transformed into an image of the obsession, and nothing is allowed to enter into the experiential framework of the person except those things that fit in with the obsession. In Poe's short stories, as in an obsession, not only are all irrelevant things excluded, but seemingly trivial things are magnified or transformed into meaningful motifs relevant to the central theme. In the romantic story, as innovated by Poe, reality is radically subjective, for the typical Poe teller is caught in a psychologically obsessive reality that swallows it up.

Reality in the modern short story, on the other hand, seems to be a purely objective event, even as at the same time the intense selectivity practised by Chekhov, Hemingway and Raymond Carver results in an intensification of reality that no longer seems objective and real, but what some critics have called 'hyperrealism'. In Hemingway and Carver's stories, reality is so attenuated and restricted (rather than developed and expanded as in the realistic novel) that it takes on a hallucinatory, dreamlike effect even when the events occur in the wide-awake daylight of the everyday world. When a story presents 'hard facts' within a symbolic structure, objects and events are transformed from mere matter into meaningful metaphors by the motivating force of the story's own thematic and structural demands. Fully mimetic characters in a short story do not make the story realistic if the situation they confront eludes their power to incorporate it within a framework of the familiar, natural world. The realistic impulse creates a realistic story only when it succeeds in convincing the involved character or the reader that the mystery confronted has been, or can be, integrated. When a character moves from ignorance to knowledge – a common structural device in the realistic novel – this indeed means that he or she has been able to bring the confronted experience or phenomenon within the realm of the naturalistic, cause–effect world. If, however, the knowledge arrived at is metaphysical and inchoate, that is, not satisfactorily the knowledge of social, natural, psychological frameworks, then it remains revelatory, intuitive, unsayable. Revelation does not necessitate change if what is revealed is an aspect of human behaviour that cannot be accounted for socially, naturalistically or psychologically, or is so morally intolerable that no change in the perceiver can effect any change in the basic situation: in short, when nothing can be done about it and when language seems inadequate to express it.

Raymond Carver knew well the short story's tradition of centring on that which can be narrated but not explained. He accepted Chekhov's demanding dictum: 'In short stories it is better to say not enough than to say too much, because, – because – I don't know why!' (Chekhov, 1994: 198). The more recent writer from whom Carver learned about the short story's shunning of explanation was Flannery O'Connor, who insisted that the peculiar problem of the short story writer 'is how to make the action he describes reveal as much of the mystery of existence as possible' (O'Connor, 1961: 98). The storyteller's effort to make the reader see what does not exist in the world of external perception is a primal source of the storytelling impulse, as old as myth, legend, folk tale, fable and romance – all forms that attempt to objectify and actualise that which exists as a purely subjective state. As O'Connor says: 'If the writer believes that our life is and will remain essentially mysterious, [...] then what he sees on the surface will be of interest to him only as he can go through it into an experience of mystery itself.' For this kind of writer, 'the meaning of a story does not begin except at a depth where adequate motivation and adequate psychology and the various determinations have been exhausted' (41–2).

The ability of the short story to reflect human reality in those moments that cannot be so easily naturalised, is, of course, what the Cardinal means in Isak Dinesen's story 'The Cardinal's First Tale' when he makes a distinction between 'story' and a new art of narration which, for the sake of realism and individual characters, sacrifices the story. Whereas this 'novel' literature, the Cardinal says, is a human product, 'the divine art is the story. In the beginning was the story' (Dinesen, 1957: 26).

Walter Benjamin (1970) also makes an important generic distinction between such primal storytelling and the novel. Indeed, the development of the novel is one of the primary symptoms of the decline of storytelling, Benjamin argues, for it signals the rise of that form of communication that has come to predominate in the modern world – 'information'. The difference between storytelling and information is that whereas storytelling always had a validity that required no external verification, information must be accessible to immediate verification. Whereas story is borrowed from the miraculous and does not demand plausibility or conformity to the laws of external reality, information must be plausible and conform to such laws. When stories come to us through information, they are already loaded down with explanation, says Benjamin; it is half the art of storytelling to be free from information. Because the reader of story is free to interpret things the way he understands them, story has an amplitude lacking in information. According to Benjamin, although realistic narrative forms such as the novel focus on the relatively limited areas of human experience that indeed can be encompassed by information, characters in stories encounter those most basic mysteries of human experience that cannot be explained by rational means.

For example, it is nonsense to talk about Sherwood Anderson's *Winesburg, Ohio* ([1919] 2005), as being merely reflective of the aimless lives of mid America, as if some sort of vague cultural wasteland of the Midwest was indeed the cause of the loneliness of the lives of those who live and die in Winesburg. It trivialises the depth of the characters' isolation and the subtlety of Anderson's art to suggest that a good social programme, perhaps with square-dance classes and Wednesday-night bingo would pull the characters out of their doldrums. To claim that had there been adequate social assistance, sufficient psychological counselling, meaningful well-paying jobs, and good health care, the characters in Turgenev's *Sportsman's Sketches* or Joyce's *Dubliners* would not have been so lonely and despairing is absurd.

Forty-five years ago, when I began my career at the age of 25, I was teaching a short story one day to a class of undergraduates and had worked the story pretty hard, I thought, doing my best to get the students to interpret, explicate, analyse – to figure out what the story meant and how it meant what it meant rather than just processing its plot and generalising about its theme. When I finished, I asked if anyone had any final questions. One older man at the back of the room, who had remained quiet through the whole proceedings, raised his hand and said, with the exasperation years of experience with the work-a-day world often brings, 'Well, hell, if that's what he meant by the damned story, why didn't he say it that way in the first place?' I took a deep breath and stumbled and stuttered about how stories could never be reduced to explanation, that they were about a reality that could not be dealt with any other way. He listened with pursed lips until I struggled to a halt, finishing hopefully, 'Does that answer your question?' He shook his head indulgently – the older man putting up with the earnestness of the younger – and said, 'It's a mystery, ain't it, son?'

Many short story writers have talked about this basic mystery. One of my favourites is Flannery O'Connor, who once explained it (without really explaining it) much more succinctly than I did to my impatient student. 'The meaning of a story has to be embodied in it, has to be made concrete in it. A story', O'Connor says, 'is a way to say something that can't be said in any other way, and it takes every word in the story to say what the meaning is. You tell a story because a statement would be inadequate' (O'Connor, 1961: 96). But what kinds of meanings cannot be expressed in a statement? Are there really such things? Later on, O'Connor says, 'There are two qualities that make fiction. One is the sense of mystery, and the other is the sense of manners. You get the manners from the texture of existence that surrounds you' (103). I understand the manners. But where do you get the mystery? She doesn't answer that.

'Mystery' is indeed Flannery O'Connor's favourite word. She says that for the writer who believes that life is essentially mysterious, 'what he sees on the surface will be of interest to him only as he can go through it into an experience of mystery itself'. For this kind of writer, the 'meaning of a story does not begin except at a depth where adequate motivation and adequate psychology [...] have been exhausted. Such a writer will be interested in what we don't understand rather than in what we do' (41–2). O'Connor says, 'The peculiar problem of the short story writer is how to make the action he describes reveal as much of the mystery of existence as possible [...] His problem is really how to make the concrete work double time for him' (98). Somehow the concrete doesn't stay concrete in the short story, but like the mystery of incarnation, is transformed into spirit or significance even as it remains mere matter.

The short story does not hold together by plot or action, but rather by reiteration through pattern, for what the short story wishes to explore is not to be discovered by recounting events organised by cause and effect in time. The implication of this – an issue I have often discussed – is that the short story seems to focus on a moment out of time, or on time as mythically perceived, the way Ernest Cassirer and Mircea Eliade have described it, something that cannot be understood as a time-bound, socially-specific event. The short story seems more apt to deal with phenomena for which there are no clearly discernible logical, sociological or psychological causes.

When Frank Kermode in his Norton lectures 30 years ago asked, 'Why Are Narratives Obscure?' he was concerned, of course, with the radiant obscurity of the parable, a word which in the Gospel of Mark is used as a synonym for 'mystery'. Flannery O'Connor says 'The type of mind that can understand good fiction is not necessarily the educated mind, but it is at all times the kind of mind that is willing to have its sense of mystery deepened by contact with reality and its sense of reality deepened by contact with mystery' (O'Connor, 1961: 79).

What makes a great short story writer, in my opinion, is sympathy for the frailty of the self, respect for the delicacy of story structure, and reverence for the precision of language. Great short story writers compellingly confront the inexplicable mysteries of what it means to be human – mysteries that cannot be solved by social reform, only gaped at with awe. The short story's lack of room to ruminate about so-called 'big' socio-political issues is one reason the form is not popular with today's so-called 'serious' critics who prefer genres that generalise. The kind of complexity that fascinates masters of the short story is not captured by using more and more words but by using just the right ones. Good stories, like good poems, don't pontificate. The best stories reflect a conscientious effort to provide a structure and a syntax for feelings unspeakable until just the right rhythm makes what was loose and lying around clench and cluster into a meaningful pattern.

Because of historical tradition and the aesthetic conventions that adhere to short narrative, great short stories do not usually focus on characters defined by their social roles. Great short stories deal with situations that compel characters to confront their essential isolation as individual human beings, not as social masks within a particular cultural context. Such an approach, which eschews the social and the polemical and instead explores the symbolic and the psychological, does not lend itself to so much contemporary criticism concerned with social issues.

The Dublin of James Joyce and the Winesburg of Sherwood Anderson, we should not have to be reminded, are lyrical literary creations, inhabited not by real people but by imaginative embodiments of desire and despair. And in spite of the fact that the stories of John Cheever and Raymond Carver are often called 'realistic', a real person couldn't live in them, for they are haunted by psychic ghosts or distorted by unshakable obsessions. We don't go to the short story for simple reality; we go to sense our secrets suggested. And the short story writer, like the poet, must restrain language and intensify experience until it is almost unbearably loaded with significance. Great short stories are infused with uneasy magic, mysterious motivation, and confounding inevitability. In all great short stories, there is mystery and not a little menace – secrets so tangled and inexplicable that efforts to explain them with the language of psychology or sociology or history are either futile or absurd.

The short story is often misunderstood and underrated because many readers try to read it the same way they do chapters of novels, following plot that rushes to its climactic end or looking for easily recognisable characters, like the folks they meet every day. Great short story writers create that scary, sacred sense that what happens is not as important as what it signifies and the shock of recognition that those you thought you knew you don't really know at all. Great short story writers know that if you remove everything extraneous from a scene, an object, a person, its meaning is revealed, stark and astonishing. I suspect that the short story writer's compulsion is similar to that of the poet – to struggle with human complexities for which psychologists, sociologists, historians, novelists and other dispensers of explanatory discourse never quite account.

Great short story writers have the artistic ability to invent characters who sound authentic, even though they are highly stylised, and to tell stories reeking of messy reality, even as they are tightly controlled artifices. Flannery O'Connor once said she loaned some stories to a country lady who lived down the road from her, and when she returned them the woman said, 'Well, them stories just gone and shown you how some folks *would* do.' O'Connor agreed: Good stories have to show how 'some specific folks *will* do, *will* do in spite of everything' (O'Connor, 1961: 90). The peculiar problem of the short story writer, O'Connor has said, is to reveal as much of the mystery of personality as possible. Great short stories are often deceptive, lulling one into a false sense of security in which time seems to stretch out comfortably like everyday reality, only to tighten so subtly and intensely that the reader is left breathless.

The secret of great short story writers is that by describing what seems to be ordinary everyday reality, they suggest universal, unspoken human desires: the desire for meaningful fantasy rather than the inconsequential actual, for aesthetic disengagement rather than physical entanglement, for the memoried past rather than the simple present. Great short stories are complex and powerful not so much because of what seems to happen in them, but because of what cannot happen except in the mysterious human imagination. In great short stories, the hidden story of emotion and secret life, communicated by atmosphere and tone, is always about something more enigmatic and unspeakable than the story generated by what happens next.

Some writers and many teachers nowadays have nothing but scorn for what they term 'the so-called aesthetic', insisting that the proper aim of literary education is righting old wrongs. For them, literature is not the mysterious exploration of the complexity that makes us human; it is sociology; it is limited by history; it is Eurocentric, phallocentric and logocentric. Originality is mere self-indulgence. Exploration of the self is narcissism. It is my opinion that the postcolonial trend of seeing literary study as social activism is finally going out of fashion in academia. The buzzwords on which such studies depend have already been so over-used and trivialised that they will soon only elicit parody. I am not sure what the new approach will be, but I suspect it will be a return to passionate engagement with the universal humanness of the work and analytical appreciation of the artistic excellence of the artist's ability to explore such humanness – not local political agendas and esoteric theories that exclude the educated reader.

I can only hope that the current trend is a fad that will pass – merely a reflection of those who are bored or baffled by literature and who wish to tame it by limiting it to historical moments or social movements. After 45 years of passion for reading and teaching, I still believe that true literature – those works that we come back to again and again because, in their beauty and complexity, they refuse to become part of our disposable society – will continue to challenge us in spite of all efforts to tame it or toss it into the dustbin of literary history.

Works Cited

Aldridge John. *Talents and Technicians*. New York: Charles Scribner's Sons, 1992.
Anderson, Sherwood. *Winesburg, Ohio*. New York: Signet Classics, 2005.
Benjamin, Walter. 'The Storyteller: Reflections on the Works of Nikolai Leskov', in *Illuminations*, trans. Harry Zohn. London: Jonathan Cape Ltd., 1970. 83–109.
Chekhov, Anton. 'The Short Story', in *The New Short Story Theories*, ed. Charles E. May. Athens: Ohio University Press, 1994. 195–8.
Dinesen, Isak. 'The Cardinal's First Tale', in *Last Tales*. New York: Random House, 1957. 3–27.
Donoghue, Denis. 'Defeating the Poem', *The New Criterion*, April 2006, 14–18.
Eagleton, Terry. *Heathcliff and the Great Hunger: Studies in Irish Culture*. London: Verso, 1995.
Eco, Umberto. 'The Analysis of Structure', in *The Critical Moment: Literary Criticism in the 1960s – Essays from the London Times Literary Supplement*. New York: McGraw-Hill, 1963. 138–45.
Farrell, James T. 'Nonsense and the Short Story', in *The League of Frightened Philistines and Other Papers*. New York: The Vanguard Press, 1945. 72–81.
Gass, William H. *Finding a Form*. New York: Alfred A. Knopf, 1996.
Geismar, Maxwell. 'The American Short Story Today', *Studies on the Left* 4 (1964), 21–7.
Howells, William Dean. 'Some Anomalies of the Short Story', *North American Review* 173 (1901), 422–32.
Jameson, Frederic. *The Prison-House of Language*. Princeton: Princeton University Press, 1972.
Kermode, Frank. *The Genesis of Secrecy: On the Interpretation of Narrative*. Cambridge, MA: Harvard University Press, 1979.

Lukács, Georg. *Writer and Critic*, trans. Arthur Kahn. London: Merlin Press, 1970.

O'Connor, Flannery. *Mystery and Manners: Occasional Prose* (eds) Sally and Robert Fitzgerald. New York: Farrar, Straus & Giroux, 1961.

Ortega y Gasset, José. *The Dehumanization of Art and Ideas about the Novel*. New York: Doubleday Anchor, 1956.

Prose, Francine. *Reading Like a Writer: A Guide for People Who Love Books and For Those Who Want to Write Them*. New York: HarperCollins, 2006.

Schlegel, Friedrich. *Nachrichten von den poetischen Werken des G. Boccaccio, 1801*, quoted in E. K. Bennett, *A History of the German Novelle*, revised by H. M. Waidson. Cambridge: Cambridge University Press, 1965.

Shklovsky, Victor. 'Art as Technique', in *Russian Formalist Criticism: Four Essays*, trans. Lee T. Lemon and Marion J. Reis. Lincoln, NE: University of Nebraska Press, 1965. 3–24.

Wharton, Edith. 'Telling a Short Story', in *The Writing of Fiction*. New York: Charles Scribner's Sons, 1925. 33–58.

9
Postgraduate Research

Ailsa Cox

This chapter focuses on two specific aspects of postgraduate research on the short story, indicating starting points for those undertaking research in this field. First of all, it looks at theoretical research dedicated to exploring the nature of the genre and the narrative strategies adopted by its authors. Secondly, it looks at practice-led research and collaborative activity linking short story writing, publication and the academy. These two categories are by no means mutually exclusive; as the Introduction points out, short story practitioners have always been leading participants in developing short story theory. The chapter's third and final section offers suggestions for a taught postgraduate programme combining both elements.

Short Story Theory

It is impossible to quantify exactly how much postgraduate study is devoted to the short story, because so much of it is embedded within a broader study of prose fiction and its authors. For instance, the range of MPhils offered at Trinity College, Dublin, including Popular Literature, Anglo-Irish Literature and Literature of the Americas, pays considerable attention to short story texts. While these and other taught postgraduate programmes include dedicated modules, at the moment of writing there appear to be no programmes focusing exclusively on short fiction. When we consider current developments, it is fair to say that research into short story texts and their authors simply follows dominant trends in literary study. However there are well established networks of scholars specialising in this field, whose activities form a useful point of reference for new researchers.

The home of short story theory has, undoubtedly, been the US. Its twentieth-century pioneers have included Charles E. May, Susan Lohafer and the late Mary Rohrberger, all leading figures in the formation of the Society for the Study of the Short Story in the late 1980s and early 1990s. It is currently directed by Maurice A. Lee of the University of Arkansas, with the writer Clark Blaise as its president. It publishes a journal, *Short Story*, and runs an international conference every two years,

Yet while the resurgence in short story theory has been US driven, it is not confined to those shores. American short story scholars often find themselves crossing the Atlantic to meet one another. The Society's founding conference was held at the Sorbonne in 1988 and its most recent venues were Lisbon, Cork and Toronto. These are not the only transatlantic links. The University of Belmont in Nashville collaborates with the Centre de Recherche Inter-Langues Angevin at the University of Angers, organising regular conferences and running the bi-annual *Journal of the Short Story in English* (founded 1983). Guests of honour at Angers have included Mavis Gallant, John McGahern, Helen Simpson and Steven Millhauser. In Norway, the Oslo Short Fiction Project, headed by Per Winther, Hans Skei and Jakob Lothe, has also organised meetings between Anglophone scholars and European researchers working on the short story in English.

Short story specialists often see themselves as mavericks, distancing themselves from the fashionable orthodoxies of the literary establishment – a view expressed by Charles E. May in the previous chapter. When Susan Lohafer gave an informal retrospective of her career in 2004 she naturally gave it the title 'Sticking to Stories: A Career Outside the Mainstream'.[1] This outsider status generates a sense of solidarity which crosses national and disciplinary boundaries, and is reflected in the eclecticism of short story theory.

Many theoreticians are also creative writers, even if, like Susan Lohafer or Maurice Lee, they are primarily known for their critical work. The Society for the Study of the Short Story has strong historical connections with the University of Iowa Creative Writing Programme, and its conference programmes feature a substantial number of readings (Amiri Baraka, Robert Olen Butler, Claire Keegan, Sandra Cisneros, Margaret Atwood). A tradition of close reading, inherited from the New Criticism, combines with the practitioner's viewpoint to create an emphasis on detailed textual analysis.

Narratology, reader response theory and, most recently, cognitive science, have all contributed to an ongoing investigation of formal characteristics. Lohafer's work on 'pre-closure' has involved a series of experiments with readers, testing their narrative expectations at points of potential closure in the text. This type of empirical approach, exploring how the text engages the reader emotionally and intellectually in real time, can be applied to other type of texts, but is becoming increasingly important to the ongoing investigation into the formal characteristics of the short story. The short story has always been attractive to linguists because it lends itself so readily to stylistic analysis; this is one reason why so much work on the short story has been carried out by European scholars. Technological advances have opened up the potential for the digitally enabled analysis of texts and the use of artificial intelligence. The new area of Cognitive Stylistics (also known as Cognitive Poetics) is being developed by the STACS Project ('Stylistics, Text Analysis and Cognitive Science: Interdisciplinary Perspectives on the Nature of Reading, Narrative Theory and the Cognitive Sciences') directed by Catherine Emmott at the University of Glasgow. A Discourse and Narrative Research Group at the State University of New York at Buffalo also conducts interdisciplinary cognitive-science research into the comprehension of narrative text.

There are two broad topics of interest to short story specialists opened up by Cognitive Stylistics. One is the identification of the linguistic strategies used to hold the reader's attention, the narrative touchstones embedded in the story-text. The other related question is the whole concept of 'storyness' as a mode of perception, hard-wired in the brain and thus an essential component in the construction of meaning.

It scarcely seems possible to talk about *the* short story, when we consider its numerous formal variations, even in terms of word count, ranging from the 'short shorts' discussed in Chapter 1 to those running to over 50 pages or more, such as Alice Munro's 'The Love of a Good Woman' (1998) or Colm Tóibín's 'A Long Winter' (2006) which might even be classed as novella, a form deserving further analysis in its own right. Then there is the question of the non-fiction short story and literary journalism. Douglas Hesse's 'A Boundary Zone: First-Person Short Stories and Narrative Essays' (first published in *Short Story Theory at a Crossroads,* 1989) pioneered a commonality between the short story and what is now called creative non-fiction. The University of Iowa's Bedell Nonfiction Now Conference, hosted every two years since 2005, includes a consideration of short forms, and students on its Nonfiction Writing Program may produce either a sustained essay or a collection of shorter pieces towards their MFA. Daniel Lehman's (1998) *Matters of Fact: Reading Nonfiction Over the Edge* re-reads texts by Sigmund Freud, Henry Mayhew, Joan Didion and others alongside Tim O'Brien's self-reflexive stories in *The Things They Carried* (1991). The generic concept of 'autofiction', applied to texts which overlap fictional content and strategies with an interrogation of the autobiographical self, might be usefully extended to O'Brien's work and to short stories by, for instance, David Sedaris or ZZ Packer.

The story sequence, cycle or 'composite novel' has received a great deal of critical attention, often centring on a debate concerning formal unity and a resistance to closure within stories published as a sequence.[2] Less attention has been paid to the structural principles behind collections without explicit themes, and to the dynamics of multi-authored anthologies. One notable exception is the work of Allan Weiss at York University, Ontario. In an as yet unpublished study, Weiss has identified the 'mini-cycle', clusters of two or three stories within an otherwise unrelated collection – for example, the 'Juliet' stories in Alice Munro's *Runaway* (2005), which return to the protagonist at key points in her life. Weiss places the mini-cycle as an intermediate form between the short story and the novella. He also refers to the short story 'series' – for instance the Sherlock Holmes stories – as another liminal form.

As these examples demonstrate, genre criticism is now shifting its focus from broad systems of classification to a more specialised consideration of disparate narrative forms, and to the shifting spaces between them. Multiplicity is celebrated, as an aspect of both form and content. Sandra A. Zagarell's concept of the 'narrative of community' (Zagarell, 1988) remains highly influential, associating the polyphonic short story cycle with collective experience. Sequences by Jean Toomer, Amy Tan, Sandra Cisneros and Jumpha Lahiri, to name but a few, have been read in this light; while the short story's roots in the oral tradition have been emphasised in studies of, for instance, Native American and Caribbean writing. In recent years, short story scholars have been particularly concerned with cultural representation, including the literature of diaspora, postcolonial theory, regionalism, links between gender and genre; and transnational/transcultural approaches.

As this volume has indicated, the term 'short story' covers a wide field, one which is even wider if we include multimedia, an area I shall briefly discuss in the following section. Online publishing has drawn attention to the permeability of generic boundaries; and some recent criticism has considered the properties shared by the short story with other art forms, rather than searching for qualities that are exclusive to short fiction. The interconnections between the short story and poetry, with drama, music, film and photography and other arts are of increasing interest to short story scholars and practitioners alike.

This volume has concentrated mostly on the teaching of twentieth-century and contemporary texts; it is, however, worth considering the large body of nineteenth-century short stories by British authors such as Charles Dickens, Anthony Trollope and Elizabeth Gaskell, which are still relatively unexamined. Thanks to the ongoing popularity of the gothic, on university courses and amongst the general public, the most widely republished Victorian stories are the supernatural tales, but Gaskell's stories, for instance, are becoming more obtainable. Her best known work *Cranford* (2008) is one of those many 'novels' that may be reclaimed as a short story cycle (and yet another 'narrative of community').

Another area of growing interest is publishing history, in all its aspects, including the circulation and reception of texts; the significance of short story reading and writing in emerging cultures; and its relevance to specific communities and social identities. The Modernist Magazines Project, directed by Andrew Thacker at De Montfort University and Peter Brooker from the University of Sussex, focuses on 'little magazines' such as John Middleton Murry's *Rhythm*, without whose existence the evolution of the modern short story is unimaginable. The first volume of *The Oxford Critical and Cultural History of Modernist Magazines* has appeared, with two more in preparation (Brooker and Thacker, 2009). The modernist project covers the years between 1880 and 1955; there is also work to be done on literary magazines in the second half of the twentieth century, for instance the short-lived but hugely influential *Bananas*, which published Angela Carter and J. G. Ballard. Nor should we forget the importance of radio; during Robert Weaver's long career at the CBC he was instrumental in the early careers of key Canadian writers including Alice Munro, Margaret Atwood and Mordecai Richler. Weaver's role, not only on the radio, but in print magazines and anthologies, provides a clear example of the interaction between short story writers and editors; recent work on Gordon Liddy's intervention in Raymond Carver's texts points the way to further research.[3] Angela Smith's *Katherine Mansfield and Virginia Woolf: A Public of Two* (1999) shows how textual analysis might be enriched by an appreciation of the ongoing process of dialogue between individual practitioners, reminding us that writers are also readers, editors and critics.

Practice-led Research

A large proportion of postgraduate research into the short story combines theory and practice through the Creative Writing MAs and MFAs offered by numerous institutions. Several specialise in prose fiction, but – surprisingly, when one considers the disparity between the word length of the standard MA dissertation and the average novel – this is more likely to be in the novel than the short story. A few, for instance Sheffield Hallam, offer dedicated pathways. At City University in London, students undertaking a postgraduate Certificate in Short Story Writing compile a portfolio of stories as the basis of a collection, and are given a systematic introduction to short story publishing. In the UK, the National Association of Writers in Education (NAWE) maintains a database of courses on its website which may be found at http://www.nawe.co.uk; in the US a similar service is offered by the Association of Writers and Writing Programs at http://www.awpwriter. org and by the Australasian Association of Writing Programs at http://www.aawp.org.au.

At PhD level, the doctoral thesis usually combines creative and critical elements; creative work in the short story will be accompanied by a reflection or statement of poetics, including the analysis of texts by published writers and a consideration of formal or thematic characteristics. Practice-led research into the short story has benefited from a systematic attempt to codify and define creative writing research in general. NAWE has issued a National Research Benchmarking Statement on Creative Writing as part of an Arts and Humanities Research Council investigation, mapping practice-led research in creative and performing arts. NAWE is also compiling a register of doctoral theses in creative writing, documenting research activities and looking at such issues as how practice-led research is valued and assessed.

Now that Creative Writing can be identified as an autonomous subject area, there are moves to break its traditional alignment with English Literature, especially in departments where practice-led research is still misunderstood or devalued. If, as Graeme Harper rightly points out, Creative Writing is not 'a branch of post-event literature analysis' (Harper, 2006: 4), why is its teaching located most often within English departments? However, as Francine Prose explains in *Reading Like a Writer* (2006), fiction writers learn their craft largely through example. In my own undergraduate teaching, I have found that those students whose joint subject is English Literature are more used to close reading, and often transfer devices they've learnt from canonical texts – modernist stream of consciousness or postmodern fragmentation – into their own writing. So far as fiction is concerned, the connection remains logical at postgraduate level, although it is important to differentiate between 'reading as a writer' and the more standard types of critical responses which do not relate literary technique to the student's own practice.

The diversity and fluidity of short story writing and reading has never been more evident. Some practitioners have returned to the oldest traditions. The National Storytelling Festival, founded in Tennessee in 1973, has helped lead a revival in oral storytelling, encompassing both traditional tales and contemporary material. Its International Storytelling Center contains a range of resources, and there is also an International Storytelling Collection at the Library of Congress. Festival at the Edge, on the Welsh borders in Shropshire, is another annual event, bringing storytellers together from across the globe; the Mythstories Museum, nearby, also offers resources and runs storytelling projects. The Society for Storytelling, the Scottish Storytelling Centre in Edinburgh and Aos Scéal Éireann (Storytellers of Ireland) all promote oral storytelling and provide useful resources.

Live literature has become very much more than promotional readings and book signings. There are an increasing number of events, such as Tales of the Decongested at Foyles Bookshop in London, which are the prose equivalent of the poetry slam. Sometimes, like the Short Fuse readings in Brighton, this is facilitated by the growth in flash fiction (see Chapter 1). As part of the 'Tilting the Mirror' project in 2007–2008, short story writers and poets worked with theatre producers, using music, lighting and other dramatic effects to stage their work.[4] WordTheatre, active in Los Angeles, New York and London, celebrates the power of the voice, using top class actors and authors to read their stories, usually as charity fundraisers.

All of these activities point to two interrelated factors which have changed the nature of short story writing, reading and dissemination – the rise of the new technology and the importance of multi-modality. Live readings and storytellings are preserved online or as podcasts; networks of writers, readers and listeners are also able to communicate and promote short story activities on the web. Collaboration with musicians, actors, visual artists and others, invites experimentation with narrative structure, style and generic properties. Bristol Stories (http://www.bristolstories.org) is a 'creative digital storytelling project' in which local people tell stories, using oral storytelling, computer graphics, film and photography. Another new project, Underwood (http://www.underwoodstories.com) has released stories by Toby Litt and Clare Wigfall as vinyl recordings. Several other publishers have launched stories as mobile 'apps'.

Many individual short story writers are working at the interface of print and digital culture; hypertext fiction, pioneered by Robert Coover, Michael Joyce, Shelley Jackson, Kate Pullinger and others, dissolves the boundaries between the visual arts, fiction and poetry. The Electronic Literature Organisation, founded in 1999 and now based at the University of Maryland, is the first port of call for writers and researchers working in this field. The ELO promotes 'works with important literary aspects that take advantage of the capabilities and contexts provided by the stand-alone or networked computer' (http://www.eliterature.org/about), including hypertext fiction, interactive fiction, stories generated by computers and stories performed online. It serves as a forum for writers, including, amongst its numerous activities, a directory, an archive and a showcase of new work. The *Iowa Review Web*, sponsored by the University of Iowa, is also a discussion forum for literary hypertext and hypermedia. In the UK, the trAce archive hosted by Nottingham Trent University at http://www.tracearchive.ntu.ac.uk houses new media material commissioned by the trAce Online Writing Centre between 1995 and 2005, critical essays, writers' journals and material documenting the project. For current discussions of hypertext literature and the relationship between contemporary fiction and network culture, researchers are advised to consult *electronic book review* (http://www.electronicbookreview.com); while the home page of Eastgate, the developers of *Storyspace*, showcases examples of hypertext fiction (http://www.eastgate.com). An online MA in Creative Writing and New Media, offered by De Montfort University, and developed from the trAce project, includes opportunities for work on short fiction. The Literary Arts Program at Robert Coover's home institution, Brown University, also offers courses in Literary Hypermedia to postgraduate student writers.

Coover's 1992 *New York Times* article 'The End of Books' lays down a challenge to conventional narrative forms, proclaiming electronic literature's ability to subvert linear narrative and empower the reader. According to Coover, the proliferation of printed material in contemporary culture is itself a symptom of terminal decline. However, the book and the magazine have not yet been superseded by the screen amongst short story writers and readers. Rather, a symbiosis has developed between print-based and digital publishing. As a fragmentary form, the short story lends itself especially well to online publication, and a great deal of new fiction appears on the web. Amongst literary e-zines, the best regarded is probably the multilingual *Barcelona Review* (http://www.barcelonareview.com). But the most influential magazines are probably those which, like *McSweeney's* and Francis Ford Coppola's *Zoetrope*, run parallel versions in print and online. *Zoetrope* acknowledges the interdependency of art forms by publishing original short fiction and one-act plays alongside stories that have been adapted for the cinema. Many of the stories published by the Manchester-based Comma Press are available as podcasts or short film adaptations. New technologies have also facilitated the growth in graphic narrative, and the emergence of the graphic short story alongside the graphic novel. Both multimedia work and graphic narrative are offered on creative writing courses at Rutgers University, New Brunswick, and similar courses are being made available elsewhere at both undergraduate and postgraduate level.

These technological interventions recontextualise short fiction within wider visual, auditory and performance culture, counterbalancing the traditional alignment of short fiction with the novel. During the *1001 nights cast*, Barbara Campbell performed a collaborative sequence of stories, each based on a word or phrase in that morning's news from the Middle East. For the 1001 nights, participants submitted stories of up to 1001 words based on the daily prompt.[5] Campbell's project would seem to fulfil Coover's vision for electronic literature, as a text which is inseparable from its technology, and cannot be experienced properly on the page. There are many other publishing ventures which harness the new technology, without fundamentally challenging print-based conventions. The Rainy City project is an 'interactive literary cityscape' locating site-specific stories on a map of Manchester (http://www.rainycitystories.com) – stories readers may well choose to download and print. However, these new formats do accentuate the fluidity of the short story form; and the nature of the anthology or the collection as a network or montage, which, freed from the finite pages of the book, has a capacity to develop and grow organically.

As we move further into the twenty-first century, it is clear that the potential for collaboration, cross-fertilisation and interdisciplinary research is increasing, as the oldest forms of storytelling interact with the new. As Andy Sawyer suggests in Chapter 6, short story criticism has tended to concentrate on 'literary' examples, almost ignoring the contribution of popular sub-genres to the form. Such barriers are breaking down completely, as existing genres develop and hybridise, bridging the plot-driven tale and image-based literary fiction. Various neologisms – 'transrealism', 'slipstream' – have been coined or revived in attempts to define a new set of conventions. According to the British writer Allen Ashley, 'Slipstream uses the tropes and ideas of science fiction, fantasy and horror but is not bound by their rules and will often make those elements only a minor feature of the story rather than its *raison d'être*' (Ashley, 2008: ii). While we may not agree with Ashley's argument that slipstream 'is the only meaningful literary response to the challenges of the new millennium' (ibid.), the appearance of new manifestos for the short story, 20 years after Raymond Carver's death, gives us some indication of debates yet to come and fresh innovations as yet undiscovered.

A Postgraduate Programme

What would an MA in the Contemporary Short Story look like? Ideally, it would continue the dialogue between theory and practice which has distinguished so much previous teaching and scholarship. This does not mean that such provision would be simply a variant of the Creative Writing MA, or that potential students would define themselves primarily in terms of their own creative practice. One possibility might be to offer creative and critical pathways. While some students might be working on their own fiction for their final dissertation, others would submit a piece of literary criticism; some might even produce hybridised forms, or fictocriticism, a mode which synthesises creative writing, critical theory and autobiographical discourse. Ali Smith's 'True Short Story' (Smith, 2008), a playful disputation on the merits of the short story over the novel, might arguably be considered an example of fictocriticism, although the term is most often associated with developments in feminist practice emerging from universities in Australia during the 1990s.

Both Paul Dawson (2004) and Hazel Smith (2005) discuss parallels between fictocriticism and the work of Charles Bernstein and other Language Poets in the US. The pioneering Poetics Program founded by Bernstein at the University of Buffalo claims that: 'its universe is an amalgam of practice, theory, and textual study, with influences from the literary avant-garde, links to the graphic arts, openness to critical theory, connections to the linguistic flux and polyphony of modern diasporas, and a keen appreciation of the cybernetic worlds of hypertext and digital media' (http://www.poetics.buffalo.edu/program/index.html). While the Buffalo manifesto incorporates prose writing in principle, its potential for teaching short story writing has yet to be fully realised. The concept of a postgraduate poetics programme aimed specifically at fiction writers offers an alternative to the broader 'pathway' model suggested above.

Dawson has some reservations about hybridisation, perceiving a danger that 'collapsing boundaries within literature, and between literature and criticism, into a generalised "writing" means *erasing* rather than celebrating or multiplying difference' (Dawson, 2005: 171). As the English Subject Centre Report, *Creative Writing: A Good Practice Guide* makes clear, 'Creative Writing is a critical discipline in its own right' (Holland,

2003: 10). It should go without saying that Creative Writing elements on an MA of this kind should be designed and delivered by practitioners; and that if, for example, a student is experimenting with pastiche or self-consciously 'plagiarising' or reworking published texts the exercise advances the writer's own practice, and is not merely an ancillary form of 'post-event' literary analysis.

When writers talk about the short story, they very often break into analogy (painting, poetry, photography) or metaphor (Boyd's bomb, Kennedy's bullet, both discussed in the Introduction). A collection of short story metaphors might even constitute a 'fictocritical' project in itself. But in fact there is no such thing as *the* short story. As I argue in the Introduction, we should be able to move on from a defensive preoccupation with generic definition. While short story scholarship and teaching will continue to be rooted in stylistic and formal considerations, a shared assumption that the short story is distinct from other literary species should be taken as a starting point and not a destination. Students would need to appreciate why the drive to distinguish the short story from the novel has been such a guiding principle behind short story criticism, while remaining resistant to the taxonomical urge. As Paul March-Russell has said, incidentally adding to my storehouse of short story metaphors, 'the short story can be likened to a black hole' (March-Russell, 2009: ix). It is apprehended through its effects, not through its essence.

All boundaries are permeable, whether formal and generic or thematic. Any student of the contemporary short story needs to have some acquaintance with, on the one hand, the modernist inheritance and the epiphanic, image-based story, still practised, for instance, by William Trevor; and, on the other, with the popular 'plot-driven' tradition, continued by writers such as Stephen King. But the strands are not polarities; they sometimes merge, as we saw with the example of 'slipstream'. King's horror yarn, 'That Feeling, You Can Only Say What It Is in French' (King, 2002) shares many techniques with the modern 'literary' story in its representation of a fluid interior consciousness.

Texts by Irish, Caribbean or US writers may be seen in the context of their respective national traditions, but these are not the only forces at work. Transnationalism is not confined to the short story, but has been especially marked in its history, not only through the migratory circumstances of its practitioners, but also through the influences of translations from writers, including Chekhov, Maupassant, Kafka and Borges, on Anglophone authors. Ideally a postgraduate course would favour a transnational perspective over a narrow focus on *the* American,

Irish and so on, short story. It would find room for short stories in translation, for instance work by Etgar Keret and Haruki Murakami; and it would refuse to discriminate between 'literary' and popular texts.

I would also hope that, in addition to textual analysis, grounded in close reading, students would have the opportunity to contextualise short stories and their authors within contemporary literary culture, publishing and the media industries. The short story flourishes when there are publishing outlets, and the nature of those outlets has formal and aesthetic repercussions. In the UK, a significant proportion of the stories in mainstream collections will have been originally commissioned by BBC Radio, and therefore addressed to a listener rather than a reader. The part played by the new media and cross-media developments in the rise of the very short story, hypertext fiction and the nature of short story writing and publication in general is crucial to any study of the short story today, whether from a critical perspective or from a practitioner's viewpoint.

No course could even begin to encompass every aspect of the contemporary short story, but in bringing together theory and practice, content, style and context, it could mark out a territory of its own, asserting a new confidence for short fiction, in all its multitudinous forms, in the twenty-first century.

Works Cited

Ashley, Allen. 'Introduction: Mapping the Unmapped', in *Subtle Edens*, ed. Allen Ashley. Norfolk: Elastic Press, 2008. i–iii.
Brooker, Peter and Andrew Thacker (eds). *The Oxford Critical and Cultural History of Modernist Magazines. Vol. 1: Britain and Ireland 1880–1955*. Oxford: Oxford University Press, 2009.
Coover, Robert. 'The End of Books'. *New York Times*, 21 June 1992.
Dawson, Paul. *Creative Writing and the New Humanities*. London: Routledge, 2004.
Fergusson, Suzanne, 'Sequences, Anti-Sequences, Cycles and Composite Novels: The Short Story in Genre Criticism'. *Journal of the Short Story in English* 41 (autumn 2003). 103–16.
Gaskell, Elizabeth. *Cranford*. Oxford: Oxford University Press, 2008.
Harper, Graeme (ed.) *Teaching Creative Writing*. London: Continuum, 2006.
Hesse, Douglas. 'A Boundary Zone: First-Person Short Stories and Narrative Essays', in *Short Story Theory at a Crossroads*, ed. Susan Lohafer and Jo Ellyn Clarey. Baton Rouge: Louisiana State University Press, 1989. 85–105.
Holland, Siobhán. *Creative Writing: A Good Practice Guide*. London: LTSN English Subject Centre, 2003.
King, Stephen. 'That Feeling, You Can Only Say What It Is in French', in *Everything's Eventual*. London: Hodder and Stoughton, 2002.

Lehman, Daniel. *Matters of Fact: Reading Nonfiction Over the Edge*. Columbus, Ohio: Ohio State University Press, 1998.
March-Russell, Paul. *The Short Story: An Introduction*. Edinburgh: Edinburgh University Press, 2009.
Munro, Alice. 'The Love of a Good Woman', in *The Love of a Good Woman*. London: Chatto & Windus, 1998. 3–78.
Munro, Alice. *Runaway*. London: Chatto & Windus, 2005.
O'Brien, Tim. *The Things They Carried*. London: Flamingo, 1991.
Poetics Program at Buffalo, The, http://www.poetics.buffalo.edu/program/index.html.
Prose, Francine. *Reading Like a Writer*. New York: HarperCollins, 2006.
Smith, Ali. 'True Short Story', in *The First Person and Other Stories*. London: Penguin, 2008. 1–18.
Smith, Angela. *Katherine Mansfield and Virginia Woolf: A Public of Two*. Oxford: Oxford University Press, 1999.
Smith, Hazel. *The Writing Experiment: Strategies for Innovative Creative Writing*. New South Wales: Allen & Unwin, 2005.
Stull, William L. and Maureen P. Carroll. 'Prolegomena To Any Future Carver Studies'. *Journal of the Short Story in English* 46 (spring 2006). 13–17.
Tóibín, Colm. 'A Long Winter', in *Mothers and Sons*. London: Picador, 2006. 225–310.
Zagarell, Sandra A. 'Narrative of Community: The Identification of a Genre'. *Signs* 13 (spring 1988) 498–527.

Notes

1. Available on http://www.english.uiowa.edu/works/lohafer.stickingtostories.html.
2. See for instance Suzanne Fergusson, 'Sequences, Anti-Sequences, Cycles and Composite Novels: The Short Story in Genre Criticism', (2003).
3. Stull and Carroll's 'Prolegomena to Any Future Carver Studies' (2006) outlines recent debates on Carver and authorship.
4. See http://www.theshortstory.org.uk/features for more information on this project.
5. See http://www.1001.net.au.

Appendix: Film Adaptations

The following is a selection of short-story-to-film adaptations, listed according to the original short story author. They are included either because of their significance as films or because they are based on work by significant writers – or in some instances because they fulfil both criteria. Some adaptations are mostly based on the title given, but incorporate elements from other stories by the same author. Some are based on collections, rather than stories. For the sake of space, most of the examples are feature films, rather than TV adaptations; the TV credits of Arthur Conan Doyle, P. G. Wodehouse or Agatha Christie would fill these pages by themselves. They are also mostly English language adaptations of English language stories. I have, however, made a number of exceptions; no such list could exclude *Rashomon*.

Ryunosuke Akutagawa
'In a Grove' (1922)
Rashomon (1950)
Writer/Director: Akira Kurosawa

Brian Aldiss
'Super-Toys Last All Summer Long' (1969)
AI: Artificial Intelligence (2001)
Director: Steven Spielberg
Writers: Ian Watson, Steven Spielberg

Sherman Alexie
'This is What it Means to Say Phoenix, Arizona' (1993)
Smoke Signals (1998)
Director: Chris Eyre
Writer: Sherman Alexie

Isaac Asimov
I, Robot (1950)
I, Robot (2004)
Director: Alex Proyas
Writers: Jeff Vintar, Akiva Goldsman

Paul Auster
'Auggie Wren's Christmas Story' (1991)
Smoke (1995)
Director: Wayne Wang
Writer: Paul Auster

Jorge Luis Borges
'The Theme of the Traitor and Hero' (1944)
The Spider's Stratagem (1970)
Director: Bernardo Bertolucci
Writers: Bernardo Bertolucci, Eduardo de Gregorio, Marilu Parolini

'Death and the Compass' (1942)
Death and the Compass (1992)
Writer/Director: Alex Cox

Ray Bradbury
The Illustrated Man (1951)
The Illustrated Man (1969)
Director: Peter Smight
Writer: Howard B. Kreitsek

'A Sound of Thunder' (1952)
A Sound of Thunder (2005)
Director: Peter Hyams
Writers: Thomas Dean Donnelly, Joshua Oppenheimer, Gregory Poirier

Thomas Burke
'The Chink and the Child' (1916)
Broken Blossoms (1919)
Director: D. W. Griffith
Writer: Emlyn Williams

Angela Carter
The Bloody Chamber (1979)
The Company of Wolves (1984)
Director: Neil Jordan
Writers: Angela Carter, Neil Jordan

Raymond Carver
Various stories, including 'They're Not Your Husband', 'Neighbors', 'Will You Please Be Quiet, Please?', 'A Small, Good Thing', 'Tell the Women We're Going', and 'So Much Water, So Close to Home', were adapted as *Short Cuts* by Writer/Director Robert Altman (1993). An anthology, *Short Cuts*, was released by the Harvill Press in 1994.

'So Much Water, So Close to Home' (1981)
Jindabyne (2006)
Director: Ray Lawrence
Writer: Beatrix Christian

Eileen Chang
'Lust, Caution' (1979)
Lust, Caution (2007)
Director: Ang Lee
Writer: Wang Hui-Ling

John Cheever
'The Swimmer' (1964)
The Swimmer (1968)
Directors: Frank Perry, Sydney Pollack
Writer: Eleanor Perry

Arthur C. Clarke
'The Sentinel' (1951)
2001: A Space Odyssey (1968)

176   Appendix: Film Adaptations

Director: Stanley Kubrick
Writers: Stanley Kubrick, Arthur C. Clarke

Joseph Conrad
'Heart of Darkness' (1899)
Apocalypse Now (1979)
Director: Francis Ford Coppola
Writers: John Milius, Francis Ford Coppola

Julio Cortázar
'Blow-Up'/'Las Babas del Diablo' (1959)
Blow-Up (1966)
Writer/Director: Michelangelo Antonioni

'The Southern Freeway' (1966)
Week End (1967)
Writer/Director: Jean Luc Goddard

John M. Cunningham
'The Tin Star' (1942)
High Noon (1952)
Director: Fred Zinnemann
Writer: Carl Foreman

Philip K. Dick
'We Can Remember It for You Wholesale' (1966)
Total Recall (1990)
Director: Paul Verhoeven
Writers: Ronald Shusett, Dan O'Bannon, Gary Goldman

'The Minority Report' (1956)
Minority Report (2002)
Director: Stephen Spielberg
Writers: Scott Frank, Jon Cohen

'Paycheck' (1953)
Paycheck (2003)
Director: John Woo
Writer: Dean Georgaris

Charles Dickens
'The Signal-Man' (1866)
The Signalman (BBC TV, 'A Ghost Story for Christmas', 1976)
Director: Lawrence Gordon Clarke
Writer: Andrew Davies

Isak Dinesen
'Babette's Feast' (1950)
Babette's Feast (1987)
Writer/Director: Gabriel Axel

Daphne du Maurier
'The Birds' (1952)

The Birds (1963)
Director: Alfred Hitchcock
Writer: Evan Hunter

'Don't Look Now' (1971)
Don't Look Now (1973)
Director: Nicolas Roeg
Writers: Allan Scott, Chris Bryant

Andre Dubus
'Killings' (1979)
In the Bedroom (2001)
Writer/Director: Todd Field

'We Don't Live Here Anymore' (1975), 'Adultery' (1977)
We Don't Live Here Anymore (2004)
Director: John Curran
Writer: John Gross

William Faulkner
'Tomorrow' (1940)
Tomorrow (1972)
Director: Joseph Anthony
Writer: Horton Foote

'Two Soldiers' (1942)
Two Soldiers (2003)
Writer/Director: Aaron Schneider

F. Scott Fitzgerald
'Babylon Revisited' (1931)
The Last Time I Saw Paris (1954)
Director: Richard Brooks
Writer: Julius J. Epstein

'Bernice Bobs Her Hair'
Bernice Bobs Her Hair (Learning in Focus, US TV film, 1976)
Writer/Director: Joan Micklin Silver

'The Curious Case of Benjamin Button' (1922)
The Curious Case of Benjamin Button (2008)
Director: David Fincher
Writers: Eric Roth, Robin Swicord

Ian Fleming
'Quantum of Solace' (1959)
Quantum of Solace (2008)
Director: Marc Foster
Writers: Paul Haggis, Neal Purvis, Robert Wade

Richard Ford
'Great Falls', 'Children' (1987)
Bright Angel (1991)

Director: Michael Fields
Writer: Richard Ford

Mary Gaitskell
'Secretary' (1988)
Secretary (2002)
Director: Stephen Shainberg
Writer: Erin Cressida Wilson

William Gibson
'Johnny Mnemonic' (1981)
Johnny Mnemonic (1995)
Director: Robert Longo
Writer: William Gibson

Graham Greene
'The Basement Room' (1935)
The Fallen Idol (1948)
Director: Carol Reed
Writer: Graham Greene

Ernest Haycox
'Stage to Lordsburg' (1937)
Stagecoach (1939)
Director: John Ford
Writer: Dudley Nichols

Henry James
'Daisy Miller' (1879)
Daisy Miller (1974)
Director: Peter Bogdanovich
Writer: Frederic Raphael

'The Turn of the Screw' (1898)
The Innocents (1961)
Director: Jack Clayton
Writers: William Archibald, Truman Capote

M. R. James
'Oh, Whistle, and I'll Come to You, My Lad' (1904)
Whistle and I'll Come to You (BBC play, 1968)
Writer/Director: Jonathan Miller

'Casting the Runes' (1911)
Night of the Demon (GB 1958 – US title *Curse of the Demon*)
Director: Jacques Tourneur
Writers: Charles Bennett, Hal E. Chester

'A Warning to the Curious' (1925)
A Warning to the Curious (BBC TV, 'A Ghost Story for Christmas', 1972)
Writer/Director: Lawrence Gordon Clark

James Joyce
'The Dead' (1914)
The Dead (1987)

Director: John Huston
Writer: Tony Huston

Eric Keown
'Sir Tristam Goes West' (1935)
The Ghost Goes West (1935)
Director: René Clair
Writers: Geoffrey Kerr, Robert Sherwood

Daniel Keyes
'Flowers for Algernon' (1959)
Charley (1968)
Director: Ralph Nelson
Writer: Stirling Silliphant

Stephen King
'The Body' (1982)
Stand By Me (1986)
Director: Rob Reiner
Writers: Raynold Gideon, Bruce A. Evans

'Rita Hayworth and Shawshank Redemption' (1982)
The Shawshank Redemption (1994)
Writer/Director: Frank Darabont

'Apt Pupil' (1982)
Apt Pupil (1997)
Director: Bryan Singer
Writer: Brandon Boyce

'1408'
1408 (2007)
Director: Mikael Håfström
Writers: Matt Greenberg, Stephen Alexander, Larry Karaszewski

W. P. Kinsella
'Shoeless Joe Jackson Comes to Iowa' (1982)
Field of Dreams (1989)
Writer/Director: Phil Alden Robinson

Rudyard Kipling
The Jungle Book (1894)
Jungle Book (1967)
Director: Rolfgang Reitherman
Writers: Larry Clemmons, Ralph Wright, Ken Anderson

'The Man Who Would Be King' (1888)
The Man Who Would Be King (1975)
Director: John Huston
Writers: John Huston, Gladys Hill

Hanif Kureishi
'My Son the Fanatic' (1997)

My Son the Fanatic (GB 1997)
Director: Udayan Prassad
Writer: Hanif Kureishi

D. H. Lawrence
'The Rocking Horse Winner' (1926)
The Rocking Horse Winner (1949)
Writer/Director: Anthony Pelissier

'The Virgin and the Gypsy' (1930)
The Virgin and the Gypsy (1970)
Director: Christopher Miles
Writer: Alan Plater

George Langelaan
'The Fly' (1957)
The Fly (1958)
Director: Kurt Neumann
Writer: James Clavell

The Fly (1986)
Director: David Cronenberg
Writers: Charles Edward Pogue, David Cronenberg

Elmore Leonard
'Three Ten to Yuma' (1953)
3: 10 to Yuma (1957)
Director: Delmer Dawes
Writer: Halsted Welles

3: 10 to Yuma (2007)
Director: James Mangold
Writers: Michael Brandt and David Haas

H. P. Lovecraft
A large body of films has been based on, or inspired by, Lovecraft's weird tales. This is a brief selection. We might also add John Carpenter's *In the Mouth of Madness* (1994), scripted by Michael de Luca, which is a re-imagining of Lovecraft's Cthulhu Mythos.

For a longer list see *The Complete H. P. Lovecraft Filmography* by Charles P. Mitchell (Westwood: Greenwood, 2001). There is a well-established H. P. Lovecraft film festival in Portland, Oregon: http://www.hplfilmfestival.com.

'Herbert West – Re-Animator: Six Shots by Moonlight' (1922)
Re-Animator (1985)
Director: Stuart Gordon
Writers: Dennis Paoli, William J. Norris, Stuart Gordon

'Dagon' (1919), 'The Shadow Over Innsmouth' (1936)
Dagon (2001)
Director: Stuart Gordon
Writer: Dennis Paoli

'The Call of Cthulhu' (1928)
The Call of Cthulhu (2005)
Director: Andrew H. Leman
(Silent production, under the auspices of the H. P. Lovecraft Historical Society)

Thomas Mann
'Death in Venice' (1912)
Death in Venice (1971)
Director: Luchino Visconti
Writers: Luchino Visconti, Nicola Badalucco

W. Somerset Maugham
Three British compilations, showcasing stories by Maugham, were released in the post-war years. The most important of these is *Quartet* (1948), with adaptations of 'The Facts of Life', 'The Alien Corn', 'The Kite' and 'The Colonel's Lady' written by R. C. Sherriff. The sections were directed, respectively, by Ralph Smart, Harold French, Arthur Crabtree and Ken Annakin. *Quartet* was followed by *Trio* (1950, directed by Ken Annakin and Harold French; writers R. C. Sherriff and Noel Langley); and *Encore* (1951, directors: Pat Jackson, Anthony Pelissier, Harold French; writers: T. E. B. Clarke, Arthur Macrae, Eric Ambler).

'Sadie Thompson' (1921) – also published as 'Rain'
Sadie Thompson (1928)
Director: Raoul Walsh
Writer: C. Gardner Sullivan

Rain (1932)
Director: Lewis Milestone
Writer: Maxwell Anderson

Miss Sadie Thompson (1953)
Director: Curtis Bernhardt
Writer: Harry Kleiner

John McGahern
'Korea' (1970)
Korea (1995)
Director: Cathal Black
Writer: Joe O'Byrne

Steven Millhauser
'Eisenheim the Illusionist' (1989)
The Illusionist (2006)
Writer/Director: Neil Burger

Prabhat K. Mukherjee
'The Goddess' (1899)
Devi (1960)
Writer/Director: Satyajit Ray

Alice Munro
'The Bear Came Over the Mountain' (2001)
Away From Her (2006)
Writer/Director: Sarah Polley

'Hateship, Friendship, Courtship, Loveship, Marriage' (2001)
Hateship, Friendship, Courtship (in production 2011)
Director: Noam Murro
Writer: Mark Poirier

Haruki Murakami
'Tony Takitani' (2002)
Tony Takitani (2004)
Writer/Director: Jun Ichikawa

Jonathan Nolan
'Memento Mori' (2000)
Memento (2000)
Writer/Director: Christopher Nolan

Joyce Carol Oates
'Where Are You Going, Where Have You Been?' (1966)
Smooth Talk (1985)
Director: Joyce Chopra
Writer: Tom Cole

Mary Orr
'The Wisdom of Eve' (1946)
All About Eve (US 1950)
Writer/Director: Joseph L. Mankiewicz

Edgar Allan Poe
'The Fall of the House of Usher' (1839)
The Fall of the House of Usher (1960)
Director: Roger Corman
Writer: Richard Matheson

'The Pit and the Pendulum' (1842)
The Pit and the Pendulum (1961)
Director: Roger Corman
Writer: Richard Matheson

'The Premature Burial' (1844)
The Premature Burial (1961)
Director: Roger Corman
Writers: Charles Beaumont, Ray Russell

'Morella' (1835), 'The Black Cat' (1843), 'The Facts in the Case of M. Valdemar' (1845)
Tales of Terror (1962)
Director: Roger Corman
Writer: Richard Matheson

'Ligeia' (1838)
The Tomb of Ligeia (1964)
Director: Roger Corman
Writer: Robert Towne

'The Masque of the Red Death' (1842)
The Masque of the Red Death (1964)
Director: Roger Corman
Writers: Charles Beaumont, R. Wright Campbell

Munshi Premchand,
'The Chess Players' (1918)
The Chess Players (1977)
Writer/Director: Satyajit Ray

Annie Proulx
'Brokeback Mountain' (1997)
Brokeback Mountain (2005)
Director: Ang Lee
Writers: Larry McMurtry, Diana Ossana

Tod Robbins
'Spurs' (1926)
Freaks (1932)
Director: Todd Browning
Writers: Willis Goldbeck, Leon Gordon

Alan Sillitoe
'The Loneliness of the Long Distance Runner' (1959)
The Loneliness of the Long Distance Runner (1962)
Director: Tony Richardson
Writer: Alan Sillitoe

Koji Suzuki
'Floating Water' (1996)
Dark Water (2002)
Director: Hideo Nakata
Writers: Yoshihiro Nakamura, Hitomi Kuroki

Dark Water (2005)
Director: Walter Salles
Writer: Rafael Yglesias

Amy Tan
The Joy Luck Club (1989)
The Joy Luck Club (1993)
Director: Wayne Wang
Writers: Amy Tan, Ronald Bass

F. X. Toole
Rope Burns (2000 – later republished as *Million Dollar Baby*)
Million Dollar Baby (2004)
Director: Clint Eastwood
Writer: Paul Haggis

Maurice Walsh
'Green Rushes' (1933)
The Quiet Man (1952)

184 Appendix: Film Adaptations

Director: John Ford
Writer: Frank Nugent

Hagar Wilde
'Bringing Up Baby' (1937)
Bringing Up Baby (1938)
Director: Howard Hawks
Writers: Dudley Nichols, Hagar Wilde

Cornell Woolrich
'It Had to Be Murder' (1942)
Rear Window (US 1954)
Director: Alfred Hitchcock
Writer: John Michael Hayes

Liu Yichang
'Intersection' (1995)
In the Mood for Love (2000)
Writer/Director: Wong Kar-Wei

Further Reading

References

Critical Survey of Short Fiction. Hackensack, NJ: Salem Publishing, 2001. Seven volumes, with information on authors listed by name.
Short Story Criticism: Excerpts from Criticism of the Works of Short Fiction Writers. Farmington Hills, MI: Gale. This is an ongoing multi-volume series featuring biographical details, bibliographies and critical excerpts.
Dictionary of Literary Biography. Farmington Hills, MI: Gale. Multi-volume encyclopedia, including many volumes devoted to short story writers within specific periods, for example *218 American Short Story Writers Since WW2*.
Baldwin, Dean and Gregory L. Morris. *The Short Story in English. Britain and North America: An Annotated Bibliography*. Lanham, MD: Scarecrow Press, 1994.
Fallon, Erin, R. C. Feddersen, James Kurtzleben, Maurice A. Lee and Susan Rochette-Crawley, eds. *A Reader's Companion to the Short Story in English*. Greenwich, CT: Greenwood Press, 2001.
Gelfant, Blanche H., ed. *The Columbia Companion to the Twentieth-century American Short Story*. New York: University Presses of California, Columbia and Princeton, 2004.
Huang, Guiyou. *Asian American Short Story Writers: An A-to-Z Guide*. Westport, CT: Greenwood Press, 2003.
Magill, Frank N. *Masterplots II. Short Story*. Hackensack, NJ: Salem Publishing, 1987.
Mann, Susan Garland. *The Short Story Cycle: A Genre Companion and Reference Guide*. Westport, CT: Greenwood Press, 1988.
Maunder, Andrew, ed. *The Facts on File Companion to the British Short Story*. New York: Facts on File Inc., 2007.
May, Charles E. *Short Story Writers*. Lanham, MD: Scarecrow Press, 2008.
Rasmussen, R. Kent and Charles E. May. *Masterplots II. Short Story Series*. Hackensack, NJ: Salem Publishing, 2004.
Walker, Warren S. and Wendell M. Aycock, eds. *Twentieth Century Short Story Explications*. North Haven, CT: Shoestring Press, 1999. With supplements and new series. Resource for finding book and journal criticism on short stories from the twentieth century and earlier eras.
Watson, Noelle. *Reference Guide to Short Fiction*. London: St James Press, 1998.
Werlock, Abby H. P., ed. *The Facts on File Companion to the American Short Story*. New York: Facts on File Inc., 1999.

Surveys and Genre Criticism

Bardolph, Jacqueline, ed. *Telling Stories: Postcolonial Short Fiction in English*. Amsterdam: Rodophi, 2001.
Bayley, John. *The Short Story: Henry James to Elizabeth Bowen*. Brighton: Harvester, 1988.

Benson, Stephen, ed. *Contemporary Fiction and the Fairy Tale*. Detroit, MI: Wayne State University Press, 2008.
Burke, Daniel. *Beyond Interpretation: Studies in the Modern Short Story*. New York: Whiston, 1991.
Cox, Ailsa, ed. *The Short Story*. Newcastle upon Tyne: Cambridge Scholars, 2009.
Dunn, Maggie and Ann Morris. *The Composite Novel: Short Story Cycle in Transition*. New York: Twayne, 1995.
Garcia, Gema Soledad Castillo, Maria Rosa Cabellos Castilla, Juan Antonio Sanchez Jimenez and Vincent Carlisle Espinola, eds. *The Short Story in English: Crossing Boundaries*. Alcalá de Henares: Universidad de Alcalá, 2007.
Gerlach, John. *Toward the End: Closure and Structure in the American Short Story*. Tuscaloosa, AL: University of Alabama Press, 1985.
Hanson, Clare. *Short Stories and Short Fictions, 1880–1980*. Basingstoke: Macmillan – now Palgrave Macmillan, 1985.
Hanson, Clare, ed. *Re-Reading the Short Story*. Basingstoke: Macmillan – now Palgrave Macmillan, 1989.
Head, Dominic. *The Modernist Short Story: A Study in Theory and Practice*. Cambridge: Cambridge University Press, 2009.
Hunter, Adrian. *The Cambridge Introduction to the Short Story in English*. Cambridge: Cambridge University Press, 2007.
Iftekharrudin, Farhat, Joseph Boyden, Mary Rohrberger and Jaie Claudet, eds. *The Postmodern Short Story*. Westport, CT: Praeger, 2003.
Ingram, Forrest L. *Representative Short Story Cycles of the Twentieth Century*. The Hague: Mouton, 1971.
Kennedy, J. Gerald, ed. *Modern American Short Story Sequences: Composite Fictions and Fictive Communities*. Cambridge, MA: Cambridge University Press, 1995.
Lohafer, Susan. *Coming to Terms with the Short Story*. Baton Rouge, LA: Louisiana State University Press, 1983.
Lohafer, Susan. *Reading for Storyness: Preclosure Theory, Empirical Poetics, and Culture in the Short Story*. Baltimore, MD: Johns Hopkins, 2003.
Lohafer, Susan and Jo Ellyn Clarey, eds. *Short Story Theory at a Crossroads*. Baton Rouge, LA: Louisiana State University Press, 1989.
Lothe, Jakob, Hans H. Skei and Per Winther, eds. *Less Is More: Short Fiction Theory and Analysis*. Oslo: Novus, 2008.
Lounsberry, Barbara, Susan Lohafer, Mary Rohrberger, Stephen Pett and R. C. Feddersen, eds. *The Tales We Tell*. Greenwich, CT: Greenwood Press, 1998.
March-Russell, Paul. *The Short Story: An Introduction*. Edinburgh: Edinburgh University Press, 2009.
May, Charles E., ed., *The New Short Story Theories*. Athens, OH: Ohio University Press, 1994.
May, Charles E. *The Short Story: the Reality of Artifice*. London: Routledge, 2002.
McSweeney, Kerry. *The Realist Short Story of the Powerful Glimpse: Carver to Chekhov*. Columbia, SC: University of South Carolina Press, 2007.
Pacht, Michelle. *The Subversive Storyteller: The Short Story Cycle and the Politics of Identity*. Newcastle upon Tyne: Cambridge Scholars, 2009.
Reid, Ian. *The Short Story*. London: Routledge, 1977.
Shaw, Valerie. *The Short Story: A Critical Introduction*. London and New York: Longman, 1983.

Toolan, Michael. *Narrative Progression in the Short Story*. Basingstoke: Palgrave Macmillan, 2008.
Winther, Per, Jakob Lothe and Hans H. Skei, eds. *The Art of Brevity: Excursions in Short Fiction, Theory and Analysis*. Columbia, SC: University of South Carolina Press, 2004.

US and Canada

Bendixen, Alfred and James Nagel, eds. *A Companion to the American Short Story*. Chichester: Blackwell, 2009.
Curnutt, Kirk. *Wise Economies: Brevity and Storytelling in American Short Stories*. Moscow, ID: University of Idaho Press, 1997.
Delville, Michael. *The American Prose Poem: Poetic Form and the Boundaries of Genre*. Gainesville, FL: University Press of Florida, 1998.
Dvorak, Marta and W. H. New, eds. *Tropes and Territories: Short Fiction, Postcolonial Readings, Canadian Writings in Context*. Montreal: McGill-Queen's University Press, 2007.
Huntington, John. *Rationalising Genius: Ideological Strategies in the Classic American Science Fiction Short Story*. New Brunswick, NJ: Rutgers University Press, 1989.
Lunden, Rolf. *The United Stories of America. Studies in the Short Story Composite*. Amsterdam: Rodopi, 1999.
New, W. H. *Dreams of Speech and Violence: Art of the Short Story in Canada and New Zealand*. Toronto: University of Toronto Press, 1987.
Nischik, Reingard M., ed. *The Canadian Short Story: Interpretations*. Columbia, MD: Boydell & Brewer Ltd., 2007.
Scofield, Martin. *The Cambridge Book of the American Short Story*. Cambridge: Cambridge University Press, 2006.

Authors and Texts

Asals, Frederick. *'A Good Man is Hard to Find': Flannery O'Connor*. New Brunswick, NJ: Rutgers University Press, 1993.
Beer, Janet. *Kate Chopin, Edith Wharton and Charlotte Perkins Gilman: Studies in Short Fiction*. London: Palgrave Macmillan, 2005.
Bell, Elizabeth S. *Kay Boyle: A Study of the Short Fiction*. New York: Twayne, 1992.
Benson, Jackson. *Wallace Stegner: A Study of the Short Fiction*. New York: Twayne, 1999.
Boswell, Marshall. *Understanding David Foster Wallace*. Columbia, SC: University of South Carolina Press, 2003.
Brantley, Susan C. *Understanding Isak Dinesen*. Columbia, SC: University of South Carolina Press, 2002.
Byerman, Keith Eldon. *John Edgar Wideman: A Study of the Short Fiction*. New York: Twayne, 1998.
Campbell, Ewing. *Raymond Carver: A Study of the Short Fiction*. New York: Twayne, 1992.
Carr, Virginia Spencer, ed. *'Flowering Judas': Katherine Anne Porter*. New Brunswick, NJ: Rutgers University Press, 1993.
Carr, Virginia Spencer. *Understanding Carson McCullers*. Columbia, SC: University of South Carolina Press, 2005.

Christian, Barbara T., ed. *'Everyday Use': Alice Walker*. New Brunswick, NJ: Rutgers University Press, 1994.
Clement, Lesley. *Learning to Look: A Visual Response to Mavis Gallant's Fiction*. Montreal: McGill-Queen's University Press, 2000.
Crowley, John W., ed. *New Essays on 'Winesburg, Ohio.'* Cambridge: Cambridge University Press, 1990.
Cummins, Elisabeth. *Understanding Ursula K. LeGuin*. Columbia, SC: University of South Carolina Press, 1990.
Davis, Philip. *Bernard Malamud: A Writer's Life*. Oxford: Oxford University Press, 2007.
Donaldson, Scott, ed. *The Cambridge Companion to Ernest Hemingway*. Cambridge: Cambridge University Press, 1996.
Earley, Margaret. *Understanding Flannery O'Connor*. Columbia, SC: University of South Carolina Press, 1997.
Evenson, Brian K. *Understanding Robert Coover*. Columbia, SC: University of South Carolina Press, 2003.
Farrier, David. *Unsettled Narratives: The Pacific Writings of Stevenson, Ellis, Melville and London*. London: Routledge, 2006.
Foster, Edward Halsey. *William Saroyan: A Study of the Short Fiction*. New York: Twayne, 1991.
Fracasso, Evelyn E. *Edith Wharton's Prisoners of Consciousness: A Study of Theme and Technique in the Tales*. Westport, CT: Greenwood Press, 1994.
Friedman, Lawrence S. *Understanding Cynthia Ozick*. Columbia, SC: University of South Carolina Press, 1991.
Fusco, Richard. *Maupassant and the American Short Story*. Pennsylvania: Pennsylvania State University Press, 1990.
Garson, Helen S. *Truman Capote: A Study of the Short Fiction*. New York: Twayne, 1992.
Gentry, Marshall Bruce and William L. Stull, eds. *Conversations with Raymond Carver*. Jackson, MS: University Press of Mississippi, 1990.
George, Dana Del. *The Supernatural in Short Fiction of the Americas*. Westport, CT: Greenwood Press, 2001.
Grassian, Daniel. *Understanding Sherman Alexie*. Columbia, SC: University of South Carolina Press, 2005.
Graulich, Melody, ed. *'Yellow Woman': Leslie Marmon Silko*. New Brunswick, NJ: Rutgers University Press, 1993.
Hallett, Cynthia Whitney. *Minimalism and the Short Story: Raymond Carver, Amy Hempel and Mary Robison*. New York: Edward Mellen Press, 1999.
Hannah, James. *Tobias Wolff: A Study of the Short Fiction*. New York: Twayne, 1996.
Henderson, Jeff. *John Gardner: A Study of the Short Fiction*. New York: Twayne, 1990.
Hibbard, Allen. *Paul Bowles: A Study of the Short Fiction*. New York: Twayne, 1993.
Jaskoski, Helen. *Leslie Marmon Silko: A Study of the Short Fiction*. New York: Twayne, 1999.
Johnson, Greg. *Joyce Carol Oates: A Study of the Short Fiction*. New York: Twayne, 1994.

Kelly, Alison. *Understanding Lorrie Moore*. Columbia, SC: University of South Carolina Press, 2009.
Kennedy, Thomas E. *Andre Dubus: A Study of the Short Fiction*. New York: Twayne, 1988.
Kennedy, Thomas E. *Robert Coover: A Study of the Short Fiction*. New York: Twayne, 1992.
Kleppe, Sandra Lee and Robert Miltner, eds. *New Paths to Raymond Carver: Critical Essays on his Life, Fiction and Poetry*. Columbia, SC: University of South Carolina Press, 2008.
Koloski, Bernard. *Kate Chopin: A Study of the Short Fiction*. New York: Twayne, 1996.
Kopley, Richard. *Edgar Allan Poe and the Dupin Mysteries*. Basingstoke: Palgrave Macmillan, 2009.
Kreyling, Michael. *Understanding Eudora Welty*. Columbia, SC: University of South Carolina Press, 1999.
Lainsbury, G. P. *The Carver Chronotope: Inside the Life-world of Raymond Carver's Fiction*. London: Routledge, 2003.
Luscher, Robert M., ed. *John Updike: A Study of the Short Fiction*. New York: Twayne, 1993.
Martin, Terry R. *Rhetorical Deception in the Short Fiction of Hawthorne, Poe and Melville*. New York: Edward Mellen Press, 1998.
May, Charles E. *Edgar Allan Poe: A Study of the Short Fiction*. New York: Twayne, 1993.
Millichap, Joseph R. *Robert Penn Warren: A Study of the Short Fiction*. New York: Twayne, 1992.
Nesset, Kirk. *The Stories of Raymond Carver: A Critical Study*. Athens, OH: Ohio University Press, 1995.
O'Hare, James. *John Cheever: A Study of the Short Fiction*. New York: Twayne, 1991.
Papinchak, Robert Allen. *Sherwood Anderson: A Study of the Short Fiction*. New York: Twayne, 1992.
Price, Joanna. *Understanding Bobbie Ann Mason*. Columbia, SC: University of South Carolina Press, 2000.
Reesman, Jeanne Campbell. *Jack London: A Study of the Short Fiction*. New York: Twayne, 1999.
Roe, Barbara L. *Donald Barthelme: A Study of the Short Fiction*. New York: Twayne, 1992.
Rood, Karen L. *Understanding Annie Proulx*. Columbia, SC: University of South Carolina Press, 2001.
Rosenfelt, Deborah Silverton, ed. *'Tell Me a Riddle': Tillie Olsen*. New Brunswick, NJ: Rutgers University Press, 2006.
Runyon, Randolph Paul. *Reading Raymond Carver*. New York: Syracuse University Press, 1992.
Schaub, Danielle. *Mavis Gallant*. New York: Twayne, 1998.
Schmidt, Peter. *The Heart of the Story: Eudora Welty's Short Fiction*. Jackson, MS: University Press of Mississippi, 1991.
Seel, Cynthia L. *Ritual Performance in the Fiction of Flannery O'Connor*. Columbia, SC: Boydell and Brewer, 2000.
Showalter, Elaine, ed. *'Where Are You Going, Where Have You Been?': Joyce Carol Oates*. New Brunswick, NJ: Rutgers University Press, 1994.

Skei, Hans H. *Reading Faulkner's Best Short Stories*. Columbia, SC: University of South Carolina Press, 1999.

Smith, Paul, ed. *New Essays on Hemingway's Short Fiction*. Cambridge: Cambridge University Press, 1998.

Smythe, Karen E. *Figuring Grief: Munro, Gallant and the Poetics of Elegy*. Montreal: McGill-Queen's University Press, 1992.

Stacy, James, ed. *Reading 'Brokeback Mountain': Essays on the Story and the Film*. Jefferson, NC: McFarland & Co, 2007.

Strengell, Heidi. *Monsters Live in Ordinary People: the Novels and Stories of Stephen King*. London: Duckworth, 2007.

Stull, William L. and Maureen Carroll, eds. *Remembering Ray: A Composite Biography of Raymond Carver*. Santa Barbara, CA: Capra Press, 1993.

Tetlow, Wendolyn. *Ernest Hemingway's 'In Our Time': Lyrical Dimensions*. Cranbury, NJ: University of Bucknell Press, 1992.

Troth, Emily. *Unveiling Kate Chopin*. Jackson, MS: University Press of Mississippi, 1999.

Volpe, Edmond L. *A Reader's Guide to William Faulkner: The Short Stories*. New York: Syracuse University Press, 2004.

Wall, Cheryl A., ed. *'Sweat': Written by Zora Neale Hurston*. New Brunswick, NJ: Rutgers University Press, 1996.

Whalan, Mark. *Race, Manhood, and Modernism in America: The Short Story Cycles of Sherwood Anderson and Jean Toomer*. Knoxville, TN: University of Tennessee Press, 2007.

White, Barbara Anne. *Edith Wharton: A Study of the Short Fiction*. New York: Twayne, 1992.

Wilhelm, Albert. *Bobbie Ann Mason: A Study of the Short Fiction*. New York: Twayne, 1998.

Wolford, Chester. *Stephen Crane: A Study of the Short Fiction*. New York: Twayne, 1989.

Wong, Hertha D. Sweet, ed. *Louise Erdrich's Love Medicine: A Casebook*. New York: Oxford University Press, 1999.

Wonham, Henry B. *Mark Twain and the Art of the Tall Tale*. New York: Oxford University Press USA, 1993.

Anthologies

The Best American Short Stories is a prestigious annual anthology, founded in 1915. Readers may want to supplement this authoritative volume with the more playful *McSweeney's* published regularly in the UK by Hamish Hamilton/Penguin.

Blackstone, Jill and Charles Talbot. *The Art of Friction: Where (Non)Fictions Come Together*. Austin, TX: University of Texas Press, 2008.

Cooper, Dennis, ed. *Userlands: New Fiction from the Blogging Underground*. New York: Akashic Books, 2007.

Eggers, Dave, ed. *McSweeney's 29*. London: Hamish Hamilton, 2009.

Ford, Richard. *The Granta Book of the American Long Story*. London: Granta, 1999.

Ford, Richard. *The New Granta Book of the American Short Story*. London: Granta, 2007.

King, Stephen, ed. *The Best American Short Stories*. Boston, MA: Houghton Mifflin, 2007.

New, W. H., ed. Canadian Short Fiction. Scarborough, ON: Prentice Hall, 1997.
Nguyen, B. Minh and Shreve Porter, eds. *30/30: Thirty American Stories from the Last Thirty Years*. New York: Longman, 2005.
Rosenthal, Lucy, ed. *The Eloquent Short Story: An Anthology – Varieties of Narration*. London: W. W. Norton & Co. Ltd., 2003.
Rushdie, Salman, ed. *The Best American Short Stories*. Boston, MA: Houghton Mifflin, 2008.
Shapard, Robert and James Thomas, eds. *New Sudden Fiction*. London: W. W. Norton & Co. Ltd., 2007.
Urquhart, Jane, ed. *The Penguin Book of Canadian Short Stories*. Toronto: Penguin, 2007.

Britain and Ireland

English, James F., ed. *A Concise Companion to Contemporary British Fiction*. Oxford: Blackwell, 2005.
Ingman, Heather. *A History of the Irish Short Story*. Cambridge: Cambridge University Press, 2009.
Malcolm, David and Cheryl Malcolm, eds. *A Companion to the British and Irish Short Story*. Chichester: Blackwell, 2008.
Orel, Harold. *The Victorian Short Story: Development and Triumph of a Literary Genre*. Cambridge: Cambridge University Press, 1986.

Authors and Texts

Baldwin, Dean. *V. S. Pritchett*. New York: Twayne, 1987.
Benzel, Kathryn N. and Ruth Hoberman, eds. *Trespassing Boundaries: Virginia Woolf's Short Fiction*. Basingstoke: Palgrave Macmillan, 2004.
Bloom, Jonathan. *The Art of Revision in the Short Stories of V. S. Pritchett and William Trevor*. Basingstoke: Palgrave Macmillan, 2007.
Bollettieri Bosinelli, Rosa M. and Harold F. Moscher Jnr, eds. *ReJoycing: New Readings of Dubliners*. Lexington, KY: University Press of Kentucky, 1998.
Brady, Kristin. *The Short Stories of Thomas Hardy*. Basingstoke: Palgrave Macmillan, 1982.
Byrne, Sandie. *The Unbearable Saki*. Oxford: Oxford University Press, 2007.
Cochran, Robert. *Samuel Beckett: A Study of the Short Fiction*. New York: Twayne, 1991.
Delville, Michael. *J. G. Ballard*. Plymouth: Northcote House, 1998.
Erdinast-Vulcan, Daphna. *The Strange Short Fiction of Joseph Conrad: Writing, Culture and Subjectivity*. Oxford: Oxford University Press, 1999.
Gamble, Sarah. *Angela Carter: A Literary Life*. Basingstoke: Palgrave Macmillan, 2006.
Gasiorek, Andrzej. *J. G. Ballard*. Manchester: Manchester University Press, 2005.
Gilmartin, Sophie and Rod Mengham. *Thomas Hardy's Shorter Fiction: A Critical Study*. Edinburgh: Edinburgh University Press, 2007.
Guignery, Vanessa. *The Fiction of Julian Barnes: A Reader's Guide to Essential Criticism*. Basingstoke: Palgrave Macmillan, 2006.
Hammond, J. R. *H. G. Wells and the Short Story*. Basingstoke: Palgrave Macmillan, 1992.

Hunter, Hayes M. *Understanding Will Self.* Columbia, SC: University of South Carolina Press, 2007.
Kemp, Sandra. *Kipling's Hidden Narratives.* Oxford: Blackwell, 1988.
Killeen, Jarlath. *The Fairy Tales of Oscar Wilde.* Aldershot: Ashgate, 2007.
Lassner, Phyllis. *Elizabeth Bowen: A Study of the Short Fiction.* New York: Twayne, 1991.
Lennon, Hilary, ed. *Frank O'Connor: New Critical Essays.* Dublin: Four Courts Press, 2007.
Norris, Leslie. *Glyn Jones.* Cardiff: University of Wales Press, 1997.
Paulson, Suzanne Morrow. *William Trevor: A Study of the Short Fiction.* New York: Twayne, 1993.
Peach, Linden. *The Prose Writings of Dylan Thomas.* London: Barnes & Noble, 1988.
Roemer, Danielle M. and Christina Bacchilega. *Angela Carter and the Fairy Tale.* Detroit, MI: Wayne State University Press, 2001.
Ryan, Kiernan. *Ian McEwan.* Plymouth: Northcote House, 1994.
Sage, Lorna. *Angela Carter.* Plymouth: Northcote House, 2006.
Smith, Angela. *Katherine Mansfield and Virginia Woolf: A Public of Two.* Oxford: Oxford University Press, 1999.
Stinson, John L. *V. S. Pritchett: A Study of the Short Fiction.* New York: Twayne, 1992.
Thacker, Andrew, ed. *Dubliners: Contemporary Critical Essays.* Basingstoke: Palgrave Macmillan, 2005.
Treglown, Jeremy. *V. S. Pritchett: A Working Life.* London: Chatto, 2004.

Anthologies

Ashley, Allen, ed. *Subtle Edens.* Norfolk, VA: Elastic Press, 2008.
Blincoe, Nicholas and Matt Thorne, eds. *All Hail the New Puritans.* London: Fourth Estate, 2000.
Byatt, A. S., ed. *The Oxford Book of English Short Stories.* Oxford: Oxford University Press, 2002.
Crossan, Maria and Tom Palmer, eds. *The Book of Leeds.* Manchester: Comma Press, 2006.
Dunn, Douglas. *The Oxford Book of Scottish Short Stories.* Oxford: Oxford University Press, 1995.
Eyre, Sarah and Ra Page, eds. *The New Uncanny.* Manchester: Comma, 2008.
Golden, Christopher, Tim Lebbon and James A. Moore, eds. *British Invasion.* Forest Hill, MD: Cemetery Dance Publications, 2009.
Kravitz, Peter, ed. *The Picador Book of Contemporary Scottish Fiction.* London: Picador, 1997.
Marcus, David. The Faber Book of Best New Irish Stories. London: Faber, 2007.
Rees, Eleanor and Maria Crossnan. *The Book of Liverpool.* Manchester: Comma Press, 2005.
Royle, Nicholas, ed. *A Book of Two Halves: New Football Stories.* London: Phoenix, 2001.
Royle, Nicholas. *Dreams Never End.* Birmingham: Tindal Street Press, 2004.
Royle, Nicholas. *68: New Stories from Children of the Revolution.* Cambridge: Salt Publishing, 2008.
Trevor, William, ed. *The Oxford Book of Irish Short Stories.* Oxford: Oxford University Press, 2001.

Unsworth, Cathi, ed. *London Noir*. London: Serpent's Tail, 2006.
Wild, Peter, ed. *Perverted by Language: Fiction Inspired by The Fall*. London: Serpent's Tail, 2007.

Africa, South East Asia and the Caribbean

Balogun, F. Odun. *Tradition and Modernity in the African Short Story: An Introduction to a Literature in Search of Critics*. Westport, CT: Greenwood Press, 1991.
Barbalsingh, Frank, ed. *Frontiers of Caribbean Literature in English*. New York: St. Martins, 1999.
Conde, Mary and Thorunn Lonsdale, eds. *Caribbean Women Writers: Fiction in English*. New York: St. Martins, 1999.
Dance, Daryl Cumber. *New World Adams: Conversations with Contemporary West Indian Writers*. Leeds: Peepal Tree, 1992.
Ramanan, Mohan and P. Sailaja, eds. *English and the Indian Short Story: Essays in Criticism*. Himayatnagar, Hyderabad: Orient Longman, 2000.

Authors and Texts

Bhattacharya, France. *Rabindranath Tagore in Perspective: A Bunch of Essays*. Calcutta: Visva-Bharati, 1989.
Chakoo, B. L. *Social Play and Metaphysical Symbolism in Raja Rao's Stories*. Amritsar: Guru Nanak De University, 2000.
Dutta, Krishna and Andrew Robinson. *Rabindranath Tagore: The Myriad-Minded Man*. New York: St. Martin's, 1995.
Edwards, Justin D. *Understanding Jamaica Kincaid*. Columbia, SC: University of South Carolina Press, 2007.
Malcolm, Cheryl Alexander and David Malcolm, *Jean Rhys: A Study of the Short Fiction*. New York: Twayne, 1996.
Mohan, T. M. J. Indra, ed. *Shashi Deshpande: A Critical Spectrum*. New Delhi: Atlantic, 2004.
Morrison, Jago. *The Fiction of Chinua Achebe*. Basingstoke: Palgrave Macmillan, 2007.
Paravisini-Gebert, Lizabeth. *Jamaica Kincaid: A Critical Companion*. Westport, CT: Greenwood Press, 1999.
Savory, Elaine. *The Cambridge Introduction to Jean Rhys*. Cambridge: University of Cambridge Press, 2009.
Sethi, Vijay Mohan. *Mulk Raj Anand: Short Story Writer*. New Delhi: Ashish Publishing House, 1990.

Anthologies

Achebe, Chinua and C. L. Innes, eds. *The Heinemann Book of Contemporary African Stories*. Oxford: Heinemann, 1992.
Brown, Stuart, ed. *Caribbean New Wave: Contemporary Short Stories*. Oxford: Heinemann International, 1990.
Chandersekaran, Achamma C., trans. *Daughters of Kerala: Twenty-Five Short Stories by Award-Winning Authors*. Tucson, AZ: Hats Off Books, 2004.
Chaudhuri, Amit, ed. *The Vintage Book of Modern Indian Literature*. New York: Random House, 2004.

Cowasjee, Saros, ed. *The Oxford Anthology of Raj Stories*. Delhi: Oxford University Press, 1998.
Cowasjee, Saros and Kartar Singh Duggal, eds. *When the British Left: Stories on the Partitioning of India*. New Delhi: Arnold-Heinemann, 1987.
Das, Monica, ed. *Her Story So Far: Tales of the Girl Child in India*. Delhi: Penguin India, 2003.
Markham, E. A., ed. *The Penguin Book of the Caribbean Short Story*. Harmondsworth: Penguin, 1996.
Morris, Mervyn, ed. *The Faber Book of Contemporary Caribbean Short Stories*. London: Faber and Faber Limited, 1990.
Ramakrishnan, E. V., ed. *Indian Short Stories, 1900–2000*. New Delhi: Sahitya Akademi, 2000.
Wickham, John and Stewart Brown. *The Oxford Book of Caribbean Short Stories*. Oxford: Oxford University Press, 2001.

Australia and New Zealand

Ben-Messahel, Salhia. *Mind the Country: Tim Winton's Fiction*. Crawley, WA: University of Western Australia University Press, 2007.
Bennett, Bruce. *Australian Short Fiction: A History*. St Lucia, Queensland: University of Queensland Press, 2000.
Dubar, Pamela. *Radical Mansfield: Double Discourse in Katherine Mansfield's Short Stories*. Basingstoke: Macmillan – now Palgrave Macmillan, 1997.
Kaplan, Sydney Janet. *Katherine Mansfield and the Origins of Modernist Fiction*. Ithaca, NY: Cornell University Press, 1991.
New, W. H. *Dreams of Speech and Violence: Art of the Short Story in Canada and New Zealand*. Toronto: University of Toronto Press, 1987.
Smith, Angela. *Katherine Mansfield: A Literary Life*. Basingstoke: Palgrave Macmillan, 2000.
Stead, C. K. *Kin of Place: Essays on New Zealand Writers*. Auckland: Auckland University Press, 2002.

Anthologies

Gelder, Kenneth and Rachael Weaver. *The MUP Anthology of Colonial Gothic Australian Fiction*. Carlton: Melbourne University Press, 2007.
Lord, Mary, ed. *The Penguin Best Australian Short Stories*. London: Penguin, 2001.
O'Sullivan, Vincent, ed. *The Oxford Book of New Zealand Short Stories*. Oxford: Oxford University Press, 1997.

Gender and Ethnicity

Bostrom, Melissa. *Sex, Race and Family in Contemporary American Short Stories*. Basingstoke: Palgrave Macmillan, 2007.
Brown, Julie, ed. *American Women Short Story Writers: A Collection of Critical Essays*. Hamden, CT: Garland, 2000.
Brown, Julie and William Cain, eds. *Ethnicity and the American Short Story*. Hamden, CT: Garland, 1997.

Dale, Corinne H. and J. H. E. Paine, eds. *Women on the Edge: Ethnicity and Gender in Short Stories by American Women*. Hamden, CT: Garland, 1999.
Ingman, Heather. *Twentieth-Century Fiction by Irish Women: Nation and Gender*. Aldershot: Ashgate, 2007.
Nagel, James. *The Contemporary American Short Story Cycle: The Ethnic Resonance of Genre*. Baton Rouge, LA: Louisiana State University Press, 2001.
Palumbo-DeSimone, Christine. *Sharing Secrets: Nineteenth Century Women's Relations in the Short Story*. Cranbury, NJ: Associated University Press, 2000.
Peach, Linden. *Contemporary Irish and Welsh Women's Fiction: Gender, Desire and Power*. Cardiff: University of Wales Press, 2007.
Wasi, Jehanara, ed. *A Storehouse of Tales: Contemporary Indian Women Writers*. New Delhi: Srishti, 2001.

Authors and Texts

Titles are listed under national categories. For American women authors, note especially the Rutgers University Press *Women Writers: Texts and Contexts* series, each of which consists of the full text of a story plus casebook.

Anthologies

Carter, Angela, ed. *Wayward Girls and Wicked Women*. London: Virago, 1986.
DeSalvo, Louise, Kathleen Walsh D'Arcy and Katherine Hogan, eds. *Territories of the Voice: Contemporary Stories By Irish Women Writers*. London: Virago Press, 1990.
Dharmarajan, Geeta and Mary Ellis Gibson, eds. *Separate Journey: Stories by Contemporary Indian Women*. Columbia, SC: University of South Carolina Press, 2004.
Gibson, Mary Ellis, ed. *New Stories by Southern Women*. Columbia, SC: University of South Carolina Press, 1989.
Hwyl, Elin ap, ed. *Luminous and Forlorn: Contemporary Short Stories by Women from Wales*. Dinas Powys, Wales: Honno, 1994.
Jones, Suzanne W., ed. *Crossing the Color Line: Readings in Black and White*. Columbia, SC: University of South Carolina Press, 2000.
Mazza, Cris and Jeffrey DeShell. *Chick-Lit: Postfeminist Fiction*. Tuscaloosa, AL: Fiction Collective 2, 1995.
Shamsie, Muneeza, ed. *And the World Changed: Contemporary Stories by Pakistani Women*. Delhi: Women United, 2005.
Ward, Candace. *Great Short Stories by English and Irish Women Writers*. New York: Dover, 2007.
Wong, Hertha Dawn, Lauren Stuart Muller and Jana Sequoya Magdaleno, eds. *Reckonings: Short Fiction by Native American Women*. New York: Oxford University Press 2008.

Publishing History

Ashley, Mike. *The Time Machines: the Story of the Science Fiction Magazines from the Beginning to 1950*. Liverpool: Liverpool University Press, 2000.
Ashley, Mike. *Transformations: the Story of the Science Fiction Magazines from 1950 to 1970*. Liverpool: Liverpool University Press, 2005.

Ashley, Mike. *The Age of the Storytellers: British Popular Fiction Magazines 1880–1950*. London: British Library, 2006.
Ashley, Mike. *Gateways to Forever: the Story of the Science Fiction Magazines from 1970 to 1980*. Liverpool: Liverpool University Press, 2007.
Brooker, Peter and Andrew Thacker, eds. *The Oxford Critical and Cultural History of Modernist Magazines. Vol. 1: Britain and Ireland 1880–1955*. Oxford: Oxford University Press, 2009.
Levy, Andrew. *The Culture and Commerce of the American Short Story*. Cambridge, MA: Cambridge University Press, 1993.
McGurl, Mark. *The Program Era: Postwar Fiction and the Rise of Creative Writing*. Cambridge, MA: Harvard University Press, 2009.

Writing Short Stories

Bailey, Tom, ed. *On Writing Short Stories*. New York: Oxford University Press, 1999.
Charters, Ann. *The Story and Its Writer: An Introduction to Short Fiction*. New York: St. Martin's Press, 1987.
Iftekharudinn, Farhat, Mary Rohrberger and Maurice Lee, eds. *Speaking of the Short Story: Interviews with Contemporary Writers*. Jackson, MS: University Press of Mississippi, 1997.
Kaylor, Noel Harold. *Creative and Critical Approaches to the Short Story*. New York: Edwin Mellen Press, 1997.
Kruk, Laurie. *Voice is the Story: Conversations with Canadian Writers of Short Fiction*. Oakville, ON: Mosaic, 2003.
Lee, Maurice A., ed. *Writers on Writing: The Art of the Short Story* Westport, CT: Greenwood Press, 2005.
Metcalf, John and J. R. (Tim) Struthers, eds. *How Stories Mean*. Ontario: Porcupine's Quill, 2001.

General Anthologies

Baldwin, Dean, ed. *The Riverside Anthology of Short Fiction: Convention and Innovation*. Boston, MA: Houghton Mifflin, 1997.
Baldwin, Dean and Patrick J. Quinn eds. *An Anthology of Colonial and Postcolonial Short Fiction*. Boston, MA: Houghton Mifflin, 2006.
Bohner, Charles and Grant Lyman, eds. *Short Fiction: Classic and Contemporary*. Indianapolis, IN: Prentice Hall, 2005.
Crossan, Maria. *Decapolis: Tales from Ten Cities*. Manchester: Comma Press, 2006.
Eugenides, Jeffrey, ed. *My Mistress's Sparrow Is Dead: Great Love Stories from Chekhov to Munro*. London: HarperCollins, 2008.
Gallagher, Tess, Claire Malcolm and Margaret Wilkinson, eds. *So, What Kept You? New Stories Inspired by Anton Chekhov and Raymond Carver*. Newcastle-upon-Tyne: Flambard, 2006.
Harrison, Stephanie, ed. *Adaptations: Short Story to Big Screen: 35 Great Short Stories That Have Inspired Great Films*. New York: Three Rivers Press, 2005.

Hartwell, David G. and Milton T. Wolf, eds. *Visions of Wonder: the Science Fiction Research Association Anthology*. New York: Tor, 1996.
Korte, Barbara and Ann-Marie Einhaus, eds. *The Penguin Book of First World War Stories*. London: Penguin Classics, 2007.
Mills, Mark, ed. *Crafting the Very Short Story: An Anthology of 100 Masterpieces*. Harlow: Prentice Hall, 2002.
Page, Ra, ed. *Comma*. Manchester: Comma Press, 2002.
Page, Ra, ed. *Hyphen*. Manchester: Comma Press, 2003.
Page, Ra, ed. *Bracket*. Manchester: Comma Press, 2004.
Page, Ra, ed. *Parenthesis*. Manchester: Comma Press, 2006.
Penzler, Otto, ed. *Dangerous Women*. London: Arrow, 2007.
Prescott, Linda, ed. *A World of Difference: An Anthology of Short Stories from Five Continents*. Basingstoke: Palgrave Macmillan, 2008.
Rabb, Jane M., ed. *Short Story and Photography 1880s–1980s: A Critical Anthology*. Albuquerque, NM: University of New Mexico Press, 1998.
Royle, Nicholas, ed. *The Time Out Book of Paris Short Stories*. Harmondsworth: Penguin, 1999.
Smith, Ali, Kasia Boddy and Sarah Woods, eds. *Let's Call the Whole Thing Off: Love Quarrels from Anton Chekhov to ZZ Packer*. London: Penguin, 2009.
Smith, Zadie, ed. *The Book of Other People*. London: Hamish Hamilton 2007.
Zimler, Richard and Raza Sekulovic, eds. *Children's Hours: Stories of Childhood*. London: Arcadia, 2008.

Science Fiction Anthologies

Fowler, Karen Joy, Pat Murphy, Debbie Notkin and Jeffrey D. Smith. *The James Tiptree Award Anthology 3*. San Francisco, CA: Tachyon Publications, 2006.
Le Guin, Ursula K. and Brian Attebery, eds. *The Norton Book of Science Fiction*. New York: Norton, 1993.
Shippey, Tom, ed. *The Oxford Book of Science Fiction Stories*. Oxford: Oxford University Press, 2003.

Journals

Journal of the Short Story in English.
Published semi-annually by the University of Angers Press, France, in association with the Department of English, Belmont University, Nashville.
http://www.belmont.edu/english/journal/index.html.

Short Story
Based at the University of Texas at Brownsville and edited by Farhat Iftekharuddin, combines original short fiction with scholarly articles.
http://www.blue.utb/.edu/eng.

Short Fiction in Theory and Practice.
Published by Intellect Press, edited by Ailsa Cox, looks at short fiction from the practitioner's perspective.
http://www.intellectbooks.co.uk/journals/view-Journal,id=196.

Studies in Short Fiction
Vols 1–36. Newbury: 1963–1999.
Although this journal has ceased publication, back issues are available in many university libraries. Issues published since Fall 1993 are available on http://www.findarticles.com. The journal was linked with the *Studies in Short Fiction* series on short story authors, published by Twayne.

electronic book review
http://www.electronicbookreview.com.
For discussion of new media and hypertext fiction.

Marvels and Tales
Interdisciplinary journal publishing scholarly work dealing with the fairy tale in any of its diverse manifestations and contexts. Published by Wayne State University Press.
http://www.langlab.wayne.edu/favicon.ico.

Eudora Welty Review (previously *Eudora Welty Newsletter*)
Published by Georgia State University.
http://www.ww2.gsu.edu/~wwwewn.

The Flannery O'Connor Bulletin, vols 1–26/27(1972–2000) and *The Flannery O'Connor Review*, vols 1– (2001–). Published by Georgia College and State University.
http://www.www2.gcsu.edu/library/sc/collections/oconnor/focreview.

The Hemingway Review
Published bi-annually by the Hemingway Society and the University of Idaho. The Hemingway Society hosts an international conference semi-annually.
http://www.hemingwaysociety.org.

Katherine Mansfield Society Newsletter
Electronic newsletter, published three times a year by the Katherine Mansfield Society, founded in 2008. A peer-reviewed journal is in preparation.
http://www.katherinemansfieldsociety.org/kms-newsletter.

The Raymond Carver Review
http://www.dept.kent.edu/english/RCR.
Electronic journal founded by the International Raymond Carver Society and hosted by Kent State University.

Websites

East of the Web. http://www.short-stories.co.uk.
Modernist Magazines Project. http://www.modmags.cts.dmu.ac.uk.
Reading the Short Story. http://www.may-on-the-short-story.blogspot.com.
The Short Story. http://www.theshortstory.org.uk.
Phil Stephensen-Payne of Galactic Central Publications maintains a useful historical database of fiction magazines, of all types and genres, which may be accessed via http://www.philsp.com/index.html.

Index

A
Aaron, Jane, 63, 69
Abbas, Khwaja Ahmed, 87
Abbasi, Talat, 91–2
adaptation, 4, 117–46, 168–9
Aidoo, Ama Ata, 71
Akutagawa, Ryunosuke, 118
Aldiss, Brian, 101
Aldridge, John, 150
All-Story, 98, 99
Alter, Stephen, 86
Altman, Robert
  Short Cuts, 10
Amazing Stories, 98, 99, 105
Analog, 112
Anand, Mulk Raj, 78, 84–5, 86, 87
Anderson, Sherwood
  Winesburg, Ohio, 7, 155, 157
anthologies, 2, 28, 60, 62–3, 65, 97–8, 104, 109–10, 164
Argosy, 98
Ashley, Allen, 169
Ashley, Mike, 98, 99, 105
Asimov, Isaac, 102, 103
Asimov's, 112
Astounding, 102
Attebery, Brian, 113
Atwood, Margaret, 162, 165
Authentic, 102

B
Babel, Isaak, 52
Bakhtin, M. M., 23
Ballard, J. G., 104, 165
Bananas, 165
Baraka, Amiri, 162
Barcelona Review, 168
Barnes, Julian
  A History of the World in 10½ Chapters, 31–6
Barthelme, Donald, 44
Barthes, Roland, 34, 134, 136
Bates, H. E., 80

Beatty, Warren
  Dick Tracy, 140
beginnings, 20–1, 44–7
Benford, Gregory, 108
Benjamin, Walter, 154–5
Bernstein, Charles, 170
Bertolucci, Bernardo
  The Spider's Stratagem, 119
Bhabha, Homi, 66
Blaise, Clark, 162
Bluestone, George, 135
Boccaccio, Giovanni, 149, 151–2
Bond, Ruskin, 89
Borges, Jorge Luis, 13, 119–46
  'Death and the Compass', 119–46
Bowen, Elizabeth, 5
Boyd, William, 2–3
Bradbury, Ray, 96, 102, 107
Branscomb, Jack, 19
Brito, Leonora, 68–9
Broderick, Damien, 106
Broderick, Peter, 140
Brooker, Peter, 165
Brown, Tony, 61, 72
Budrys, Algis, 101
Buffon, George-Louis Leclerc, Comte de, 43
Bulman, Colin, 13
Burroughs, Edgar Rice, 99
Butler, Robert Olen, 162
Buxton, Jackie, 32

C
Cammell, Donald
  Performance, 120
Campbell, Barbara, 169
Campbell, John W., 102, 105, 11
Capek, Karel
  Rossum's Universal Robots, 103
Carnell, John, 102
Carr, Nicholas, 8
Carroll, Maureen P., 59, 173

199

Index

Carter, Angela, 61, 67, 70–1, 73–4, 165
Carver, Raymond, 5, 10, 43–59, 148, 153, 154, 157, 165
Casares, Adolfo Bioy, 119
Cassirer, Ernest, 156
Cavalier, 99
Chakoo, B. L., 86
Charters, Ann, 63, 64
Chatman, Seymour, 133, 136–7
Chatterji, Bankimchander, 83
Chaudhuri, Amit, 79
Chekhov, Anton, 48–9, 61, 63, 80, 153, 154
Chesney, George, 98
Chiang, Ted, 103
Chopin, Kate
 'Ripe Figs', 18–23
Cisneros, Sandra, 162, 164
Clarke, Arthur C., 100, 102
Clinton, Alan, 34
closure, 162–3, 164
 see also endings
Clute, John, 97, 100
Cognitive Stylistics, 162–3
Colliers, 102
Conrad, Joseph, 109
Coover, Robert, 167–8, 169
Coppola, Francis Ford
 Zoetrope, 168–9
Cowasjee, Saros, 78, 87
Cox, Alex, 120–46
 Death and the Compass, 120–44
Cozarinsky, Edgardo, 146
Creative Writing, 2, 4, 15, 25, 26, 27, 60, 61–2, 162–3, 165–72
Crowley, John, 107

D
Dabydeen, David, 66
Das, Monica, 92
Dawson, Paul, 170
Delany, Samuel R., 106, 108
Derrida, Jacques, 36
Desai, Anita, 90
DeSalvo, Louise, 65
Deshpande, Shashi, 76
Dick, Philip K., 97
Dickens, Charles, 3, 165
Didion, Joan, 163

Dinesen, Isak, 154
Divakaruni, Chitra Banerjee, 91
Donoghue, Denis, 147
Donoghue, Emma, 69–72
Doyle, Arthur Conan, 99, 120
 Sherlock Holmes stories, 164
du Maurier, Daphne, 10, 118, 120
Dumas, Alexandre, 80
Dutta, Krishna, 79
Dybek, Stuart, 148

E
Eaglestone, Robert, 35
Eagleton, Terry, 151
Eco, Umberto, 151
Egan, Greg, 100
Eisenberg, Deborah, 148
electronic book review, 168
Eliade, Mircea, 156
Ellis, Edward S., 98
Ellison, Harlan, 103, 104, 106
Emmott, Catherine, 163
endings, 21–2, 25, 47–50, 52–3, 56–8, 104–5, 152
 see also closure
epiphany, 48–50, 53, 90, 151, 171
Extrapolation, 97

F
Fantastic Metropolis, 113
Farrell, James T., 150
Faulkner, William, 85
Fergusson, Suzanne, 173
fictocriticism, 170
flash fiction, 167
 see also short shorts
Flaubert, Gustave, 80
Ford, John
 The Quiet Man, 117
Foundation, 96, 97, 112
Fowler, Karen Joy, 110
Freud, Sigmund, 163
Friedman, Norman, 6

G
Gallant, Mavis, 148, 162
Gaskell, Elizabeth, 165
Gass, William H., 148
Geismar, Maxwell, 150

Index 201

gender, 24, 35, 36–41, 62–75, 90, 107, 108–9, 110–12, 164
genre, 38–9, 60–2, 96–8, 99, 101–7, 119, 120–1, 134, 145
genre theory, 1, 4–6, 13–14, 25–6, 28–9, 34–6, 147–60, 161–5
Gentry, Marshall Bruce, 45, 47, 48, 50, 54, 56
Gerlach, John, 6, 47
Gernsback, Hugo, 98–101, 105–6
Gessell, Paul, 13
Gibson, William, 97, 103, 105–6
Gillespie, Bruce, 97
Gioffre, Rocco, 143
Godwin, Tom
'The Cold Equations', 100, 103, 104–5, 107, 108
Gogol, Nikolai, 83
Gordimer, Nadine, 5
Gorky, Maxim, 83
Greene, Graham, 119
Greimas, A. J., 15, 16, 15, 25
Griffiths, George, 99
Gunn, James, 104

H
Halliday, M. A. K., 15, 16, 17, 25
Hanson, Clare, 5–6, 36, 72
Hardy, Thomas, 3
Harper, Graeme, 166
Hartwell, David G., 98, 99
Head, Bessie, 71
Heinlein, Robert A., 102, 106, 107
Helix, 113
Hemingway, Ernest, 13–18, 28, 50, 53, 56, 153
'The Revolutionist', 14–18, 26
Henry, O., 80, 85
Hesse, Douglas, 6, 163
Hillis Miller, J., 30–1
Hitchcock, Alfred
Rear Window, 117
Holland, Siobhan, 170–1
Howells, William Dean, 150
Hugo, Victor, 80
Huntington, John, 104
Hurley, Ursula, 14, 26, 27
Hussein, Aamer, 92
hypertext, 4, 167–9

I
Infinity Plus, 113
intertextuality, 13–14, 16, 21, 22, 25, 144–5
Interzone, 109, 112
Iowa Review Web, 168
Irving, Washington, 153

J
Jackson, Shelley, 167
James, Henry, 53, 109
James, Siân, 66–8, 70
Jameson, Frederic, 115, 150
Jhabvala, Ruth, 89
Johnson, Samuel, 55
Joshi, Arun, 76
Journal of the Fantastic in the Arts, 97
Journal of the Short Story in English, 6, 162
Joyce, James, 28, 157
Dubliners, 29–31, 155
Joyce, Michael, 167

K
Kafka, Franz, 13
Kay, Jackie, 5
Keegan, Claire, 162
Kennedy, A. L., 1
Kenyon Review, The, 2
Keret, Etgar, 172
Kermode, Frank, 156
Kessel, John, 97–8, 109–10
Keyes, Daniel
'Flowers for Algernon', 103
Kincaid, Jamaica, 71
Kincaid, Paul, 106
King, Stephen, 171
Kipling, Rudyard, 78, 80, 96
Knights, Ben, 2
Kristeva, Julia, 36
Kurosawa, Akira
Rashomon, 118

L
Lahiri, Jumpha, 76, 164
Langford, David, 115
Le Cain, Maximilian, 121, 133, 134
Le Guin, Ursula K., 97, 103, 106, 107, 110

Lee, Maurice A., 162
Leebron, Fred
  'Water', 14, 23–6
Lehman, Daniel, 163
Levy, Andrew, 5
Liddy, Gordon, 165
Litt, Toby, 167
Lohafer, Susan, 6, 161–2
Lothe, Jakob, 162
Lucy, Niall, 29
Lukács, Georg, 151

M
Mansfield, Katherine, 5, 61, 63–5, 71, 73, 165
  'The Doll's House', 64–5
March-Russell, Paul, 171
Maunder, Andrew, 3
Maupassant, Guy de, 61, 63, 79–80, 85
May, Charles E., 4, 6, 8, 96, 161–2
Mayhew, Henry, 163
McAllister Bruce, 115
McEwan, Ian, 3
McFarlane, Brian, 135–6
McGahern, John, 162
McSweeney's, 168
Mendlesohn, Farah, 100
Merril, Judith, 104
microfiction, 13
  see also flash fiction
Miles, Rosalind, 70
Miller, Walter A.
  A Canticle for Leibowitz 103
Millhauser, Steven, 162
modernism, 63, 98, 117, 166, 171
Montgomery, Martin, 16–17, 25
Moorcock, Michael, 102, 104
Morrison, Toni, 69
Múgica, René
  El Hombre de la Esquina Rosada, 119
multimedia, 118, 167–9
Munro, Alice, 5, 118, 148, 163, 164, 165
Munto, Saadat Hasan, 87
Murakami, Haruki, 172
Murry, John Middleton, 165

N
Narayan, R. K., 78, 85–6, 87
Nebula, 102

New Worlds, 102, 104
New York Review of Science Fiction, 97
Nicholls, Peter, 97, 100
Nilsson, Leopoldo Torre
  Días de Odio, 119
non-fiction short story, 163
novella, 4, 101, 149, 163, 164

O
Oates, Joyce Carol, 3
O'Brien, Edna, 65
O'Brien, Tim, 163–4
O'Connor, Flannery, 4, 148, 154, 155–7, 158
O'Connor, Frank, 5
O'Faolain, Sean, 5
O'Halloran, Kieran, 14
oral storytelling, 34, 149, 164, 167
Ortega, José, 148

P
Packer, ZZ, 164
Page, Ra, 1
Paley, Grace, 64
Pall Mall Magazine, 99
Pearson's, 99
Perrin, Alice, 78
Poe, Edgar Allan, 4–5, 80, 96, 99, 100, 120, 152–3
Pohl, Frederik, 107
Polley, Sarah
  Away From Her, 118
Pope, Rob, 2
Porter, Katherine Anne, 61
postcolonialism, 76–95, 159, 164
postmodernism, 35, 66–7, 97, 106, 119, 166
Pound, Ezra, 30, 56
Practice-led Research
  see Creative Writing
Prairie Fire, 13
Pratt, Mary Louise, 13, 20, 34
Premchand (Dhanpat Rai Srivastava), 79, 82, 86
Pritchett, V. S., 5
Prose, Francine, 147–8, 166
Pullinger, Kate, 167

R

Rabaté, Jean-Michel, 30, 41
Raengo, Alesandra, 118, 121
Ramakrishnan, E. V., 80, 87
Rao, Raja, 78, 86
Reid, Ian, 61, 63
relevance theory, 13–27
Rhythm, 165
Richler, Mordecai, 165
Robinson, Andrew, 79
Robinson, Kim Stanley, 107
Roeg, Nicolas
   Don't Look Now, 10, 118, 120
Rohrberger, Mary, 6, 161–2
Rose, Bernard
   Ivansxtc, 10
Rousseau, Jean Jacques, 83
Rubin, David, 79, 82
Rushdie, Salman, 90–1
Russ, Joanna
   'When It Changed', 107

S

Saint, Tarun K., 87
Saki, 80
Santiago, Hugo
   Invasión, 119–20
Sarshar, Ratannath, 83
Saturday Evening Post, 102
Schlegel, Friedrich, 149
Scholes, Robert, 14, 16, 17, 18
Science Fiction, 96–116, 169–70
Science Fiction Studies, 97
Sedaris, David, 164
Senares, Luis, 98
Serviss, Garrett P., 99
Sethi, Vijay Mohan, 84
Shamsie, Muneeza, 92
Shaw, Bob, 106
Shaw, Valerie, 61, 63
Shklovsky, Victor, 150
short FICTION, 2
short shorts, 13–27
   See also flash fiction
Short Story, 162
short story cycle
   see short story sequence
short story sequence, 4, 28–42, 103, 164–5, 169

Simpson, Helen, 162
   Hey Yeah Right Get a Life, 36–41
Singh, Bhupal, 79
Singh, Kushwant, 87, 88–9
Skei, Hans, 162
slipstream, 169–70
Smith, Ali, 170
Smith, Angela, 73, 165
Smith, Hazel, 170
Smith, Paul, 15, 16
Sorabji, Cornelia, 80–1
Spencer, Dorothy, 80
Sperber, Dan 14
Stam, Robert, 118, 121
Stand, 2
Steel, Flora Annie, 78
Stevenson, Robert Louis, 47
Strange Horizons, 113
Strand, The, 96, 99
Stross, Charles
   Accelerando, 103
Strychacz, Thomas, 15, 18
Stull, William L., 45, 47, 48, 50, 54, 56, 173
sudden fiction, 13
   See also short shorts
Suhrawardy, Saista Akhtar Banu, 79
Suvin, Darko, 106–7

T

Tagore, Jyotirindranath, 79
Tagore, Rabindranath, 79–80, 82, 83, 86
Tales of Wonder, 102
Tan, Amy, 164
Thacker, Andrew, 165
Thomas, James, 13
Thurgar-Dawson, Chris, 2
Tiptree Jr., James
   'The Women Men Don't See', 100–1
Tóibín, Colm, 163
Tolstoy, Leo, 10, 38–9, 40, 83
Toomer, Jean, 164
Tremaine, F. Orlon, 102
Trevor, William, 148, 171
Trollope, Anthony, 165
Troth, Emily, 21
Turgenev, Ivan, 80, 155

V

van Vogt, A. E.
   The Voyage of the Space Beagle, 102
Vatsyayan, S. H., 80
Verne, Jules, 98, 99

W

Wagner, Geoffrey, 134–5
Walsh, Maurice, 117
Wasi, Jehanara, 92
Weaver, Robert, 165
Weinbaum, Stanley
   'A Martian Odyssey', 108, 111–12
Weird Tales, 98
Weiss, Allan, 164
Wells, H. G., 80, 96, 98, 99, 101–2, 104, 109
Westfahl, Gary, 101, 104–5
Weston, Peter, 97
Wharton, Edith, 152
Wiene, Robert
   Das Cabinet des Dr Caligari, 138
Wigfall, Clare, 167
Williams, Joy, 148
Williams, William Carlos, 56
Williamson, Jack, 107, 115
Wilson, Deirdre, 14
Winther, Per, 162
Wolfe, Gary, 109
Wool, Dan, 143–4
Woolf, Leonard, 78
Woolf, Virgina, 61, 63, 64, 73, 74, 165
Woolrich, Cornell, 117

Z

Zagarell, Sandra A., 164